D1710218

Rouget de Lisle's famous anthem *La Marseillaise* admirably reflects the confidence and enthusiasm of the early years of the French Revolution. But the effects on music of the Revolution and the events that followed it in France were more far-reaching than that. Hymns, chansons and even articles of the Constitution set to music in the form of vaudevilles all played their part in disseminating Revolutionary ideas and principles; music education was reorganized to compensate for the loss of courtly institutions and the weakened maîtrises of cathedrals and churches. Opera, in particular, was profoundly affected, in both its organization and its subject matter, by the events of 1789 and the succeeding decade.

The essays in this book, written by specialists in the period, deal with all these aspects of music in Revolutionary France, highlighting the composers and writers who played a major role in the changes that took place there. They also identify some of the traditions and genres that survived the Revolution, and take a look at the effects on music of Napoleon's invasion of Italy.

Music and the French Revolution

Music and the French Revolution

edited by
MALCOLM BOYD

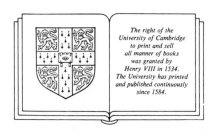

CAMBRIDGE UNIVERSITY PRESS

Cambridge

New York   Port Chester   Melbourne   Sydney

Published by the Press Syndicate of the University of Cambridge
The Pitt Building, Trumpington Street, Cambridge CB2 1RP
40 West 20th Street, New York, NY 10011–4211, USA
10 Stamford Road, Oakleigh, Victoria 3166, Australia

© Cambridge University Press 1992

First published 1992

Printed in Great Britain at the University Press, Cambridge

A catalogue record for this book is available from the British Library

Library of Congress cataloguing in publication data
Music and the French Revolution / edited by Malcolm Boyd.
p.   cm.
Rev. and expanded papers from a conference organized by the Centre
for Eighteenth-century Musical Studies, University of Wales College
of Cardiff, and held at Dyffryn House in July 1989.
Includes index.
ISBN 0 521 40287 5 (hardback)
1. Music – France – 18th century – Congresses.
2. France – History – Revolution, 1789–99 – Songs and music – Congresses.
3. Revolutionary music – Congresses.
I. Boyd, Malcolm.
II. University of Wales. Centre for Eighteenth-Century Musical
Studies.
ML270.3.M88 1992
780'.944'09033–dc20   91–10775   CIP

ISBN 0 521 40287 5 hardback

.

Contents

Preface   *page* ix

DAVID CHARLTON
Introduction: exploring the Revolution   1

ELEMENTS OF CONTINUITY

JULIAN RUSHTON
'Royal Agamemnon': the two versions of Gluck's *Iphigénie en Aulide*   15

MICHAEL ROBINSON
Opera buffa into *opéra comique*, 1771–90   37

CATHERINE MASSIP
Periodical editions of music at the time of the French Revolution   57

PHILIPPE OBOUSSIER
The French string quartet, 1770–1800   74

ROGER COTTE
François Giroust, a Versailles musician of the Revolutionary period   93

REVOLUTIONARY OPERA

M. ELIZABETH C. BARTLET
The new repertory at the Opéra during the Reign of Terror:
Revolutionary rhetoric and operatic consequences   107

DAVID GALLIVER
Léonore, ou L'amour conjugal: a celebrated offspring of the Revolution   157

DAVID CHARLTON
On redefinitions of 'rescue opera'   169

MUSIC AND THE NEW POLITICS

CYNTHIA M. GESSELE
The Conservatoire de Musique and national music education
in France, 1795–1801   191

ORA FRISHBERG SALOMAN
French Revolutionary perspectives on Chabanon's *De la
musique* of 1785   211

JEAN-LOUIS JAM
Marie-Joseph Chénier and François-Joseph Gossec: two artists
in the service of Revolutionary propaganda   221

HERBERT SCHNEIDER
The sung constitutions of 1792: an essay on propaganda in the
Revolutionary song   236

NAPOLEON AND AFTER

GABRIELLA BIAGI RAVENNI
The French occupation of Lucca and its effects on music   277

BEATE ANGELIKA KRAUS
Beethoven and the Revolution: the view of the French musical
press   300

Index   313

Preface

The essays in this volume result from papers read at an international musicological conference organized by the Centre for Eighteenth-Century Musical Studies, University of Wales College of Cardiff, and held at Dyffryn House, near Cardiff, in July 1989. The papers have for the most part been revised and expanded by their authors, and David Charlton has added a general introduction to the volume. The editor makes no apologies for adding to the voluminous literature that the bicentenary of the French Revolution has already spawned. Musical sources are usually ignored by political and social historians, and yet, as several of the essays in the present volume demonstrate, they can provide an interesting and illuminating commentary on how the changing events of a momentous period affected those who lived through it. Besides, the music itself is less well known outside (and perhaps even inside) France than it should be.

In acknowledging the assistance I have received in bringing this volume to press, I must mention first Dr Michael F. Robinson, head of the music department at the University of Wales College of Cardiff, without whose initiative and drive neither the conference nor the publication of these essays would have happened. Financial assistance towards publication was received, either directly or indirectly, from the university music department and from the French Embassy in London. I received invaluable help from my colleagues at Cardiff, particularly from Caroline Rae, who advised on numerous points in the translations from French and German, and David Wyn Jones, who kindly assisted with proof-reading. I am grateful, too, to Penny Souster at Cambridge University Press for guiding and chiding as occasion demanded.

THE FRENCH REVOLUTIONARY CALENDAR

The Revolutionary calendar was calculated from 22 September 1792 (the first day of the republic), adopted on 5 October 1793 and finally abandoned in 1806. It divided the year into twelve months of thirty days each, which were given seasonal names: Vendémiaire, Brumaire, Frimaire, Nivôse, Pluviôse, Ventôse, Germinal, Floréal, Prairial, Messidor, Thermidor and Fructidor. Each month had three ten-day weeks, or *décades*, the last day of the week (*décadi*) being a rest-day, as also were the five days remaining at the end of the year.

Dates from the republican calendar are shown in the present volume as, for example, '20 pluviôse an IV', or (with capitals) '20 Pluviôse An IV', according to whether the context is French or English; in many cases the Gregorian equivalent (in this example, 9 February 1796) follows after a diagonal stroke (/).

MALCOLM BOYD, Cardiff, September 1990

DAVID CHARLTON

Introduction: exploring the Revolution

One should not be surprised that there is no coherent body of musical writings, even in France, on the music of the crucial last decade of the eighteenth century. Napoléon and the Bourbon Restoration in 1815 effectively legitimized their music in areas already strong before 1789: a concert life with strongly international connections and an operatic life imbued with influences from Italy. Native French musicians in the early nineteenth century played their part, and their music publishers and instrument-makers continued to hold a world position. Yet events served to obscure a decade when the Revolution and its wars obliged music to serve many new needs, and to define for itself something of a new 'national character'.[1] And had not 'official' art become stained by association with the Revolutionary scaffold? Has not the art even of Jacques-Louis David been somehow found wanting because of his active Revolutionary roles and his vote for Louis XVI's death in January 1793? Musical composition in France, less fortunate than painting, possessed no single figure who could rival the stature of David, his command of different genres and his versatile technique.

At the same time, contradictory messages have come down to us through our involvement with music by the Revolution's contemporaries: Haydn, Mozart, Beethoven. If freemasonry and its music was significant in Vienna, surely France's 600 masonic lodges, and the commissioning of six symphonies from Haydn by the Loge Olympique in Paris, must signify common aims and experiences?[2] If Mozart and Da Ponte adapted the recent play *Le mariage de Figaro* by Beaumarchais, and Mozart borrowed ideas for it from a French opera staged in Paris in 1778 after he left, surely that reflects favourably on the vitality of theatre there?[3] As for Beethoven, few can have doubted his approval for

1 See the chapters within this book by Cynthia M. Gessele and Ora Frishberg Saloman.
2 Roger Cotte, *doyen* of research into music and French freemasonry, discusses a composer who bestrode Catholic, masonic and Revolutionary music, François Giroust. See pp. 93–104.
3 The borrowing was from Grétry's *L'amant jaloux*; this is discussed in the present author's *Grétry and the Growth of Opéra-comique* (Cambridge, 1986), Chapter 21.

the ideals of the First Republic, and many have pondered his debt to the styles of Cherubini and his contemporaries in Revolutionary Paris. In Winton Dean's formulation, 'it would scarcely be too much to say that Beethoven's entire instrumental style, in the symphonies and overtures as well as in *Fidelio*, is a transfiguration of Cherubini's, with its balance of structural masses, its combination of a rhetorical melodic thrust with seething orchestral textures, its sharply contrasted dynamics, and intense rhythmic energy'.[4]

The truth is that the French Revolution offers an as yet unmatched challenge to musical historians. It challenges the accepted ways we write about music. It challenges us to explore the musical experience of men and women over a wider-than-usual spectrum. Because a revolution re-examines and re-creates its institutions, studying the 1789 period also means looking at a quickly changing pattern of musical patronage, whether state-inspired or individually organized. The evaluation of anything becomes a challenge because of the temporal concentration of events and the politicization of so much musical art. And, we must add, there are difficulties of access to even those repertories which have long been known to survive: a prime example of this is the fact that hardly any music composed for the major festivals of the Revolution has ever been made available in full score, as opposed to piano reduction.[5]

Let us pause to look at one case of such a challenge. *Fidelio* (by Sonnleithner and Beethoven) began as a virtual textual translation of the opera *Léonore, ou L'amour conjugal* by Bouilly and Gaveaux (February 1798). Pierre Gaveaux, born in 1760, was a prolific opera composer, but also a good tenor and actor, taking major roles at the Théâtre Feydeau in Paris.[6] He had been educated at a traditional choir school (the normal route for pre-Revolution musical boys) at Béziers Cathedral in the deep south of France. The Feydeau was a centre of anti-Jacobin reaction. In the aftermath of the fall of Robespierre and the Terror (9 Thermidor An II/27 July 1794) there was sharply increasing tension between what we would call 'Left' and 'Right'. In January 1795 Gaveaux composed a political song to words by J. M. Souriguère, 'Le réveil du peuple contre les terroristes'.[7] He sang its text of open revenge against the 'monstres du

4 W. Dean, 'German Opera', in *The Age of Beethoven, 1790–1830 (The New Oxford History of Music*, viii), ed. G. Abraham (Oxford, 1982), p. 472.
5 The standard reference works are by C. Pierre: *Musique exécutée aux fêtes nationales de la Révolution française* (Paris, 1893–4), *Le magasin de musique à l'usage des fêtes nationales et du Conservatoire* (Paris, 1895), *Musique des fêtes et cérémonies de la Révolution française* (Paris, 1899, containing piano scores of much music) and *Les hymnes et chansons de la Révolution* (Paris, 1904), the main documentary volume. References to work by A. Coy and J.-L. Jam will be found in a bibliography devoted to the Revolutionary decade in *Le tambour et la harpe*, ed. J. Mongrédien and J.-R. Julien (Paris, 1991), pp. 280–316.
6 On Gaveaux, Bouilly and *Léonore*, see also the essay by David Galliver in the present volume.
7 Pierre, *Musique des fêtes*, p. 484. For a relevant secret police report, see M. E. C. Bartlet, 'Politics and the Fate of *Roger et Olivier*', *Journal of the American Musicological Society* xxxvii (1984), pp. 137–8.

Ténare', the 'drinkers of human blood', at both the Feydeau and the Café de Chartres.[8] His song immediately became a rallying cry for the Right, and, as had been the case during the Revolution, theatre audiences split apart in acute, sometimes violent, struggles. The *Marseillaise* was renewed as the musical call of the Left. Actors and even theatre musicians were coerced or abused. A July law, prohibiting all unofficial singing, was simply disregarded. Another, banning Gaveaux's song, was passed in January 1796. But as late as 14 July 1797, and into 1798, the song accompanied public provocations and demonstrations.

When *Léonore* was first seen, at the Théâtre Feydeau, Gaveaux himself sang the role of Florestan. The libretto makes it clear that Florestan is not a criminal: his two years' incarceration in Pizare's dungeon is the result of personal vengeance on the part of one who fears political exposure.[9] Florestan's description of his captor, in Act 2 scene i, as 'un tyran', 'un monstre exécrable', was a plain Robespierrist reference to anyone watching Gaveaux in 1798. And on the previous 10 December Bonaparte, in full military dress, had enjoyed a hero's return after victories in Italy, welcomed by the Directory executive, officials, and 200 musicians performing Méhul's *Le chant du retour* for the first time. Anyone instinctively seeking a parallel for Bouilly's 'strong man', the Dom Fernand who restores justice, would not have had far to look.

This case history illustrates the tangled interrelationship of possible meanings in one opera; keeping it in mind, we can now examine some areas of concern to musicians of the time, following the thematic outlines provided in this book itself. First, continuity. France had a population of some twenty-six million inhabitants, ninety per cent of whom worked on the land. Of the total number, about two hundred thousand could be classed as people of title or nobility; far from all had fortunes, but they enjoyed all the privileges and the influential jobs. The Revolution saw the abolition of privileges, of the monarchy and of the hugely wealthy and conservative Catholic Church. But the Church was re-established by Napoleon, though its influence had vanished, and the nobility was quick to recover itself. Many nobles served the Revolution and Directory, and only nine per cent of the victims of the Terror were of this class. The bourgeoisie's fortunes simply changed round; pre-1789 civil servants and property owners made losses, while bankers, dealers and buyers of national assets made money. The latter became a ruling element under the Directory (1795–9). Continuity obtained in life as a whole. For example, although the Republican calendar was officially adopted in 1793 (Year I was deemed to have begun on 22 September

---

8 Pierre, *Les hymnes et chansons*, pp. 746–7.
9 Pizare: 'ce Florestan ... dont j'ai tant sujet de me venger ... qui voulut me dévoiler aux yeux de l'état'. J.-N. Bouilly, *Léonore, ou L'amour conjugal* (Paris, an VII), p. 14.

1792, the birthday of the Republic),[10] Gregorian Sundays were still being observed as rest days in many quarters even five years later.

Basic industries continued, including manufacture of musical scores and parts. At least fifteen piano makers continued working in Paris during the decade.[11] Artists continued to live by their art as far as possible. In music the continuities are chiefly visible in opera (see below), but were still present in concert-giving and the practice of domestic chamber music. The famous Lenten Concert Spirituel series finally ended on 13 May 1790[12] (by which date church land was being sold off and its Civil Constitution was being prepared). But, as *Les spectacles de Paris* for 1792 noted, under the heading of 'Concert Spirituel':

Vingt autres concerts ont pris sa place, et les plus célèbres Virtuoses se font entendre, soit au Cirque, soit au Musée; le Théâtre de la rue Feydeau particulièrement a satisfait des amateurs; & les Concerts qu'on y a donné les jours de *Fêtes Solemnelles* ont été très brillants.

Twenty other concerts have taken its place, and the most famous virtuosos have been heard, whether at the Cirque [a new theatre erected in the Palais-Royal] or at the [Hôtel du] Musée; the Théâtre de la rue Feydeau has particularly pleased the music lovers; and the [six] concerts there on solemn feast days were most brilliant.

The last-mentioned concerts were given under Viotti in the Feydeau's brand-new theatre during April 1791. Entrepreneurs supplied concerts as long as people would pay to hear them. Managements tried hard: 'The auditorium [of the Feydeau] was laid out so as to flatter the eye of spectators, and in order that no sound should be lost' ('On a disposé la salle de manière à flatter l'oeil des Spectateurs et à ce qu'aucun son ne fût perdu').[13] Social unrest, of course, caused some personnel to leave (Viotti went to London in July 1792), but theatres and their orchestras stayed working. The real turning-point for the *émigrés* was the defeat of the monarchy on 10 August 1792, originating in the attempted emigration of the royal family in June 1791 and succeeded by the September Massacres. But such events did not spell the end of public concerts or private music. Indeed, 1792–3 saw the beginning of concerts designed for a wider public, some given by the band of the National Guard. Here is the programme for the people's concert in the Tuileries Gardens on 14 July 1794, played by musicians of the new Institut National de Musique, together with some 240 extra singers and players from various theatres:

10 See above, pp. ix–x.
11 Others left Paris around 1790; see A. de Place, *Le piano-forte à Paris entre 1760 et 1822* (Paris, 1986), pp. 180–5.
12 C. Pierre (ed. A. Bloch-Michel), *Histoire du Concert Spirituel, 1725–1790* (Paris, 1975), pp. 68 and 344.
13 *Almanach général des spectacles ... Seconde année, 1792*, p. 27. The standard handbook in English is B. Schwarz, *French Instrumental Music Between the Revolutions (1789–1830)* (New York, 1987).

Overture to *Démophon* (Vogel)
'Hymne à l'Etre Suprême' (Gossec)
The Battle of Fleurus (Catel), for voices and ensemble
Oath from *Ernelinde* (Philidor)[14]
Minuet from Symphony in C (Haydn)
'Le chant du départ' (Méhul)
Finale from Symphony in C (Haydn)
The Taking of the Bastille, a 'hiérodrame' (Désaugiers)
'Poursuivons jusqu'au trépas', from *Armide* (Gluck)[15]
The *Marseillaise*
'Le chant de Châteauvieux' (Gossec)
Ça ira
La Carmagnole
'Le pas de charge des armées de la République'

More orthodox concerts were soon flourishing under the Directory. The Feydeau played Méhul's early Symphony in C in January 1797;[16] the new Conservatoire held its first prize-giving concert in October 1797; the Concerts de la rue de Cléry started in 1798, in the town house of the art dealer J.-B.-P. Lebrun.

Publishing seems to have enjoyed a boom period. Typical musical and entertainment guides have been cited earlier. Newspapers sprang up in abundance, some geared to theatre life and concerts, far too numerous to list here. One journal is discussed in detail by Catherine Massip in the present volume. Large quantities of musical material were issued, to judge from information in catalogues or journals. Jean Gribenski discovered an increase in symphonic works available between 1788 and 1796: Imbault, the publisher, listed thirty-one such in 1788 and 126 in 1796.[17] Adélaïde de Place has published a list of French piano music issued during the period (see note 11). Already the works of Mozart were finding their way into shops, and Beethoven's sonatas were sold from 1800 onwards.[18] If Mozart's music was little played in public up to 1800, 'his name had never been forgotten in Paris', and publishers there under the Directory issued the late G minor Symphony, several piano concertos, quartets, quintets and extracts from *Così fan tutte*.[19] 'However', Jean Mongrédien adds, 'it is obvious that many foreign editions, especially by J. André (Offenbach) or Simrock (Bonn) were [also] in circulation ...'

14 Operatic oath scenes are discussed by M. E. Bartlet in the present volume; see pp. 117–24.
15 The exciting choral and vocal ensemble ending Act 1 of the opera (Paris, 1777).
16 I.e. the fragmentary 'no. 0', heard on 28 January and 7 February. See Etienne-Nicolas Méhul, Symphony no. 1 in G minor, ed. D. Charlton (Madison, 1985), p. ix.
17 Verbally communicated at the conference *Le tambour et la harpe*, Université Lumière, Lyons, 2 October 1989.
18 G. Favre, *La musique française de piano avant 1830* (Paris, 1953), p. 103.
19 J. Mongrédien, *La musique en France dès Lumières au Romantisme (1789–1830)* (Paris, 1986), p. 315.

The evidence, presented in Philippe Oboussier's essay, of lively chamber-music activity, can be seen against a background of continuity suggested by the work of Michèle Garnier.[20] Publications for string quartet remained buoyant, though the type of music changed from more traditional genres towards those including arrangements, transcriptions, and picturesque pieces. Over 500 quartet publications, by some eighty composers, were issued in the 1790s. On the social context and function of this music, much work remains to be done.

By contrast, the musical life of Revolutionary theatres in Paris has always been a subject of historical interest. There was essential continuity, despite changes of name, location and management, in the life of the Paris Opéra: its collections have remained largely together to this day. In a parallel manner, the traditional home of *opéra comique* had the stability to survive, though only just: the Comédie-Italienne, later Opéra-Comique National, in the Salle Favart.[21] Also a bedraggled survivor of the decade was the Théâtre Feydeau, which – as Michael Robinson describes below – was originally started in 1789 under the Italianizing patronage of the king's art-loving brother (the Comte de Provence) as the Théâtre de Monsieur.

Yet the differences in the musical theatre of the 1790s overall, when compared with the decades on either side, are far greater than the similarities. First, the 'liberty of the theatres' was decreed in January 1791: anyone could build a theatre and mount a work in any genre. Second, the ancient *privilège* of the Paris Opéra, to which annual dues had formerly to be paid by all smaller theatres, was of course abolished. Third, there was an enormous increase in the number of new theatres, great and small, often with their complement of musicians: 'Without counting auditoria converted within existing buildings (convents, churches, town houses), there were about ten important building-sites between 1790 and 1793 that gave rise to theatres, and important ones at that.'[22] Fourth, the politicized nature of life in general could make for all kinds of intensifications. If Gluck's *Iphigénie en Aulide* reflected political perceptions in 1774–5 (see the essay within by Julian Rushton), the same work provoked open conflicts in October 1790. In the second-act solo with chorus, 'Chantons, célébrons notre reine', Etienne Lainez, as Achille, was deemed too enthusiastic in his singing by a Revolutionary section of the public. On a following night the royalists were in the majority and obtained an encore for the piece. On a third

20 'Les avatars d'un genre élitiste, le quatuor à cordes', in *Le tambour et la harpe*, pp. 189–207.
21 See C. D. Brenner, *The Théâtre Italien: its Repertory, 1716–1793* (Berkeley, 1961); D. Charlton, *Grétry*, Chapter 26; and M. E. C. Bartlet, 'Etienne Nicolas Méhul and Opera During the French Revolution, Consulate and Empire' (PhD diss., Chicago University, 1982).
22 N. Wild, 'Les théâtres parisiens sous la Révolution', in *Orphée phrygien: les musiques de la Révolution*, ed. J.-R. Julien and J.-C. Klein (Paris, 1989).

occasion, Revolutionaries were in the majority, forcing Lainez to kneel in a gesture of forgiveness and to tread on a crown to prove his patriotism.[23]

We forget, in our electronic age, the natural association between a theatre, its rhetoric and communal expression of will. In an age when operas and associated genres could be written and revised quickly, that which was on offer could act almost like a cinema or a videotape newsreel today. Actual events were hastily dramatized and 'replayed': the siege of Lille by the Austrians, lifted on 7 October 1792, was set to music by A. E. Trial *fils*, and given at the Opéra-Comique six weeks later.[24] Similar works at the Opéra are mentioned by Elizabeth Bartlet in her essay. Extraordinary ends call for extraordinary means, so it was not unnatural that operatic scores in general should contain numerous points of interest suggestive of the future rather than the past: substantial choruses (discussed by Edward Dent, among others);[25] advanced use of harmonic dissonance or unorthodox progressions;[26] use of new orchestration techniques, even by older composers like Grétry; and the appearance of new timbres such as the serpent, the tam-tam and bells, or of novel muting techniques.

When the poet Wordsworth wrote in *The Prelude* of his first-hand experiences during the Revolution, he linked music with the moral exultation, felt intensely, which liberating events seemed continually to produce:

> Even files of strangers merely, seen but once,
> And for a moment, men from far with sound
> Of music, martial tunes, and banners spread,
> Entering the city, here and there a face,
> Or person singled out among the rest,
> Yet still a stranger and beloved as such;
> Even by these passing spectacles my heart
> Was oftentimes uplifted, and they seemed
> Arguments sent from Heaven to prove the cause
> Good, pure, which no one could stand up against ...
>
> (Book IX, 1850 version, lines 275–84)

23 M. Dietz, *Geschichte des musikalischen Dramas in Frankreich während der Revolution bis zum Directorium* (Vienna, 2nd edn, 1886), p. 147; also J. Favier and others, eds., *Chronicle of the French Revolution* (London and Harlow, 1989), p. 178.

24 *Cécile et Julien, ou Le siège de Lille*, words by Joigny, 21 November 1792. Trial's father, a well-known operatic singer-actor since the days of Monsigny, was an ardent Robespierrist. He poisoned himself in February 1795 in the midst of the troubles alluded to earlier in connection with Gaveaux's song, after being forced to read an anti-Robespierre text on stage.

25 E. J. Dent, *The Rise of Romantic Opera*, ed. W. Dean (Cambridge, 1976); W. Dean, 'French Opera', in *The Age of Beethoven*, pp. 26–119.

26 E.g. the parallel fifths motif in H.-M. Berton's *Le délire* (1799) or the ten- and twelve-note dissonances in J. P. A. Martini's *Sapho* (1794).

Later, under the Terror, Wordsworth could not escape the feeling of

> ...a kind of sympathy with power,
> Motions raised up within me, nevertheless,
> Which had relationship to highest things

and found in the following metaphor an apt image to express the clash between Revolutionary sympathy and his religious instincts of prophetic doom:

> Wild blasts of music thus did find their way
> Into the midst of terrible events
>
> (Book X, 1805–6 version, lines 420–21)

– which could well serve as an epigraph for our volume.

Some of the most memorable 'wild blasts' were those heard in the contexts Wordsworth first recalls: public gatherings and festive ceremonies. As will be seen in the third section of essays in this book, these festivals produced some of the most original and yet typical music of their time. At least three categories were developed: celebratory choral works, with mixed or male-voice choirs, in various forms, usually accompanied by wind groups; funerary music, either with or without voices, and including Gossec's *Marche lugubre* as a prototype; and one-movement 'symphonies' or 'overtures', often in sonata form, for wind ensemble.[27] In these 'democratic' genres, composed between 1791 and 1799, France came nearest to creating her new 'national' music, with Gossec as the most prolific contributor, followed (in no particular order) by Steibelt, Pleyel, Martini, Méhul, Cherubini, Le Sueur and many others.

A key figure in this *milieu*, however, was the founder of the National Guard band and instigator of the Institut National de Musique, whose musicians formed the festival wind ensembles: Bernard Sarrette (1765–1858)[28]. The Paris Conservatoire was the direct outcome in 1795 of the Institut; so Sarrette, who nurtured the Conservatoire for its first twenty years, and the Revolution itself are actually the parents of music education in modern Europe. But we should not forget that the Conservatoire was established partly in order to train musicians for public festival performance. Looking back at the results of Sarrette's initiatives and of state patronage, Gossec wrote:

27 See bibliography in note 5, and also W. S. Dudley, Jr, 'Orchestration in the Musique d'harmonie of the French Revolution' (PhD diss., University of California at Berkeley, 1968); and D. P. Swanzy, 'The Wind Ensemble and its Music During the French Revolution' (PhD diss., Michigan State University, 1966). On the festivals themselves, see D. L. Dowd, *Pageant-Master of the Republic: Jacques-Louis David and the French Revolution* (Lincoln, Nebraska, 1948) and M. Ozouf, *Festivals and the French Revolution*, trans. A. Sheridan (Cambridge, MA, and London, 1988).

28 C. Pierre, *B. Sarrette et les origines du Conservatoire National de Musique et de Déclamation* (Paris, *c.* 1895).

L'enthousiasme qui anima le peuple Républicain dans ses brillants succès, inspira ses poëtes et ses musiciens; des compositions d'un caractère absolument neuf furent entendues, et dans le nombre le *Chant du départ* fut choisi par le soldat français et consacré par sa valeur.... Telle fut la musique nationale, énergique et intacte ...[29]

The enthusiasm animating Republican people at the moment of their [military and civil] success inspired her poets and musicians. Compositions of an absolutely new character were heard, among which [Méhul's] *Le chant du départ* was chosen by the French soldier and consecrated by his valour.... Such was our national music, energetic and unimpaired ...

Even the greatest of the festivals, with their very different organic natures, their various political motivations, must remain static images on paper to us, if they were illustrated or described at all. But the music of the festivals, still chiefly unperformed and unpublished in full score, remains to lend us temporal and sensuous witness to occasions like the Federation (14 July 1790), the reburial of Voltaire in the Panthéon (11 July 1791), the Festival of the Supreme Being (8 June 1794) or the five annual Directorial ceremonies (14 July, 10 August, 1 Vendémiaire, 21 January, 9 Thermidor). With inspirations like Gossec's *Marche lugubre* before us,[30] we cannot agree with Anthony Lewis (assuming we wish to talk of aesthetics) that 'The importance of this music of the French Revolution lies not so much in its intrinsic value, as in the role it plays in a great social movement', even though we agree that 'Organised music, which had for so long served lords spiritual or temporal, now made articulate the will of the people'.[31] There is simply too much still to assess.

The people's will, musically expressed, did not, however, necessitate great levels of organization. Claude-Joseph Rouget de Lisle's *La Marseillaise*, of which he wrote both words and melody, was the work of an army engineer, stationed in Strasbourg, during a single night in April 1792.[32] Simon Schama has dubbed it a 'swelling anthem', for ever and inimitably 'expressing the comradeship of citizens in arms'.[33] It was, though, only one song. In fact there existed thousands of popular songs, some with new tunes, some just adapting existing ones. In observing such 'light music' we must not think in terms of any simple congruence

29 F.-J. Gossec, *Rapport de la classe des beaux-arts de l'Institut* (1803), reprinted in J. Le Breton, *Rapports à l'Empereur sur le progrès des sciences, des lettres, et des arts depuis 1789* (Paris, 1989), v, p. 271.

30 Full score in Pierre, *Musique exécutée*, pp. 47–50; recording by The Wallace Collection on Nimbus, NI 5175. Another recording of interest is *Révolution française*, conducted by Michel Plasson on EMI, CDC 749470 2.

31 A. Lewis, 'Choral Music', in *The Age of Beethoven*, p. 657.

32 Pierre, *Les hymnes et chansons*, pp. 225ff. Its official title was *Chant de guerre pour l'armée du Rhin*.

33 S. Schama, *Citizens: a Chronicle of the French Revolution* (New York and London, 1989), pp. 598–9.

between idiom and audience. Yesterday's *opéra comique* audiences were enjoying the same tunes as today's street singers, or even today's worshippers. The gaiety of late *ancien régime* church music was everywhere apparent. 'During the elevation of the host and the chalice, they play ariettes and sarabandes', noted Louis-Sébastien Mercier in Paris.[34] In June 1781 the Bishop of Rennes complained about music at vespers, forbidding the singing in future of 'opera arias that cannot match the decency and majesty of Divine Service'.[35] (From this perspective, the sheer dignity and quality of much Revolution festival music presents a revolution in itself.) Conversely one might observe, reading Herbert Schneider's essay in the present book, that street tunes – if given exceptional social conditions – were often the bearers of deadly serious secular messages.

Perhaps we shall never manage to recapture the true contexture of musical experience at this time. But unless we try to enter it further, we shall remain outside the historical and musical significances of its own gestures. We shall mistake its various intentions. Scholars today are surely right to look more closely at the sound-world that reached forwards towards Romanticism and which inspired a Beethoven. Only some areas permit the musical historian, at this stage, to study concrete relations between theory and practice, and to apply analytic methods. Jean-Louis Jam's chapter, within, shows how this can be achieved. Other musicologists, apart from those mentioned so far, are looking at a variety of issues: musical copyright law,[36] patterns of theatre pricing and attendance, exact dating of theatre works,[37] visual evidence[38] and the music of political reaction.

Do revolutions create their own art, or do they simply modify existing forms? Opposing views are apparent even in the twin introductions to *Orphée phrygien* (see note 22). Jean Mongrédien quotes Henri Focillon in order to support the second thesis: '[revolutions] act on institutions ... But they use preceding forms'. J. R. Julien and J.-C. Klein propose the notion: '[a decade] is a very short time in which to revolutionize both the conditions of production and the production itself'. They throw the weight of achievement forward to the era of the pupils of Méhul (that is, Hérold), Le Sueur (Berlioz) and Cherubini (Boieldieu, Auber and Halévy). On the other hand, the present Introduction has mentioned

34 L.-S. Mercier, 'Orgues', in *Le tableau de Paris* (Amsterdam, 1782–8), ii, Chapter 131, pp. 81ff, quoted in J.-R. Julien, 'Paris: cris, sons, bruits', in *Orphée phrygien*, p. 46.
35 M.-C. Le Moigne-Mussat, 'Les musiciens à Rennes pendant la Révolution', in *Orphée phrygien*, p. 75.
36 F. Karro, 'Le musicien et le librettiste dans la nation: propriété et défense du créateur par Nicolas Dalayrac et Michel Sedaine', in *Etudes sur le XVIIIe siècle*, xvii: *Fêtes et musiques révolution-naires: Grétry et Gossec*, ed. R. Mortier and H. Hasquin (Brussels, 1990), pp. 9–52.
37 M. Noiray, 'Les créations d'opéra à Paris de 1790 à 1794', in *Orphée phrygien*, pp. 193–204.
38 Articles by R. Legrand and D. Lauvernier, in *Etudes sur le XVIIIe siècle*.

both the concept of 'national' music and the manifold circumstances in which different musics were created. We are still looking for the best questions to ask. Future writers will doubtless address new aspects: the Revolution and musical women (considering, *inter alia*, the new provision for their education after 1795), music in various parts of the French territories, typologies of musical material and the knowledge of French music abroad. Eventually, perhaps, we shall also come to study *ordinary* musical experience in the German-speaking countries during the Revolutionary decade.

ELEMENTS OF CONTINUITY

JULIAN RUSHTON

'Royal Agamemnon': the two versions of Gluck's *Iphigénie en Aulide*

Like the year 1789, 1774 represents for French opera not the first, but one of a series of upheavals – perhaps the one that marked a point of no return. It was a critical commonplace to call Gluck a musical revolution-ary.[1] In Paris the sixty-year-old composer put into effect his belief in the reunion of national styles: by way of *opera seria*, *opéra comique* and his own Viennese reform with Calzabigi, he synthesized the modern musical idiom learned in Italy with *tragédie lyrique*. He also insisted on a performing style to match his version, and not only vocally: by 'le travail d'un sergent instructeur'[2] he persuaded cast and chorus alike to present not an operatic entertainment with ballets, but a unified theatrical action.

Yet reform of French opera was already a live issue when Gluck reached Paris in November 1773. In December, at the marriage of the dauphin's younger brother, the Comte d'Artois (later Charles X), the court at Versailles witnessed no fewer than five operas, including three of reforming tendency by composers under Italian influence. Philidor's *Ernelinde* was a revival; at the Opéra in 1767–9 it had challenged traditional *tragédie lyrique* by its naturalistic, political plot and eschewal of the 'merveilleux'. It had also anticipated *Iphigénie en Aulide* in having three acts, but for Versailles it was arranged in the conventional five, allowing for additional ballets. Gossec's *Sabinus*, given for the first time, followed Philidor's musical lead but retained a supernatural element. Both operas are replete with chorus, spectacle and dance, and both end

---

1 G. M. Leblond, *Mémoires pour servir à l'histoire de la révolution opérée dans la musique par M. le Chevalier Gluck* (Naples, 1781), includes J. F. Marmontel, *Essai sur les révolutions de la musique en France* (Paris, 1777); reprinted in *Querelle des Gluckistes et des Piccinnistes*, ed. F. Lesure (Geneva, 1984), i. A critical analysis of *Iphigénie en Aulide* appears in my 'Music and Drama at the Académie Royale de Musique, Paris, 1774–1789' (Ph.D diss. Oxford University, 1969); the present article modifies this. T. la May discusses the opera in the light of social and political issues in 'The Search for an Epic Hero: French Serious Opera in Pre-Revolutionary Paris' (Ph.D. diss., Oxford University, 1978).
2 Castil-Blaze, *Théâtres lyriques de Paris: l'Académie Impériale de Musique* (Paris, 1855), i, p. 324.

with a 'ballet des nations'. When presented at the Académie Royale in Paris (February 1774), *Sabinus* was reduced to four acts to remove 'ce qui était rélatif à l'objet des fêtes de la cour'.[3] Grétry's *Céphale et Procris*, a bold attempt to reform the pastoral, was not seen in Paris until 1775. These works might have had a better chance with the Opéra audience, and *Ernelinde* might have been revived in Paris before 1777, had the controversy surrounding Gluck and the Italians not begun to dominate Parisian operatic life.

After a week's postponement, *Iphigénie en Aulide* was performed on 19 April 1774 in the presence of the dauphin and his wife, Gluck's former pupil Marie Antoinette, and other royalty. On 10 May Louis XV died and the Opéra was closed after five performances. When the theatre reopened it presented revivals of traditional repertory while preparing Gluck's *Orphée*, performed on 2 August; the sixth performance of *Iphigénie en Aulide* was on 10 January 1775, by which time it had been revised. Since *Orphée* is a work *sui generis* and hardly to be imitated, it was the ultimate success of *Iphigénie*, with renewed royal approval, that definitively launched French opera in a new direction. Although over-shadowed by its successors, *Iphigénie en Aulide* deserves especial attention as the first and decisive gesture in this phase of Gluck's campaign. Whereas his Orpheus and Alcestis operas were translated and virtually recomposed for Paris, the changes made to *Aulide* for the 1775 revival are not extensive; they nevertheless impinge upon its political, even revolutionary, nature.

The subject of Iphigenia in Aulis had been used by Gluck in a ballet, and was known in *opera seria* versions which, however, are unlikely to have affected the French opera.[4] There is no earlier *tragédie lyrique* despite, or perhaps because of, the familiarity of the subject to French audiences through Racine's *Iphigénie* (1674), a work both sternly political and, its reception suggests, lachrymose. Its published form has a trenchant preface setting forth Racine's views on the use of mythological material for modern tragedy. Gluck's librettist, du Roullet, was criticized for his treatment of the dramatic outline and the actual verses. Nevertheless his *Iphigénie en Aulide* is a respectable piece of work and Gluck's opera has been unduly neglected. Among his Parisian masterpieces it is a worthy

---

3 *Mercure de France*, April 1774, p. 160; reprint (Geneva, 1971), vol. cvi, p. 264.
4 Earlier settings include Capece and D. Scarlatti (1713); Zeno, set by Caldara (1718), Orlandini (1732) and Porta (1738); Rolli and Porpora (1735); Verazi and Jommelli (1751); Cigna-Santi, set by Bertoni (1762) and Franchi (1766); and Bottarelli and P. A. Guglielmi (1768). Gluck's Iphigenia ballet (1765) is lost; its music may have contributed to *Aulide*, just as *Semiramis* is recycled in *Tauride* (see G. Croll, 'Gluck, Christoph Willibald', in *The New Grove Dictionary of Music and Musicians*, ed. S. Sadie (London, 1980), vii, p. 462).

companion to *Armide* and *Iphigénie en Tauride*, and in its original form it is perhaps more radical than either; it is, however, not the original but the revised form that has been enshrined in two scholarly editions.[5]

The Greek army, ready to attack Troy, is becalmed at Aulis through the wrath of Artemis (Diana). The sacrifice of Iphigenia is ordained in propitiation. After Aeschylus, dramatic treatments tend to avoid Iphigenia's actual death, but they vary in contriving endings with or without the conventional descent of the goddess *ex machina*. The exact nature of the dénouement affects our understanding of the principal character, who in both play and opera is not the eponymous heroine but the elected leader of the Greek forces, her father Agamemnon.

In adapting Racine's play of nearly 2000 alexandrines, du Roullet perforce reduced Agamemnon's self-justificatory tirades, and cut the wonderful confrontations with his wife Clytemnestra and with Iphigenia herself (Act 2 scene ii; 3, i; 4, iii–iv). Few among the Athenian audience, or the Parisians of 1674 and 1774, can have been unaware of the sequel to the ancient story: after the conquest of Troy Iphigenia (presumed or actually sacrificed) was avenged by her mother, and Agamemnon avenged in turn by their son Orestes. This terrible chain of events, recounted in *Iphigenia in Tauris*, casts an ironic shadow over Gluck's *Aulide*: Iphigenia bids Clytemnestra 'Vivez pour Oreste mon frère' (3, v).

It is not surprising that French opera, generally concerned to promote a positive image of kingship, should have ignored Agamemnon for so long. He is in the power of the seer-priest Calchas, who dominates by exploiting the vulnerability of the merely human (even a king rules only by divine sanction); his chief weapon is the superstition of the army. Racine may even have intended a warning against the weakness of merely elective leadership such as Agamemnon's.[6] In his play Calchas casts a long shadow over the action without ever appearing on stage.[7] This image of religious tyranny, which may be compared with the hold of the Grand Inquisitor over Philip II in *Don Carlos*, is one of du Roullet's finest contributions. Like Verdi, Gluck embodies the Church–State conflict in a single disputation which lies at the heart of one of his most magnificent dramatic periods, from the opening of Act 1 to its mid-point, when the appearance of Iphigenia and her affairs of the heart reduce the surface, if not the underlying, tension.

5 *Iphigénie en Aulide*, ed. F. Pelletan and B. Damcke (Paris, 1873); ed. M. Flothuis in Christoph Willibald Gluck, *Sämtliche Werke*, Abteilung I (hereafter sw): vol. 5a (Kassel, 1987) contains the score, vol. 5b (Kassel, 1989, hereafter sw5b) the foreword, facsimiles and notes.
6 L. Dubech, *Jean Racine politique* (Paris, 1926), p. 214.
7 Calchas's role in the play has been assessed by R. Barthes, *Sur Racine* (Paris, 1963) and M. Delcroix, *Le sacré dans les tragédies profanes de Jean Racine* (Paris, 1970), and in the opera by W. Weismann, 'Der Deus ex machina in Gluck's "Iphigenie in Aulis"', *Deutsches Jahrbuch zur Musikwissenschaft*, vii (1962), p. 7.

Agamemnon's appalling dilemma is perhaps the most harrowing of all legendary child-sacrifices. For Abraham, in a less sophisticated culture, the Lord's word suffices: Isaac must be offered up. Jephtha and Idomeneus, their victims chosen by tragic coincidence, are bound by unbreakable oaths; but their other battles are over and each has received the boon for which his child's life is the price. Agamemnon has to pay in advance. He can save his daughter only by renouncing leadership, thus suffering a terrible humiliation: Iphigenia must die to save his face and ensure his glory. Unpleasant as this is, both Racine's poetry and Gluck's music contrive to make him sympathetic, particularly when his last move is another attempt, overwhelmed by the pace of events, to save his daughter. 'Agamemnon n'est pas un monstre, c'est un *médiocre*, une âme moyenne'.[8]

Gluck and du Roullet begin magnificently, with Agamemnon's lone defiance of Artemis ('Diane impitoyable', linked to the overture and using its opening motif). He turns for help to the sun, Helios, or possibly Apollo ('Brillant auteur de la lumière, Verrais-tu sans pâlir le plus grand des forfaits?'). Gluck underlies the change by replacing tight contrapuntal textures with a high-pitched homophony for 'Brillant auteur', the strings joined by the strained sonority of a tenor-register bassoon. From flat minor keys (G and C) and Eb major, he has reached a strikingly remote E minor, the tonal distance symbolizing a divided mind. In scene iii Agamemnon returns to C minor for further defiance of Artemis (and Calchas: 'Je n'obéirai point à cet ordre inhumain' (not 'divin')). In the central section sustained wind add melancholy appoggiaturas, also anticipated in the overture, for 'le cri plaintif de la nature'.[9]

In Euripides, Racine's principal source, Iphigenia is finally saved by metamorphosis, to pass many years in Tauris before she is taken home by Orestes. Racine concludes not with this equivocally 'happy' ending, but instead with the essential ingredient of comedy, a wedding. Agamemnon's tergiversation gives Iphigenia's betrothed Achilles the excuse and opportunity to intervene. The Great King and High Priest, militarily nonplussed if not defeated, can restore their authority only by the immediate cessation of hostilities, and their legitimacy by reference to its divine origin: supernatural intervention, pretended or real, is indispensable to them. The difference between the 1774 and 1775 versions of Gluck's opera is the difference between pretence and reality.

Gluck's portrayal of Calchas is given added weight by motivic cross-reference. Weismann points out that Calchas's dialogue with

---

8 R. Barthes, *Sur Racine*, p. 111.
9 This scene is analysed by Tovey in *Essays and Lectures on Music* (London, 1949), p. 92. Tovey's dictum that 'Gluck's highest pathos is expressed in the major mode. He uses the minor mode chiefly to express protest or energy' (pp. 96–7) is borne out by this aria, but modified by the rest

Agamemnon (1, iii) is introduced by a ferocious gesture ('Vous voyez leur fureur extrême', Ex. 1a), reproduced precisely, but in a smoother form, at the dénouement ('Votre zèle des Dieux a fléchi la colère', Ex. 1b). He also notes the resemblance between the powerful cadence in his public prayer to the goddess (1, ii, 'l'ordre que tu prescris') and his sardonic warning to Agamemnon (1, iv; Ex. 2a and b).[10] Another allusion to this musical shape, again in Bb, comes at the dénouement (Ex. 2c, one falling third now a rising sixth); this reinforces the connection between the opening and closing scenes which F. W. Sternfeld has compared to the ritornello effect of oracles and divine appearances in *Orfeo* and *Alceste*.[11] Both these cross-references lose

of Agamemnon's music: E minor (1, i) and A minor (2, vii) are used for prayer, self-communion, even pathos, while his protest at the end of Act 2 is in A major.

10 Weismann, 'Der Deus ex machina', p. 10.
11 F. W. Sternfeld, 'Expression and Revision in Gluck's "Orfeo" and "Alceste"', in *Essays presented to Egon Wellesz*, ed. J. Westrup (London, 1966), p. 129. (Sternfeld names not Artemis but Athene.)

Ex. 3

point in the second version when the goddess intervenes in person: Ex. 1b is used for her rather than for Calchas.

Calchas's 'Au faîte des grandeurs' sets up another sinister chain of resonance. The dotted rhythm is a normal attribute of eighteenth-century ceremonial music, but in the fifth bar it outlines a motif (Ex. 3a) which reappears to open the Act 2 quartet, 'Jamais à tes autels' (Ex. 3b). This is irony; the ceremonial anticipated in Act 2 is a wedding, but moments later we learn that Agamemnon is at the altar not to marry, but to sacrifice, his daughter. Ex. 3b is reproduced in D minor during the last quartet, after the dénouement (Ex. 3c). Calchas has fallen silent; but his power is confirmed. The dotted rhythm informs the *Marche* of the Act 2 divertissement (Ex. 3d, used in both versions: see Table 2), which provides the motif for the sacrificial hymn of Act 3 (Ex. 3e).

These passages share strong religious feeling. They are also examples of a degree of integration which reflects careful thought by the composer during a long period of gestation: Einstein goes so far as to suggest that *Aulide* is 'in a sense devised on a basis of *Leitmotiv*'.[12] Nevertheless, Gluck made several changes after the interruption of performances in 1774. They affect mainly the divertissements and have been largely ignored, presumably because critical orthodoxy would not include them in the dramatic part of an opera. This represents a mistaken view of the

12 A. Einstein, *Gluck* (London, 1936), p. 140. On gestation, Burney reported that Gluck played the unwritten opera to him in September 1772. See P. Scholes, ed., *Dr Burney's Musical Tours in Europe*, ii (London, 1959), p. 91.

ideal, a union of arts, which informs the best *tragédie lyrique* as it does Gluck's Viennese reform operas. *Orfeo ed Euridice*, which as *Orphée* was an immediate success in Paris, is rightly admired for its integration of dance and choral elements into the dramatic whole. If the dances in *Iphigénie* are a backward step, they are, like those of *Alceste* if not *Paride ed Elena*, a step from the *festa teatrale* towards *tragédie lyrique*. Nevertheless several early French critics considered the composer of *Don Juan* ineffective in dance music, and even the generally friendly *Mercure de France* referred to *longueurs* in the divertissements.[13] Choreography and costumes may have contrasted unfavourably with the dynamic staging insisted upon by Gluck elsewhere. The extent of the revisions to the divertissements suggests an attempt to meet this criticism.

The change that has received most critical attention – although several writers on Gluck omit to mention it – is the dénouement, where the music was hardly altered at all. A miraculous ending is indispensable to the Tauris story (Artemis intervenes to save her statue from profanation by human sacrifice), but the Aulis story offers other possibilities. Racine's sources furnished him with an alternative human sacrifice, Eriphile, who for some critics is the truly tragic character. This mysterious figure, whose real name proves also to be Iphigenia, enabled Racine to dispense both with the sacrifice of Agamemnon's daughter and with divine intervention:

Quelle apparence que j'eusse souillé la scène par le meutre horrible d'une personne aussi vertueuse et aussi aimable qu'il fallait représenter Iphigénie? Et quelle apparence encore de dénouer ma tragédie par le secours d'une déesse et d'une machine et par une métamorphose, qui pouvait bien trouver quelque créance du temps d'Euripide, mais qui serait trop absurde et trop incroyable parmi nous?[14]

How would it have seemed if I had besmirched the scene with the dreadful murder of someone as virtuous and likeable as Iphigenia must appear? And how would it have seemed to resolve my tragedy with the help of a goddess, a machine and a transformation, which might have found some credence in Euripides's time, but would be too absurd and unbelievable to-day?

The dénouement is described by Ulysses (5, vi): with a thunderclap, the funeral pyre spontaneously burst into flame. The apparition of Artemis is merely rumour:

---

13 *Mercure de France*, May 1774, p. 175; reprint, cvi, p. 374. See also the anonymous 'Lettre a Madame de ***, sur l'Opéra d'Iphigénie en Aulide', in *Querelle des Gluckistes*, ii, pp. 21f.
14 J. Racine, 'Préface' to *Iphigénie*. The conventions of neo-classical tragedy precluded presenting the dénouement on stage.

> Le soldat étonné dit que dans une nue
> Jusque sur le bûcher Diane est descendue
> Et croit que, s'élevant au travers de ses feux,
> Elle portait au ciel notre encens et nos voeux.

The astonished soldier says that Diana descended in a cloud onto the pyre, and believes that, rising through the flames, she carried our incense and our vows to heaven.

The fire and the opportune change in the weather may be viewed as miraculous, or taken as a combination of chicanery and luck: Calchas, noticing the impending storm, and unable to overcome Achilles and impress his priestly authority through the sacrifice, has the pyre surreptitiously lit and claims a miracle to satisfy the credulous troops. The possibility of interpreting apparent miracles as a concatenation of natural phenomena and human acts recalls the tenets of Jansenism, to which Racine subscribed.[15]

A 1769 production presented Racine's dénouement directly, like an opera. Ulysses's reported speech was turned into dialogue and action, with a few additional lines, resembling an opera libretto.[16] In 1773 Algarotti's *Saggio sopra l'opera in musica* was published in a translation by Chastellux, including an Iphigenia libretto.[17] Though a *philosophe* by conviction, Algarotti resorts to the *merveilleux*. He omits Eriphile; instead he revives Euripides's ending, in which a doe miraculously appears as an alternative offering (compare the sacrifice of Isaac).

Du Roullet's 1774 dénouement, which like the 1769 Racine pastiche includes no inescapably visible goddess, lacks any sacrifice. The wedding of Achilles and Iphigenia is perceived as the prelude to the invasion of Troy, a motif present in Racine but reinforced in the opera by a full-length divertissement, culminating in a bellicose chorus. In the score published in 1774 there is a pause shortly before the end of the huge and apparently final D major chaconne. Calchas sings 'Partez, volez à la victoire'; the chaconne concludes; and the chorus takes up these words to a sinuous unharmonized melody in D minor, unison almost to the end (Ex. 4). This strange music makes the ending feel

15 The 1676 edition of Racine's play has a frontispiece illustrating the goddess descending on a cloud, but Ulysses's apparent scepticism is supported by Racine's scorn for such devices. See also below, note 22.

16 G. F. P. de Saint Foix, *Dénouement d'Iphigénie* (Paris, n.d.). Staged on 13 July 1769 at the Comédie-Française, this ending was not a success because the stage was too small to accommodate the armies. It would be interesting to know whether du Roullet knew of this production, which preceded by a few months his proposal of this subject to Gluck.

17 That Algarotti's treatment affected du Roullet's (P. J. Smith, *The Tenth Muse* (London, 1971), p. 153; D. Heartz, 'Algarotti', *The New Grove* vol. 1, p. 256) is not clear from internal evidence; Algarotti, writing in French, keeps Ulysses, does not let Calchas appear, and adheres much more closely to Racine's dialogue. See also D. Heartz, 'Sacrifice Dramas', in *Mozart's Operas* (Berkeley, 1990), pp. 1–13 and Y. Giraud, 'Iphigénie entre Racine et du Roullet', in *L'Opéra au XVIIIe siècle* (Aix, Université de Provence, 1982), pp. 163–84.

Ex. 4

remote from the conventional *lieto fine*,[18] but the conception is original even in the libretto. *Ernelinde* also ended with a dramatic rescue at the sacrificial altar, but divine intervention could not arise in that case, since there is no divine motivation for the action; with Greek subjects it was expected. The 1774 ending echoes Racine's Jansenism, effectively questioning whether the gods exist.

In 1775 du Roullet and Gluck rendered the motivation of the action and its conclusion unambiguous by a short speech from Artemis. The tumult is quelled and she bids the young lovers live in happiness (which must appear fatuous to any spectator with knowledge of subsequent events). This depressingly conventional solution, like that of *Alceste* the following year, responds to negative criticism of the original. The only support for the first ending came from the sycophantic *Mercure de France*: 'Without the help of machines, and without the intervention of gods, a brilliant and majestic spectacle has been produced' ('Sans le secours des machines, et sans l'intervention des dieux, on a fait un spectacle brillant et majestueux').[19] The *Correspondance littéraire* found it unconvincing, while hinting at how it was staged:

Calchas, qui venait tout à l'heure de déclarer aux Grecs que la volonté inéxorable des dieux demandait le sang de la fille d'Agamemnon, change soudain d'avis et les assure prudemment que le ciel est satisfait; on jette une petite fusée sur le bûcher et tout est dit.[20]

---

18 On the dénouement within the tradition of the *lieto fine* see L. Finscher, 'Gluck und das lieto fine', *Musica*, xviii (1964), p. 296, and 'Gluck e la tradizione dell'opera seria', *Chigiana*, xxx (1975), p. 263; and Weismann, 'Der Deus ex machina'.
19 *Mercure de France*, May 1774, p. 170; reprint, cvi, p. 369.
20 F. M. von Grimm and others, *Correspondance littéraire* (Paris, 1877–82), x (1879), p. 416. This description is followed by J. G. Prod'homme, one of the few modern writers to notice the revised dénouement: see his *Gluck* (Paris, 1948), p. 214. Yet Calchas, in the original ending, admits military defeat: 'Et du fils de Thétis la valeur immortelle force leur justice éternelle de révoquer leurs ordres rigoureux'.

Calchas, who has just declared to the Greeks that the inexorable will of the gods demands the blood of Agamemnon's daughter, suddenly changes his mind and is at pains to assure them that heaven is satisfied; a small flare is thrown on the pyre and no more is said.

The *Journal encyclopédique* anticipated the eventual outcome:

L'action d'Achille, en arrachant la victime, est peu faite pour calmer une divinité du paganisme, toujours jalouse et délicate sur ce point. Ce serait une correction aisée de montrer Achille menaçant, et prêt à violer le respect des autels, mais arrêté par la descent subite de Diane.[21]

Achilles's action in seizing the victim is scarcely calculated to soothe a pagan goddess who is jealous and sensitive on this issue. It would be a simple improvement to show Achilles in a threatening attitude, ready to violate the respect due to the altars, but prevented by the sudden descent of Diana.

So simple, indeed, that Gluck added only a few bars. Work was in hand by May 1774:

On verra paraître Diane dans les nues, le ciel s'expliquera avec plus de dignité, et Iphigénie n'aura plus l'air de devoir ses jours à la frayeur du fourbe Calchas.[22]

Diana will be seen to appear in the clouds, the will of heaven will be expounded with more dignity, and Iphigenia will no longer seem to be about to owe her life to the cowardice of the cheat Calchas.

Because it was published and clearly had the composer's approval, the 1774 score acquired an authority out of proportion to the number of Paris performances it represents, a state of affairs which enabled Wagner to claim the introduction of Artemis in his 1847 version as his own invention.[23] Gluck's three Calzabigi operas all end with divine intervention, and the decision to end *Aulide* without cannot have been taken lightly. Weismann grants the 1774 score prime, as well as prior, status, claiming the alterations were made against Gluck's will.[24] This theory is attractive, but cannot be proved. Du Roullet, on the contrary, gave reasons for including the goddess:

Il est d'ailleurs essentiel dans l'Opera-Tragédie que le dénouement soit heureux ... Toute l'action du sujet d'Iphigénie en Aulide a pour base la colère de Diane. Les

---

21 *Journal encyclopédique*, May 1774, p. 519; reprint (Geneva 1967), xxxvii, p. 426.

22 *Correspondance littéraire*, p. 416. Grimm's tone suggests that this new dénouement did not necessarily meet with his approval; he shared Racine's view of supernatural intervention. See R. Angermüller, 'Reformideen von Du Roullet und Beaumarchais als Opernlibrettisten', *Acta musicologica*, xlviii (1976), p. 236.

23 Wagner's version is quite different from that of 1775, of which he may not have been aware. He had access to the printed (1774) score and to a manuscript score which he describes as 'the Berlin performing edition' (*My Life* (*Mein Leben*, trans. A. Gray and ed. M. Whittall, Cambridge, 1983), p. 337). This is now lost. It probably included alterations made by Spontini, who if he saw the work in Paris must have known the 1775 version. I am grateful to Horst B. Loeschmann for information concerning Wagner's version.

24 Weismann, 'Der Deus ex machina', p. 14.

prières et la soumission des Grecs peuvent désarmer le Déesse, et la clémence étant un attribut de la Divinité, il est dans la nature du sujet que Diane révoque ses ordres rigoureux; *qu'elle vienne elle-même* enlever Iphigénie de l'autel, où elle avait ordonné qu'on la sacrifiât, qu'elle la transporte en Tauride, etc. Ce dénouement surnaturel est dans le sujet …[25]

It is, moreover, essential in tragic opera that the ending is happy. … The entire action of the story of Iphigenia in Aulis is founded upon the anger of Diana. The prayers and submission of the Greeks can disarm the goddess, and, clemency being an attribute of Divinity, it is in keeping with the subject that Diana should revoke her strict orders; *that she should herself come* to abduct Iphigenia from the altar on which she had ordered her to be sacrificed, that she should transport her to Tauris etc. This supernatural dénouement is part of the subject. …

As a defence of the 1775 ending this is disingenuous; Iphigenia is not transported to Tauris. Du Roullet was perhaps confused because at this period he was apparently working on an *Iphigénie en Tauride*.[26]

The score published in 1774 was certainly prepared before the reception of the opera indicated to Gluck that alterations might improve its chances of continuing success. The new version, which remained in the repertory until the 1820s, survives in two manuscript scores in the Paris Opéra.[27] The earlier of these was used in the 1774 performances and adapted for those of 1775 and beyond. The later score was a replacement, certainly made after Gluck ceased to interest himself directly in this opera. Their successive readings are also recorded in the performing material.[28]

The librettos, however, offer little help. Some of them are commercial products, profiting from a revival, their texts simply copied from earlier publications. Table 1 lists seven librettos in the library of the Paris Opéra; only the last corresponds to the 1774 score.[29] If the librettos were our only source we might assume that the version printed in score was never performed. The handsome no. 1 has all the signs of being a

25 Du Roullet, 'Lettre sur les drames-opéra' (Paris, 1776), pp. 14–15; in *Querelle des Gluckistes* ii, pp. 120–21 (my italics).

26 See Gluck's letter to du Roullet of 1 July 1775; H. and E. H. Mueller von Asow, *The Collected Correspondence and Papers of Christoph Willibald Gluck* (London, 1962), p. 67.

27 Bibliothèque-Musée de l'Opéra, Paris (hereafter *F-Po*), A.229.a, the score used in 1774 and revised; and A.229.b. The latter, as sw5b points out (pp. xi and 583), uses a later notational style; it should follow that it is not an authentic source.

28 *F-Po* Matériel 18 [139. I am indebted to the library of the Paris Opéra for assistance in studying this material. sw5b (p. 583) states that nothing survives from 1774. Several parts were copied freshly at an unknown date (1775 or later), but many others show clear signs of origination in 1774, and like the earlier score are patched up to conform to later versions.

29 I have not seen the specimen listed in sw5b (p. 580) as 'Paris 1774', but the facsimiles and collation suggest identity with no. 1. In Table 1, no. 2 corresponds to sw 'Paris 1777', no. 3 to 'Paris 1782', no. 4 to 'Paris o.J.', nos. 5 and 6 to the two called 'Paris 1783', and no. 7 to 'Paris 1796'. sw also lists two librettos from Bordeaux, one from Stockholm (in Swedish!), one from Brno (in German) and two late examples from Paris (1788 and An VI (1797–8)); like no. 7, these are not authentic (du Roullet died in 1786).

Table 1   Librettos of *Iphigénie en Aulide*

	Date	Publisher	*F-Po* Liv. 18	No. of pages	Version[a]
1	1774	Delormel [*sic*]	367	63	2A[b]
2	1777	Ballard	369	67	2B[c]
3	1782	Ballard	370	62	2B
4	[1783]	Roullet	368	54	2A[d]
5	1783	De Lormel [*sic*]	371	28	2A
6	1783	Marchard de pièces de théâtre	896	24	2C[e]
7	1796	Marchands de nouveautés	372	39	1

Notes:
[a] Versions:
   1 corresponds to the 1774 score
   2 has the 1775 dénouement
     2A: with original form of Act 2
     2B: with revised form of Act 2, without Patroclus's solo
     2C: as 2A, but lacking the final words of Calchas and chorus
[b] 'Approbation' dated 19 March and wrong first performance date (12 April), copied in all the others.
[c] Nos. 2 and 3 related to court performances; in 1777 Iphigénie was sung by Sophie Arnould, in 1782 by Rosalie Levasseur, after their retirements.
[d] Undated. The cast list shows it to be no earlier than 1783 (Clytemnestra was sung by Maillard, who made her début that year; Iphigenia was sung by Mme Chéron, Agamemnon by Chéron, Achilles by Lainez, and Calchas by Adrien).
[e] No. 6 is the only libretto without the final chorus. The cast list is the same as for no. 4.

first publication, including the premature announcement of the first performance (12 rather than 19 April); but this error, followed in the full score (of which the *privilège* is as late as August 1774) and reproduced in later librettos, tells us nothing. Nevertheless no. 1 already has the dénouement with the goddess *ex machina*, although 'Diane' does not appear in the cast-list.[30]

SW is undoubtedly correct in regarding the intervention of Artemis as Gluck's final word on the dénouement, but we may question whether it is the best, or even his preferred, solution. Certainly he made no attempt to alter the printed score before relinquishing his rights to it in March 1775, after the success of the revival.[31] Not all later readings are necessarily improvements, and there is room for doubt about the authorship of some changes. Agamemnon's second great monologue (2, vii) reaches the heart of his struggle between injured pride, paternal love

30 The mystery of this libretto is that it contains the revised dénouement but the original Act 2. Conceivably du Roullet always intended Artemis to intervene, and the libretto was prepared on this understanding, in which case the score reflects Gluck's preference.
31 The negotiations, undertaken by the Austrian ambassador Franz Kruthoffer, to whom Gluck gave power of attorney on leaving for Vienna, are documented in Mueller von Asow, *The Collected Correspondence*, pp. 50ff.

and fear of retribution, and Gluck composed it with particular expressiveness. Having heard the 'plaintive cry of nature' (woodwind stilling his fury), Agamemnon perceives his own barbarity: 'Père inhumain! n'entends-tu pas les cris des Eumenides?'. According to SW the orchestra illustrates this with crude punctuating chords. The 1774 score includes sharply-etched semiquaver figures from flutes, second violins and violas, a far more telling expression of the forces, real or imagined, impinging on the king. SW corresponds to the final reading of the second Opéra score and the performance material, in all cases tipped in or glued over the original reading. Can Gluck, who in a later scene of imagined torment by the Eumenides (*Iphigénie en Tauride*, 3, iv) envenomed similar chords with sweeping grace notes and varied the texture with sustained wind and tremolo, really be responsible for weakening the invention of the *Aulide* scene, whose 'sifflements des Eumenides' were remarked on at the time?[32]

Nearly all the other variants are in the divertissements, although Act 1 was almost unaltered in 1775. It consists of a celebration of the youth and beauty of Iphigenia, and gains piquancy through irony: she has arrived as a victim, not a bride.[33] The Act 2 divertissement celebrates the prowess of Achilles. Although the framing chorus and quartet remained, much of this ballet was renewed in 1775 (see Table 2), with a significant shift of emphasis: instead of the future conquest of Troy (Patroclus vibrantly asserts that 'Hector et les Troyens vont mordre la poussière') we hear of Achilles's recent conquest of Lesbos, underlining his military power and capacity to defy Agamemnon and Calchas. Despite its length, which was probably reduced in most performances, this revision is an improvement, avoiding tautology in key (all three 1774 divertissements proceed from C to D) and dramatic meaning: it is for the final divertissement to anticipate the conquest of Troy.

Iphigenia's acceptance by the Thessalian troops (for whom she is a foreigner) led to a happy incident at the seventh performance (13 January 1775). Joseph Legros, who sang Achilles, gestured towards the royal party as he sang 'Chantez, célébrez votre reine', signifying that the

---

32 *Journal encyclopédique*, May 1774, p. 517; reprint, p. 426. The Eumenidian figure appears in all vocal scores consulted, including the earliest (1809), and was noted approvingly by Hoffman in a review (1810); see D. Charlton, ed., and M. Clarke, trans., *E. T. A. Hoffman's Musical Writings* (Cambridge, 1989), pp. 259–60. In F-Po Matériel 18 [139, there is one very clean first violin part, which SW5b agrees was evidently copied well after the others; it uses different paper (upright, white; not oblong, blue) and appears unused, but still contains the Eumidean figure as a cue. The 1873 score (see note 5) unequivocally brands this emendation a performer's simplification.

33 The ironic divertissement goes back at least to Lully's *Roland*. A comparable example is *Hippolyte et Aricie*, Act 3, where Theseus, like Agamemnon, suffers a divertissement while condemning his child to death.

Table 2   Act 2 divertissements

1774		'Chantez, célébrez votre reine' (in C) 1775	
Marche	G	Marche (air gai) (bis)	G
Moderato			
Patroclus and chorus	A		
Une Grecque	A	Une Grecque (air gracieux)	A[a]
Passacaille	D–A		
Gavottes	A–a–A		
Passacaille	A–D[b]		
		Choeur (*Paride*)	C
		Moderato (*Don Juan*)	C[c]
		Ballet	
		(Air des athlètes: *Paride*)	a
		Lentement	C
		Chaconne	C
		Gavotte gracieuse	
		(Entrée des esclaves)	a[d]
		Choeur des esclaves	a
		Recit	a–C[e]
		Air pour les esclaves	
		(two movements)	F[f]
		Quartet and Chorus: 'Jamais à tes autels' (in F)	

Notes:
[a] 1774: 'Son front est couronné'; 1775: 'Achille est couronné'.
[b] Passacaille and Gavottes used in Act 3 in 1775.
[c] Transposed to D in *F–Po*, A.229.b, where it and the following two numbers are marked to be omitted.
[d] Originally 'Gavotte gracieuse' in G. Throughout, 'Esclaves' are 'Esclaves lesbiennes'.
[e] Iphigenia gives the slaves their freedom.
[f] Taken from Act 3 of the 1774 score.

Scores and parts contain directions like 'Bruit de guerre', 'Roulement', 'Bruit de timballes' etc. at three points. These clearly represent performing practice, but are omitted from published scores.

Austrian dauphine was now the Queen of France: a moment of patriotic acclaim for the new reign and its deceptive promise (it is hard to see Louis XVI as Achilles). Perhaps this moment symbolized the acceptance of Gluck at the Paris Opéra.[34]

The Act 3 divertissement is essential to the opera's apparent plan. It ends with the unison chorus in D minor ('Partons, volons à la victoire'), restoring Agamemnon to the centre of attention; the army is setting forth under his leadership, and he introduces each verse before the chorus; the entire cast is united with a single political will.[35] Du Roullet (see above)

34 The incident is reported by Grimm, *Correspondance littéraire*, xi, p. 12, and by the *Mercure*, January 1775, p. 170 (reprint, cviii, p. 161).
35 This reading appears in the score used for performance (*F-Po* A.229.a) but not the printed score, which assigns all the music to the chorus.

said that the motivation of the opera was the anger of Artemis, but its subject is the price exacted by a concerted military venture. To end without reference to this is to falsify the whole structure.

Yet SW omits the final divertissement altogether, ending with the briefest mention of the future amidst the choral acclaim for the heroic young couple:

> Et leur hymen est le présage
> De nos triomphes glorieux.

The sources are by no means unanimous about the content of this *fête*, but it was standard practice at the Opéra to select from available music according to the ideas of the choreographer. There is no indication that any composer's sanction was sought for changes in the ballet after the earliest performances, and the importance of the ending as a block of time underlining a dramatic point is unaffected by detailed alterations. In this case its importance to Gluck may be gauged from the extent of the revision; the 1774 printed version disappears almost entirely from the Opéra scores. Table 3 compares 1774 with the later Opéra score, carefully copied from its exhausted predecessor.[36] Although they share so little music, both versions describe a tonal progression in which D, the eventual goal, is approached from C major by way of G, with a preliminary excursion to F. In 1775 the move is emphasized by the extension of the sharp side to A in the Gavottes.

No musical source implies unequivocally that the final divertissement should be suppressed, and certainly none close to Gluck, who left Paris for the last time in 1779. The orchestral parts, which indicate changing performance practice over fifty years, show a number of cuts and the removal, at a date impossible to determine, of the final unison chorus, 'Partons, volons à la victoire'.[37] Not even the most carefully prepared librettos (nos. 1, 2 and 3 in Table 1), unfortunately, list the actual dances; but they have the word 'DIVERTISSEMENT' at the appropriate place in each act and include the final chorus. Nos. 2 and 3 list new

---

36 Unlike the rest of the score, the final divertissement (including the unison chorus) in *F-Po* A.229.b shows no sign of use. But it is unlikely to have been copied unless some use of it was anticipated.

37 The avowed aim of sw is to reconstruct the version seen in 1775. The editor is not unaware of the problem: 'Da es an jeglicher Angabe, *wann* diese stattgefunden haben, fehlt – somit auch nicht feststellbar ist, ob sie vom Komponisten autorisiert wurden –, ist es sinnlos, sie in einer Neuausgabe der Partitur zu berücksichtigen' (p. 10). However no evidence is offered to show that Gluck was personally responsible for omitting the final divertissement. On the contrary, the performing material suggests that a final divertissement was usually given, and that some, at least, of the music was Gluck's. The material was presumably used over some fifty years and should perhaps not have been the edition's 'Hauptquelle'; more regard might have been paid to an earlier edition with the same objective (p. xi), that of 1873 (see note 5), which omits the final chorus, ending with the passacaille (see Table 3). Only the clean first violin part (see note 32) lacks the divertissment; but this was copied much too late to be evidence of Gluck's intentions.

Table 3 Act 3 divertissements

Quartet: 'Mon coeur ne saurait contenir' and chorus: 'Jusqu'aux voûtes éthérés' (in F–C)			
1774		1775	
Amabile	C	Amabile moderato (3/4)	C[a]
		Allegro moderato (2/4)	G
Grazioso	C	Allegro moderato (2/4)	G
		Aria 'Heureux guerriers'	C
Danse d'esclaves	F[b]	Gigue	F
Air gai	G		
Tambourins	D–d–D		
		Air gracieux	C
Menuetto	G–g–G	Gavottes	G–g–G
		Gracieux	C
Menuet	G	Andante (3/4)	G
Air: une Grecque (*Paride*)	C		
Ariette (Aria) D (Achille: 'J'obtiens Iphigénie')[c]			
Chaconne	D[d]	Passacaille	D–A[e]
		Gavottes	A–a–A
		Passacaille	A–D
Choeur: 'Partons, volons à la victoire' in D minor[f]			

Notes:

[a] The same piece in both versions.

[b] Taken into Act 2 in 1775.

[c] Headed 'Ariette' in A.229.a. The use of 'Aria' instead of this precise French term is a symptom of the relatively late date of A.229.b.

[d] 279 bars. 37 bars from the end is the recitative for Calchas: 'Partez, volez à la victoire'. Transferred to *Orphée*, 1774.

[e] The Passacaille–Gavotte–Passacaille sequence (284 bars) comes from 1774, Act 2. F–Po A.229.a and the parts show several cuts within the movement, implying continued use.

[f] F–Po, A.229.a (but not the 1774 score) includes a Moderato [Andante] in D minor, after which 'on reprend le choeur' (i.e. the second verse).

The divertissement copied into F–Po A.229.b is probably a repertory, not designed to be used as a whole. A.229.a shows minor variants, adding an Air in A and a Gigue in D. In their final state, the parts suggest that the vocal items came to be omitted, but there is no indication when. The final chorus survives in some parts; most end with the Passacaille.

dancers for the final act.[38] Two of the librettos published in 1783 mention the final divertissement, and these take us well beyond the time when Gluck had any say in the matter. Only one libretto (no. 6), which has no particular authority, omits the final chorus and Calchas's final injunction ('Partez, volez ...', for which, however, there is no music in the 1775 version; its inclusion in other librettos must be an oversight).

38 'Prêtres et prêtresses'. Unless the divertissement was unusually simple for a court production, other dancers will have reappeared in previous roles; for both Acts 2 and 3, libretto no. 1 lists

Under the *ancien régime* a final divertissement was usual unless the ending is tragic, as in *Armide* (which nevertheless has a divertissement in each act). Gluck did not compose one for *Iphigénie en Tauride*, but one was performed, with music by Gossec. Divertissements conclude adaptations of old librettos as late as Sacchini's *Dardanus* (1784). Grétry's *Andromaque* (1780) mitigates Racine's tragic ending in favour of a wedding and final ballet, and a new final divertissement was added to Piccinni's *Atys* when it was revived in 1783 with a *lieto fine*.

In July 1775, several months after the Aulide revival, Gluck revealed how criticism of his dance music had hurt him:

I will have no more ballet airs in my operas apart from those which occur during the action of the opera, and, if people should be dissatisfied with this, then I will do no more operas, for I will not let myself be reproached in all journals that my ballets are weak, mediocre, etc., and so the scoundrels shall hear no more by me . . .[39]

Having studied the market, Gluck would not have wilfully neglected the ballet in his first offering to French audiences. We ought, therefore, to take the divertissements seriously, as, clearly, did Gluck and the contemporary critics who disliked them. The apparent rejection of divertissement after the dénouement is the effect of pique, and refers specifically to *Cythère assiégée*; if anything, it implies that there had been a final divertissement in the recent performances of *Aulide*.

The revised divertissements in Acts 2 and 3 and the new dénouement are Gluck's work. But given the care with which the 1774 version was composed, none of the changes needs be accepted without question unless 'Fassung letzter Hand' is the only criterion of authenticity. The new dénouement changes the meaning of the opera, giving it a conservative, albeit Enlightenment, outlook; it is surely legitimate to agree with Racine's view on divine intervention, even if the source play should not, as a rule, be used to evaluate the solutions adopted in an opera. The divertissements may well be pruned in performance, but the more relevant dramatic thrust of the second-act revision is worth preserving. The Act 3 versions make the same tonal bridge and are of equivalent quality; the transferred Passacaille prohibits mixing 1774 Act 2 with 1775 Act 3. Either way, the D minor chorus (which makes just as good sense after the passacaille as after the chaconne) is essential to the work's proper balance.

Iphigénie en Aulide is one of the most integrated operas of its time: among associated repertory it yields only to the ephemeral Lemoyne

'Grecs et Grecques, Guerriers Thessaliens, Aulidiennes, Esclaves Lesbiennes' (facsimile, sw5b, p. xv).

39 Letter to Franz Kruthoffer, 31 July 1775, cited in Mueller von Asow, *The Collected Correspondence*, p. 68.

(*Electre*) and *Idomeneo*. The opening scenes are fluid but dramatically cogent, a sequence of musical characterizations built into a dramatic tableau unmatched by the huge musical blocks in *Alceste*. The overture, measured by the precepts of the *Alceste* preface, is Gluck's finest, presenting the principal thematic (in the broader sense) elements of the opera in the manner of a prologue.[40] The plaint of Agamemnon, the inexorable unison later associated with the armies, the bustle of the camp, the cry of nature (woodwind semitones as in Agamemnon's Act 1 defiance): all are represented. But, *pace* Einstein (see note 12), Gluck does not use his overture as a source of reminiscence motifs or leitmotifs; his methods are less overt. Some of these motifs, or images, are inarticulate signs, cross-references without clear denotation: 'motifs' may be too specific a term. The army's G major unison (not a consistent texture, but prominent at cadences) has different melodies in Acts 1 and 3; the unison idea reaches from the overture to the final chorus. The 'cri plaintif' is a semitone in the overture and 1, iii, where at its most complaining it is an appoggiatura; in Agamemnon's second monologue it is reduced to frozen dyads and descending chromatic 6–3 chords.

Study of tonality yields no simple associations between keys and characters or events, except perhaps between Bb and Calchas. Table 4 indicates the broad tonal areas, but keys in opera probably make less impact than more immediate elements. D major is recognizably brilliant in eighteenth-century terms, but when Achilles explodes into 'Calchas, d'un trait mortel blessé' it is the entry of the trumpets after a long silence that makes the effect; it does not matter whether he sings in D (the 1774 score) or C (1775).

The only tonal pattern is the regular progression to sharper keys within acts. After the overture, C is quitted in a flatward direction, with the striking exception of Agamemnon's E minor air. Eb and Bb characterize Calchas and the army's prayer (they recur in Act 3, for the sacrificial hymn and 'Adorez la clémence'). Gluck sets passages of wide-ranging modulation against areas of stability. C major returns for Iphigenia's entrance, and the divertissement moves steadily to D. This prepares G minor for Iphigenia's finest aria ('Hélas, mon coeur sensible et tendre'), but her quarrel with Achilles goes as far sharp as A in their arias; D returns when harmony is restored in the duet.

Act 2 also begins in C major, and it is used decisively for a chorus ('Chantez, célébrez'): in 1775, two choruses. The 1775 divertissement reverses the usual trend (see Table 2), concentrating on C major, A minor and F; F is taken up in the celebratory 'Jamais à tes autels' (losing a noble opening gesture in D minor, however, which links it to the

40 See R. Wagner, 'Glucks Ouvertüre zu "Iphigenia in Aulis"', *Gesammelte Schriften*, v (Leipzig, 1872), p. 149; and C. Floros, 'Das "Programm" in Mozarts Meisterouvertüren', *Beihefte zur Denkmäler der Tonkunst in Oesterreich* (1964), p. 145.

Table 4 Summary of tonality and recurring motifs

	Motifs[a]	Keys[b]	Outline keys
Act I			
Overture			C major
	(1, 2, 3)		
Scenes 1–5			C major
1	(1)	g, Eb, e	
2	(2, 4, 1 inverted)		
		G, g, Eb, c, Eb	
3	(2, 3)	Eb, c, C	
4–5	(5, 4)	Bb, C	
Divertissement			G to D
		G, D, A, D	
Scenes 6–8			F to D
		F, g: A, a, D	
Act II			
Scenes 1–2–3		C, F:	C to F
Divertissement (1774)			G to D
		G, C, D, A, D	
Divertissement (1775)			G to F
		G, C, a, C, a, F	
	(5)	F	
Scenes 4–7			F to A
4–5		c, f: b, C, G:	
6–7	(3)	F: a–A	
Act III			
Scenes 1–3 (1774)			G to D
	(2)	G: Bb, Eb, D	
Scenes 1–3 (1775)			G to C
	(2)	G: Bb, Eb, C	
Scenes 4–7			G to Eb
	(2)	G, g, Eb	
Scene 8			G to C
	(2, 4, 5)	c, G, b: Bb, F, C	
Divertissement			C to D
(1774)		C, F, C, G, D/d	
(1775)		C, F, C, G, D, A, D/d	

Notes:
[a] Motifs (1) Agamemnon ('Diane impitoyable')
(2) Unison texture (army)
(3) 'Cri plaintif'
(4) Calchas (Exx. 1.1 and 1.2)
(5) Ceremonial motive (Ex. 1.3)
[b] Tonalities: these are seldom juxtaposed. A colon indicates that the bridge (usually recitative) makes a tonal *relation* very tenuous.

passacaille in 1774). A disruptive sequence (F major, B minor, C major) marks the peripeteia. Recitative destroys the sense of progression, but F, established for the angry duet, extends into the final scene, Agamemnon's monologue; here the pace of modulation in the obbligato recitative is precipitate and recalls his previous solo scene, before he settles into A minor and major.

In Act 3 G major is firmly associated with the barbaric unison of the army. Iphigenia's arias are in Bb and Eb; the inveterate seeker after key symbolism will note that resignation has brought her into Calchas's region. This flatward movement parallels Act 1, culminating in Clytemnestra's G minor aria and the sacrificial hymn in Eb. The fighting begins in C minor; the army restores G major. Tonal movement accelerates, Calchas using B minor and Bb. The final sharpward movement begins with the F major of the reconciliation quartet ('Mon coeur ne saurait contenir') and the C major chorus with which, according to SW, the opera ends. This progression nearly reverses that of the opening scenes, but the drama does not end where it began and Gluck planned to conclude on a higher note: defiance of Troy brings D minor, hitherto little used. This progressive system, in which each act ends with reconciliation (of the lovers; of Agamemnon with himself; of everything) and in a sharper key, is another reason for retaining the final divertissement.

If the story is founded on the anger of Artemis, its central action is a purely human struggle. One pity of war is that judgment and natural affection become clouded by the desire for glory. We need not believe in the gods; what matters is that Gluck convincingly presents people in the grip of that belief. The dramatic tension is surely stronger, as Racine implicitly recognized, if Artemis remains unseen. The apparent incomprehension of the 1774 audience is understandable, but should not prevent us from valuing the original conception.

So many forces contend with the flawed humanity of Agamemnon that one cannot simply condemn his vacillations. No Gluck opera is richer in characterization: Clytemnestra, worthy mother of Mozart's Electra; the vacuously resplendent Achilles; and Agamemnon's sole support and cruellest enemy, the filial compliance of Iphigenia. Gluck's music achieves as much as Racine's supple alexandrines, and with Agamemnon he reached new heights. We cannot equate this 'Macbeth of the enlightenment'[41] with the dying Louis XV, but drama in all its forms has no finer image of majestic impotence. Is this, perhaps, why *Iphigénie en Aulide* continued to interest Paris into the 1790s and beyond, and why as late as 1797 the audience greeted with delight the

---

41 W. Dean, in *The New Grove*, vii, p. 471.

farewell performance by the sixty-year-old Larrivée in the role he created in 1774?

Gluck does not appear revolutionary outside the particular cultural ambiance of Paris in the 1770s; pensionnaire of emperors, composer for archdukes and archduchesses, he is a figure of the *ancien régime*. Yet *Iphigénie en Aulide* is intensely political, without being propaganda for one faction or another. Like the greatest art, it can survive incompatible interpretations. The *ancien régime* might see legitimacy restored in a triumphal D major, revolutionaries an image of a rotten, priest-ridden body politic, and a new hope in youth (Achilles, ancestor of Siegfried).

Such fruitful ambiguity, however, depends on keeping the original dénouement. If we accept that Gluck's rejection of it need not be definitive, the opera is enriched. The marriage and reconciliation of the Greek powers become sub-plots, adequately finished in the quartet and C major chorus. The super-plot is the dangerous delay in moving against Troy; in passages of (for him) exceptionally wide-ranging modulation, and in the magnificent choruses of the outer acts, Gluck shows a community turned against itself. Only the final divertissement and chorus suffice to symbolize the restored political will of the people gathered in Aulis.

The final chorus goes further. Its sentiments may seem unequivocal, it is supported by the unison which we associate with the army, and Gluck cast it in the minor, with unison orchestration apart from the bass drum,[42] belying the confidence of the words ('Que notre gloire soit des siècles futurs l'éternel souvenir'): this D minor is equivocal in harmony, uncertain in its scale, and unstable in its modulations, defined only by the melodic line with its fleeting suggestion of the Dorian mode (see Ex. 4). The significance of this unprecedented gesture is clear: the dotted rhythm recalls earlier references to sacrificial ritual, but the victims will be the flower of Greek and Trojan manhood, including Achilles.

By calling into question the integrity of Calchas, the original dénouement threatens the legitimacy of Agamemnon's leadership on which the unity of the army depends. Weismann considers this inspired ending to be characteristic of the Enlightenment.[43] But it is surely more original than that, and more prophetic, even if the endings of *Orfeo*, *Alceste* and *Idomeneo* are perceived as typical. The *philosophes* were not generally in favour of anarchy or atheism, and the most widely-held

42 This rare use of the bass drum was praised by Berlioz in *A travers chants* (ed. L. Guichard (Paris, 1971), pp. 124 and 195). Berlioz makes it plain that this chorus had been omitted (he cannot have heard it in performances of the 1820s); on this slender evidence the 1873 edition confidently infers its omission as early as 1775.

43 Weismann, 'Der Deus ex machina', p. 14. Although I diverge from his conclusions (as perhaps from his ideological standpoint), Weismann's is the most thorough attempt to get to grips with the question.

political ideal was an ordered society under an enlightened ruler, a Sarastro: at various times Joseph II of Austria, Gustav III of Sweden, and Algarotti's patron, Friedrich II of Prussia, aspired to this Platonic role of Enlightened monarch ruling not by Divine Right but by divinely ordained duty.

Ambiguity is scarcely characteristic of Enlightenment thought, and given the artificiality of the exercise of working out a modern version of a Greek drama, the intervention of Artemis could be accepted as more rational than the 1774 ending: she symbolizes harmony and reconciliation, and reinforces the authority of the priest and hence of the king. Flothuis goes so far as to call the new ending 'logical'.[44] Youthful vigour must be turned from rebellion towards conquest; if a king yields power to youth it should be an organic process, as in *Die Zauberflöte*. In 1774 the success of Achilles questions the legitimacy of the system, but in 1775 his rebellion, motivated by love, is assimilated into the higher order. The latter, surely, is the Enlightenment solution, comparable to *Idomeneo*. The original version, by contrast, can be seen as revolutionary: without a visible goddess there is a residue of doubt, and the unison chorus sets the seal on a feeling of impermanence. So original, so chilling, is this invention that it is hard to believe Gluck consented to its removal. I hope, indeed, that my analysis of progressive tonality is not merely a rationalization of my feeling that the true message of *Iphigénie en Aulide* is its grim depiction of the fleeting nature of reconciliation, the inevitability of further conflict. Today as much as in 1789 there can be little doubt of the relevance of such an image.

44 sw5b, p. xi.

MICHAEL F. ROBINSON

Opera buffa into opéra comique, 1771–90

The long-term effects of the so-called Querelle des Bouffons of 1752–4 upon the relationship of Italian and French opera in France can be summarized in two ways. The Querelle made little impact upon the century-old policy of the Académie Royale de Musique, which held the monopoly of opera set throughout to music, to preserve the distinctive, national character of its productions. Little or no Italian influence therefore permeated the types of opera, notably *tragédie lyrique*, that the Académie habitually promoted on its own stage. Upon the artistic product of the other Parisian lyric companies, the Comédie-Italienne and the Opéra-Comique, however, the Querelle had a more profound effect. Earlier in the century these companies had customarily staged *comédies-vaudevilles*, comedies in which sections of the text were set to pre-existing popular music. After the Querelle both developed the so-called *comédie mêlée d'ariettes*, a genre in which sophisticated, Italian-style music in the form of arias (*ariettes*, as they were called in French) and ensembles alternated with the dialogue. The arrival in Paris of the Italian Egidio Duni in 1757 to compose some of these new *comédies mêlées d'ariettes* and the adoption by many of the best French composers – Philidor, Dauvergne, Monsigny and then Grétry – of the basically Italian techniques of aria and ensemble writing strengthened the development of this type of opera. Henceforth the new *comédie* had the advantage over the older *comédie-vaudeville* of being able to combine, at least in theory, a well-organized, coherent plot (such as was found in the best French comedies) with music capable (as Italian music was particularly capable) of portraying human sentiments and personalities in a comical and psychologically apt manner. There is not the space here to discuss whether the French made the most of this advantage in their *comédies mêlées d'ariettes* generally. But how well did they succeed when they took already existing Italian operas and transformed them into *comédies*? This essay provides information about the social and political background affecting the production of Italian opera in France in the years leading to the start of the French Revolution and offers tentative views about whether the particular Italian operas rearranged as *comédies* did incorporate the best qualities of French and Italian theatre.

The takeover of the Opéra-Comique by the Comédie-Italienne in 1762 gave further impetus to the development of Italian features within the new genre. The *comédie mêlée d'ariettes* was henceforth unequivocally associated with the Comédie, which was the 'Italian' theatre of Paris in the double sense that it included plays in Italian among its productions as well as operas with Italian-style music.[1] In 1769, in fact, its actors were forbidden to perform plays in French and thereafter had to rely on comic operas and on plays in Italian to stay in existence as a company. Although the operas staged in the 1760s in this theatre owed much to Italian example, they included no 'parodies'[2] of existing Italian operas written for Italian audiences. Parodying, the art of applying new texts to old music, had been a time-honoured technique in the French theatre; it had been a crucial factor during the Querelle, of course, when several Italian operas, including Pergolesi's *La serva padrona*, had been adapted and staged in French.[3] The absence of Italian parodies from the *comédies mêlées d'ariettes* staged during the 1760s means that at that time the French thought they were producing as good music for their purposes as the Italians. This attitude was to change a decade later as the desire arose again to hear not merely operas composed by Frenchmen in the Italian manner but operas composed by Italians for theatres in Italy.

The point at issue, still relevant long after the Querelle was over, was whether or not the French should do more to assimilate the good aspects of Italian music. Several of the *littérateurs* who had been among the original supporters of the Italians in the disputes of the early 1750s continued a decade or more later to be exasperated by conservative aspects of French grand opera and to extol the virtues of Italian opera as an alternative. One finds instances of their pro-Italian sentiment in articles in the later volumes of the *Encyclopédie*[4] and in Grimm's *Correspondance littéraire*. In an extreme form one finds it in sections of Rousseau's *Dictionnaire de musique*, where in the article on 'Génie', for example, the author proclaims that only Italian composers like Durante, Pergolesi and Jommelli have 'genius', and that if other composers cannot hear this they should turn to writing French music[5] (music which

---

1 C. D. Brenner, *The Théâtre Italien: its Repertory, 1716–1793, with a Historical Introduction*, (Berkeley and Los Angeles, 1961), pp. 9–10.
2 See the definition of 'Parodie' in J.-J. Rousseau, *Dictionnaire de musique* (Paris, 1768), pp. 367–8: 'Dans une Musique bien faite le Chant est fait sur les paroles, & dans la *Parodie* les paroles sont faites sur le Chant'.
3 I. Mamczarz, *Les intermèdes comiques italiens au XVIIIᵉ siècle en France et en Italie* (Paris, 1972), pp. 236–7.
4 See especially the *Encyclopédie* articles on 'Musique' (vol. x (1765), pp. 898–902) and 'Poème lyrique' (vol. xii (1765), pp. 823–36).
5 J.-J. Rousseau, *Dictionnaire*, pp. 320–21.

Rousseau had earlier, in his *Lettre sur la musique française* of 1753, professed to abhor). The ideas of the pro-Italian Encyclopedists were much permeated by the sense of admiration they felt for the works of the immediately preceding Italian generation: Vinci, Hasse, Durante and, especially, Pergolesi.[6] This was the generation which, to their way of thinking, had achieved perfection in music by combining simplicity of style with intensity of expression.[7] But this interpretation of the past implicitly raised the question whether contemporary Italians were maintaining the high standards that earlier composers like Pergolesi had attained. Grimm, who during the period 1758–62 had written strongly in support of Duni's comic operas in French, wrote on 1 February in the *Correspondance littéraire*:

Il est vrai que le goût a changé en Italie; que M. Duni, sorti de la même école à qui nous devons les Vinc [*sic*], les Hasse, les Pergolèse, est trop simple, que son goût a un peu vieilli, qu'il n'a pas ce nerf ni ce style vigoureux par lequel les compositeurs modernes ont cherché à remplacer le génie des grands hommes que je viens de nommer.[8]

It is true that taste has changed in Italy; that M. Duni, who emerged from the same school to which we owe Vinci, Hasse and Pergolesi, is too simple, that his taste has become a little too old, that he has neither the zest nor the vigorous manner with which modern composers have tried to replace the genius of the great men I have just named.

The re-emergence of the Italian parody in France in the 1770s must therefore be interpreted in part against a background of literary propaganda by the Encyclopedists that both fanned the curiosity of the French about Italian music and, paradoxically, helped keep French doubts about it alive. The specific issue – whether or not new Italian-style music could suit French theatre – was very much prompted by these mixed feelings. It was central of course to the Gluckiste-Piccinniste squabble fought between groups of patrons of the Académie Royale de Musique. But it had equal relevance in the case of comic operas, and especially parodies of Italian comic operas, produced by the Comédie-Italienne and other, smaller theatre groups.

One should not overemphasize the importance of Italian parodies in the French operatic world before the Revolution. The number of such works produced during the 1770s and 1780s was quite small, a tiny proportion in fact of the total number of comic operas then being performed in France. It is difficult to say whether the small number was

---

6 M. F. Robinson, *Naples and Neapolitan Opera* (Oxford, 1972), p. 30.
7 This opinion of Italian composers of the 1720s–40s was still being expressed at the end of the century; see A.-E.-M. Grétry, *Mémoires, ou Essais sur la musique* (Paris, 1789), pp. 505–7.
8 F. M. Grimm, D. Diderot and others, *Correspondance littéraire, philosophique et critique*, ed. M. Tourneux, vi (Paris, 1878), p. 189.

proportionate to the actual demand. The facts suggest that the demand for the most recent Italian music was as strong in the 1780s as it had ever been, and that perhaps it was increasing. The formation of an extra company producing Italian operas and Italian parodies (the Théâtre de Monsieur, which opened its doors on 26 January 1789) is one piece of evidence supporting this view. The Appendix, below, lists *opera buffa* parodies known to have been produced between 1771 and 1790. It reveals that the Comédie-Italienne was the first company to promote such works in the 1770s, but that it largely abandoned them in the 1780s. It provides evidence of the constant interest in these works at court (where musical taste was largely controlled by Marie Antoinette) up to the start of the Revolution. And it shows how, during 1789 and 1790, the number of parodies suddenly increased as a result of the activities of the Théâtre de Monsieur and then of the Théâtre Montansier.

The Appendix also indicates which particular Italian comic music was staged as parody; this music was presumably what the French imagined they were not getting in their own *comédies mêlées d'ariettes*. A glance at the list reveals from the start the reliance upon a rather limited group of Italian sources: either upon certain Italian operas which had been particularly successful at home, for example Piccinni's *La buona figliuola*, or upon the music of composers who enjoyed an exceptional reputation, such as Paisiello. It is noticeable how the arrival of both Piccinni and Sacchini in France (the first in 1776 and the second in 1781) was preceded by the production of a parody of one of their more successful works. Piccinni's *La bonne fille* was presented in 1771, *La colonie* (the parody of Sacchini's *L'isola d'amore*) in 1775. With both Piccinni and Sacchini in France during the 1780s (Sacchini died there in 1786), there was of course little need to bring their music to performance in the form of parody; both composers were producing new operas in French for the French stage. Paisiello's case was different. The French librettist N. E. Framery tried hard in 1781 to persuade Paisiello to write the music of a new opera in French, but the composer, who was in St Petersburg at the time, would not agree.[9] The only way, therefore, to present his operas in French was to parody them. This, plus the fact that Paisiello was probably the greatest single name among Italian composers during the 1780s and 90s, explains why he appears so prominently in the Appendix.

The reason why the Comédie abandoned Italian parodies in the 1780s was that it lost its legal right to perform them. In the second half of 1779 new agreements were drawn up which completely transformed what it

---

9 Framery's letter of invitation to Paisiello, dated 5 May 1781, is in F. Schizzi, *Della vita e degli studi di Giovanni Paisiello* (Milan, 1833), pp. 89–90.

was permitted to stage. As a result of these agreements it recommenced productions of spoken comedy in French on 15 July 1779. It abandoned plays in Italian at the end of that season (that is, in April 1780). And, as a result of a new contract (*bail*) signed between it and the Académie which came into force on 1 January 1780, it renounced the production of new parodies of Italian opera. In return the Académie agreed not to introduce foreign music into its ballets.[10] What the *bail* reconfirmed, in practice, was the Académie's right to place restrictions on the activities of its chief rival when they appeared to challenge its privileges. Henceforward the Comédie was unable commercially to exploit Italian music. It could continue to stage its pre-1780 parodies. But the only new operas with an Italian connection that it could produce were *opéras comiques* (i.e. *comédies mêlées d'ariettes*) with original music by Italian composers.[11]

The new arrangement was supposed to give the Comédie a monopoly over *opéra comique*, but it failed to do so. One reason was that it was operative within Paris only. Every other company therefore could perform comic opera in the provinces. But equally injurious to the Comédie's monopoly was its inability, and that of the Académie, to keep other companies out of Paris. A small troupe called the Théâtre Beaujolais started to perform *opéras comiques*, including occasional parodies, at the Palais Royal in 1784.[12] And in 1789, as already stated, a new company called the Théâtre de Monsieur drove a complete horse and carriage through the existing arrangements by reinvoking an old privilege granted to a private company by Monsieur, brother of Louis XIV, and getting it resuscitated in the name of the present Monsieur, the Comte de Provence. The Théâtre set out to produce operas in Italian, comic operas (including operatic parodies) in French and French spoken plays, an infringement in practice upon the old rights of all the privileged companies in Paris: the Académie, the Comédie-Italienne and the Comédie-Française.[13]

The Académie's motives for signing the 1780 agreement had been affected as much by pique at its own recent failures to exploit Italian music commercially as by envy of the Comédie-Italienne. Its major mistake in this context had been the hiring of an Italian troupe during the 1778–9 season to perform *opere buffe* in the original language. The singers turned out to be mediocre, and once the novelty of their

---

10 Brenner, *The Théâtre Italien*, pp. 13–14.
11 Piccinni composed a number of *opéras comiques* for the Comédie during the 1780s.
12 M. Noiray, 'L'opéra de la Révolution (1790–1794): un "tapage de chien"?', in *La carmagnole des muses: l'homme de lettres et l'artiste dans la Revolution*, ed. J. C. Bonnet (Paris, 1988), p. 361.
13 N. E. Framery, *De l'organisation des spectacles de Paris, ou Essai sur leur forme actuelle* (Paris, 1790), pp. 149–52. Framery adds that the Comédie-Française quickly prevented the Théâtre de Monsieur from staging French comedies in more than two acts.

performances wore off the audiences disappeared.[14] From 1780 onwards the Académie wanted neither to have anything to do with Italian opera itself nor to let others have anything to do with it. During the 1780s, therefore, it did very little to satisfy the public demand for the latest Italian music. It did not repeat the 1778–9 experiment of inviting an Italian *buffa* troupe to perform on its stage. And it produced but three parodies of existing Italian operas, Anfossi's *L'incognita perseguitata*, Paisiello's *Il barbiere di Siviglia* and his *Il re Teodoro in Venezia*. All three operas, it will be noted, had already been parodied by other companies in France, and one gets the impression that the Académie staged new versions only because the operas in question had achieved a degree of success already.

The first of the three, *L'inconnue persécutée*, had originally been produced by the Comédie-Italienne at Fontainebleau with words by P. L. Moline. When the work, with a new text by de Rozoy, appeared at the Académie in 1781, Moline republished his libretto with a preface claiming: first of all, that the Comédie had been prevented from performing his version in Paris after its production at Fontainebleau 'par ordre supérieur' (had the Académie anything to do with this order, one wonders?); secondly, that he had lost his own rights as author of the text with the signing of the new *bail*; and thirdly, that the Académie had in effect expropriated his text, inserting some of it into its own production without acknowledgment. The same Moline however must have been on better terms with the Académie by 1787, for it was he who provided the texts for the Académie's parodies of Paisiello's two most famous operas, *Il barbiere* and *Il re Teodoro* that year. The publication of the score of his version of *Il re Teodoro* (by Cousineau *père et fils*) came several months before its stage production and may even have predated the Académie's decision to put it on stage. An advertisement for the score appeared in the *Mercure de France* for 12 May 1787, but the work was not premièred until 11 September. One could guess in any case that the score was not specifically published with the Académie in mind from the fact that it contains spoken dialogue rather than passages of recitative in between Paisiello's items (by convention the Académie's productions had accompanied recitatives). In many other particulars the score differs from the version actually staged in September.[15]

A little of the frustration some Parisians felt at the Académie's policy of keeping the Italian influence at bay can be sensed in comments in the

---

14 Some further remarks on the 1778–9 season are in D. Charlton, *Grétry and the Growth of Opéra-comique* (Cambridge, 1986), pp. 181–2. See also T. de Lajarte, *Bibliothèque musicale du Théâtre de l'Opéra* (Paris, 1878), p. 313, for comments on the financial failure of the last opera of the Italian series.

15 Paris, Bibliothèque-Musée de l'Opéra, MSS A 322[I–III] contain the version of the opera more or less as it was performed.

Mercure de France on 3 March 1787, in an article entitled 'Réflexions sur quelques objets particuliers aux Théâtres Français et Italiens'. The author, after commenting on how the *bail* had been to the advantage neither of the Académie nor of the Comédie-Italienne, went on:

> On a couru en foule à Fontainebleau, à Versailles, pour entendre la délicieuse musique du *Roi Théodore*, & la Capitale n'en peut jouir! On en permettra l'exécution à de mauvais Batteleurs à vingt pas au-delà des barrières; mais les productions divines des Paesiello, des Sarti, des Anfossi, des Cimarosa seront arrêtées aux murs de Paris comme de la contrebande.

> The crowds have been flocking to Fontainebleau and Versailles to hear the delicious music of *Roi Théodore* [a reference to the Dubuisson parody performed in 1786], but the capital is not allowed to enjoy it! Incompetent 'batteleurs' may perform it twenty paces outside the barrier, but the divine creations of Paisiello, Sarti, Anfossi, Cimarosa, are stopped at the walls of Paris as if they were contraband.

When the Académie Royale de Musique imposed this rigorous restriction on the *comédiens italiens*, the writer continued, it did so on the pretext of using this music itself and performing it on its own stage. But it had not done this, nor was it capable of doing so in a satisfactory way, because, in the writer's opinion: comic music was more effective when heard in a smaller theatre; French actors were unaccustomed to performing action of the 'grotesque' kind; Italian operas were too long and needed to be shortened so that ballets could be introduced; and the simple recitatives had to be replaced by accompanied. All these circumstances combined to ensure that the French comic operas specially written for the Académie, for example, Grétry's *Colinette à la cour*, *La caravane du Caire* and *Panurge dans l'isle*,[16] were the best contemporary operas in the comic vein that the Parisians could hope to see.

The remark that any 'batteleurs' could perform Italian opera outside the gates of Paris seems to have caused offence on the grounds that it could be taken to refer to, among others, the actors at Versailles. So on 17 March 1787 another, shorter article appeared in the *Mercure* called 'Notice sur le spectacle de Versailles', saying that no criticism of the opera there had been intended. It praised especially the 1786 production of *Roi Théodore*, and reinforced the point that, whereas any team could perform this opera outside the capital, only the Académie could perform it within and that it was not doing so. The appearance of a new published score of *Roi Théodore* (Moline's) in May and the Académie's production of it in September have therefore to be seen against a background of public pressure for productions involving Italian music to occur inside as well as outside Paris.

The other circumstance producing a groundswell of opinion in favour

---

16 These three Grétry operas were first performed at the Académie in 1782, 1784 and 1785 respectively.

of a reintroduction of Italian parodies on the Parisian stage was the successful appearance in the summer of 1787 of an Italian troupe at Versailles performing *opere buffe*. This troupe was basically the one then engaged at the King's Theatre in London. Having the summer free, it came across to Versailles for a limited season of thirty performances that included Cimarosa's *L'italiana in Londra* and *Giannina e Bernardone* and a pastiche of Paisiello's *Le gare generose* (now renamed *Gli schiavi per amore*).[17] These performances achieved a standard by which any future Italian opera at the Académie was inevitably going to be judged. Much therefore depended on the quality of the first Parisian production of *Roi Théodore*, premièred on 11 September. In the event the Académie proved unequal to the challenge. The *Mercure* edition of 29 September reported that the work had not met with acclaim. It criticized Moline's text, the inappropriate ballets and the recitatives sung by the performers in a stodgy manner unsuitable for comedy. The great success of the earlier *Roi Théodore* at Versailles, it went on, had led the Académie to think that any version would create the same effect because of its music. The Versailles version, however, had been better written (by P. U. Dubuisson), and 'above all better arranged, because, being in simple dialogue, it was better performed' ('sur-tout mieux arrangé, puisqu'il est en simple dialogue, & par conséquent il a été mieux exécuté').

There seems no doubt that the Académie's inability at this time to satisfy the demand for comic opera in the Italian style helped pave the way for the formation of the Théâtre de Monsieur. The Théâtre de Monsieur from its inception had two opera troupes, one Italian and one French. All the contemporary reports confirm that initially the French troupe was more favourably received than the Italian. As 1789 progressed, however, the situation went into reverse, and the Italian one gradually acquired the better image. Some of the reasons for this reversal of fortune are clear. The list of operas staged by the Italian members of the company between 1789 and 1791 is impressive, both in terms of the comparatively large number of different operas and the number of composers represented – beside the names of Piccinni, Paisiello, Anfossi, Cimarosa and Sarti, already mentioned, one finds those of Tritto, Mengozzi, Martín y Soler, Guglielmi, Salieri, Storace, Tarchi and Gazzaniga – a wide spectrum, in fact, of contemporary Italian talent. By comparison the French list is more limited; one can see from the Appendix how the parodies on this list are based (at least officially) on the music of a very few composers, Paisiello prominent among them. The French troupe had as its function the task of 'playing these same [Italian] operas in translation, imitated and parodied in French, and

---

17 *Mercure de France*, 18 August 1787.

[playing] other authorized works' ('jouer ces mêmes Opéras traduits, imités, parodiés en Français, & autres pièces autorisées').[18] But here there was a problem. Audiences might prefer parodies, which after all were in the vernacular, to Italian operas, but only if they were in their own way as good as, or better than, the originals. In point of fact, as the Appendix shows, a large proportion of the French repertory was made up not of parodies of recognizable works but of musical pastiches with new plots – perhaps so that comparisons would not be easy to make. Nonetheless the audiences did draw comparisons between the two troupes, much to the disadvantage of the French one in the long term. Both its repertory and its singing were judged more and more unfavourably. As Framery explained:

Il arriva que les amateurs du genre Français se degoûtèrent; ils cédèrent aux Ultramontains une place qui ne leur paraissait pas valoir la peine d'être défendue, & l'enthousiasme exclusif de ceux-ci décida, sans contradiction, que jamais l'Opéra Français ne serait en état de soutenir la concurrence contre l'Opéra Italien.[19]

It happened that the lovers of the French genre became displeased, and yielded to the Italians the [superior] place which they no longer considered it worth while to defend. The enthusiasm exclusively reserved to the [lovers of Italian music] determined once and for all that never again would French opera be in a condition to challenge the Italian.

As a postscript Framery added some extra comments upon the most recent events in the theatrical world of Paris in the middle of the year 1790, including the fact that the Théâtre Montansier, the company which had begun performances at the Palais Royal in April under 'demoiselle Montansier' (previously manager of the theatre at Versailles), was doing well;[20] also that the Monsieur was building itself a new theatre in the Rue Feydeau and that it was trying to reanimate its production of French opera. On the latter point the author had doubts. It would need good actors and good works, he wrote, neither of which is common.[21] He was right in assuming that the French section of the company was in no immediate position to challenge the Italian. It entered 1791 with a minimal repertory and in no position to embark upon a large number of new parodies of Italian operas.[22]

It was mentioned earlier that parodying was a way of supplying a demand both for Italian-style music in general and for certain Italian operas in particular. Before making an assessment whether, during the period preceding and overlapping the start of the Revolution, the French

---

18 Framery, *De l'organisation*, p. 151.   19 Ibid., p. 155.
20 Ibid., p. 256. The Montansier company replaced the Beaujolais company at the Palais Royal.
21 Ibid., pp. 255–6.
22 Cf. the Monsieur repertory for 1790–91 as listed in M. Noiray, 'Les créations d'opéra à Paris de 1790 à 1794', in *Orphée phrygien: les musiques de la Révolution* (Paris, 1989), pp. 196–9.

art of parodying the Italians was, on balance, successful, it is perhaps useful to consider in more detail what the techniques of the art actually were. In theory, of course, the words were supposed to be built around the music, so the words were changeable but the music was not. The opening sentences of Dubuisson's Preface ('Avertissement') to the 1786 libretto of *Hélène et Francisque* air the general views and the general policy that most *parodistes* adopted.

Le désir de faire connaître aux Amateurs de la bonne Musique le chef-d'oeuvre du célébre [*sic*] PAESIELLO, me fit naître l'idée de traduire en François son Opéra du ROI THÉODORE A VENISE, fait & joué à *Vienne* en 1784, par l'ordre de S. M. l'Empereur.

   Cet entreprise présentait plusieurs difficultés. Le Poème Italien, quoique d'un Auteur renommé, ne pouvait être adapté à la Scène Française sans de très-grands changemens: mais, en se les permettant, il fallait aussi conserver les plus beaux morceaux de Musique du grand Maître dont le génie est empreint par-tout dans cet Ouvrage, & c'est à quoi je me suis principalement appliqué; c'est, aussi, ce qui doit servir de réponse à toutes les objections que l'on pourrait faire contre un plan dont la coupe a dû necessairement être fort gênée.

   The desire to introduce lovers of good music to the masterpiece of the celebrated Paisiello instilled in me the idea of translating into French his opera of *Re Teodoro in Venezia*, composed and performed at Vienna in 1784, by order of His Imperial Majesty.

   This undertaking presented many difficulties. The Italian poem, although by a well-known author, could not be adapted to the French stage without major changes. While making them, care had to be taken to preserve the most beautiful pieces of music by the great master whose genius is everywhere stamped on this work, and this was my principal objective. The same argument [about preserving the music] must serve as reply to all the criticisms that can be made of a [textual] structure much cramped and restricted of necessity.

   In practice the amount of change in both text and music very much depended upon the degree of respect the adapter felt for the original. One extreme is represented by the 1784 parody of Paisiello's *Il barbiere di Siviglia*, in which the parodist, Framery, did the minimum necessary to change the Italian opera into a French one, merely by translating the words of the arias and ensembles from one language to the other and replacing the simple recitatives by dialogue from Beaumarchais's original play. He felt no need to do more for the simple reason that the opera itself follows the play in all its details − in a manner unique in an 18th-century *opera buffa*. Paisiello's major decision, once he had decided to compose the work, had been to choose which parts of the action he would set as recitative, aria or ensemble. Once these choices had been made, he had simply arranged for the French text to be translated into the right kinds of Italian verse, which he then set to music accordingly. The reverse process, from *opera buffa* to *opéra comique*, was an easy one for Framery to instigate. He was even able to re-use

Beaumarchais's original words for the two songs that in the opera appear as the Count's serenade in Act 1 and Bartolo's *seghidiglia* in Act 3 (because Paisiello had preserved the Frenchman's metre and verse lengths).

Quite the opposite procedure was followed by Framery in his parody of Paisiello's *La frascatana*, entitled *L'Infante de Zamora*. Madame De La Haye, reporting in the *Mercure* (9 June 1781) on the previous success of *L'Infante* at Strasbourg, was quite right when she described this work as 'parodied on the music of *La frascatana*, although the two subjects have no connection one with the other' ('parodié sur la musique de la *Frascatana*, quoique ces deux sujets n'aient ensemble aucune espèce de rapport'). The story of *La frascatana* concerns a young girl from Frascati, Violante, who is courted not only by the man she loves, Nardone, but also by two other admirers whom she regards as tiresome: a Cavaliere Giocondo and her miserly guardian, Don Fabrizio. The cavaliere, however, is already 'promesso' to a high-class lady called Donna Stella. Two servants, one male and one female (Lisetta and Pagnotta), complete the cast. The ending can be guessed long before it occurs: Violante marries her sweetheart, Giocondo marries his Donna Stella (as he is committed to do before the start) and the two servants marry also. Framery, on the other hand, concocts a story of a chivalrous Breton knight, Chevalier Monrose, who on his way to Toledo to marry a Lady Olympia meets in mysterious circumstances a beautiful woman (actually L'Infante de Zamora), with whom he falls in love but whom he tries to avoid as he imagines she is an enchantress. She is equally in love with him, and tests his affection by following him around dressed as a male page. At the end of the opera, after Monrose has declared (on the point of endangering his life in a tournament) that his heart is still with his enchantress, there is an extraordinary change of scenery (reminiscent of the *merveilleux* element in grand opera):

Le mur du fond s'écroule, et laisse voir un Palais magnifique; L'Infante est sur un trône, à ses côtés est Dona Mendoça; au milieu d'elles une place vide. Toute la Cour de l'Infante environne le trône.[23]

The back wall collapses, and there appears a magnificent palace; the Infante is on a throne, to her side is [her friend] Dona Mendoça, and in the middle is an empty space. All the Infante's court surrounds the throne.

Needless to say, Monrose's desires are fulfilled, as he is invited to fill the empty place by the side of his beloved.

The only episode in the plot of *L'Infante* which is clearly influenced by the action of *La frascatana* is the one at the end of Act 2. In the Italian

---

23 Stage direction at the start of Act 3 scene vii in the score, published by d'Enouville (Paris, [1790]).

opera Don Fabrizio locks up Violante in a tower in the forest and then tries to abduct her in the middle of the night. She, however, is saved by the timely intervention of Nardone and others. In *L'Infante* there is a rather similar scene in which Monrose, hearing that his page has disappeared in the forest, follows her to the tower and saves her from a group of 'géants'. The similarity of the two scenes allows, of course, for the use of the same music. Elsewhere, however, Framery has to match Paisiello's music with a different dramatic plan. He has managed to retain fourteen of the original twenty-four arias and ensembles of *La frascatana* more or less in the original order. But he has also inserted six items from another Paisiello opera, *Il tamburo*, at various places, and also a piece from a third Paisiello opera, *Il gran Cid*.[24] What cannot be answered at the present time is why he decided to use the music he did. Did he initially plan to use just the music of *La frascatana* but then change his mind, or had he the intention of using pieces from *Il tamburo* from the moment he began the project?

One thinks one can see the librettist's way of working rather more clearly in the case of *Le tuteur avare*, performed by the small Beaujolais company in 1787. Gabiot de Salins had definite intentions at the start of creating a parody of Anfossi's *L'avaro* – in Act 1 of *Le tuteur* five of the six lyrical items, including the finale, are taken from Anfossi's score. But in Act 2 only two of the six items are traceable to *L'avaro* (and one of these has an altered ending by G. M. Cambini), while in Act 3 none of the five items is from Anfossi's opera. The published score of the French work credits most of the music not attributable to Anfossi to Cambini, who was in Paris at the time, while Anfossi was not. It therefore seems likely that Salins, who had little experience of parodying, started with the intention of using Anfossi's pre-existing music but found it increasingly difficult to do so as he altered details of the story here and there. His solution was to ask a composer to complete the rest of the music after the words – the work therefore starts as a parody but ends as an ordinary *opéra comique*.

There were other reasons, too, why an adapter might have felt the need to change aspects of the music. Maybe the original music was too difficult for the singers. In the parody of Piccinni's *La buona figliuola* of 1771, for example, the adapters have left out the two important 'serious' characters, the Marchesa Lucinda and the Cavaliere Armidoro, who play such a major role in the Italian original since they are the two who object to the marriage of the 'good maid' (Cecchina in the Italian opera, Rosette in the French) to the marchesa's brother, the Marchese della Conchiglia, and effectively prevent it until the young girl is discovered to

24 More information on the sources of this parody is in M. F. Robinson, *Giovanni Paisiello: a Thematic Catalogue of his Works*, i (New York, 1991), p. 185.

be of noble birth herself. As a replacement character who can object to the marriage, they have created an elderly comtesse. The suspicion that maybe the music of the marchesa and cavaliere was too difficult and too much in the style of *opera seria* for the singers of the Comédie-Italienne is aroused by the fact that the comtesse's part is much less technically demanding than theirs. It is worth noting, by the way, that the long chain finales of Acts 1 and 2 have been severely cut, not for any dramatic reason that one can see but because, in all likelihood, they were once again musically too difficult or too complex.

The other point of interest about this particular parody is that in Act 3 a further new character appears, namely the Colonel, father of Rosette, in time to recognize his daughter and give his blessing to her marriage with the marquis. Perhaps dissatisfied with the rather casual way in which the Italian librettist, Carlo Goldoni, unravels his dénouement – an offstage disclosure by an old woman of Cecchina's past history, and the production of a letter that conveniently confirms her noble birth and convinces the marquis's family that she can marry into it – the adapters have added some extra touches to the ending to make the marriage more socially acceptable: the father gives his consent in person, and Rosette is re-established within her own parents' circle at the same time that she marries into the family of the marquis. This extra episode underlines two further reasons why parodists made often quite drastic changes to the original work. One reason was that they did not wish characters to behave in ways offensive to French standards of social propriety. The other was that they wanted the episodes to follow one another with some degree of verisimilitude and lead to a well-founded dénouement. For the sake of imprinting French social and intellectual values upon the text, parodists were prepared to sacrifice the original music if need be.

Other obvious cases of alteration for the sake of manifesting correct propriety occur at the endings of Dubuisson's and Moline's versions of Paisiello's *Il re Teodoro in Venezia*. In the Italian opera Teodoro is a deposed king living in Venice with no money and endeavouring to survive on charity. His debts become so large that finally he cannot repay them; he therefore finishes up in a debtors' prison.[25] The moment of his arrest occurs in the middle of the finale of the last act. Afterwards he appears in prison where various companions come to console him. Whether he regains his freedom, however, is a matter left unresolved. The opera ends with the cast providing no material aid to the king; instead it sings the moral that whoever rises to the top can easily fall downwards again on the wheel of fortune. This ending was clearly felt

25 The plot is inspired by Chapter 26 of Voltaire's *Candide*, in which six deposed monarchs, including a King Theodore, are described staying at a Venetian inn. Voltaire's character is in turn based on the historical figure of Baron Theodor von Neuhof, who in 1736 fought for the independence of Corsica and became its king for a short while.

by both Dubuisson and Moline, when they undertook their parodies, to be unsatisfactory – it does not take too much imagination to understand why in the political context of 1786–7. In neither of their versions does Théodore end in gaol. Both of them altered the story at the moment of his arrest, creating a situation whereby his debts could be immediately repaid in full. Moline managed to preserve the music of the prison scene more or less intact, superimposing new words, but Dubuisson cut most of it out.[26] Both, though, kept the final moral; the 'happier' context in which it now appears softens, of course, its apparent cynicism at the way the world goes.[27]

The most common motivation for major changes, however, was the French disdain for what they regarded as incoherent or ludicrous episodes in the works they were adapting. Throughout the period in question barely a voice was raised in France, not even by the most ardent Italophile, in support of the skills of Italian librettists as creators of sensible plots.[28] The following extract from the Preface of the printed score of *L'esclave, ou Le marin généreux*, a 1773 parody of Piccinni's *Gli stravaganti*, gives an indication of the level of scorn many Frenchmen felt. It summarizes the scenario of the original work thus:

Au fait, une jeune fille tient un Caffé, pour parler décemment, et loge sans façon le prémier venu; son amant dans sa tendre fureur court aprés elle, l'épée á la main; surpris, il s'excuse disant qu'il poursuivoit un chat: Un Capitaine qui se dit l'egal d'Hercule, qui a défait lui seul, les Maures, les Turcs et les Arabes, débarque tout exprés pour venir débiter des platises, et a peur des Ours dans un pays oú il n'y en a point; son Esclave plus courageuse, sort de nuit d'une ville qu'elle ne connoit pas, pour courrir des bois qu'elle n'a jamais vûs; L'amant de Caffetiére devenu perfide,

26 There is no prison scene in the full score of either the Dubuisson version (published by Huguet and Leduc) or the Moline (published by Cousineau *père et fils*). However, in the printed 1786 libretto of the Dubuisson version (published by F. Hayez) Théodore does go to gaol before being released. This illustrates the difficulties of determining the precise form in which some parodies were produced on stage.

27 *Il re Teodoro* was produced in Italian with its original ending at the Monsieur in February 1789. The *Mercure* (14 March 1789) reported that complaints had been made about leaving the king in prison at the end, and added: 'C'est une faute sans doute, quoiqu'il y ait beaucoup de philosophie dans cette idée.'

28 Italian plots had already been criticized by Grimm in 1762:

> ... ce qui empêche qu'on ne devienne absolument fou des opéras bouffons d'Italie, c'est que le poeme d'ordinaire n'a pas le sens commun. Ce n'est pas que le dialogue n'en soit facile et vrai, ou qu'il manque de situations très-plaisantes et vraiment comiques, mais l'intrigue qui les amène est presque toujours détestable, et, après l'air le plus sublime qui transporte d'admiration pour le musicien, on est livré aux plus plates bouffonneries du poete.

See. F. M. Grimm, D. Diderot and others, *Correspondance littéraire*, v (1878), p. 192.

Later W. A. Mozart was a witness to how the music sustained *opere buffe* in Paris despite their poor librettos. He wrote to his father on 13 October 1781: 'Why do Italian comic operas please everywhere – in spite of their miserable libretti – even in Paris, where I myself witnessed their success? Just because there the music reigns supreme and when one listens to it all else is forgotten'. See *The Letters of Mozart and his Family*, ed. E. Anderson (London, 2nd edn, 1966), ii, p. 773.

cherche la belle Esclave dont il s'amuse á tracer le nom sur les arbres, et ce nom paroit tout eclatant au milieu des ombres; il la trouve enfin endormie par ses soucis; elle s'eveille, elle lui parle, loin d'etre enchanté de trouver l'objet qu'il cherche, il en a peur et le prend pour une ombre des champs elisées quoi qu'ils se soient quittés il y a un quart d'heure, en trés bonne santé. Enfin aprés bien de Contradictions et mille autres facéties de cette espéce, le dénouement arrive á l'ordinaire, par une lettre aussi peu vraisemblable que tout le reste, dans un jardin fort éclairé oú ils se retrouvent subitement tous quatre et oú ils se marient, comme s'ils n'avoient ni deraisonné ni courru toute la nuit. C'est tout ce fatras qu'on nommoit *les Extravagants*; il faut avouer que jamais titre n'a mieux été rempli.[29]

As for the facts: a young girl is proprietress of a coffee house, to use the decent expression, and provides lodging without ceremony to the first gentleman who comes along. Her lover, furious at this, runs after her with drawn sword. Surprised [while in the act of chasing her], he excuses himself, saying he was pursuing a cat. A sea captain who calls himself the equivalent of Hercules, who single-handedly defeated Moors, Turks and Arabs, disembarks to say some silly things. He has great fear of bears, although the country which he is in has none of them. His female slave, who is more courageous than he is, slips at night out of the town, which she does not know, into woods she has never seen before. The lover of the coffee house owner, with perfidious intent, searches for the beautiful slave and amuses himself trying to trace her name on the trunks of the trees. Her name, indeed, appears all sparkling in the midst of the shadows. At last he finds her asleep, exhausted as a result of her cares and sorrows. She wakes and speaks to him, but far from being delighted to find the person he is seeking, he takes fright and imagines her to be a ghost from the Elysian Fields – this although he had left her only a quarter of an hour earlier in very good health. At last, after all the contradictions and the thousand other sillinesses of this work, the dénouement is reached in a very ordinary way, by means of a letter which is no more probable than any of the rest, in a well-lit garden in which all four characters suddenly find themselves and in which they all get married, as if they had never for a moment been deranged or run about for the entire night. All this rubbish is called *Les extravagants*. One must confess that never has a better title been discovered.

One needs at this moment to distinguish between episodes in Italian opera that are far-fetched because they create a farcical situation and those that stretch credulity because they lack motivation and link badly with what occurs before and after. The French were quite right in saying that Italian opera had too many episodes of the latter kind. In partial defence of Italian librettists one could argue that theatrical conventions at home were such that they had to pay more attention to the demands of singers to sing the requisite number of arias and ensembles in the right order (and to leave the stage after their arias) than to the demands of audiences for plots that were perfectly logical. If in an Italian *opera buffa* characters come on stage without any particular motive for doing so, or at times when reason dictates they should not be there, this is usually

---

29 The spelling is as in the full score published by Rigel (Paris, ?1774).

because the librettist has calculated that their turn for an aria or ensemble is due shortly; the performance of this aria or ensemble is even more important than the need to maintain dramatic coherence. The French had never been slave to a tradition which laid down that characters had to sing such-and-such a number of items in turn, and at the end of each leave the stage. A comparison of an *opera buffa* and its French parody usually brings the different theatrical traditions of the two nations clearly to light. In the parody such arias and ensembles as are retained will often be found to be both in a rearranged order and shifted from the end of 'scenes' to the beginning or middle of them (that is, moved to places where the singer cannot depart immediately afterwards). This greater freedom to place the music wherever they wanted ought to have given parodists the opportunity satisfactorily to amalgamate Italian music, with its particular comic and psychologically apt qualities, with a plot coherent enough to please the severest French intellectual.

More research needs to be carried out before anyone can properly assess how well they succeeded. But if, as seems likely, the final verdict is that most parodies are rather mediocre, the reason for the mediocrity has to be sought as much in the unsatisfactory nature of the art of parodying as in the lack of genius they displayed. In the first place it was not always possible to change the details of an Italian opera to please French sensibilities without destroying many of its good qualities. Part of the fun of many an *opera buffa* is that its characters often seem socially to act 'out of character': men of rank may, for example, behave or talk stupidly; girls of the bourgeois class may flirt in a brazen fashion most unbecoming of respectable young maidens. By comparison, the characters in the parodies have better drawing-room manners and tend to lack the multiplicity of facets, the mixture of conventional and bizarre qualities, of their Italian counterparts. But the music they sing occasionally suffers too. One is not just thinking here of the fact that spoken dialogue replaces the simple recitatives, so that the parody provides less of a musical experience throughout than the original opera.[30] One is also aware that some French librettists were insensitive to the rhythms and flow of the original vocal lines and superimposed ungainly translations.[31] A further point is that (almost by the nature of things) where the sense of the words is changed, the new words and the old music tend to match imperfectly rather than perfectly.[32] By the 1770s–80s *opera buffa*

---

30 Parodies with music throughout (i.e. with accompanied recitatives rather than spoken dialogue) were rare because they were permitted only at the Académie.

31 Instructive in this context is the comparison of Framery's and Moline's versions of *Le barbier de Séville*; Framery's translation preserves Paisiello's musical prosody much more carefully and sensitively than Moline's.

32 The view that parodying rarely produces satisfactory results for the reason that the words naturally inspire music rather than vice-versa was one commonly held in the eighteenth century.

music was displaying an increasing diversity of forms and textures to fit the dramatic situation of the moment. Being composed for one particular dramatic episode, an aria or an ensemble could not easily be adapted to suit a different purpose. The replacement of one piece of music by another, or the use of a piece in a different dramatic context, required more sensitive treatment than some parodists applied.[33]

All the evidence is therefore that, during the period leading to the start of the Revolution, French adapters of Italian opera never quite overcame the peculiar problem they were faced with of preserving as much of the original music as possible and, at the same time, of making the plot coherent and socially acceptable. Alone among Italian operas *Il barbiere di Siviglia* presented them with no problem for the reason that its plot derived directly from a French play of recognized worth. Framery expressed the sort of difficulties that they faced in most other cases in the Preface to the printed libretto of his *La colonie*. Obliged to conserve all Sacchini's musical pieces, so he claimed, he had been forced to keep to the same basic action ('fonds de sujet') as in the original opera and almost follow the same details ('marche'), whence were derived 'the faults of the structure, the entries, the badly motivated exits, the weakness of many scenes which do not keep the action moving. These faults are in the original work' ('les vices de contexture, les entrées, les sorties mal motivées, les langueurs de quelques scènes qui ne marchent pas assez vîte vers l'action. Ces défauts sont de l'original'). Only for the words of the spoken dialogue, he continued, did he take complete responsibility and accept any possible blame. What he was in fact saying was that Sacchini's music was sufficiently good to compensate for the faults of his libretto. This was an excuse both for creating the parody in the first place and for not making it better than it was. The final conclusion must be, therefore, that although parodists had the theoretical chance to unite much of the best in French and Italian theatre, many of them had more limited ambitions. Their aim, in short, was to create opportunities for Italian supporters to hear the music they wanted in an agreeable environment. It is against this background that their work awaits the judgment of posterity.

See M. Duchow, 'Musico-textual criticism in the Correspondance littéraire', *Canadian Music Journal*, i (1957), pp. 7–10, for the opinions of Grimm and Madame D'Epinay on this subject.

33 The decision by the creators of *Orgon dans la lune*, the 1777 parody of Paisiello's *Il credulo deluso*, to reshuffle the musical items so that the finales no longer come at the end of the acts seems particularly inappropriate.

APPENDIX
French operatic parodies, 1771–90

The following list presents details of all known *opera buffa* parodies produced in France (mainly in Paris and Versailles) between 1771 and 1790. The information consists in each case of the French title and number of acts, the material on which the parody is based (in parentheses), the names of those responsible for the adaptation, and the place and date of the parody's first performance. Much of it is drawn from lists of theatrical repertory in M. Noiray, 'Les opéras des compositeurs originaires des Pouilles représentés à Paris au XVIIIe siècle: liste chronologique et données bibliographiques', in *Atti del convegno internazionale di studi, Lecce, 6–8 dicembre 1985* (Rome, 1988), pp. 272–9; and M. Noiray, 'Les créations d'opéra à Paris de 1790 à 1794', in *Orphée phrygien: les musiques de la Révolution* (Paris, 1989), pp. 196–203; also from A. Loewenberg, *Annals of Opera, 1597–1940* (London, 1943; 3rd edn, revised, 1978); and from information kindly given the author by Elizabeth Bartlet.

ARM – *Paris, Académie Royale de Musique*   CI – *Paris, Comédie-Italienne*
TdM – *Paris, Théâtre de Monsieur*   TM – *Paris, Théâtre Montansier*
(single figures refer to the number of acts)

1 *La bonne fille*, 3 (*La buona figliuola*, 3, 1760: music by Niccolò Piccinni)
Cailhava d'Estandoux (text), Domenico Baccelli (music): CI, 17 June 1771; repeated Versailles, 2 December 1775

2 *L'esclave, ou Le marin généreux*, 1 (*Gli stravaganti*, 2, 1764: music by Piccinni)
According to libretto, 'représenté en province', 1773

3 *La colonie*, 2 (*L'isola d'amore*, 2, 1766: music by Antonio Sacchini)
Nicolas Etienne Framery (text): CI, 16 August 1775; repeated Fontaine-bleau, 4 November 1775

4 *Le duel comique*, 2 (*Il duello*, 1, 1774: music by Giovanni Paisiello)
Pierre Louis Moline (text), N.-J. Le Froid de Méreaux (music): CI, 16 September 1776; repeated Fontainebleau, 10 October 1777

5 *L'inconnue persécutée*, 3 (*L'incognita perseguitata*, 3, 1773: music by Pasquale Anfossi)
P. L. Moline (text), N.-J. Le Froid de Méreaux (music): Fontainebleau (by CI company), 12 November 1776

6 *Orgon dans la lune*, 4 (*Il credulo deluso*, 3, 1774: music by Paisiello)
M. J. Mattieu de Lépidor (text): according to Loewenberg, Versailles, before 11 June 1777; repeated TdM, 27 April 1789

7 *Pomponin*, ? (*Lo sposo burlato*, 2, 1769: music by Piccinni)
Pierre Louis Guinguené (text): Fontainebleau, 3 November 1777

8 *Les deux amis, ou Le faux vieillard*, 3 (based on music by 'several Italian masters')
Barnabé Farmain de Rozoy (text): Versailles (by CI company), 19 February 1779

9 *L'infante de Zamora*, 3 (*Il tamburo*, 3, 1773, and *La frascatana*, 3, 1774: music by Paisiello)
N. E. Framery (text): Strasbourg, 1779; repeated Versailles, 1781; TdM, 22 June 1789

10 *Le philosophe imaginaire*, 3 (*I filosofi immaginari*, 2, 1779: music by Paisiello)

Paul Ulric Dubuisson (text): Paris, Tuileries and Palais Royal, 1780

11 *Les deux comtesses*, 2 (*Le due contesse*, 2, 1776: music by Paisiello)

N. E. Framery (text): prepared for Paris but performed Strasbourg, 1781

12 *L'inconnue persécutée*, 3 (*L'incognita perseguitata*, 3, 1773: music by Anfossi)

B. F. de Rozoy (text), Jean-Baptiste Rochefort (music): ARM (Tuileries), 21 September 1781 (containing some sections of Moline's earlier text on the same subject); ARM (Pont St-Martin), 12 May 1782 (with alterations); ARM, 14 December 1783 (with new finale from Anfossi's *Il geloso in cimento* (3, 1774))

13 *Le barbier de Séville*, 4 (*Il barbiere di Siviglia*, 4, 1782: music by Paisiello)

N. E. Framery (text): CI (Trianon), 15 September 1784; repeated Versailles, 29 October 1784

14 *Le Roi Théodore à Venise*, 3 (*Il re Teodoro a Venezia*, 2, 1784: music by Paisiello)

P. U. Dubuisson (text): Brussels, ?1786; repeated Fontainebleau, 28 October 1786, and Versailles, 18 November 1786

15 *Hélène et Francisque*, 4 (*Fra i due litiganti*/*Le nozze di Dorina*, 3, 1782: music by Giuseppe Sarti)

P. U. Dubuisson (text): Versailles, 1786; repeated TM, 20 April 1790

16 *Le tuteur avare*, (*L'avaro*, 3, 1775: music by Anfossi)

Gabiot de Salins (text) and Giuseppe Maria Cambini (music): Paris, Théâtre Beaujolais, 15 March 1787; repeated Versailles, 15 August 1788

17 *Le barbier de Séville*, 4 (*Il barbiere di Siviglia*, 4, 1782: music by Paisiello)

P. L. Moline (text), August Heinrich Wenck (music): ARM (Tuileries), 1787.

18 *Le roi Théodore à Venise*, 3 (*Il re Teodoro a Venezia*, 2, 1784: music by Paisiello)

P. L. Moline (text), L. C. A. Chardiny (music): ARM, 11 September 1787

19 *La grotte de Trophonius*, ? (*La grotta di Trofonio*, 2, 1785: music by Paisiello)

P. U. Dubuisson (text): according to the *Mercure de France* (27 March 1790), performed at Versailles 'il y a quelques années', i.e. 1786–8

20 *Le maître généreux*, ? (*Le gare generose*/*Gli schiavi per amore*, 2, 1786: music by Paisiello)

P. U. Dubuisson (text): Versailles, 1788; repeated Paris, TM, 28 May 1790

21 *Le philosophe imaginaire*, 3 (*I filosofi immaginari*, 2, 1779: music by Paisiello)

Paris, Théâtre Beaujolais, 15 January 1789 (it is unclear whether this was a new work or a repeat of the 1780 parody)

22 *Le Marquis Tulipano*, 2 (*Il matrimonio inaspettato*, 1, 1779: music by Paisiello)

C. Joseph Antoine de Gourbillon (text): TdM, 28 January 1789

23 *La feinte jardinière*, 2 (*La finta giardiniera*, 3, 1774: music by Anfossi)

?Balle (text): TdM, 5 February 1789

24 *L'Antiquaire*, ? (?)
   TdM, 9 March 1789

25 *L'île enchantée*, 3 (parody based on music by Antonio Bartolomeo Bruni)
   Sedaine de Sarcey (text): TdM, 3 August 1789

26 *Les fourberies de Marine*, ? (parody based on Goldoni's *La notte critica* and
   on music by Piccinni)
   B. F. de Rozoy (text): TdM, 11 September 1789

27 *Le valet rival et confident*, ? (parody based on music by Paisiello)
   ?Hippolyte (text): TdM, 27 October 1789

28 *Le directeur dans l'embarras*, ? (*L'impresario in angustie*, 2, 1786: music by
   Domenico Cimarosa)
   P. U. Dubuisson (text): Théâtre Beaujolais, 23 December 1789

29 *Le valet rival*, ? (parody based on music by Paisiello)
   Pierre Germain Pariseau (text): TdM, 6 February 1790 (according to the
   Mercure de France (20 February 1790), the music was that of *Le valet rival
   et confident* (see no. 27), but the text was basically new)

30 *Le bon maître ou Les esclaves par amour*, 4 (*Le gare generose/Gli schiavi
   per amore*, 2, 1786: music by Paisiello)
   C. J. A. de Gourbillon and P. G. Pariseau (text): TdM, 20 March 1790

31 *Les époux mécontents*, ? (*Gli sposi malcontenti*, 2, 1785: music by Stephen
   Storace)
   P. U. Dubuisson (text): TM, 12 April 1790

32 *Livia, ou L'italienne à Londres*, 3 (*L'italiana in Londra*, 2, 1778: music by
   Cimarosa)
   TM, 13 April 1790 (printed score gives TdM as venue but no date)

33 *L'arbre de Diane*, ? (*L'arbore di Diana*, 2, 1787: music by Vicente Martín y
   Soler)
   TM, 6 May 1790

34 *Les trois mariages*, ? (parody based on music by Paisiello)
   P. U. Dubuisson (text): Paris, Théâtre Français Comique et Lyrique, 26
   June 1790

35 *Le curieux indiscret*, ? (*Il curioso indiscreto*, 3, 1777: music by Anfossi)
   P. U. Dubuisson (text): TM, 23 September 1790

Periodical editions of music at the time of the French Revolution

Until recently confusion persisted over the term 'périodique musical'. It was used sometimes for the periodical publishing of music itself, and at other times to designate a periodical containing writings about music. The publications of Imogen Fellinger have served to clarify the terminology and to draw attention to the quantitative and qualitative importance of each type as a source of information about music-making.[1] Her latest bibliography, *Periodica musicalia*, published in 1986, covers only those periodicals founded from 1789 onwards, leaving in obscurity a section of French music publishing particularly active in the years 1770–80. To mark the bicentenary of the French Revolution, Professor Pierre Rétat published a bibliography of journals in the French language that appeared in 1789, and this takes account of music journals.[2] As for the *Répertoire international des sources musicales*, the volume dedicated to eighteenth-century collections lists such publications, together with the names of the composers represented in them.[3] The existence of these various research tools makes it possible now to study and analyse this important output of the eighteenth century. The word 'periodical' is here taken in its strict sense, that is to designate a regularly spaced publication delivered on subscription payable in advance.

Why, it may be asked, did publishers at certain periods dispose of part of their production in the form of periodical editions? The most important reason seems to have been to create a faithful following among musical amateurs. The practice itself does not date from the eighteenth century, but already existed in the seventeenth in the collections of *airs* published by successive members of the Ballard family in Paris. These collections appeared annually to start with; they were

1 I. Fellinger, *Verzeichnis der Musikzeitschriften des 19. Jahrhunderts* (Regensburg, 1968); *Periodica musicalia (1789–1830)* (Regensburg, 1986).
2 P. Rétat, *Bibliographie des journaux de langue française paraissant en 1789* (Paris, 1989) (including citations of 194 new Parisian journals).
3 F. Lesure, ed., *Répertoire international des sources musicales* [hereafter RISM], series B II: *Receuils imprimés, XVIIIe siècle* (Munich and Duisburg, 1964).

issued monthly for a short period towards the end of Louis XIV's reign.[4] At this time they were devoted almost entirely to vocal music. After a long interruption the practice became fashionable again in the years 1760–70, when it manifested itself in various ways. The venture of the *Bureau d'abonnement musical*, for example, responded to a desire to rationalize the distribution of music. This lending library, founded in 1765 by Antoine de Peters and Jean-Baptiste Miroglio,[5] itself became, under pressure from other publishers, a publishing house. To it we owe, among other things, a collection entitled *Raccolta dell'harmonia: colletione del Magazino musicale*, which played an effective role in the dissemination of instrumental music, publishing works by Dittersdorf, Boccherini, Felice Bambini, J. G. Bürckhoffer, Felice Giardini, J. P. A. Schwarzendorf (known as Martini) and even the quartets of Gossec; one notes in a French publication the use of an Italian title, calculated to attract interest.[6]

It was at this time that the publication of music in periodical editions began. In 1762 a certain Charles-François Clément launched the *Journal de clavecin composé sur les ariettes des comédies, intermèdes et opera-comiques qui ont eu le plus de succes*;[7] it continued until 1772 and already showed characteristics to be found in similar later publications. One observes in it the association of a fashionable instrument with a repertory of song arranged and simplified for domestic music-making. Other ventures were addressed more to semi-professionals: the *journaux d'orgue* of Jean-Jacques Beauvarlet-Charpentier[8] and Guillaume Lasceux,[9] which were of assistance to organists in convents and parishes who wished to maintain music in their churches without always having the resources for it. Unlike many other periodical editions, they included original pieces: masses, *proses*, hymns for the main religious festivals, Magnificats and *Noëls*.

In the 1760s the publisher La Chevardière began to issue the *Journal hebdomadaire, ou Recueil d'airs choisis dans les opéra-comiques. Mêlé de vaudevilles, rondeaux, ariettes, duo, romances ... avec accompag-*

---

4 See particularly the *Receuils d'airs sérieux et à boire de différents auteurs* published between 1701 and 1724 (RISM, series B II, pp. 311–15).

5 See A. Devries and F. Lesure, *Dictionnaire des éditeurs de musique français* (Geneva, 1988).

6 In its rate of production (it ran to about sixty fascicles spread over the years 1765–73) this collection closely resembles a periodical series. The other composers included in it were Benevento di San Rafaele, Eugène Godecharle, Ignazio Celoniati, Gaetano Chiabrano (or Chabran), G. Francisconi, Alessandro Mario Antonio Fridzeri, Theodore Smith, Philippe-Jacques Meyer and Andreas Och; see F. Lesure, ed., *Catalogue de la musique imprimée avant 1800 conservée dans les bibliothèques publiques de Paris* (Paris, 1981).

7 RISM, series B II, p. 206; Lesure, ed., *Catalogue de la musique*, p. 123.

8 *Journal d'orgue à l'usage des paroisses et communautés religieuses* (c. 1783–4); see Lesure, ed., *Catalogue de la musique*, pp. 35–6.

9 Lesure, ed., *Catalogue de la musique*, p. 370. During the years 1774–8 Benaut had issued the same kind of didactic pieces without calling the series a 'Journal'. To this list may be added a certain Leclerc, of whose *Journal de pièces d'orgue* there exists one fascicle, dating from 1780.

nement de violon et basse chiffrée pour le clavecin. This enjoyed an exceptionally long life – from 1764 to 1808 – since La Chevardière's successor, Leduc, in 1784 was bent on continuing a publishing enterprise which had been crowned with success, merely changing its title slightly. Its unique success perhaps inspired other publishers whose fortunes turned out somewhat differently: seven titles were founded during the years 1760–80, sixteen in 1780–90 and four in 1790–98.[10]

The years 1780–4 were particularly auspicious; each year saw new initiatives, especially 1784, when the *Journal de violon dédié aux amateurs ... composé d'airs d'opéras sérieux et comiques, airs de ballets, arietes italienes, rondeaux, vaudevilles et chansonettes arangés par le meilleur maîtres, pour deux violons ou deux violoncelles* was founded, as well as the *Feuilles de Terpsichore*, two periodicals for harp and clavier issued by the instrument makers Cousineau *père et fils*, and Boyer's *Journal de pièces de clavecin*, discussed below. The length and explicit wording of the titles constitute in themselves a kind of advertising: they frequently associate vocal music with a fashionable musical instrument. A title-page attractively illustrated, preferably with the instrument concerned (see Fig. 1) is often another means to attract attention, at least for the first number, and often for those following. Several periodical editions stopped appearing in 1789, but the life of these publications was in any case so unpredictable that this need not necessarily be attributed to political events. Thus the *Courrier lyrique et amusant, ou Passe-temps des toilettes par Mme Dufresnoy*, a fortnightly which began in 1785, ceased publication in 1789, while 180 issues of the *Journal d'airs italiens et français avec accompagnement de guitare*, a daily published by Leduc, appeared that year; the *Journal de violon*, already mentioned, also ceased in 1789 after five years of existence. Others survived troublous times without difficulty; life continued, and so did music. The *Journal d'ariettes italiennes* of Bailleux; the *Journal de harpe*, a weekly published by Leduc from 1781 to 1795; the *Journal hebdomadaire*, already mentioned; Leduc's *Journal de clavecin* and Cousineau's *Feuilles de Terpsichore* all appeared regularly during the period 1789–95. These journals, comprising quarterlies, monthlies, fortnightlies, weeklies and even dailies, bear witness to an astonishing vitality and to the existence of an avid and faithful public eager to get to know new things, especially from the lyric theatre.

Can one identify and define the public that bought these publications? They are addressed, of course, to 'amateurs', a word that appears frequently in titles, as also does the word 'dames' ('ladies'). A pedagogical intent is also clear in the title of the *Feuilles de Terpsichore*:

10 This information is derived from titles listed in RISM, series B II.

Fig. 1: Title-page of an issue of *Feuilles de Terpsichore* published by Cousineau *père et fils* (Paris, 1784)

Feuilles de Terpsichore, ou Nouvelle étude de clavecin dédiées aux dames dans lesquelles on trouvera successivement l'*agreable*, l'*aisé* et le *difficile*, composés par les professeurs les plus recherchés de cet instrument.

Feuilles de Terpsichore, ou Nouvelle étude de clavecin dedicated to the ladies, in which will be found in succession the *pleasant*, the *simple* and the *difficult*, composed by the most learned professors of that instrument.

The dedication to the ladies contains the statement, 'to earn your approval is, for the artist who dedicates his efforts to your amusement, the most flattering of rewards' ('mériter votre bienveillance est pour l'artiste qui consacre ses veilles à votre amusement le prix le plus flatteur'). What one finds in these *Feuilles* – well-named, since they take the form of two folio leaves ('feuillets') – are *airs* from operas and *opéras comiques* arranged by the best organists in Paris (Nicolas Séjan, Jean-Jacques Beauvarlet-Charpentier, Grenier (perhaps Gabriel Grenier) and Guillaume Lasceux) and by the well-known harpsichordists Carolus Emanuel Fodor and Rigel. The *airs* are arranged either for harpsichord alone or for voice and harpsichord. The *métier* of arranger seems already to have been a flourishing one.

The choice of a particular instrument accords with the period when its popularity was at its height. A chronology may be established based on the dates when the journals were founded. The harpsichord takes pride of place at first (with Clément's *Journal*, 1765), then the cittern in 1778, the harp (Leduc's *Journal de harpe*, 1781 and the *Feuilles de Terpsichore*, 1784) and the organ. The harpsichord and pianoforte were offered as alternatives in the *Variétés à la mode* of César (1785) and the *Journal d'ariettes arrangées pour le piano forte ou clavecin et violon* of Mezger (1787–8). The guitar comes to the fore towards 1786–8 with the *journaux* of Vidal and Porro, as well as the *Journal d'airs italiens avec accompagnement de guitare* of Leduc (1789), while the pianoforte is finally dissociated from the harpsichord after 1792.

Although the whole of this production was based on the French and Italian vocal repertory, one must stress the originality of the *Journal d'ariettes italiennes*, a fortnightly published from 1779 to 1795; this allowed the performance of Italian arias with complete instrumental accompaniment, issued in the form of separate parts, and with a French translation of the words. This *journal* acted as a remarkable 'Trojan horse' for Italian opera, which made inroads into France by means of the most important arias in the contemporary Italian repertory; the list of composers represented runs from Accorimboni to Zingarelli, taking in Andreozzi, Bianchi, Gazzaniga, Sarti and Traetta.

A last group of *journaux* was devoted to ensemble music. The *Journal de violon*, published monthly from 1784 to 1789, contained only arrangements for two violins or two cellos of items from *opéras comiques.* Another publication for instrumental ensembles was the *Receuil d'airs nouveaux français et étrangers, en quatuors concertans, ou Journal de violon, flûte alto et basse* (1784–95), which extended instrumental forces to the quartet.

The last title I shall examine presents, by contrast, an original repertory, made up of editions of new works and reissues of others already published abroad. This is the *Journal de pièces de clavecin par differens auteurs contenant des sonates avec ou sans accompagnement, des duo, trio, quatuor, quinque, simphonies, simphonies concertantes et concerts*, published by Boyer from 1784 to 1794. Boyer made several ventures into periodical publishing, collaborating each time with 'experts' well-versed in the particular field covered by the publication. With Ozi he published between 1786 and 1791 the *Nouvelle suite de pièces d'harmonie contenant des ouvertures, airs et ariettes d'opéra et opéra comiques. Arrangées pour deux clarinettes, deux cors et deux bassons.* From about 1783 to 1786, with Pierre-Antoine César, an inveterate arranger of contemporary operas, he issued the *Variétés à la mode ... arrangées pour le clavecin ou le forte-piano.* A little later, in 1788, he collaborated with Wenck and Baillon to launch (again) the *Variétés musicales pour le piano forte ou clavecin*; finally, in the same year he bowed again to the fashion for arrangements and topicality with a *Journal d'ariettes choisies dans les meilleurs opéras exécutés au théâtre de Monsieur.*

But the most interesting and longest-lived of his *journaux* was without doubt the *Journal de pièces de clavecin*, which showed numerous original features, including that of picturing on the title page of the first issue a piano accompanied by a violin, rather than the harpsichord (*clavecin*) of the title (see Fig. 2). The price of the subscription was rather high: 24 lt (*livres tournois*) (that is, 2 lt per issue) for Paris and 30 lt for the provinces. The declaration of intent that appears at the beginning of the first number was to be quite faithfully carried out by the publisher:

L'editeur espere que ce nouveau genre de production ne pourra qu'etre accueilli favorablement par MM les amateurs tant par sa variété que par le choix des morceaux: il se flatte que MM les compositeurs voudront bien coopérer par leurs ouvrages au succès de ce journal.

The publisher hopes that this new kind of production will not fail to be received favourably by the lovers of music on account of both the variety and the choice of pieces; he flatters himself that composers will wish to assist in the success of the *journal* with their works.

To each monthly issue Boyer added a catalogue of the works he published, and so extended the publicity attracted by the journal itself. The twelve issues of the first year (the only one preserved complete) successfully mix composers of local and international repute. Among the

Fig. 2:   Title-page of the third issue of Boyer's *Journal de pièces de clavecin* (Paris, 1784)

local 'stars' are Henri-Joseph Rigel, then *maître de musique* at the Concert Spirituel; Jean-François Tapray, organist at the Ecole Royale Militaire; Charles Fodor; François Devienne and Jean-Louis Adam. The international masters are Haydn, the favourite of Parisian music publishers, represented by a symphony and a concerto; Clementi; Vanhal and J. F. X. Sterkel. In the second year the names of Mozart, Hüllmandel and Kozeluch appear, and in 1789 that of Viotti. The names that, for us, represent music at the time of the Revolution, figure in the *journal* from 1787: Ignace Pleyel, Louis-Emmanuel Jadin and Daniel Steibelt in 1788 confirm their budding celebrity. Among others may be mentioned Franz Mezger, who settled in Paris, and Benoit Mozin: both were to found their own musical *journaux*, for which they made their own arrangements.

In the Appendix, below, every number of the journal has been included, in order to show the lacunae as clearly as possible and to stress the tentative character of any conclusion one might wish to draw as to its contents and orientation. A glance at the number of issues extant for each year will underline this:

1784: 12	1788: 10	1792: 1
1785: 9	1789: 2	1793: 4
1786: 5	1790: 2	1794: 2
1787: 8	1791: 1	

– in all, fifty-six out of the 132 issued during the eleven years of publication. It follows that the number of times a particular composer is represented cannot be taken as an indication of his popularity (or lack of it), but the following analysis does reflect a distinct interest in those German and Austrian composers who had settled in Paris:

represented six times	Steibelt and Sterkel
five times	Mezger
three times	Mozart, Kozeluch, Clementi and Haydn
twice	Devienne, J. L. Dussek, Louis-Emmanuel Jadin and Henri-Joseph Rigel
once only	Adam, Fodor, Hemmerlein, Hüllmandel, Küffner, Kuhn, Le Pin, Mozin, Pleyel, Ragué, Rasetti, Henri-Jean Rigel, Schröter, Tapray, Vanhal, Viotti and Vogler

Table 1, which lists the various instrumental combinations called for in Boyer's publication, reflects the unusual diversity of its contents and the quality of the works it promoted. It shows an intelligent selection such as is not to be found, except in a few cases, in later publications of this kind. How did Boyer make his selection? Did he have an adviser, or a correspondent who drew his attention to foreign publications? Does

Table 1 Instrumental combinations represented in Boyer's *Journal de pièces de clavecin*

bn – bassoon	hpschd – harpsichord	pf – pianoforte	vla – viola
fl – flute	orch – orchestra	vcl – violoncello	vln – violin

Instrumentation	Composers (issue no.)
1 instrument	
hpschd/pf	Clementi (6, 56); Küffner (21); Mozart (38); Dussek (51); Steibelt (53, 82, 127); Sterkel (66); Mozin (103); Haydn (113)
hpschd/pf (3 hands)	Mezger (43)
hpschd/pf (4 hands)	Sterkel (3); Kozeluch (11): Vogler (16); Mezger (111)
2 instruments	
2 pfs	Rigel (119)
vln and hpschd	Vanhal (2); Fodor (5); Adam (9); Clementi (10); Hüllmandel (13); Mozart (18); Mezger (19, 35, 55); Sterkel (23, 34); Steibelt (97)
fl and hpschd	Devienne (8); Jadin (44, 52)
3 instruments	
hpschd/pf, fl/vln and vcl/'quinte'/'basse'	Ragué (20); Haydn (50); Schröter (57); Steibelt (75, 122)
hpschd/pf, fl and vla	Kuhn (30)
fl, bn and hpschd	Devienne (39)
4 instruments	
hpschd/pf, fl/vln, vla and vcl/'basse'/bn	Tapray (6); Rasetti (42)
pf, 2 vlns and 'basse'	Pleyel (37)
more than 4 instruments	
hpschd/pf and orch	Rigel (1); Haydn (7); Mozart (14); Kozeluch (24, 49); Sterkel (25); Dussek (41); Hemmerlein (46); Le Pin (59)
hpschd/pf, vln and orch	Rigel (36); Viotti (65)

the *journal* consist only of reprints, or does it include first publications? Because most music publications of the period were undated, it is difficult to answer such a question. The issues of 1790–4 reveal certain concessions to the changing fashions of the period: a taste for *potspourris* and for musical depictions of battles, and the disappearance of any mention of the harpsichord in favour of the piano. The *Journal de pièces de clavecin* runs counter to the usual production of musical *journaux*, and the interest it aroused was due precisely to its originality.

In conclusion, I would say that the accepted historical chronology is of little relevance when one comes to examine the musical facts. Musical *journaux* reflect certain tendencies foreign to the way things developed: the great predominance of vocal music, a fragmentary and incomplete perception of the repertory of the lyric stage (a finding which contradicts the impression created by the multitude of arias and short operatic extracts that were actually known), curiosity about the instruments in vogue (though possibly the *journaux* themselves helped to create a particular vogue) and the popularizing and developing of certain genres (the quartet, for example). The publishing phenomenon itself deserves our interest, insofar as it was not confined to France. In Europe as a whole there seems to have been a golden age for periodical music: *modinhas* in Portugal, the journals of Johann André produced in Offenbach, the *Journal d'airs italiens, français et russes avec accompagnement de guitare* published at St Petersburg from 1796 to 1798, and other periodicals in Hamburg, Brussels and The Hague bear witness to the extent of a phenomenon which cannot be explained only by reference to the Parisian vogue for these things. Numerous questions remain, which cannot be answered because of the considerable gaps in the series and in the surviving copies of them: questions about the print runs, the kind of people who subscribed to the series, the precise repertory and the roles of the various 'partners' in this minor industry – the editors, composers, arrangers, engravers of text and music and the distributors. And yet, the very existence of these enterprises shows that a regular body of amateurs flourished on the margins of the official and institutional music-making which created, during the same epoch, its own avenues of production and distribution (as the *Magasin de musique à l'usage des fêtes nationales* testifies).

Translation by the editor

APPENDIX
The contents of the *Journal de pièces de clavecin par différens auteurs*, published in Paris by Boyer and Le Menu (1784–94)[11]

Pa: Paris, Bibliothèque de l'Arsenal   *Pn*: Paris, Bibliothèque Nationale

No.	Composer	Title	No. of pages/ inst. parts	Locations
1st Year (1784) (*Pn*, X.364 (1–12))				
1	Rigel, Henri-Joseph	Concerto pour le clavecin ou le forte piano avec accompagnement de deux violons, alto et basse ...	4 parts	*Pn*, D.12123, L.4619(3), K.7931
2	Vanhal, Johann	Sonate pour le piano forte ou le clavecin avec accompagnement de violon, ad libitum	1 part	*Pn*, K.8284
3	Sterkel, Johan Franz Xaver	Sonate a 4 mains pour le clavecin ou le forte piano	17 pp.	*Pn*, A.48293, Vm7 5666
4	Clementi, Muzio	Sonate pour le piano forte ou le clavecin, op.10, no.1	9 pp.	—
5	Fodor, Charles	Sonate pour le clavecin ou le forte-piano avec violon et basse	2 parts	*Pn*, A.33984
6	Tapray, Jean-François	Quatuor concertans pour le clavecin ou le forte piano, flûte, alto et basson ... Oeuvre XIX ... La flûte et le basson peuvent être remplacés par un violon et un violoncelle	4 parts	*Pn*, K.8249; *Pa*, M.355(a–b)
7	Haydn, Joseph	Concerto pour le clavecin ou le forte piano [Hob.XVIII: 11]		—
8	Devienne, François	Sonate pour le clavecin ou le forte piano avec accompagnement de flûte obligé	11 pp.	*Pn*, A.33775
9	Adam, Jean-Louis	Sonate pour le clavecin ou le forte piano avec accompagnement de violon	9 pp.	—
10	Clementi, M.	Sonate pour le forte piano ou le clavecin avec accompagnement de violon, op. 10, no.3	9 pp.	—
11	Kozeluch, Leopold	Duo pour le clavecin ou le piano forte ... Oeuvre IX	27 pp.	*Pn*, A.34590

11 Compiled from information in Lesure, ed., *Catalogue de la musique*, RISM, series A 1, and card-indexes in the Bibliothèque Nationale, Paris

| 12 | Haydn, J. | Simphonie pour le clavecin ou le forte piano avec accompagnement de deux violons, alto et basse [Hob. I: 76] | 4 parts — | |

2nd Year (1785)

13	Hüllmandel, Nikolaus Joseph	Sonate pour le clavecin ou le piano forte avec violon obligé (en ut)	1 part	*Pn*, Vm7 5500, D.6171(8)
14	Mozart, Wolfgang Amadeus	Premier concerto pour le clavecin avec accompagnement de deux violons, alto, basse, hautbois, flûte et cors ad libitum [K175]	8 parts	*Pn*, K.25469
15				
16	Vogler, Georg Joseph	Sonate a quatre mains pour le piano-forte ou le clavecin	13 pp.	*Pn*, A.49487
17				
18	Mozart, W. A.	Sonate pour le clavecin ou le piano forte avec accompagnement de violon obligé [K454]	2 parts	*Pn*, Rés.F.1511
19	Mezger, Franz	Sonate pour le forte piano ou le clavecin avec accompagnement de violon ad libitum	2 parts	*Pn*, K.7715
20	Ragué, Louis-Charles	Trio pour le clavecin ou le forte piano avec accompagnement de flûte ou violon et de violoncelle ou quinte	2 parts	*Pn*, K.3664(1–2), K.7879
21	Küffner, Johann Jakob Paul	Sonate (en ut) pour le clavecin ou piano forte	9 pp.	*Pn*, A.41802
22				
23	Sterkel, J. F. X.	Grande sonate pour le clavecin ou le forte piano avec accompagnement de violon obligé … (en si^b)	2 parts	*Pn*, Vm7 5665
24	Kozeluch, L.	6e concerto pour clavecin et orchestre en la majeur, op.XVI	2 parts (1st and 2nd oboes)	*Pa* M.357

3rd Year (1786)

| 25 | Sterkel, J. F. X. | Premier concerto pour le clavecin ou le forte piano avec accompagnement de violons, alto, basse, deux cors et hautbois ad libitum … Oeuvre 18e | | *Pn*, Vm7 6006 [1 part] |

26				
27				
28				
29				
30	Kuhn, Anton Leoni	Trio concertant pour le clavecin ou le forte piano flûte et alto …Oeuvre Ve	3 parts	*Pn*, Vm7 5721
31				
32				
33				
34	Sterkel, J. F. X.	Simphonie pour le clavecin ou le forte piano avec accompagnement d'un violon et d'un violoncelle … Oeuvre XXe	2 parts	*Pn*, Vm7 5764
35	Mezger, F.	Sonate pour le clavecin ou le forte piano avec accompagnement de violon	2 parts	*Pn*, Vm7 5540
36	Rigel, H.-J.	Concerto concertant pour le clavecin et violon principal avec accompagnement de deux violons, alto, violoncelle, deux cors et deux hautbois ad libitum … Oeuvre 20	10 parts	*Pn*, Vm7 6033

4th Year (1787)

37	Pleyel, Ignace	Simphonie … avec 2 violons et basse	4 parts (vls 1 and 2, bass, pf)	*Pn*, Vm7 5583
38	Mozart, W. A.	Sonate (avec variations) [K284/205b]	18 pp.	*Pn*, Vm7 5549
39	Devienne, F.	Sonate (en ut) avec flûte et basson obligés	3 parts	*Pn*, Vm7 5749
40				
41	Dussek, Jan Ladislav	Concerto pour le piano-forte ou le clavecin avec accompagnement de deux violons, alto, deux hautbois, deux cors, deux flûtes et basse ad libitum … Oeuvre 3e	9 parts [one oboe part missing]	*Pn*, Vm7 5979
42	Rasetti, Amadeo	Quatuor pour le piano-forte avec accompagnement de violon, alto et basse … Oeuvre 5e	4 parts	*Pn*, Vm7 5746
43	Mezger, F.	Sonate à trois mains pour le piano forte ou le clavecin …Oeuvre 5e	21 pp.	*Pn*, Vm7 5722, Vm12 i 5969

44	Jadin, Louis-Emanuel	Sonate pour le clavecin ou le forte piano avec accompagnement de flûte (en sol)	2 parts	*Pn*, Vm7 5504, A.34452
45				
46	Hemmerlein, Joseph	Concerto pour le clavecin ou le forte piano avec accompagnement de deux violons, alto, basse, deux flûtes et deux cors ad libitum ... Oeuvre 73	9 parts	*Pn*, Vm7 5986
47				
48				

5th Year (1788)

49	Kozeluch, L.	Septième concerto pour le clavecin ou le forte piano avec accompagnement de deux violons, alto, basse, cors et hautbois (ad libitum) exécuté au Concert spirituel ... Oeuvre 25	9 parts	*Pn*, Vm7 5996, A.34576
50	Haydn, J.	Septième Symphonie ... intitulée la Reine de France [Hob.I:85], arrangée pour le clavecin ou le forte piano avec accompagnement de violon et basse par M. Charpentier		*Pn*, Vma.2449(6)
51	Dussek, J. L.	Sonate pour le clavecin ou le forte-piano (en sol)	9 pp.	*Pn*, Vm7 5431
52	Jadin, L.-E.	Sonate avec flute en ré	2 parts	*Pn*, Vm9 2527, Vm7 5503
53	Steibelt, Daniel	Pot pourri d'airs connus et autres pour le forte piano ou le clavecin ...(Premier) [plate no.249]	13 pp.	*Pn*, A.4820(1)
54	Sterkel, J. F. X.	Sonate avec violon et violoncelle en sol maj. Op. VII/3	3 parts	*Pn*, Vm7 5677
55	Mezger, F.	Sonate pour le clavecin ou le piano forte avec accompagnement de violon ad libitum	2 parts	*Pn*, Vm7 5541
56	Clementi, M.	Sonate pour le clavecin ou forte-piano suivie d'un air varié [op.24, no.1]	13 pp.	*Pn*, D.16408(5)
57	Schröter, Johann Samuel	Sonate pour le clavecin ou le forte piano avec accompagnement de violon et basse ...Oeuvre XI	3 parts	*Pn*, Vm7 5625, Vm17 860
58				
59	Le Pin, Henry-Noël	(Concerto en la)	5 parts	*Pn*, Vm7 6032
60				

70

6th Year (1789)

61			
62			
63			
64			
65	Viotti, Giovanni Battista	Première symphonie concertante ... arrangée pour clavecin ou forte-piano et violon obligé avec accompagnement de deux violons, alto et basse, cors et hautbois (ad libitum) par D. Steibelt ... P. Nadermann, Mme Le Menu; Bordeaux, Phelippeaux	*Pn*, L.10015(5)
66	Sterkel, J. F. X.	Air varié pour le piano forte ou le clavecin (en sol)	RISM, series A I, S 6020
67			
68			
69			
70			
71			
72			

7th Year (1790)

73				
74				
75	Steibelt, D.	Ouverture turque pour le clavecin ou forte-piano, violon et violoncelle ... Oeuvre 3e	3 parts	*Pn*, L.5675 IV, 26
76				
77				
78				
79				
80				
81				
82	Steibelt, D.	Deuxième pot pourri d'airs connus arrangés pour clavecin ou forte-piano	12 pp.	*Pn*, A.48201(2)
83				
84				

8th Year (1791)

85
86
87
88

89				
90				
91				
92				
93				
94				
95				
96				
97	Steibelt, D.	Sonate pour le forte-piano avec accompagnement de violon ad libitum	2 parts	*Pn*, Vm7 5636

9th Year (1792)

98				
99				
100				
101				
102				
103	Mozin, Benoit-François	Sixième pot-pourri d'airs connus arrangés pour le forte-piano [plate no.174]	12 pp.	*Pn*, Vmg.19642
104				
105				
106				
107				
108				
109				

10th Year (1793)

110				
111	Mezger, F.	Ouverture de Démophon arrangée à quatre mains pour le forte-piano		*Pn*, K.7712
112				
113	Haydn, J.	Sonate pour le piano forte [Hob.XVI:49]	14 pp.	*Pn*, Vmg.15134
114				
115	—	La bataille de Prague		*Pn*, Vm12 675
116				
117				
118				
119	Rigel, H.-J.	Duo pour deux forte piano	1 part	*Pn*, D.12127
120				
121				

11th Year (1794)

122	Steibelt, D.	Ouverture et marche de Roméo et Juliette pour le forte piano avec accompagnement de violon, et basse	3 parts	*Pn*, Vm15 5527
123				
124				
125				
126				
127	Steibelt, D.	Défaite des Espagnols par l'Armée française, sonate militaire pour le piano-forte	18 pp.	*Pn*, Vm7 5658, Vm12 26958 (or 26875)

The French string quartet, 1770–1800

From about 1770 to the end of the eighteenth century a strong international market existed for music for string quartet. For instance, in 1786 over 2000 quartets were advertised as being available from Parisian publishers.[1] These were composed not only by French musicians; composers from many countries had their works printed, and pirated, in Paris, London, The Hague and Amsterdam, and it is often difficult to identify the first issue of a particular work. The fact that opus numbers frequently differ between one edition and another further complicates the problem.[2]

Who performed these quartets, and where were they played? There is no evidence of public performance by professional musicians in France before the nineteenth century.[3] Chamber music was written principally for amateurs, joined on occasion by professionals, who gave private concerts in Parisian salons, whether of the nobility or of wealthy financial operators such as the *fermier-général* de la Haye or the Baron d'Ogny.[4] Among the most important patrons were the Baron de Bagge (himself a composer of quartets), who was reputed to promote the best private concerts in Paris, and the Prince de Conti, whose personal orchestra was led by Pierre Vachon and for whom Gossec directed after 1766.

It is clear that the development of the quartet in France was fashioned by foreign composers. Haydn's earliest quartets, published in Paris in 1764, were of prime importance in establishing the genre in the French capital. Equally significant was the influence of Boccherini, whose first

---

1 C. Johansson, *French Music Publishers' Catalogues of the Second Half of the Eighteenth Century* (Stockholm, 1955). For a list of quartets published in Paris between 1770 and 1787, see D. L. Trimpert, *Die Quatuors concertants von Giuseppe Cambini* (Tutzing, 1967), pp. 313–23.
2 For example, in the case of Davaux's set published as op. 9 by Bailleux in Paris (1779) and as op. 6 by Hummel in The Hague (n.d.). However, a set of parts of the latter edition in the library of King's College, Cambridge, was bound into a collection dated 1777.
3 J. Mongrédien, *La musique en France des Lumières au Romantisme, 1789–1830* (Paris, 1986), p. 229.
4 M. Brenet, *Les concerts en France sous l'ancien régime* (Paris, 1900; reprinted 1969), pp. 358ff.

Ex. 1   Baudron: Quartet no. 4 in F

sets were issued in 1767 and 1769. Parisian editions of quartets by Carl Friedrich Abel, Carl Stamitz and Antonín Kammel appeared in 1770. The only set by a Frenchman known to be earlier than this is one by Antoine Laurent Baudron, dating from 1768.[5] His six quartets, all in major keys, are three-movement works. The slow middle movements are tonally related to the others, three of them being in the dominant major, two in the dominant minor and one (the Andante of the fourth quartet in F) in the more unusual mediant minor (Ex. 1).

As in so much other music of the period, the melodic material of these quartets is basically triadic, and the sharing of the argument between the four instruments qualifies them as *quatuors concertants*. The viola and cello are at times treated as soloists, as they were also in later quartets, especially those of Jean-Baptiste Davaux. This style of writing may have been influenced by the success of the *symphonie concertante*, for which Davaux is particularly important; his works in this genre were a popular addition to the increasingly secular programmes of the Concert Spirituel and the later Concert de la Loge Olympique.

François-Joseph Gossec, although Belgian, was a powerful influence in Parisian musical circles. He published two sets of quartets, op. 14 in 1770 and op. 15 in 1772. Compared to Baudron's quartets, Gossec's show a more assured technique, as one would expect from a skilled composer. The sixth quartet of op. 15, for example, is livelier and the sonata form more fully structured, with both main subjects returning (if in shortened form) in the recapitulation, while the coda theme is clearly defined. The 1772 quartets are in only two movements, both in the same

Ex. 2   Gossec: Quartet op. 15 no. 6 in A

---

5 Baudron played first violin at the Comédie-Française from 1760. His set of *Sei Quartetti / Per due Violini, Alto, e Violoncello / obligati*, once thought to be lost, is in the Library of Congress, Washington (M452.B333).

key, and the frequent repetition of two- and four-bar phrases results in a
lack of the variety essential to the dramatic character of sonata form.
However, the concluding movements have a certain charm, as that of the
sixth quartet illustrates (Ex. 2).

Davaux's first set of quartets was advertised as op. 6 in Paris in 1773.[6]
A study of the op. 9 quartets (Paris, 1779)[7] shows that all but one are in
two movements: a sonata-form movement followed by a rondo or
Presto. The exception is the last of the set, in three movements, with a
Largo in the dominant. This characteristic cantilena type of slow
movement, found in the works of many composers, is in a kind of rondo
form. Example 3(a) shows the third and last statement of the opening
melody over a cello solo which previously sounded a fifth higher in
C major, taking the instrument up to a very exposed top f''. The Presto
(Ex. 3(b)) is lively and has much imitative repartee, without being a true
fugue.

Among French quartets published in the 1770s and 80s, those by
Pierre Vachon show the greatest assurance, in terms of both expression
and structure. Born in Arles in 1731, Vachon came to Paris in 1751 to
study the violin with the Italian Chiabrano.[8] He appeared at the Concert
Spirituel in the mid-1750s in his own and other composers' concertos.
By 1761 he was *premier violon* in the Prince de Conti's orchestra. He
came to London in about 1772,[9] and his quartets were soon published

6 Published also as op. 6 by J. T. Crajenschot (Amsterdam), but as op. 1 by Hummel (The Hague).
7 Published as op. 6 by Hummel (The Hague, n.d.).
8 Biographical details from F.-J. Fétis, *Biographie universelle des musiciens* (2nd edn, Paris, 1860–81).
9 J. Harden, 'Vachon, Pierre', in *The New Grove Dictionary of Music and Musicians*, ed. S. Sadie (London, 1980), xiv, pp. 482–3. The London visits are not mentioned by Fétis.

Ex. 3(a) Davaux: Quartet op. 9 no. 6 in Bb, slow movement

there by Napier.[10] He went to Germany in about *1784* and became
maître de concert of the royal orchestra in Berlin, a post he held until
1798. He died there in *1803*.

As with Davaux's quartets, it is difficult to establish where and when
Vachon's works were first issued. Judging by the number of copies
surviving in libraries,[11] his quartets had wide distribution. Napier issued
his opp. 5, 6 (dedicated to the Earl of Kelly) and 7, only the last of which
is known in a Parisian edition. Of Vachon's two later sets, both

10 The op. 7 set was dedicated to the Comte de Guines, the French ambassador to London from
  1770 to *1776*, who later commissioned Mozart to write the Concerto for Flute and Harp
  K299/297c.
11 For details, see G. Haberkamp and H. Rösing (eds.), *Repertoire international des sources
  musicales* [RISM]: *Einzeldrucke vor 1800*, ix (1981), pp. 1–2.

The French string quartet, 1770–1800

(b) third movement

published by Sieber (op. 9 in 1774 and op. 11 in 1782), copies are very rare.[12] Dating the Napier publications is difficult, but a copy of the op. 7 set in King's College, Cambridge, is bound into a collection dated 1772, the property of Henry Dashwood, almost certainly the owner of Kirtlington Hall north of Oxford.[13]

A study of Vachon's quartets opp. 5, 6, 7 and 11 reveals a composer who understood string texture and sonority.[14] Instead of Davaux's soloistic cello parts we find a simple harmonic bass line, figured in the London imprints, as was the case with many of Haydn's early quartets. In every other way these are concertante quartets, with the three upper voices treated as equals. Of the twenty-four quartets in these four sets, twelve have three movements, ten have two and only two have four movements. Over the four sets there is no evident difference in the balance between more or fewer movements.

The three-movement quartet in G minor, op. 5 no. 2, illustrates well Vachon's style. As usual, there is no slow introduction but, untypically, the Allegro is in triple time,[15] opening with a four-bar unison phrase, elements of which, together with those of the second phrase, more subtle in its rhythmic accentuation and harmony, are later developed in various ways (Ex. 4(a)). Solos from the second violin and viola lead to the second subject, a figure just two bars long, thrown between upper and lower pairs of voices in thirds (Ex. 4(b)). Scales lead to the closing section over chords which derive from the second part of the opening passage. A codetta brings the exposition to a close in Bb major (Ex. 4(c)). The short development of forty-one bars is based largely on familiar material, modulating to D minor and finally to the dominant of G minor. As in a number of Davaux's quartets, the recapitulation omits the opening material, going straight to the tonic minor version of the second subject, with the order of instruments reversed. The same codetta passage closes

12 RISM lists only one exemplar of op. 9 (Berlin, Deutsche Staatsbibliothek) and two of op. 11 (Munich, Bayerische Staatsbibliothek, and Washington, Library of Congress).
13 Henry Dashwood (1745–1828), third Baronet from 1779. The memorial chapel in the church of St Mary the Virgin, Kirtlington, provides much information about the family; see *The Victoria History of the Counties of England: Oxfordshire*, vi: *Ploughley Hundred*, ed. M. D. Lobel (London, 1959), p. 219. Henry Dashwood is quoted as being 'encumbered by debt'. There is no reason to doubt that the set of part books in the Rowe Library at King's College (where there is also a copy of Giardini's string trios op. 17, dedicated to Henry Dashwood) belonged to the Kirtlington family, and not to that of Sir Francis Dashwood of West Wycombe Park, notorious member of the Hellfire Club.
14 It is impossible to date the publication of these sets with any accuracy. The Napier issues of opp. 5, 6 and 7 must date from the early 1770s in view of the dated copy of op. 7, which is unnumbered by Napier but is the same as that published by Venier as op. 7a (*second livre*). Napier also issued two miniature quartets on favourite airs 'selected from the English, Scotch, Irish, German and Italian musick'. The first is based on tunes from Dibdin's version for London of *Le déserteur* by Monsigny, published in 1773. Opp. 5 and 7 have been published in a modern edition by P. Oboussier (Exeter, 1987).
15 Only seven of the twenty-four quartets have first movements in triple time and, of these, five are in the op. 7 set.

Ex. 4   Vachon: Quartet op. 5 no. 2 in G minor
      (a) Allegro (opening)

(b) Allegro (2nd subject)

(c) Allegro (codetta and opening of development section)

Ex. 5 Vachon: Quartet op. 5 no. 2 in G minor
(a) Andante gratioso (opening)

(b) Andante gratioso (middle section)

the movement, which in many ways has a coherent structure, with contrast in its opening eight bars and variety in the mixing of triadic and linear outlines, as well as touches of colour in the harmony.

The G major Andante gratioso is in ternary form, a structure commonly found in the three-movement quartets. An elegant four-bar phrase introduces the main aria-type melody (Ex. 5(a)), repeated with violins at the octave and brought to a close with a cadential phrase. The middle section, also basically in G and its dominant, provides a complete contrast in character (Ex. 5(b)). A linking passage, based on the introduction, brings the music back to the tonic for the reprise.

The last movement, Allegro, is in sonata form; it divides into exposition (39 bars), development (30 bars) and recapitulation (29 bars). A vigorous opening provides all the material for the development

Ex. 6   Vachon: Quartet op. 5 no. 2 in G minor

(Ex. 6). As in the first movement, this material is omitted from the recapitulation.

The features of Vachon's style exemplified in this quartet can be summarized as: a strong melodic content, especially elegant in slow movements; imitative rather than contrapuntal textures; and harmonic colouring, usually sensitive but with climactic diminished sevenths at dramatic moments (see Ex. 4(c): opening of the development). Musical ideas are worked out within a coherent framework in the sonata-form movements. Although conceived on a small scale, the quartets nevertheless display an elegance in their overall musical style.

One further constituent of Vachon's quartets merits discussion: the last movements entitled 'Tempo di Minuetto', or simply 'Menuet'. These extended minuets occur only in two- and three-movement quartets. Some, as in op. 6 nos. 1 and 2, are in effect rondo-minuets, while others

Ex. 7   Vachon: Quartet op. 5 no. 6 in Eb
    (a) Tempo di minuetto

    (b) Minuetto 2°

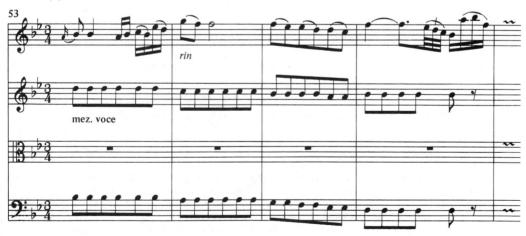

are double minuets, as in a minuet and trio pairing.[16] However, there are some which show elements of sonata form, for example that of op. 5 no. 6, a two-movement work.

Menuet I of op. 5 no. 6 has 52 (24+28) bars and Menuet II 36 (20+16) bars, making a total (with all repeats) of 228, against the 106 of the first movement (including the exposition repeat). The first minuet (Ex. 7(a)) has two themes, in tonic (Eb) and dominant keys, and some development takes place before the reprise of the first theme. The second minuet, in Bb (Ex. 7(b)), is quite contrasted in character – simpler in structure but more complex in texture. This contrast is more marked than is normally the case in the 'dance' minuets of the four-movement works.

Vachon was among the most prolific French composers of string quartets. While not displaying the structural coherence and contrapuntal mastery of Haydn's quartets, Vachon's are well-contrasted in character, and he shows confidence in handling string textures within the technical limitations of his day. What distinguishes the lesser talents from Haydn is the virtual absence of any advance, from one set to the next, in compositional technique or stylistic language. Towards the end of the century, however, virtuosity for its own sake began to affect chamber music. Viotti, who came to Paris in 1782, became an important figure in French musical life. During his stay of some ten years, he published two sets of *quatuors brillants*, which, like those of Cambini, feature his own instrument at the expense of the lower parts and are essentially a vehicle for the virtuoso violinist. It is therefore perhaps unexpected to find that quartets which largely maintain a balance of interest between the voices were composed by another instrumental virtuoso – a brilliant young pianist who was appointed professor at the newly founded Conservatoire in 1795, at the age of nineteen.

Hyacinthe Jadin[17] wrote four sets, each of three quartets, between 1795 and 1798. Copies of the original publications are scarce.[18] They are clearly the work of a young man, but display compositional skills far

16 Extended minuet movements are not found in the op. 11 set, where final movements have an Allegro character.

17 Jadin was the son of a Belgian violinist who served the court at Versailles. Fétis (*Biographie universelle*) states that he was born in 1769 and died in 1802, but Arthur Pougin's *Supplément* (1880) to Fétis's work cites an obituary notice, clearly written by an intimate friend, from the *Courrier des spectacles* (19 vendémiaire an IX/11 October 1800), announcing Jadin's death: 'Hyacinthe Jadin vient de mourir à l'âge de vingt-quatre ans'. This suggests that he was born in 1776, a fact verified by research into the records at Versailles. The author is grateful to Nathalie Castinel of the Université Lumière, Lyons, for this information.

18 Quartets opp. 1, 2 and 3 are in the Comte d'Oetting archive at Český Krumlov in Czecho-slovakia. A second copy of op. 1 is in the Kongelige Bibliotek, Copenhagen. The only known copy of op. 4 is in the Bibliothèque Nationale, Paris. The first three sets were published by the Magasin de Musique in 1795, 1796 and 1797 respectively. Pleyel published the (unnumbered) last set early in 1798. Op. 1 no. 3 and op. 2 no. 1 have been published in a modern edition by P. Oboussier (Exeter, 1989).

Ex. 8   H. Jadin: Quartet op. 2 no. 1 in E♭

superior to those found in his piano sonatas. In both genres there is a penchant for chromatic colouring, but in the quartets the ideas are more imaginatively developed, and the musical language foreshadows Romanticism. Jadin's first set was dedicated to Haydn and the third to Baillot, the celebrated violinist and protégé of Viotti. However, even in this set the first violin part is not over-emphasized. Only the first quartet in the fourth set has fewer than the standard four movements, consisting of an Allegro followed by a Rondo-Allegro. All the other quartets have a Minuet and Trio, placed second or third.

Three of Jadin's first movements open with a Largo introduction. Allegro sections in sonata form follow, and in a number of cases the main subject is tonally ambivalent – sufficiently often, in fact, for this to be regarded as a feature of Jadin's style. For example, op. 2 no. 1 in E♭ opens with a pedal A♭ on the cello, the upper strings coming in mysteriously at odd intervals, until the bass finally settles on a long B♭

Ex. 8   (cont.)

pedal, the dominant of the Allegro moderato that follows. The resemblance to the opening of Mozart's 'Dissonance' Quartet, K 465, written ten years earlier, is striking (Ex. 8). The Eb tonic of the Allegro is barely established before the music, now over an F pedal, arrives at the bridge passage. Although the first subject does not reappear at the recapitulation, the rising and falling semitone motif, first heard in the Largo, permeates the whole movement.

Jadin can be surprisingly dramatic in his development sections, and a good example is found in the C major quartet, op. 3 no. 1. The codetta, which is based on the opening theme's triplet figure, ends with a dominant seventh over a pedal G. At the double bar Jadin moves the bass up by semitones, passing rapidly through the keys of C major, Eb major, Gb major, Bb minor, F minor and A minor, mainly by way of diminished sevenths, to end on a dominant (E) pedal (Ex. 9). A noticeable feature of Jadin's first-movement form, and one already

Ex. 9   H. Jadin: Quartet op. 3 no. 1 in C

Allegro moderato

Ex. 9 (cont).

noted in Vachon's quartets, is the absence of the first subject from the recapitulation; this is to be observed in six of the last nine quartets. It would seem that, since it is often only the first subject that is developed, there is no reason to return to it in the reprise, which in these cases starts with the second subject.

Jadin's slow movements are mainly of the aria type, characterized by accompaniments involving elaborately figured and chromatic inner parts; there is also a pastorale, an Andante *louré* and, in the last of his quartets, a set of variations whose rich harmonic accompaniment to what is a very simple melody reminds one at times of Schubert. Minuet and trios are generally short and simple in character. Jadin is fond of hemiola accentuation, though not in the Baroque cadential context. Unusually, his Quartet in F minor, op. 1 no. 3, has a minuet in octaves, with some surprising, harmonically generated melodic outlines (Ex. 10(a)). The sweet tone of the trio makes an effective contrast (Ex. 10(b)).

Speaking generally, Jadin's last movements are his weakest. However, his very first quartet recalls the unpredictability and humour of Haydn's music, and one presumes that this is intended to be a compliment since Haydn was the dedicatee of the op. 1 set. The insertion of two silent bars at the beginning of the development, followed by the sudden entry of the main theme in Db (after the codetta's firm and final F major cadence), is one of several surprises, another being a coda which, in the event, is not the real end of the work. In other finales, mostly in sonata form, Jadin shows a light touch, but in general these are not very convincing.

It is somewhat surprising that Jadin's quartets were composed between 1795 and 1798, during the Directory, when France was in turmoil and Napoleon was establishing his empire in Italy and Egypt, and when composers were officially urged to write popular music for the *fêtes nationales*. Jadin, like his elder brother Louis, did write music for wind band, and his song for a Festival of Agriculture has survived.

Ex. 10   H. Jadin: Quartet op. 1 no. 3 in F minor
   (a) Menuet

   (b) Majeur [Trio]

However, the musical language of Jadin's quartets is witness to the development in sonata form and stylistic idiom that took place during the thirty years after Baudron's publication. Those early, rather tentative essays in the medium have been succeeded by others which reflect the influence of Haydn and point forward in idiom to the Romantic movement. Who played these works we do not know. Possibly they were professionals, like Baillot, in the privacy of their homes, students at the Conservatoire, or gifted amateurs who continued to make music in spite of the dangerous times in which they lived. What is certain is that the best of Jadin's quartets deserve a place in concert programmes alongside those of his better-known contemporaries.

François Giroust, a Versailles musician of the Revolutionary period

François Giroust, one of Mozart's most brilliant contemporaries, has unfortunately suffered for over a century and a half from a quite incompetent, meaningless and pretentious statement by one of the most influential critics and musicologists of the nineteenth century. In his famous *Biographie universelle des musiciens* François-Joseph Fétis (famous himself for the 'corrections' he made to the symphonies of Beethoven) wrote in about 1835:

La collection des partitions originales de Giroust a été acquise par la bibliothèque du Conservatoire de Paris; j'ai examiné cette musique, et je puis déclarer que tout y est misérable, d'un mauvais style et mal écrit.[1]

The collection of Giroust's autograph scores has been acquired by the library of the Paris Conservatoire; I have examined this music and can declare that everything in it is of inferior quality, in a poor style and badly written.

The recent revival of Giroust's music in both concert hall and recordings, due originally to the efforts of the *abbé* Jean Prim and subsequently to those of others as well,[2] has given the lie to Fétis's judgment in no uncertain manner.

François Giroust was born in Paris on 9 April 1737. At the age of seven he was sent to the choir school of Notre Dame, where he received a general and musical education. His first teacher was a certain Louis

---

1 F.-J. Fétis, *Biographie universelle des musiciens et bibliographie générale de la musique* (Brussels, 1835–44; 2nd edn, 1860–65; supplement ed. A. Pougin, Paris, 1878–80), iv, p. 16.
2 J. Prim, 'Giroust', in *Die Musik in Geschichte und Gegenwart*, v (Kassel, 1956), cols. 167–72. In addition to the literature cited in the notes to the present article, the following are important for the study of Giroust and his music: M.-F. Beaumont d'Avantois, *Notice sur François Giroust* (Versailles, n.d. [1799]); R. Cotte, *La musique maçonnique et ses musiciens* (Paris, 1975; 2nd edn 1987), and 'Les musiciens franc-maçons à la cour de Versailles et à Paris sous l'ancien régime' (Ph.D. diss., University of Paris, 1982; in course of publication); J. Ehrard and P. Viallaneix, *Les fêtes de la Révolution, colloque de Clermont-Ferrand (juin 1974): actes* (Paris, 1977); *Mélanges historiques, choix de documents, TII: sur l'administration de l'argenterie, menus plaisirs et affaires de la chambre du roi en 1784* (Paris, 1877); C. Pierre, *Notes inédites sur la musique de la Chapelle royale* (Paris, 1899); E. Thoinant, *Catalogue des registres de la cour des aides, maisons du roi et des princes* (MS in Paris, Bibliothèque de l'Opéra).

Homet, a former pupil of Nicolas Bernier. Later, from the age of eleven, he received lessons from Antoine Goulet, *maître de chapelle* at Saint-Germain l'Auxerrois, and when he was fourteen his first important work, a motet for full choir, was performed. From this period until the time of the Revolution he made a reputation chiefly as a church musician. In 1756 he was appointed *maître de chapelle* at Orleans Cathedral, and in 1768 he entered two works anonymously for a competition organized by the Concert Spirituel in Paris. This was for a motet on Psalm 137 (136 in the Vulgate), *Super flumina Babylonis*. A prize of a medal worth 300 *livres* had been offered by a rich amateur for the best entry, to be judged by Antoine Dauvergne, director of the Concert Spirituel, assisted by the *abbé* Blanchard, former *directeur des pages de la musique du roi*, and Charles Gauzargues, *maître de musique de la chapelle du roi*. The work was to be of 25–30 minutes' duration, the composer's name being hidden from the jury in a sealed envelope until after the public performance of the short-listed entries. Two of the scores were judged to be of equal merit, and it was therefore decided to create a second prize. A small clique led by D'Alembert favoured one of these scores in particular, thinking it to be the work of François Danican Philidor. To everyone's surprise, when the envelopes were opened they revealed that both works were by the same François Giroust. He carried off the two prizes and, as the author of the *Mémoires secrets* wrote, no-one failed 'to admire the supple genius of this artist, who could so vary his works that he could be different from himself with almost equal superiority' ('d'admirer le génie souple de cet artiste, qui savait varier ses productions au point d'être aussi différent de lui-même avec une presque égale superiorité').[3] The two scores were performed alternately on numerous occasions at the Concert Spirituel, and later elsewhere each year with equal success.

No time was lost in inviting Giroust to Paris, where he first directed the choir of the Saints-Innocents, a church in the Rue Saint Denis which disappeared at the end of the *ancien régime*, three years before the Revolution. Before long he left this relatively modest post to become *sous-maître de musique* and finally *surintendant de la musique du roi* at Versailles.

Under Louis XVI Giroust's activities were almost entirely devoted to sacred music, but his association with musicians from the *chapelle du roi* began to lead him towards a new spiritual and musical orientation. Many of these musicians (in fact, a fifth of the singers and about half of the instrumentalists) belonged to the masonic lodges known as 'de

---

3 L. Petit de Bachaumont, *Mémoires secrets pour servir à l'histoire de la république*, (London [?Amsterdam], 1777–89), cited in C. Pierre, *Histoire du concert spirituel 1725–1790* (Paris, 1975), p. 141.

l'Orient de la Cour'. Having been initiated in about 1777 in the Parisian Lodge 'Saint-Louis de la Martinique', Giroust (or 'Giroux') became a member of the Lodge 'Le Patriotisme' at the Orient de la Cour in 1784 or 1785. Going with the grain of Enlightenment thought, Giroust would have found there a spiritual (or, one might say, philosophical) orientation already close to Revolutionary ideas. The name of the 'Le Patriotisme' should not, however, mislead one into thinking that these freemasons already heralded, in premonitory fashion, the soldiers of An II. Having achieved a privileged position, the forty or so musicians belonging to the lodge were intent on conserving their privileges for ever. One of their brethren, Louis Basset de la Marelle, a member of the musicians' lodge known as 'L'Olympique de la Parfaite Estime', admirably summarized the intentions of the founders of 'Le Patriotisme' with the words: 'the love of the French for their sovereign is the strongest support the State possesses, and the firmest possible base for the power and glory of that monarchy; that is what French patriotism is' ('L'amour des Français pour leur souverain est le plus ferme appui de l'Etat, la base inébranlable de la puissance et de la gloire de cette monarchie: c'est là le patriotisme français').[4] For the rest, the activities of the lodge (apart from an impractical attempt in 1783 to collect enough money for a ship to be offered to the royal navy, then occupied in America's War of Independence) amounted to the organization of pompous ceremonies and charitable fêtes, in the course of which were performed little operas on moral, initiative or philosophical subjects, some of which might be described as 'pre-Revolutionary', despite their Biblical inspiration.

Let us return for a moment to François Giroust himself. His physical appearance is known to us, thanks to an invention by one of his musicians, the cellist Gilles-Louis Chrétien. A talented instrumentalist, Chrétien was also an able engineer who developed a teaching system based on audio-visual methods comparable to those used, with varying degrees of success, for instructing schoolchildren to-day. Fétis, of course, did not fail to heap ridicule on him. A crazy inventor, Chrétien had nevertheless perfected a kind of photographic apparatus, the *physionotrace*, which remained in use until the cameras of Niepce and Daguerre came on the scene. According to contemporaries, this instrument produced portraits of a perfect likeness which were reproduced on engraved discs. Although hundreds of pages, and even a French doctoral dissertation,[5] have been written on the subject, it is still not known how the apparatus functioned; the only drawing of it (see Fig. 1) is hardly

4 Quoted in W. Krauss, '"Patriote, patriotique, patriotisme" à la fin de l'ancien régime', in *The Age of Enlightenment: Studies Presented to Theodore Besterman*, ed. W. H. Barber (Edinburgh, 1967), pp. 393–4.
5 R. Hennequin, *Les portraits au physionotrace* (Troyes, 1932). See also G. L. Chrétien's collection of physionotrace portraits in the Bibliothèque Nationale, Paris (Estampes Dc65c).

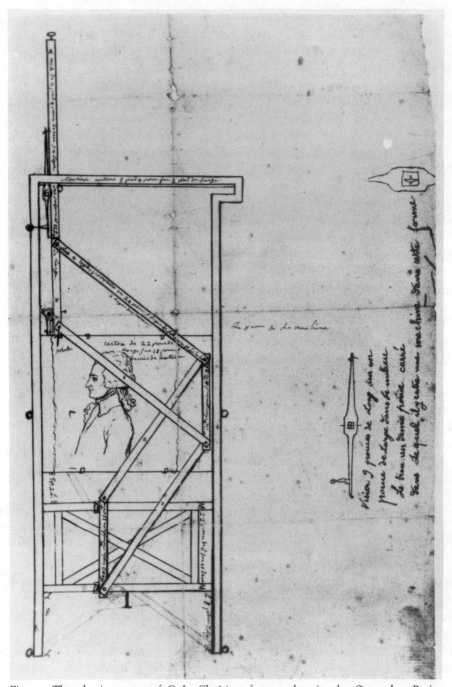

Fig. 1: The physionotrace of G. L. Chrétien, from a drawing by Quenedey. Paris, Bibliothèque Nationale.

Fig. 2: François Giroust: a physionotrace portrait by G. L. Chrétien. Paris, Bibliothèque Nationale.

explicit. But the invention at least enables us to know what François Giroust looked like: Fig. 2 shows him as an elegant court musician. This, then, was the person entrusted with the most important musical functions at the court of Louis XVI and, at the same time, those of the freemasons at Versailles.

A poet was obviously needed for the non-religious works of Giroust, and this was Félix Nogaret, an official in the Ministry of the King's Household and later librarian and *lecteur* to the Countess d'Artois, wife of the future Charles X. Pensioned off – or superannuated, as we might say to-day – in 1791, he embraced with suspicious enthusiasm both the Revolutionary cause and, later, that of the Empire, under which he was appointed a theatre censor. He was dismissed by Napoleon's chief of police, Fouché, and lived the rest of his life under the courtesy title of *Doyen de la littérature française*. A member, then an officer and finally, from 1786 to 1788, Worshipful Master of 'Le Patriotisme', he supplied the composers of the lodge, Mathieu de l'Epidor and, above, all, François Giroust, with numerous texts for musical setting: poems for cantatas, rituals for masonic ceremonies (notably a superb funeral ritual) and many small operas which were put on to assist the charitable or social activities of the lodge. The aims of these performances were, firstly, to raise funds for the *frère hospitalier* (the lodge brother in charge of charitable work), 'whose principal care was to provide for the comfort of widows, orphans, the aged and the infirm, and of all those poor people ... whose misfortune was not their own fault' ('dont le soin principal était de pourvoir au soulagement des veuves, des orphelins, des vieillards et des infirmes et de tous les pauvres ... qui n'étaient pas malheureux par leur faute')[6] and, secondly, to spread moral and initiative, or philosophical, instruction by introducing the teachings of masonic ritual to the uninitiated. As far as the second point is concerned, this was a move parallel to that of the author and composer of *Die Zauberflöte*. The performances took place in the temple of 'Le Patriotisme' itself (unfortunately destroyed during the period of the Revolution, but known from Nogaret's descriptions as having been a model of its kind), at the Hôtel des Chevau-légers (to-day the Versailles auction rooms), or at the Théâtre Montansier (now the town's municipal theatre). Audiences were generous. In 1788, when a production was given 'in the presence of the entire court ... for the benefit of poor octogenarians adopted by "Le Patriotisme"' ('en présence de toute la Cour ... au profit des pauvres octogénaires adoptés par le "Patriotisme"'),[7] a collection taken at two performances produced the sum of 6000F (equivalent in modern currency to about 150,000F). Such productions stand out in the life of a lodge!

As already mentioned, some of these miniature operas develop a philosophy which could already be described as Revolutionary. One example is *Gédéon, ou L'amour de l'égalité*, as it was called in the edition of 1787, or *Gédéon, ou Le renoncement au pouvoir absolu*, as it became in the edition of 1807 (the year in which Napoleon's chief of police withdrew the post of theatre censor from the poet). The music was almost certainly by Giroust. It was deposited along with all his other operas in the library of the Conservatoire, which at that time lent scores to whoever wished to borrow them, and is now thought definitely to be

6 F. Nogaret, *L'isle des sages* (Paris, 1785), p. 4.
7 F. Nogaret, *Fictions, discours, poèmes lyriques et autres pièces adonhimites* (Paris, 1787; 2nd edn, Paris, 1807), p. 17.

lost. The title itself strikes a decidedly anti-monarchist note. The plot is borrowed from the Book of Judges, Chapter 8 verses 22–3:

Then the men of Israel said unto Gideon, Rule thou over us, both thou, and thy son, and thy son's son also; for thou hast delivered us from the hand of Midian.

And Gideon said unto them, I will not rule over you, neither shall my son rule over you: the Lord shall rule over you.

The edition of 1807 mentions an incident at once curious and revealing about the reception of sung drama at the time: 'This little drama ... was performed with success at Compiègne by the brethren of this 'Orient' on a small stage. Lacking the music, it was all spoken' ('Cette petite pièce ... a été jouée avec succès à Compiègne par les FF.°. de cet Orient sur un petit théâtre. Faute de musique on a tout déclamé'). It is thus not even certain that this text was ever set to music, despite the fact that it was explicitly designed for musical setting; above all, the observation confirms the importance accorded in early French opera to the supremacy of the libretto over the music.

Another opera, *Les inquiétudes et les charmes de l'amitié*, the music of which (now lost) was certainly by Giroust, brings forward ideas that were even more modern, although they revived those of the famous *Ballet de la paix* written by Descartes almost a century and a half earlier (in 1649) for the birthday of Queen Christina of Sweden. Nogaret accompanies his verses with a severe anti-militarist commentary:

L'instant de la scène est celui où Philippe [II de Macédoine], ayant usé de représailles, & vengé les dégats commis sur les terres de son royaume, vient d'accorder la Paix: ce qui ne rend pas aux laboureurs les récoltes que la guerre a moissonnées pour eux.

The action takes place as Philip [II of Macedonia], having made reprisals and avenged the havoc wrought on the territories of his kingdom, comes to grant peace, which fails to give back to the farmers the harvest that the war has reaped for them.

It seems that this piece re-used the libretto, and perhaps the music, of a cantata composed earlier for the recovery of the Countess d'Artois after an illness.

Another *poème lyrique* on which Giroust and Nogaret collaborated was *Irruption de l'Ocean dans la partie du Globe appelée aujourd'hui la Méditerranée*. This concludes with an affirmation already (in 1780!) in agreement with the future spirit of the constituents of 1789: 'aimons-nous, tous les hommes sont frères', asserted and developed in the final chorus. On the other hand, an oratorio, *L'ombre de Samuel*, given its first performance in 1781, takes up an idea cherished by the Enlightenment, that of the benevolent despot. Taking its inspiration from Chapter 8, verses 20–2 of the First Book of Samuel, it proclaims:

> D'un roi juste et valeureux
> Tout aime et craint la présence,
> Son peuple qu'il rend heureux
> Sait périr pour sa défence ...

Everyone loves and fears the presence of a just and valorous king. His people, whom he makes happy, are ready to die in his defence ...

Other operas and lyrical works by Nogaret and Giroust allude clearly to masonic rituals, and are of comparatively little interest here.

It would be gratifying to hear this music. Unfortunately the generosity of nineteenth-century librarians at the Conservatoire has deprived us of the pleasure. But, thanks to some happy mischance, a single overture escaped the abuses of those who freely borrowed material from the library and has remained in the Conservatoire's collection, now deposited in the Bibliothèque Nationale. According to Prim's slender hypothesis, this is the overture to the lost opera *Thélèphe*,[8] but it is more likely to belong to one of the little masonic operas. It has the characteristics of such works: C minor tonality (with its symbolic key signature of three flats) and a bipartite structure consisting of a slow introduction, rhythmically and harmonically unstable, followed by an Allegro built on the motifs of Giroust's own masonic funeral music, which is punctuated with, and at times halted by, recurrent and symbolic triplet figures.[9]

The events of 1789 in the end disrupted Giroust's career as much as that of his librettist. Of course, the ideas which they, in the role of amateur philosophers, had defended until then were about to be legalized and put into practice (at a price!), and for some time things continued as usual. On the day the States General were inaugurated (5 May 1789) Giroust conducted a Haydn symphony 'pendant le lever de Sa Majesté';[10] Nogaret remained in the service of the Countess d'Artois until 1791, and about that time was granted a pension by the government of 1500F a year.

Giroust had already, in 1788, made a good bargain by selling the reversion, or succession, of his post as *surintendant de la musique du roi* for the enormous sum of 10,000 *livres* (250,000F at today's values); the purchaser was Johann Paul Ægidius Martini (or Schwarzendorf), remembered today as the composer of the over-celebrated song *Plaisir d'amour*. In October 1789, when the royal family were obliged to leave Versailles for the palace of the Tuileries in Paris, Giroust followed

---

8 J. Prim, 'Giroust', col. 170.
9 The overture has been recorded by the Nouvel Orchestre Symphonique Belge, conducted by Roger J. V. Cotte, on a tape to be issued in conjunction with the author's *Les musiciens francs-maçons* (see note 2, above).
10 J. Tiersot, *Les fêtes et les chants de la Révolution française* (Paris, 1908).

them, remaining as *maître de chapelle* until the fall of the royalty. He then returned to Versailles in order to place his talents at the service of the new regime, who were not overwhelmed by the offer. With the cooperation of former members of the king's *musique*, he formed a large orchestra which he placed at the disposal of the département and the town to add lustre to patriotic festivals. From then on the style of his output changed – at least in appearance.

Giroust now allowed himself to be inspired by events of the moment, for example by the transference to the Panthéon of the ashes of Marat and Lepeletier, the republican 'martyrs' assassinated for their views (the first by Charlotte Corday, admirer of the Girondins, the second by the Parisian bodyguards for having voted for the king's death). Giroust marked this double commemoration no fewer than five times, with as many musical scores. The first was a grand chorus entitled *Apothéose de Marat et Le Peletier* to a poem by Delrieu, a native of Versailles, where he taught rhetoric; it is some 600 bars long with accompaniment of strings and wind, and was probably used for some ceremony at Versailles. An *Invocation pour la plantation de l'arbre de la liberté* for three voices and orchestra with reduced wind, was played on 28 February 1794 at the inauguration of the busts of Marat and Le Peletier during a civic festival attended by members of the *gendarmerie* of the commune of Versailles. Constant Pierre dismissed the piece as 'insignificant'.[11]

A similar fête, again for the inauguration of two busts of the same martyrs, was organized by the office of the 'Comptabilité nationale' a little earlier, on 4 November 1793 (14 Brumaire An II in the Revolutionary calendar), and it was no doubt for this occasion that Giroust produced his *Hymne des versaillais*. Two further hymns with words by Félix Nogaret were composed for other similar occasions.

From time to time Giroust drew on earlier compositions, modifying the text to a greater or lesser extent. These are usually masonic works, such as the *Scène dityrambique: chant républicain exécuté le 20 vendémiaire, an III* [12 October 1794] *à l'occasion de l'anniversaire de l'installation de la Manufacture d'armes de Versailles*. The manuscript in the Bibliothèque du Conservatoire includes two poetic texts, the first of which has been crossed through and is no longer legible; the other is republican in tone, evidently adapted to already existing music. Clear masonic expressions are everywhere present in the second version, from which it may be inferred that a composition originally intended for a ceremony or concert at a lodge has been re-used in the context of a republican festival. For example:

C'est aujourd'hui l'anniversaire ...,

11 C. Pierre, *Les hymnes et chansons de la Révolution française* (Paris, 1904), p. 304 (note 41).

Tubalcain! buvez, chantez,
Chantons l'amitié ...
Célébrons les douceurs de la Fraternité ...

To-day is the anniversary ... Tubalcain! drink, sing, let us sing of friendship ... let us celebrate the comforts of Brotherhood ...

Stranger still is the sequence of transformations undergone by the *Hymne à l'Éternel* sung at the Musée de Paris, an academic society which sprang from the reorganization of the former Société Apolonienne. In this Nogaret's text was presented as 'a kind of free imitation of several passages from the Psalms ...' ('une espèce d'imitation libre du plusieurs passages tirés des psaumes ...').[12] The music of this first version was by Dannery, *maître de chapelle* at Soissons Cathedral. Some years later the same text, set by an unknown composer (possibly Giroust), became the masonic *Hymne au Grand Architecte de l'univers*. Finally, in 1794 (Year II), Giroust presented to the Convention a newly composed score on the same text, with the title *Cantate à l'Éternel, présentée au Comité d'Instruction Publique le 20 brumaire, an II ... pour être chanté[e] au temple de la Raison*. This 'Temple of Reason' was none other than the church of Notre Dame at Versailles, transformed to suit what might be called an atheist cult devised by the Revolutionaries for citizens who were too much in the habit of frequenting churches on Sunday (or rather on 'décadi', the 'Sunday' of the ten-day week in the Revolutionary calendar). Giroust's score, now lost, must have been quite substantial, since in a petition presented on 11 Pluviôse An III/ 2 February 1795 it is regretted that only extracts could be given at Versailles, and the hope is expressed that it might be presented in Paris, 'where alone may be found the forces necessary for its performance' ('[qui] seul fournirait les moyens nécessaires à son exécution').[13] Giroust himself kept some copies which he distributed without charge to those who requested them.

Another protean text, the *Concert des octogénaires*, is known in three versions. The first, intended for charitable events organized by the Lodge 'Le Patriotisme' prior to 1787 at the Montansier theatre in the presence of the court, raised more than 6000F, which was all distributed among the poor. Giroust's music, like so much else deposited in the Conservatoire, is of course lost. After 1793 this was transformed into a Revolutionary and republican work by the simple addition of three couplets and a change of title to *Concert au profit des indigents*. Nogaret, the poet, calls on young composers to be inspired anew by his text, wishing 'that they, like Giroust, may have the pleasure of seeing their listeners

---

12 Nogaret, *Fictions, discours*, pp. 175ff.
13 Pierre, *Les hymnes et chansons*, pp. 619–20 (note 1002).

tremble and weep ...' ('qu'il leur arrive, comme à Giroust, de jouir du plaisir de voir frémir et pleurer leurs auditeurs ...').[14] Another comment by Nogaret goes even further:

Citoyens indigents! c'est pour vous que j'écris. Je reprends cette plume qui fut autrefois consacrée dans le Temple de la Sagesse où vécurent amis des poètes, dont les productions [furent] embellies par les accents vainqueurs de la musique ...[15]

Poor citizens! It is for you that I write. I take up again that pen that was in former times consecrated in the Temple of Wisdom [referring, obviously, to the Lodge] where lived poets whose works were embellished by the persuasive tones of music ...

And, to conclude on a frankly indecorous note from the pen of a former servant and beneficiary of the fallen monarchy: 'and while the head of some poor wretch ceases to blaspheme as it drops into the bag, I run into my garden crying: Long live l'Etude! long live la Montagne! long live the Republic!' ('et tandis que la tête d'un coquin achève de blasphémer en tombant dans le sac, je cours à mon jardin criant: vive l'Etude!, vive la Montagne!, vive la République!').[16]

But the career of the poem, and of the music, was not yet finished. The poem appeared again in 1795, when the Versailles publisher, M.-D. Cosson, issued it with music (possibly new) by Giroust, manuscript copies of which he offered to supply free of charge. Finally, in 1807, Nogaret refashioned the text in a new edition, this time divided into recitatives, arias, duets and choruses, under a fresh title, *Appel à la bien faisance*. While mentioning Giroust's score as being 'en dépôt au Conservatoire', he accompanied his verses with another call to composers 'to exercise their talents on some of these words' ('à exercer leur talent sur quelques unes de ces paroles'). In that way, he adds without modesty, 'the good I propose to do would extend to a larger number of people' ('le bien que je me suis proposé de faire s'étendrait sur un plus grand nombre d'individus').

Giroust wrote several dozen more songs on texts, mostly by Nogaret, which hymned the changing virtues of the new regimes: martial songs in honour of republican soldiers, various devout songs for use by the Cult of Reason, then (this latter having been abolished by Robespierre, who considered it to be atheist and blasphemous) for the Cult of the Supreme Being and finally, from 1797, for that of the Theophilanthropists (the lovers of God and men), which proved to be no more durable.

Instead of the plum jobs offered to his colleagues in the musical

14 Anonymous [F. Nogaret], *Concert au profit des indigents* (Versailles, n.d.), 'Préface'.
15 Ibid.
16 'La Montagne' ('the Mountain') was the name given to the left-wing deputies, led by Robespierre, who occupied the upper tiers in the National Assembly. By 'l'Etude' Nogaret refers to his philosophical and poetical work.

establishment of the National Guard or at the newly formed Conservatoire, Giroust received only the modest sinecure of *concierge du palais national* at the former palace of Versailles. There he died on 28 April 1799. The composer's last appointment led his former collaborator, Félix Nogaret, to give him the name of 'génie-concierge'. Unable to appreciate his true worth, the Revolutionary authorities showed themselves no better qualified in music than did the unfortunate Fétis at a later date.

Translation by the editor

REVOLUTIONARY OPERA

The new repertory at the Opéra during the Reign of Terror: Revolutionary rhetoric and operatic consequences[1]

For more than a century after its foundation the Opéra took pride in its close association with the monarchy and indeed benefited greatly from prerogatives granted it under royal *privilège*. Its very name, Académie Royale de Musique, was a constant public reminder of its favoured position. The decade following the death of Rameau in 1764 was one of little activity, but the institution gained new vitality during the reign of Louis XVI (1774–92). The foreigners Gluck, Piccinni, Sacchini and Salieri, as well as Grétry, composed works for Paris which were to dominate the repertory well into the nineteenth century. Debates between Gluckistes and Piccinnistes enlivened the conversation in salons and the contents of the press: not since the mid-eighteenth-century Querelle des Bouffons had operas at the Académie Royale been of such concern to the élite of French society.[2] The musical qualities of 'reform' opera and its contrast to Rameau's style were, of course, important. But the fact that attending opera was once again the fashionable thing to do for the upper class, thanks in part to Queen Marie Antoinette's patronage, should not be underestimated.[3]

1 This is one of a series of articles devoted to the Opéra in 1793–4. In 'Revolutionschanson und Hymne im Repertoire der Pariser Oper, 1793–1794', in *Die französische Revolution als Bruch des gesellschaftlichen Bewusstseins*, ed. R. Reichardt and R. Koselleck (Munich, 1988), pp. 479–507 (translated into German by H. Schneider), I examined the symbolic use of the *chanson* and *hymne* and pieces in similar style. State-theatre relations, as well as an overview of the whole Opéra repertory (new works and old favourites), is the subject of 'From *Académie Royale de Musique* to *Opéra National*: the Republican "Regeneration" of an Institution', a paper given at Michigan State University, 27 April 1989. The interchange between opera and Revolutionary *fête* will be the focus of a forthcoming study.
2 On the 1750s controversy, see L. Reichenburg, *Contribution à l'histoire de la 'querelle des bouffons': guerre de brochures suscitées par le 'Petit prophète' de Grimm et par la 'Lettre sur la musique française' de Rousseau* (Philadelphia, 1937) and D. Launay, ed., *La querelle des bouffons: texte des pamphlets avec introduction, commentaires et index* (Geneva, 1973). On the 1770s debate, see especially Gaspar Michel, *dit* Leblond, ed., *Mémoires pour servir à l'histoire de la révolution opérée dans la musique par M. le chevalier Gluck* (Naples and Paris, 1781; reprinted Amsterdam, 1967), which includes many of the Gluckistes' letters to newspapers, replies to reviews, pamphlets etc.
3 About her patronage of the Opéra, see A. Jullien, *La cour et l'Opéra sous Louis XVI: Marie-Antoinette et Sacchini; Salieri; Favart et Gluck; d'après des documents inédits conservés*

In the early years of the Revolution (1789–92) little seemed to change on the surface. The theatre's name remained the same (except for a brief period after the king's attempt to flee, on 21 June 1791);[4] the works given premières since 1774 continued to be performed often and well attended; new operas (like Lemoyne's *Louis IX en Egypte* and Méhul's *Cora*), though sometimes critical of abuses of power, nonetheless contained praise for good governance in the figure of the monarch and references to his subjects' affection in the tradition of the *ancien régime*;[5] the audience applauded the queen on her quite frequent appearances. Indeed, one of the last times she and the royal family were seen in public was at this theatre, on 20 September 1791.

Yet, after the fall of the monarchy (10 August 1792) and the declaration of the Republic (22 September following), the Opéra made a successful transition from the most royalist of Parisian public institutions to one committed to the new order. To do so required timely political manoeuvring on the administration's part. Still, they succeeded in ensuring that the Opéra remained the theatre for the élite. The élite changed but, in common with that of the 1770s and 1780s, they were those with money and power. Nor were the administration's actions merely self-seeking. Just as the Académie Royale de Musique had promoted the glory of Louis XIV, so the Opéra National had a mission to serve the Republic. The administration felt a genuine responsibility to promote certain moral and patriotic sentiments through theatrical works. The efficacy of such lessons was assumed: for the medieval church stained-glass windows and statues were the most direct way of teaching the congregation, and for the French of the 1790s the arts, including lyric theatre, could fulfil a similar function for citizens. As one critic remarked in a review of one opera's première:

Tous les Arts doivent célébrer la Liberté, & la Musique aussi. C'est par des chants que les Peuples honorent la Divinité, & la Liberté est la Divinité des Peuples Républicains.[6]

All the arts must celebrate liberty, and music as well. It is through songs that people honour the divinity, and liberty is the divinity of republican peoples.

aux Archives de l'état et à l'Opéra (Paris, 1878) and 'Marie-Antoinette musicienne', in *La ville et la cour au XVIIIe siècle* (Paris, 1881), pp. 61–101. About her support of the Comédie-Italienne (Opéra-Comique), see M. E. C. Bartlet, 'Grétry, Marie-Antoinette and *La rosière de Salency*', *Proceedings of the Royal Musical Association*, cxi (1984–5), pp. 92–120.

4 It reverted to its royal name when Louis XVI accepted the constitution the following September. For a list with dates, see J. G. Prod'homme, *L'Opéra (1669–1915): description du nouvel Opéra, historique, salles occupées par l'Opéra depuis son origine, dénominations officielles, directions, répertoire, principaux artistes, bibliographie* (Paris, 1925; reprinted Geneva, 1972), p. 56.

5 For several examples, see M. E. C. Bartlet, 'Etienne Nicolas Méhul and Opera during the French Revolution, Consulate, and Empire: a Source, Archival, and Stylistic Study' (PhD diss., University of Chicago, 1982), pp. 1041–2.

6 *Affiches, annonces et avis divers, ou Journal général de France*, 23 nivôse an II/12 January 1794, p. 5670 [review of *Toute la Grèce, ou Ce que peut la liberté*].

The parallel between sacred and secular, the implied substitution of republican values promoted in theatrical works for those of religious rites, are evidence of the standards of morality required by contemporaries.

The Opéra's administration often used this very argument in seeking support from the Committee of Public Safety (to replace that lost with the dissolution of the court's civil list). Old operas could be revised; new ones, extolling republican virtues through the selection of appropriate topics from classical history, rehearsed and staged; even ballet, that decadent and voluptuous art, made pure and moral.[7] The representatives of artists responsible for managing the theatre went further; at the height of the Terror they wrote to the Committee:

L'Opéra National doit sa conservation au Comité de Salut Public. Les secours qu'il a bien voulû donner à ce théâtre lui ont fourni l'heureux moyen de porter l'esprit public au degré d'énergie qu'exigent les circonstances. L'Opéra sera toujours une Ecole de Patriotisme.

Les Grecs se réunissoient pour célébrer leurs Jeux Olimpiques et pour y voir revivre, sous le pinceau des Poëtes dramatiques, les magnifiques Epôques de leur histoire.

Il est tems que les Français jouissent avec enthousiasme du plaisir d'admirer leurs exploits et de voir représenter leur gloire.

Citoyens, les Artistes de l'Opéra se sont réunis aux Auteurs dramatiques. Ils ont trouvé dans nos Annales révolutionnaires une foule de sujets propres à exercer leurs talens et à enflâmer toutes les passions généreuses et républicaines.

Ces Artistes donnent tous leurs soins à la composition d'un nouveau Répertoire qui présentera à l'enthousiasme et à la reconnaisance des Citoyens les grands événemens, les beaux traits qui ont signalé notre révolution.[8]

The Opéra owes its survival to the Committee of Public Safety. The aid it kindly gave to this theatre provided the means to arouse public spirit to the degree that current circumstances require. The Opéra will always be a school of patriotism.

The Greeks used to gather to celebrate their Olympic Games and to see the magnificent eras of their history revived in the verses of dramatic poets.

It is time for the French to enjoy with enthusiasm the pleasure of admiring their own exploits and to see staged their own glory.

Citizens, the artists of the Opéra have joined ranks with the dramatic authors. They have found in our Revolutionary annals a host of subjects appropriate to testing their talents and to arousing all those generous and republican passions.

These artists are making every effort to establish a new repertory which will present to the enthusiastic and grateful citizenry the great events and the fine deeds that have marked our Revolution.

7 For a transcription of several representative documents and a fuller examination of them, see my paper 'From *Académie Royale de Musique* to *Opéra National*'.
8 Petition dated 7 Ventôse An II/25 February 1794; Paris, Archives Nationales, AJ[13] 44 [III].

In this petition the emphasis on the didactic purpose of theatre is clear, but what is new for the Opéra is a conscious pride, even a sense of superiority, in France's contemporary achievements. Whereas even during the reign of Louis XVI serious operas based on French history were rare – and these few (like *Louis IX* and *Peronne sauvée*) restricted to medieval and Renaissance subjects – now current events illustrating valour, love of country and self-sacrifice were worthy of the *premier théâtre lyrique*. As we shall see later, classical models remained important, although now the stories were taken from the histories of republican Greece and Rome, rather than their imperial heritage or their myths, and frequently they were modified to reflect current French ideals and concerns. It is also to be noted that the artists claim to have taken the initiative, in tandem with authors, to renew their repertory. No works were imposed on the theatre; only one performed (*La réunion du dix août*) had strong government backing. It is significant, perhaps, that the two works which the Committee of Public Safety strongly recommended (*Brutus* and *La journée du dix août*) were never staged.[9]

Revolutionary rhetoric mirroring the spirit of the times had an impact on new works for the Opéra from the years 1793 and 1794 (see Appendix, below).[10] A few may be omitted from consideration here. In spite of the artists' committee's pronouncement, neither of the ballets deviated substantially from *ancien régime* procedures.[11] Beaumarchais was a special case; and *Le mariage de Figaro* (music by Mozart) did not enter the repertory at this time.[12] The two works by Grétry were not performed during the Terror, for good reason, and are therefore excluded. The remaining items never made up the repertory exclusively, for at this, the most traditional of French lyric theatres, earlier operas by Gluck and Sacchini and ballets by Miller (choreographed by Gardel) continued to be performed and to draw audiences throughout the period. Nevertheless, singling out recent acquisitions is a legitimate test of artistic response to changing political and social conditions, at least in part.

To establish the context, I shall use sources besides the works themselves, including official pronouncements, as in speeches in the

9 F. V. A. Aulard and others, eds., *Recueil des actes du Comité de Salut Public, avec la correspondance officielle des représentants en mission et le registre du Conseil Exécutif provisoire* (Paris, 1889–1971), xi, p. 214 [deliberation of 29 Pluviôse An II/17 February 1794, *re Brutus*]: and xii, p. 342 [deliberation of 13 Germinal An II/2 April 1794, *re La journée du dix août*].

10 On the importance of rhetoric in the broad sense during the Revolution, see L. Hunt, *Politics, Culture, and Class in the French Revolution* (Berkeley and Los Angeles, 1984).

11 Only the choreographer's dedication of *Les muses* to 'ses braves frères d'armes, les sans-culottes' and, in the final scene, Apollo's orders to Melpomene to trample a crown under foot reflect the temper of the times; neither is of importance for the work.

12 W. S. Dudley, 'Les premières versions françaises du *Mariage de Figaro* de Mozart', *Revue de musicologie*, lxix (1983), pp. 55–83.

National Assembly and Convention and submissions by its committees. Among the latter the report by Léonard Bourdon de la Crosnière (who was himself a librettist) in the name of the Committee of Public Instruction, entitled *Recueil des actions héroïques et civiles des républicans français* (Paris, an II/1794), is particularly important, for the National Convention sanctioned it as a catechism for republican patriots to replace, as they saw it, the superstitions of the Christian religion as practised by the Roman Catholic church. It was distributed to schools, city officials and others at government expense. The arts, both high and popular, provide interesting parallels.

My goals are to show the continuity of some themes with *ancien régime* precedents, but at the same time to indicate differences in interpretation or emphasis; to demonstrate how the Opéra sought to fulfil its mission of moral, republican theatre; and, finally, to assess the musical consequences of any shifts or changes. Among the vast possibilities, several more limited interrelated aspects will elucidate the matter. Here an examination of the dynamics of group commitment, attitudes towards leadership and heroism, and roles that every section of society (even the disenfranchised) could undertake will contribute to our understanding of Revolutionary *mentalité*. In order to provide a clearer focus, reaction to suicide, the status of women and the collective oath will provide concrete examples. In all of these, the contemporary definition of republican ideals is more important than an assessment of how imperfectly they were realized.

ASPECTS OF REVOLUTIONARY RHETORIC

New emphasis on collective action and, for the republicans of 1793–4, the terrifying examples of individuals who one day were held high in public esteem and the next branded as traitors to their country led to a reconsideration of heroism. In the early years of the Revolution living generals and politicians were cited as models of military and civic behaviour, much as they had been in the previous decade. But after the cases of La Fayette, the highly respected commander of the National Guard in the years 1789–91, who fled France in 1792; Bailly, the first elected mayor of Paris, guillotined on 21 Brumaire An II/11 November 1793; Mirabeau, a popular orator in the National Assembly, whose double-dealings with the court were discovered after his death; Danton, demagogue and leader, guillotined on 16 Germinal An II/5 April 1794; Dumouriez, the victor at Valmy (20 September 1792) and turncoat less than a year later – after these cases and many others there was an increasing reluctance to exalt the individual in a position of power.

'Fraternité' and 'égalité' were, of course, key words for the period. Bourdon argued that, to interpret the concepts that they represented, due credit for all participants was essential; in examining cases from 1789 on for his republican catechism he regretted that:

Nous avons marqué avec peine, que, lorsqu'il s'agit d'un trait de vertu commun à plusieurs défenseurs de la patrie, on a eu soin de nous transmettre le nom de l'officier, et que souvent on a laissé dans l'oubli celui des soldats; nous prendrons les mesures nécessaires pour réparer cet oubli qui semble tenir aux injustices de l'ancien régime, et qui est si opposé aux principes de la révolution.[13]

We have noticed with chagrin that when a virtuous deed common to several of the country's defenders was at issue, the reporter was careful to tell us the name of the officer, but often left out those of the soldiers. We shall take the necessary steps to correct this neglect which seems to perpetuate the injustices of the *ancien régime* and which is so contrary to the principles of the Revolution.

In consequence, he continued, he will cite an officer's name only in cases of exceptional personal bravery.

Bourdon lived up to his claim. Tales of group heroism, both military and civilian, form a significant part of his collection. Names, when given, are usually placed at the end of the anecdote, almost as an after-thought.[14] Furthermore, individuals are often not named, even when they could have been identified easily. In the case of soldiers, of those explicitly named, nearly all from lower ranks, most died or were seriously wounded because of their actions to serve the Republic. Among the identified civilians, again most fall into a limited number of categories: those who could not be corrupted by royalists, those tortured and killed by the enemy and those from classes of society not generally associated with heroic feats (the very poor, women and children). There are no generals, no commanders, no ministers of state. A large part of Bourdon's intention was to provide models: the omission of names helps to give the stories a universality and to encourage the reader to identify with at least some of the heroes depicted.

One special form of a leader's individual heroism did meet with official approval during the early Republic: suicide in the face of overwhelming enemy odds. While opinion was not unanimous, that suicide was on occasion glorified is further evidence of the break with received Christian precepts, which condemned self-destruction as a mortal sin. Bourdon related the case of Duchemin, a battalion chief, who, when his capture was inevitable, cried out 'Long live the Republic!' and, 'preferring death to the shame of surrendering the arms that the country had confided to him for its defence, shot himself in the head' ('Il crie: *Vive la République!* ... Duchemin, préférant la mort à la honte de rendre les armes que la patrie lui a confiées pour la défendre, se brûle la

13 Bourdon de la Crosnière, *Recueil*, no. 1, p. 5.
14 As in the tale of sixteen day labourers who, because of a dearth of horses, pulled supply wagons for the army (no. 1, pp. 9–10).

cervelle'). Bourdon continued the moral lesson by pointing out that the enemy was so wicked that they massacred even those who had given up.[15] A more important example was that of Beaurepaire, commander of the first battalion of Mayenne and Loire, who, when municipal representatives decided to cede Verdun to the enemy, preferred death to dishonour. The deputy Delaunay argued that Beaurepaire deserved the state's recognition: to deny him this due would be a vestige of 'the senseless prejudice that for far too long a time led us to term weak and mad the courage of Brutuses and Catos' ('le prégugé insensé qui trop longtems nous a fait donné le nom de faiblesse et de fureur au courage des Brutus et des Caton'). He did not take this action simply to flee, to avoid pain, Delaunay continued; rather

Il a jugé que sa mort nous serait plus utile que sa vie, qu'il fallait que cette grande et terrible leçon encourageât les timides, reffermit les chancelans, qu'elle devînt le premier supplice des coeurs lâches qui ont abjuré la liberté, et qu'enfin elle apprît aux satellites de la Prusse et de l'Autriche, qu'on n'asservit point un pays tant qu'il existe des hommes qui n'ont pas vainement juré de vivre libres ou mourir.[16]

He decided that his death would be more useful to us than his life, that it would be essential to give a grand and awesome lesson to encourage the faint-hearted and strengthen the waverers, that it would become the first punishment of those cowards who renounced liberty, and finally that it would teach the henchmen of Prussia and Austria that one does not enslave a country as long as there are men who did not swear in vain to live as free men or to die.

The Assembly approved his proposal for Beaurepaire's burial in the Panthéon and the inscription on his tombstone, 'He preferred suicide to surrender to tyrants' ('Il aima mieux se donner la mort que de capituler avec les tyrans').

Individual heroism, which provided models of behaviour for others, was possible, but most often occurred when the person was isolated by the wickedness of enemies, and the results were usually tragic. Suicide for moral reasons was condoned. Republican virtue, in itself a form of heroism, could be achieved by every stratum of society, according to Bourdon: wounded soldiers declared, echoing Horace, 'We still have blood to spill for our country; oh! how sweet it is to die for her!' (no. 4,

---

15 Bourdon, *Recueil*, no. 3, p. 9.
16 *Gazette nationale, ou Le moniteur universel*, 14 September 1792, p. 1095 [minutes of the session of the National Assembly of 12 September]. Beaurepaire's heroism inspired several artists. In Pierre Berthault's engraving after Jacques François Swebach-Desfontaines, 'Prise de Verdun, mort de Beaurepaire', his body, which is being taken from the city, is barely discernible; the style is conservative, and the view of the city dominates. The lesson presented is that his sacrifice was not in vain, for Verdun has been recaptured. Two coloured engravings in a far less polished style, 'Mort de Beaurepaire', one by Labrousse and the other anonymous, seek to emphasize the shock value of the actual suicide for popular market consumption. All are reproduced in M. Vovelle, *La Révolution française: images et récit, 1789–1799* (Paris, 1986), iii, p. 159.

p. 21: 'nous avons encore du sang à répandre pour la patrie; représentans, ah! qu'il est doux de mourir pour elle!'); enlisted men turned over a village collection in their favour to help the poor (no. 1, p. 12); peasants donated some of their crops to neighbours, whose harvest was destroyed by hail (no. 2, p. 12); members of the working class, *sansculottes*, gave their shoes to the country's barefoot defenders (no. 3, p. 16); the fourteen-year-old Joseph Barra proved youth capable of an honourable death while crying 'Long live the Republic' (no. 1, pp. 22–3)[17] and so on. Mutual support in the face of adversity is frequently the lesson. The participation of women was similarly extolled, but before turning to a few examples in the *Recueil* and other publications, we must trace changes in attitude during the period 1789–94.

In the early years of the Revolution, the role of women was a topic of debate.[18] Although a consensus was not achieved, arguments for improvements in female education, for allowing women a place in the political system (at the most extreme giving them the vote) and for a bill of rights for them paralleling that for men were taken seriously. Women participated in several clubs with men and even had some of their own.[19] Women edited newspapers not confined to feminine topics and wrote political tracts. Officials praised the heroism of women: one was listed among the conquerors of the Bastille, and female soldiers (in male disguise) were mentioned favourably in military dispatches.[20] The law on marriage and its dissolution of 20 September 1792 gave women new rights to request and obtain divorce. In short, during the period 1789 to early 1793 there were signs of, if not emancipation, at least a liberalization in their status.

With the Terror a strong reaction set in. The Constitution of 24 June 1793 excluded women from political rights. They were barred from hitherto mixed clubs, and their own were suppressed by law (29 Vendémiaire An II/20 October 1793); they were prevented from participating in political debates.[21] Except for approved suppliers, women were

---

17 Robespierre, among others, promoted Barra as a martyr; see his speech in the National Convention, 8 Nivôse An II/28 December 1793 (published in *Le moniteur universel*, 10 nivôse an II/30 December 1793, p. 403). A *fête* was planned in his honour and that of another youthful victim, Agricole Viala; David's plans for it were presented to the Convention on 23 Messidor An II/11 July 1794 (published in *Le moniteur universel*, 5 thermidor an II/23 July 1794, pp. 1247–8). But it was postponed, and after Robespierre's downfall cancelled by the Convention on 9 Thermidor An II/27 July 1794 (*Le moniteur universel*, 12 thermidor an II/30 July 1794, p. 1277).

18 For an overview of the status of women see C. Marand-Fouquet, *La femme au temps de la Révolution* (Paris, 1989) and P.-M. Duhet, *Les femmes et la Révolution, 1789–1794* (Paris, 1971). For a fine collection in facsimile of contemporary documents relating to these issues see *Les femmes dans la Révolution française* (Paris, 1982).

19 See M. Cerati, *Le club des citoyennes républicaines révolutionnaires* (Paris, 1966).

20 J.-P. Bertaud, *La vie quotidienne des soldats de la Révolution* (Paris, 1985).

21 A little later (4 Prairial An III/23 May 1795) the Convention passed a law institutionalizing this by prohibiting women from even attending as spectators.

ordered from combatant roles and barred from following the army on
14 Brumaire An II/4 November 1793, although there were still a few
cases where the ban was defied. Several leading feminists were publicly
disgraced, imprisoned or guillotined, among them Olympe de Gouges
and Claire Lacombe – just punishment in the eyes of many for forgetting their proper station.[22] Both in assemblies and in the press, men
sharply criticized women who sought a public role. The female virtues
extolled were again (as they had been before 1789) those of the private
sphere: obedience to the husband, dedication to him and the family,
charity to the unfortunate, caring for the sick. As for serving the
Republic, women did so by raising children, teaching them love of
country and its values, rejoicing in France's victories and reacting
stoically to the losses of sons and spouses in the war and other necessary sacrifices.[23] Bourdon singled out an extremely poor woman who
nevertheless returned a lost *assignat* to its owner and thereby permitted
him to buy food for his children (no. 1, p. 13), a daughter who
sacrificed a fine position to take care of her ill mother for seventeen

22 *Le moniteur universel*, 29 brumaire an II/19 November 1793, p. 237, recommended women to
learn from the examples of three recent executions. Marie Antoinette, ambitious in political
schemes to benefit the enemy Austria, was 'mauvaise mère, épouse débauchée'. 'Son nom sera à
jamais en horreur à la postérité.' Olympe de Gouges 'voulut être homme d'Etat, et il semble que
la loi ait puni cette conspiratrice d'avoir oublié les vertus qui conviennent à son sexe'. Mme
Roland, wife of the fallen Girondin leader, though a mother, 'avait sacrifié la nature, en voulant
s'élever au-dessus d'elle; le désir d'être savante la conduisait à l'oubli des vertus de son sexe, et
cet oubli, toujours dangereux, finit par la faire périr sur l'échafaud'. Cited in P.-M. Duhet, *Les
femmes*, pp. 205–6.
23 Two examples illustrate the accepted view. André Amar's report in the name of the Committee
for General Security, which led to the suppression of women's clubs, noted:
    Quel est le caractère propre à la femme? Les moeurs et la Nature même lui ont assigné ses
    fonctions: commencer l'éducation des hommes, préparer l'esprit et le coeur des enfans
    aux vertus publiques, les diriger de bonne heure vers le bien, élever leur âme et les
    instruire dans le culte politique de la liberté: telles sont leurs fonctions, après les soins du
    ménage; la femme est naturellement destinée à faire aimer la vertu ... doivent-elles
    prendre une part active à des discussions dont la chaleur est incompatible avec la douceur
    et la modération qui font le charme de leur sexe? ... L'honnêteté d'une femme
    permet-elle qu'elle se montre en public, et qu'elle lutte avec les hommes, de discuter à la
    face d'un peuple sur des questions d'où dépend le salut de la République? En général, les
    femmes sont peu capables de conceptions hautes et de méditations sérieuses: et si, chez
    les anciens peuples, leur timidité naturelle et la pudeur ne leur permettaient pas de
    paraître hors de leur famille, voulez-vous que, dans la République Française, on les voye
    venir au bareau, à la tribune, aux assemblées politiques comme les hommes; abandon-
    nant et la retenue, source de toutes les vertus de ce sexe, et le soin de leur famille? (*Le
    moniteur universel*, 10 brumaire an II/31 October 1793, p. 164; cited in P.-M. Duhet,
    Les femmes, p. 156).
On Amar, see also Cerati, *Le club*, pp. 163–7. The *Feuille du salut public*, a Jacobin newspaper
close to the government, urged its female readers:
    Femmes! voulez-vous être républicaines? Aimez, suivez et enseignez les lois qui rappel-
    lent vos époux et vos enfants à l'exercice de leurs droits; soyez glorieuses des actions
    éclatantes qu'ils pourront compter en faveur de la patrie, parce qu'elles témoignent en
    leur faveur; soyez simples dans votre mise, laborieuses dans votre ménage; ne suivez
    jamais les assemblées populaires avec le désir d'y parler; ... alors la patrie vous bénira,
    parce que vous aurez réellement fait pour elle ce qu'elle a le droit d'attendre de vous
    (cited in Duhet, *Les femmes*, p. 206).

years (no. 4, p. 20), a couple of humble means who took in an abandoned child (no. 1, pp. 19–20) and others conforming to the ideals of 1793–4.[24]

One public gesture, particularly though not exclusively associated with women, continued to receive official approbation, and it had classical precedents admired during the *ancien régime*: the patriotic gift. The incident from Roman history where Camilla gave the proceeds of the sale of her jewels to the senate and was imitated by other ladies in order to raise the necessary funds to fulfil a state vow to Apollo was the subject for several French artists. At the 1785 salon Nicolas Guy Brenet exhibited his picture 'Piété et générosité des dames romaines'. A few years later Louis Gauffier treated the same theme and showed his painting in the 1791 salon.[25] In between these public exhibitions one event provided a vivid example of life imitating art. Twenty wives and daughters of several leading French artists, at the instigation of Mme Moitte, wife of the sculptor Jean Guillaume Moitte, decided to perform a similar service for France. During the session of the National Assembly on 7 September 1789, all dressed in white, 'decorated only by that beautiful simplicity which characterizes virtue' (according to the official account),[26] they entered the chamber and made a donation of their jewellery to be sold to help pay the nation's debt. Too modest to deliver her speech on the ladies' behalf, Mme Moitte had one of the deputies read it. After citing the Camilla episode, it went on to say that 'they would blush to wear jewels when patriotism required their sacrifice' and encouraged others, especially those with greater means, to follow their example.[27] One member praised their generosity, which he rated above what had happened in Rome;[28] the president of the Assembly complimented them and their names were formally inscribed in the minutes.

The organizers were conscious of setting a precedent for the French. Their clear call to equal, if not better, classical precedent, the theatrical effect in their deliberate simplicity of dress and their emphasis on ostentatious modesty were all calculated to impress by emphasizing virtues for women held in high esteem. In a pamphlet issued after the event, Mme Moitte urged others to contribute and in the form of a prayer stressed that all had a part to play. Note again the religious inflection given to patriotic actions:

24 In his only tale of a female soldier he made it clear that she was following her brother and husband, and, though courageous in battle, afterwards in tending to her wounded husband 'en lui prodiguant les soins de la tendresse conjugale, elle prouve qu'elle n'a pas renoncé aux vertus de son sexe' (Bourdon, *Receuil*, no. 1, pp. 23–4). The anecdote dates from Brumaire An II/October–November 1793.
25 Brenet's painting is in the château at Fontainebleau. Gauffier's 'Générosité des dames romaines' is reproduced in Vovelle, *La Révolution française*, i, p. 205.
26 *Le moniteur universel*, 8 September 1789, p. 223: 'ornées de cette belle simplicité qui caracterise la vertu'.
27 A. M. A. C. Moitte, *Suite de L'âme des romaines dans les femmes françaises* [Paris, 1789].
28 *Courier français*, 8 September 1789, p. 315. The sum raised was approximately 6000 *livres*.

Oh! toi, Dieu des Puissances, protecteur des bienfaits, répands tes faveurs célestes sur cette noble entreprise; et que chacun de nous à l'envi, sans distinction de sexe ni de rang, marche avec rapidité vers l'Autel de la Patrie.[29]

Oh! Thou all-powerful God, protector of good deeds, bestow your heavenly blessing on this noble undertaking; and may each one of us in emulation of one another, without making distinction between sex or rank, march quickly to the Country's altar.

Their example was indeed followed, as the press reported, but the size and frequency of such donations were insufficient to make much difference to France's sorry economic plight. Still, the incident provided enormous propaganda value and found its place in contemporary art[30] and in Bourdon's *Recueil*.[31]

In spite of Mme Moitte's fervent wish, the collective actions of the soldiers, the poor and the women, praised and idealized by Bourdon and others, demonstrate distinctions by occupation, class and sex, even though the moral is that republican virtue could be attained by everyone. The patriotic oath, on the other hand, became a symbol for the unity of all the French. Surveying briefly the changing attitude to the oath in the late eighteenth century will help us understand its importance.

According to the modern scholar Jean Starobinski,

Le sacre, cérémonie d'instauration, conférait, au monarque, par une intervention d'en haut, au nom d'un Dieu transcendant, les signes surnaturels de son pouvoir. Le serment révolutionnaire *crée* la souveraineté – alors que le monarque le *recevait* du Ciel. La volonté singulière de chaque individu se *généralise* dans l'instant où tous prononcent la formule du serment: c'est du fond de chaque vie individuelle que monte la parole dit en commun, où la loi future, tout ensemble impersonelle et humaine, trouvera sa source.[32]

Through a supreme intervention in the name of a transcendent God, the coronation, the ceremony of initiation, conferred on the monarch supernatural insignia of his power. The republican oath *creates* sovereignty – whereas the king *received* it from

29 A. M. A. C. Moitte, *Suite*, p. 4.
30 Berthault's engraving after Jean Louis Prieur, 'Députation des femmes artistes à l'Assemblée', stresses the solemnity and the decorum of all present: the women form only a small part of the conception; the representatives are as important. Lesueur's gouache 'Des citoyennes de Paris offrent leurs bijoux à la Convention Nationale' makes them more central and more real, but has them anachronistically wearing sashes of patriotic red, white and blue (the terms 'citoyennes' and 'Convention' are also several years out). Not all artistic comment was as positive. In the anonymous coloured engraving 'Oh bravo mesdames, c'est donc votre tour' the message is clear: these well-off *bourgeoises* should take their turn in contributing to the national coffers; for too long peasants have borne the burden. All are reproduced in Vovelle, *La Révolution française*, (i, p. 204; iii, pp. 288–9; and ii, p. 120–21) and the first in Jean-Jacques Lévêque, *L'art et la Révolution française, 1789–1804* (Neuchâtel, 1987), p. 100.
31 Bourdon, *Recueil*, no. 3, pp. 19–20. According to him, the youngest, who had the honour to present the box, had 'une grâce et une timidité qui ajoutent à ses charmes'. This was one of the cases where he cited all the names at the end of the anecdote.
32 J. Starobinski, *1789: les emblèmes de la raison* (Paris, 1979), pp. 66–7.

Heaven. The separate will of each person *becomes general* at the moment when all utter the oath's formula: it is from the essence of each individual life that the words said in common achieve the level which will serve as the source for future law, at the same time both impersonal and human.

An analysis of public ceremonies (and of a few of the works of art that they inspired) supports Starobinski's interpretation and, further, permits us to see the importance oath-taking had for republicans.

Louis XVI at his coronation took a vow to God only. His oath placed Christian values first: protection of the Church, maintenance of justice and peace in the realm, the extermination of heresy. As head of the Order of the Holy Spirit, he declared:

Nous, Louis, par la grâce de Dieu, Roi de France & de Navarre, jurons & vouons solemnellement en vos mains, à Dieu le créateur, de vivre & mourir en sa sainte foi & religion Catholique, Apostolique & Romaine, comme à un bon Roi très-chrétien appartient.[33]

We, Louis, by the grace of God King of France and of Navarre, swear and vow solemnly to God the Creator to live and die in His holy faith and Catholic, Apostolic and Roman religion, as it behoves a good, most Christian king.

The élite of society (aristocratic and wealthy) were witnesses. As tradition dictated, the ceremony took place in an enclosed space (the Cathedral of Rheims), from which people not invited were excluded. To be sure, during the rites the archbishop formally asked those present if they accepted Louis XVI as their king: their 'respectful silence' was taken as their consent.[34]

Jacques Louis David's famous painting, 'Le serment des Horaces',[35] first shown in the 1785 salon, boldly proclaims a new view of the oath and one that in this context seems to have originated with the painter, even now one who did not hesitate to challenge authority[36] and later a fervent Jacobin republican, organizer of Revolutionary *fêtes*[37] and member of the government. The eyes of all men are on the hilts of the

---

33 Abbé Pichon, *Le sacre et le couronnement de Louis XVI, Roi de France et de Navarre, dans l'église de Reims, le 11 juin 1775; précédé de recherches sur le sacre des Rois de France, depuis Clovis jusqu'à Louis XVI; et suivi d'un journal historique de ce qui s'est passé à cette auguste cérémonie* (Paris, 1775), p. 41; see also pp. 40–43. The medal struck to commemorate the event continues this theme of the monarch's direct accountability to God first and foremost; it shows Louis, crowned, kneeling to receive divine blessing from an angel, with the legend 'to God the Consecrator'; no priests or people are represented. Pichon shows a reproduction on p. 50.

34 Jean Michel Moreau's engraving 'Serment de Louis XVI à son sacre' serves the official view of kingship: the splendour of the setting and the rich attire of those present indicate the exclusivity of the ceremony. It is reproduced in Lévêque, *L'art et la Révolution*, p. 15.

35 Reproduced in Vovelle, *La Révolution française*, i, p. 16, and in Lévêque, *L'art et la Révolution*, p. 222.

36 See Thomas Crow's masterly study 'The *Oath of the Horatii* in 1785: Painting and Pre-Revolutionary Radicalism in France', *Art History*, i (1978), pp. 424–71.

37 D. L. Dowd, *Pageant Master of the Republic: Jacques-Louis David and the French Revolution* (Lincoln, Nebraska, 1948).

Fig. 1: Jacques-Louis David, sketch of the *Serment du Jeu de Paume*, Salon of 1791. Versailles, Musée national du château.

swords; the brothers' outstretched arms (also pointing to the same spot – not Heaven) and aggressive stride reflect a unity of purpose and equality in commitment.[38] The work is an extraordinarily powerful image and one that strongly impressed David's contemporaries. They identified personally with the action. Even after the declaration of the Republic it continued to be an important model. In the *fête* of 20 Prairial An II/8 June 1794, for example, those present, when taking the oath, deliberately assumed a pose inspired by that in the painting.[39] In a patriotic chanson entitled 'Le serment' Thomas Rousseau cited with fulsome praise David's picture as an inspiration for the French and specifically for legislators, the 'fathers' of the country.[40]

Another David work, his design for a painting commemorating the *Serment du Jeu de Paume* (the Tennis Court Oath), first shown at the 1791 salon, unites art and politics (see reproduction facing p. 118).[41] The event was, of course, the decision of the deputies of the Third Estate, representing the large majority of the French but with far less political power than the first two estates (the clergy and the nobles), to declare themselves the National Assembly and to swear not to disband until they had formulated the Constitution. In so doing they defied the king's orders. It was a major challenge to royal authority, for the claim to sovereignty of the people was explicit. Soon the French viewed 20 June 1789, as well as 14 July (the storming of the Bastille), as days that marked the beginning of a new order. Soon numerous papers and political tracts gave their year of publication as 1789, the 'first year of liberty'. The Tennis Court Oath quickly became a favourite topic for pictures and engravings. To return to David's, which is not historically accurate in all its details, the strict neo-classical unity of 'Le serment des Horaces' has given way to an exuberance. But the collective oath remains a powerful theme. As one contemporary critic remarked,

On ne pouvait pas mieux varier les caractères & les expressions des figures. Elles

---

38 As the art historian Michael Fried has stressed:

> The swearing of an oath provides a powerful, and perhaps unique, means of involving a multiplicity of figures in a single action *in the same way*. That is, the nature of the action of swearing an oath ... makes possible what in the *Horatii* is experienced as a perfect matching or fusion – a further, deeper synchrony – of the moral or spiritual and the physical or bodily: as though the inner meaning, the private intensity of swearing an oath, were *entirely* manifest in its outward, public expression.

See 'Thomas Couture and the Theatricalization of Action in 19th Century French Painting', *Art Forum*, viii/10 (1970), p. 46; cited by P. Bordes, *Le serment du Jeu de Paume de Jacques-Louis David: le peintre, son milieu et son temps de 1789 à 1792* (Paris, 1983), p. 58.

39 Dowd, *Pageant Master*, p. 123.

40 *L'âme du peuple et du soldat: chants républicains*, 2ᵉ cahier [Paris, 1793], pp. 7–9.

41 For a fine documentary study, see Bordes, *Le serment*. It is reproduced in Vovelle, *La Révolution française*, i, pp. 100–01 (Vovelle also presents several other artists' treatments of this theme on pp. 102–5) and Lévêque, *L'art et la Révolution*, p. 11.

respirent l'amour de la patrie, de la vertu & de la liberté. On reconnoît par-tout des Catons prêts à mourir pour elles. On se sent transporté en voyant ce dessin.[42]

One could not better vary the characters and expressions of the figures. They exude love of country, of virtue and of liberty. One recognizes everywhere Catos ready to die for these principles. One feels transported on seeing this drawing.

He was right. Individuals, each one with his own personality, are recognizable, reacting positively to the exhortation of Bailly, president of the Assembly, standing in the centre – with one exception: the seated deputy, Martin d'Auch, the only one to oppose it. The three in the centre foreground, for example, are men of the first estate: a curate (*abbé* Grégoire), a monk (Dom Gerle) and a Protestant minister (Rabaut Saint-Etienne), and their fraternal embrace symbolizes the unifying power of the oath, transcending classes and religious sects. Women and children from the windows on the left and members of the National Guard from those on the right are enthusiastic.

The image of the Tennis Court Oath rapidly seized the imagination of the French. The swearing of fidelity was no longer to one superior (God or king), but to the nation or constitution or law. It became a group action representing strength through unity. The formulas of oaths changed. In the early years of the Revolution (before 1792) soldiers did not take an oath only to the king, as commander-in-chief – the traditional one of the *ancien régime* – but 'to the nation, and to the king, [as] leader of the nation'.[43] The monarch was not the embodiment of the country (as is implied by the phrase apocryphally attributed to Louis XIV, 'L'état, c'est moi'), but he was worthy of respect as its head.

Public oath-taking became a virtually obligatory feature of celebrations. At the Festival of the Federation on 14 July 1790, commemorating the fall of the Bastille and the unity of France, La Fayette, in the name of the troops, swore to preserve the country and its constitution (in this case, the Declaration of the Rights of Man and Citizen), and political leaders followed suit.[44] Nor was the king exempt. At the same ceremony Louis XVI affirmed publicly: 'I, King of the French, swear to the nation to use all power given me by constitutional law of the state to maintain the constitution and have the laws upheld' ('Moi, Roi des François, je jure à la Nation d'employer tout le pouvoir qui m'est délégué par la Loi constitutionelle de l'Etat, à maintenir le Constitution et à faire exécuter

---

42 M. D., *Explication et critique impartiale de toutes les peintures, sculptures, gravures, dessins, etc., exposés au Louvre au mois de septembre 1791* (Paris, 1791), p. 21. The passage quoted is cited in Bordes, *Le serment*, p. 71.

43 Starobinski, *1789*, p. 67.

44 See the anonymous painting 'La Fayette prêtant serment à la fête de la Fédération', in which his action is presented in heroic terms and seems to receive divine blessing. Reproduced in Vovelle, *La Révolution française*, ii, p. 146; Vovelle includes several other works of art depicting the *fête* (ii, pp. 108–23).

les Loix').[45] In short, he recognized the authority of a document drafted by representatives of his 'citizens', no longer merely his 'subjects'. This declaration took place not indoors before chosen witnesses (as was the case at the coronation), but on the Champ-de-Mars, where anyone could attend and hundreds of thousands did, including many from outside Paris. Louis XVI's acceptance of the new constitution on 14 September 1791 marked an additional stage in the public realization that a monarch did not receive his authority from on high, but served the collective will of free Frenchmen.[46]

Another measure of the importance attached to the oath was the major crisis provoked in 1790 by the Assembly's decision to insist that all clergy swear to uphold the civil constitution. This action implied the recognition of the primacy of state over church in certain matters. It met much resistance at home and the Pope's anathema abroad. The split in the ranks of the clergy between those who obeyed French law and those who obeyed the Church hierarchy contributed to the rise of a strong anti-Catholicism movement within both the government and society. The situation was not improved for more than a decade.[47] But even this negative result proves the significance of the oath as symbol during the Revolution.

As well as soldiers and members of the National Guard,[48] citizens also took oaths to constitution and country.[49] One, the playwright La Harpe,

---

45 *Le moniteur universel*, 16 July 1790, p. 807.
46 In his proclamation Louis declared 'j'emploîrai tous mes efforts à la maintenir & à la faire exécuter. Le terme de la révolution est arrivé: ... il est temps de fixer l'opinion de l'Europe sur la destinée de la France, & de montrer que les François sont dignes d'être libres' (*Détail de tout ce qui s'est passé à l'Asse[m]blée Nationale et les cérémonies qui ont eu lieu à l'arrivée du Roi, et la réponse du président* ([Paris], 1791), pp. 4–5). François David's engraving after Nicolas Le Jeune, 'Louis XVI à l'Assemblée Nationale accepte solemnellement la constitution', has strong traces of the earlier iconographic tradition, such as the hovering angel trumpeter hailing the event and the allegorical figure of France presenting the king with a wreath of laurels; however, this older approach serves the new order, for the constitution's authors figure prominently, and the spectators welcome the monarch's acquiescence. It is reproduced in Lévêque, *L'art et la Révolution*, p. 95, and Vovelle, *La Révolution française*, ii, p. 305, where other works of art on the same theme are presented (ii, pp. 304–5).
47 See T. Tackett, *La Révolution, l'église, la France* (Paris, 1986), and M. Vovelle, *Religion et révolution: la déchristianisation de l'an II* (Paris, 1976).
48 In the anonymous painting 'Un officier de la garde nationale prêtant serment' the officer swears on the constitution, depicted as a book, set on a pedestal which has Louis XVI's portrait in its base – a clear representation of the primacy of the law. Lesueur's gouache 'Le serment des districts' emphasizes the unifying power of the oath; young boys join the volunteers in swearing it. Both are reproduced in Vovelle, *La Révolution française*, (ii, p. 160 and iii, p. 286) and the Lesueur in Lévêque, *L'art et la Révolution*, p. 14.
49 One popular engraving, 'Le serment de la Nation' commemorating the ceremony of 14 July 1790, reproduces in its caption the civic oath:
    Nous jurons de rester à jamais fidèle à la Nation, à la Loi et au Roi, de protéger conformément aux Loix la sûreté des personnes et des propriétés, la libre circulation des Grains et subsistances dans l'Intérieur du Royaume et la perception des Contributions publiques sous quelque forme qu'elles existent, [&] de demeurer unis à tous les français par les liens indissoulubles de la fraternité.

expressed well the 1790 view that such oath-taking negated traditional hierarchic views:

Je me souviens en même temps de mon serment civique, le seul que j'aie prononcé en ma vie, & que je n'ai prononcé en vain. Je méprise les écrivains sans pudeur qui ont outragé un roi citoyen: ils ont oublié ce qu'ils devoient au chef d'un peuple libre, & que, manquer parmi nous à la dignité royale, c'est attenter à la majesté nationale. J'aime et je respecte mon roi dans la personne de Louis XVI, mais c'est précisément parce qu'il n'est pas *mon maître*, & que, d'après mon serment & le sien, je n'ai de *maître* que la loi.[50]

At the same time I recall my civic oath, the only one that I ever uttered in my life, and one that I did not swear in vain. I despise unscrupulous writers who have insulted a citizen king: they have forgotten the respect they owe to the leader of a free people, and that in our society to commit a breach towards royal dignity is to attack national majesty. I love and respect my king in the person of Louis XVI, but this is precisely because he is not my *master*, and because, according to my oath and his, I have no *master* but the law.

With such standards accepted, it was soon to become thinkable to try a king who failed to live up to his commitments. After Louis's attempt to flee in June 1791 one Jacobin pamphlet addressed him in strong language: 'Oh, perfidious perjurer, you have violated the most sacrosanct vows' ('Oh perfide et parjure, tu as violé les sermens les plus sacrés!'),[51] referring not to his coronation oath, of course, but to those of 1790 and 1791. He was therefore no longer protected by constitutional safeguards for the monarchy. In Bourdon's republican catechism, of all Louis XVI's 'crimes' his breaking of his oath to the constitution was the one singled out and, according to Bourdon, a woman from the common people was the only one at that time brave enough and astute enough to challenge him, pointing to his previous deceptions and predicting his

See D. Bindman, *The Shadow of the Guillotine: Britain and the French Revolution* (London, 1989), pp. 93–4 (there is no reproduction). An anonymous watercolour, 'Serment civique à Saint-Etienne-du-Mont', shows a village ceremony on 5 February 1790; this is reproduced in Vovelle, *La Révolution française*, ii, p. 19.

50 J. F. de la Harpe, *Discours sur la liberté du théâtre; prononcé par M. de la Harpe le 17 décembre 1790, à la Société des Amis de la Constitution [des Jacobins]* (Paris, 1790), p. 8. La Harpe soon afterwards became an early supporter of the Republic, but, revolted by the excesses of the Terror, he joined the side of the opposition to the Jacobins by the mid-1790s.

51 *Louis XVI et Antoinette traités comme ils le méritent* (Paris, [6 July 1791]), p. 3. See also *La fédération de Louis XVI aux Tuileries et les reproches que les patriotes français lui font sur son serment* [Paris, 14 July 1791], p. 6: 'Quels étaient donc tes sermens, quels sont ceux des Rois? De n'en tenir aucun. Voilà tous vos crimes!' [also an ostensible address to Louis]. Later the author includes an oath put in the mouths of all true citizens:

Voilà nos dernières résolutions, que nous jurons à la face de l'Univers entier de soutenir jusqu'à la dernière goutte de notre sang, et nous protestons de plutôt mourir que de souffrir que l'ennemi de notre constitution [Louis XVI], digne ouvrage de nos représentans, vienne nous asservir sous l'ancien despotisme que nous avons anéanti au péril de notre vie (p. 8).

future behaviour: 'In what you have just undertaken, she said to him, are you truly sincere? Will these fine new promises again be broken? Eh! Won't the same thing happen again today as happened before?' ('Ce que tu viens de faire, lui dit-elle, est-il bien sincère? toutes tes belles protestations seroient-elles de nouveaux parjures? eh! ne sera-ce pas encore aujourd'hui comme il y a quinze jours?').[52]

Revolutionary rhetoric thus sought to reflect a new image of the relationship between an individual and society. How the reality corresponded (or did not correspond) is beyond the scope of this article. Rather, in an examination of works given premières in 1793–4 at the Opéra we can see the authors' reactions to current concerns and their pursuit of the goal to provide moral theatre worthy of republicans.

REFLECTIONS OF REVOLUTIONARY RHETORIC IN LIBRETTOS, 1793–4

L'Opéra National est sans contredit le spectacle qui a le plus contribué, cette année, à échauffer l'esprit public par des scènes patriotiques faites pour électriser les âmes les plus froides. ... il a donné tant de preuves de civisme qu'il a mérité une attention particulière de la part de la Convention Nationnale, & de la Commune de Paris, qui n'ont rien négligé pour soutenir le zèle & donner de l'extension aux talens des Artistes Patriotes qui le composent. ... Il est tems en effect d'oublier ces vieilles chimères de nos pères &, de ne plus offrir, sur nos Théâtres que des modèles d'un Patriotisme ardent & d'un amour brûlant pour la Patrie, la Liberté & l'Egalité.[53]

The National Opéra is without question the theatre that has contributed the most this past year to raise the public spirit by patriotic scenes designed to electrify the coldest souls. ... It has given so many proofs of [fine] civic attitudes that it earned special attention from the National Convention and the Paris Commune, who overlooked nothing that might support the zeal and extend the talents of the Artist-Patriots who make up the company. It is time indeed to forget those old myths of our fathers and to offer on our stages only models of an ardent patriotism and a passionate love for country, liberty and equality.[53]

In public estimation, then, the Opéra fulfilled its mission in its new works, reflected the ideals accepted by society as approved by its representatives and helped to convey these in a persuasive form to citizens.

Like Bourdon and other government leaders, librettists sought to universalize the lessons presented and did so in two main ways. First, by choosing classical subjects they could at the same time continue the traditions of the theatre and capitalize on the cult of antiquity among Revolutionaries (as we have seen, comparisons with the precedents of

52 Bourdon, *Recueil*, no. 2, p. 11.
53 *Les spectacles de Paris et de toute la France, ou Calendrier historique & chronologique des théâtres* (1794), i, pp. 99 and 119–20.

republican Greece and Rome were frequent in official speeches).[54] Inviting audiences to see parallels between their own day and classical history was, of course, not new in France. Quinault and Lully had established a pattern more than a century before. But now it was not the grandeur of a king lauded in a prologue; patriotism formed the core of the action.

The *Journal de Paris national* opened its review of *Miltiade à Marathon* with:

La célèbre victoire de Marathon, & la situation d'Athènes lors de l'invasion des Persans, présentent, par leur analogie frappante avec l'état actuel de la République, un sujet bien digne de la Scène Françoise.[55]

The famous victory at Marathon and the situation in Athens at the time of the Persian invasion present, because of their striking analogy with the current state of the Republic, a truly worthy subject for the French stage.

The writer went on to point out how well the librettists had handled it. *Toute la Grèce* was highly praised since 'one could easily recognize under the Greek costumes Frenchmen excited by the most ardent love of liberty' ('l'on distinguait aisément sous des costumes grecs des Français animés du plus ardent amour de la liberté').[56] Since the goal was to address the concerns of the present, librettists felt justified in changing historical facts or introducing anachronisms in order to make clear the moral message for their own day and society. About *Fabius* another critic noted justly:

Mais il paraît que l'auteur a tout sacrifié au désir de présenter une foule d'allusions aux circonstances présentes, et de développer les sentimens du patriotisme le plus pur et le plus ardent. Il a parfaitement réussi dans ces deux points; les allusions y sont d'autant plus sensibles, que l'auteur ne s'est pas cru obligé de se conformer à l'histoire, dont il s'écarte à tout moment.[57]

But it seems that the librettist has sacrificed everything in order to include a multitude of allusions to present circumstances and to expound on feelings of the purest and most fervent patriotism. He has succeeded perfectly in both; the allusions are so much the more evident since the librettist did not consider himself bound to follow history, from which he deviates frequently.

54 See H. T. Parker, *The Cult of Antiquity and the French Revolutionaries* (Chicago, 1937).
55 *Journal de Paris national*, 19 brumaire an II/9 November 1793, p. 1260. The reviewer of *Affiches, annonces et avis divers*, 17 brumaire an II/7 November 1793, pp. 4721–2, also praised it for being 'propre, plus que tout autre, à électriser les âmes les plus froides dans les circonstances présentes' and 'parfaitement à l'ordre du jour'. He continued:
   Quoi de plus intéressant pour des Républicains, que de voir un Peuple Républicain travaillant, comme eux, pour affermir son indépendance, éprouvant comme eux des trahisons intestines, l'attaque précipitée de tous les Despotes qui les environnent, & triomphant comme eux d'un million de bras armés pour arracher l'arbisseau naissant de sa liberté!
56 *Le moniteur universel*, 1 pluviôse an II/20 January 1794, p. 488.
57 *Le moniteur universel*, 16 August 1793, p. 969.

He continued that Barouillet knew that at the time depicted Carthage was as much a republic as Rome, but, by making the enemy a monarchy in league with others, effective tirades could be included.

Second, by choosing examples of contemporary French heroism, librettists could exalt the principles of the Republic. This was a greater challenge, for there were no clear precedents. The desire to present models and to avoid hero-worship of living people led to the suppression of many French names that were a matter of public record. In *Le siège de Thionville* the three brave hussars, the mayor and the artillery commander remain unidentified; of the major characters only Wimpfen, father and son, are named, and the son dies at the end of the opera. In *Toulon soumis*, none of the French based on real people receives more than a title ('le représentant du peuple', for example); two fictional lovers do, but the audience would have no difficulty in seeing them as types, idealizations of patriotism in the common people. By this procedure librettists sought to put on stage fine examples of the right behaviour for mayors, soldiers and others. The treatment of dramatic action was also at times generic (in other words, the siege of Thionville could represent any siege), specific incidents were often the librettists' inventions and factual details were ignored. Tolerant of manipulation of classical history, critics were much less so here. For them, authors had not yet found the proper balance between a universal model and a glorification of a specific French achievement.[58]

The subjects of all these operas emphasize the group more than the individual, whether the French people's joy (as in *Le triomphe de la République* and *La réunion du dix août*) or grief (as in *La patrie reconnaissante*) or valour, directly (in *Le siège de Thionville* and *Toulon soumis*) and indirectly (in *Fabius*, *Miltiade à Marathon*, *Toute la Grèce* and *Horatius Coclès*). Since so many dealt with war (at a time when France had most of Europe united against her), the question of the portrayal of leadership in conformity with republican principles was crucial. The solutions varied. One was to split traits of leadership and individual heroism among several (*Toulon soumis* and *Horatius Coclès*), another to have the most valiant die (*Le siège de Thionville*). Most librettos had lines extolling the bravery of the group and crediting them all with the successes. Several have the leader declare his refusal of any position of absolute authority. Fabius did so, and further emphasized that the victory belonged to the Romans and their allies (Act 3). When the Greeks credited him with the victory, Miltiade protested that it belonged to all the warriors (Act 2 scene v), but in the opening scene he had accepted the command all too readily, according to several. In an

58 See, for example, the *Abréviateur universel*, 20 ventôse an II/10 March 1794, p. 1735, and the *Affiches, annonces et avis divers*, 16 ventôse an II/6 March 1794, pp. 6474–5, on *Toulon soumis*.

otherwise strongly positive review, one writer felt obliged to criticize the emphasis on the hero:

Il semble que ce Général soit le seul soutien de la Grèce & de la Liberté. Cette confiance aveugle n'est pas très-républicaine: nous avons été, jusqu'à présent, si cruellement trompés par nos Généraux, que l'expérience nous a appris à ne pas nous fier entièrement à eux du salut de notre Patrie! … Nous le répétons, ces éloges sont indignes d'un Peuple libre: ce sont des Soldats citoyens qui sauvent une République; c'est une Armée Républicaine qui triomphe en masse, & qui doit recevoir en masse les bénédictions de la Patrie.[59]

It seems that this general was the only mainstay of Greece and of liberty. This blind confidence is not very republican: up till now we have been so cruelly betrayed by our generals that experience has taught us not to entrust entirely to them the safety of our country! … We repeat, these praises [of Miltiade] are unworthy of a free people; it is citizen soldiers who save a Republic; it is a Republican Army who triumphs *en masse*, and who should receive *en masse* the country's thanks.

This critique shows what a fine line was drawn in assessing whether works measured up to standards; contemporary application was assumed even for this classical work.

Self-sacrifice, even suicide, is a theme developed in several of the librettos. Of course, suicides in opera were not new; Piccinni's *Didon* (one of a long line of works on the subject) was familiar to Parisian audiences. But *ancien régime* treatment of the topic was restricted to classical stories where the character's fate is the outcome of a love-versus-honour dilemma. Now authors sought to make suicide serve patriotic ends. In *Miltiade à Marathon* the report of Nitoclès's suicide, under circumstances very like Beaurepaire's, inspires the soldiers to fight for liberty (Act I scene ii). The most obvious example is *La patrie reconnaissante, ou L'apothéose de Beaurepaire*. Here, however, Leboeuf hesitated to present the actual event; in his preface he claimed that such a scene would have resulted 'only in declamatory tirades' to be set in 'a cold, monotonous récitative'; but more likely, as a literary conservative, he still felt bound by the theatrical convention not to show the death of a contemporary hero on stage.[60] Like Delaunay, he makes several parallels with classical precedents. In the memorial service the mayor stresses:

> Je vous ai rassemblés pour vous parler d'un homme,
> Qui, semblable au Caton de la superbe Rome,
> Préféra, comme lui, la mort au déshonneur,
> De ramper sous les lois d'un insolent vainqueur. (scene ii)

I have brought you together to speak to you about a man, who, like Cato in proud Rome, preferred death to the dishonour of grovelling under the laws of an insolent victor.

59 *Affiches, annonces et avis divers*, 17 brumaire an II/7 November 1793, p. 4722.
60 See H. Lancaster, *French Tragedy in the Reign of Louis XVI and the Early Years of the French Revolution, 1774–1792* (Baltimore, 1953).

The opera closes with a call to imitate Brutus, stamp out crime and celebrate virtue.

More interesting is the treatment of the self-sacrifice theme in *Le siège de Thionville*. Again the historical figure of the French commander is cited as a model by both Wimpfen, father and son. Indeed, the younger yearns for a similar test of his patriotism:

> Ce Brutus des Français, qui pour la Liberté
> A bravé du trépas la terreur impuissante,
> Va jouir des honneurs de l'immortalité.
> Que ne puis-je à ce prix sacrifier ma vie!
> Quel plaisir pour mon coeur! Eh! Quel destin plus beau
> Que celui d'emporter dans la nuit du tombeau,
> Les regrets de mon Père et ceux de ma Patrie? (Act 1 scene iv)

This Brutus among the French, who for liberty braved the impotent terror of death, will possess immortal honours. May I not at this cost sacrifice my life! What a pleasure for my heart! Oh! What finer fate than taking to the grave my father's regrets and those of my country?

At the climax of the opera, the final assault, an Austrian officer threatens to kill the captured youth if the French advance. As the stage directions indicate, 'the alarmed French stop; but the young Wimpfen, in order to leave them free to press home their victory, grasps one of the bayonets aimed at him and stabs himself'. His wish was fulfilled. This episode, the librettist's invention,[61] received unanimous praise from critics, and the secret police agent reported with satisfaction the audience's warm response.[62]

The presence of representatives from the lower classes in the operas was still rare, and confined to works with contemporary French settings. *Le triomphe de la République* follows traditional depictions of idealized happy villagers in the characters of Laurette and Thomas. The heroism of the convict in *Toulon soumis* did mark a break with the past, but in this instance the librettist was inspired by published accounts of the convicts, although the specific deed is his own invention.[63] *La réunion du dix août*, which sought to put on stage the *fête* of 10 August 1793,[64] had perforce to include urban lower classes in a favourable light. This, too, was a novelty. One critic remarked:

Le pas des Forts de la Halle remplit l'âme des Spectateurs de la joie la plus douce &

---

61 For the official account of the siege, see *Le moniteur universel*, especially 22 and 29 September and 11 October 1792 (pp. 1126, 1159 and 1205–8).

62 A. Schmidt, ed., *Tableaux de la Révolution française, publiés sur les papiers inédits du département de la police secrète de Paris* (Leipzig, 1867–70), ii, pp. 66–7 (quoting Perrière).

63 See Barère's praise of them and subsequent decree in the National Convention on 14 Nivôse An II/3 January 1794, published in *Le moniteur universel* the following day.

64 Described in the *Journal de Paris national*, 9 August 1793, p. 890, and 10 August 1793, pp. 892–4.

la plus pure. Qu'on nous pardonne de rappeller que *jadis*, c'est à-dire, il y a quatre ou cinq ans, il n'étoit possible d'introduire ces personnages sur la scène qu'en les avilissant. Dans cette Pièce, au contraire, leurs costumes & leurs attitudes les plus habituelles y sont parfaitement conservés, mais sans charge.[65]

The dance of the porters of Les Halles filled the spectators' souls with the greatest joy. May our readers pardon us for reminding them that formerly, that is to say, four or five years ago, it was not possible to introduce such characters on stage without debasing them. In this work, on the contrary, their usual customs and attitudes are perfectly rendered, but without exaggeration.

The Opéra's attempt at 'égalité' was noticed and lauded, although another reviewer pointed out accurately that fishmongers and vegetable merchants did not express themselves as they did here.[66] For the most part librettists contented themselves with giving a more prominent role to the united patriotic people in general, as we shall see below.

Compared with the often heroine-dominated works of the late *ancien régime*, the operas of 1793–4 seem almost devoid of strong women. Adèle in *Toulon soumis* acts virtuously in repulsing an enemy's advances, but fortunately she is saved before he can harm her (scene vi). Beaurepaire's widow also does what is expected of her: she takes care of her child and calls for vengeance for her husband's death (*La patrie reconnaissante*, scene iv). Even the heroine of the October days (during which, in reality, women took the initiative and acted with violence) now regrets the absence of 'our brave warriors who are fighting for the country' and will give them the wreaths of laurels they received – that is to say, the fighting and feats of heroism will be left to the men in future (*La réunion du dix août*, Act 2 scene ii).

Only the sacrifices of women (financial and other) are extended representations of specifically female patriotism at the Opéra during the Reign of Terror. Both *Fabius* and *Toute la Grèce* have donation ceremonies, but, unlike the Camilla legend, they are not merely helping their city to fulfil a vow after the fact; they, like the modern French, are contributing to meet current national requirements, more specifically the war effort. Eucharis, the women's leader in *Toute la Grèce*, expresses their hopes:

> Qu'ils partent, nos guerriers!
> Qu'au prix de ces bijoux leur conquête s'assure! (scene iii)

Let them depart, our [valiant] soldiers! May the proceeds from [the sale of] these jewels assure their victory!

After she leads the Roman women in their gesture, Valérie in *Fabius* avers:

---

65 *Journal de Paris national*, 21 germinal an II/10 April 1794, p. 1880.
66 *Journal des théâtres et des fêtes nationales*, 5 vendémiaire an III/26 September 1794, pp. 321–2.

> Si nos malheurs sont grands,
> Les sublimes sentimens
> Que le patriotisme inspire
> Sont encor plus puissans. (Act 2 scene i)

If our misfortunes are great, the fine sentiments that patriotism inspires are even more powerful.

In both cases the women's actions receive official praise for the example they set. Their fate was to await anxiously the return of their loved ones, but when Valérie sighs too loudly her friend reminds her of their duty to endure this hardship and trust that they will be victorious. Both agree on women's place:

> Notre sexe est exclus des emplois difficiles,
> Et la foiblesse de nos bras
> Nous défend de tenter les hasards des combats;
> Mais nous pouvons inspirer aux soldats
> Le dévouement et les vertus utiles,
> Qui font la force des Etats. (Act 2 scene i)

Our sex is excluded from hard work, and our physical weakness prevents us from daring the risks of combat; but we can inspire in soldiers devotion and useful virtues which give strength to the state.

Such self-effacement and willingness to fulfil a supporting role (within the home is implied) would have met with official approval in the Terror.

The importance of the people, their unity and their patriotism is most clearly seen in the oath. So obvious a public symbol by the early Revolution, it was quickly taken up by librettists, and all the serious operas of 1793–4 had at least one, and often more. Unlike the typical expressions of a desire for vengeance found in *ancien régime* works (more often in *airs* than in choruses), which cannot be easily categorized because of their variety, in the oath choruses of the 1790s a limited number of phrases and constructions provide clear indications of genre. First, the hoped-for result (nearly always involving violence) takes the form 'Que' plus subjunctive. In *La patrie reconnaissante*, the citoyenne Beaurepaire exclaims:

> Que le Peuple, armé de sa foudre,
> Anéantisse et mette en poudre
> Les assassins de mon époux. (scene iv)

May the people, strongly armed, wipe out and reduce to dust my husband's assassins.

The patriotic French swear that they will.

Second, concrete reference to the practice of oath-taking (following current French forms) is frequent. In *Le siège de Thionville* the mayor urges patriotic citizens:

> Sur cet autel sacré faisons tous le serment
> De mourir dans nos murs ou d'y vivre sans tache.

On this sacred altar [of the country], let us all take an oath to die here or to live without guilt.

And they reply:

> Sur cet autel sacré nous faisons le serment
> De ne jamais nous rendre,
> Et nous jurons de nous défendre
> Jusqu'à notre dernier moment.
> Si l'un de nous était capable
> De songer à capituler;
> Son trépas est inévitable:
> Nous vous jurons de l'immoler. (Act 1 scene vii)

On this sacred altar we take the oath never to surrender, and we swear to defend ourselves with our dying breath. If one of us is capable of even considering surrender, his fate is sealed: we swear to you to sacrifice him.

Note that the citizens have not merely mechanically repeated the mayor's instructions; they have taken the initiative to go further, and their patriotism moves them to undertake to rid the country of traitors within – which, as we have seen (as in the cases of Louis XVI and La Fayette), was a current concern. The staging with a prominent altar to the country, around which the French gather, is, of course, borrowed from republican ceremonies.

Third, 'nous le jurons' (or a similar phrase), often repeated for emphasis, occurs in more than one work. The resonance of the first person plural imperative had a special impact on the audience. In a litany-like arrangement, for example, it is prominent in the first-act finale of *Fabius*:

PAUL-EMILIE: Jurez de rétablir l'autorité de loix.
CHORUS: Nous le jurons.
PAUL-EMILIE: Jurez, au prix de votre vie,
      De sauver la Patrie.
CHORUS: Nous le jurons.
PAUL-EMILIE: Jurez que les propriétés,
      Que les hommes par vous seront tous respectés,
      Et de la liberté pourront goûter les charmes.
CHORUS: Nous le jurons.

Swear to re-establish the authority of law.
We so swear.
Swear at the price of your lives to save our country.
We so swear.
Swear to respect other men's property so that they may benefit from the charms of liberty.
We so swear.

Even though this opera is set in classical Rome, Paul-Emilie and his fellow citizens anticipate the Declaration of Rights: the authority of law resulted from the fact that it 'is the expression of the general will; all citizens have the right to contribute personally or by their representatives in its formation' (Article 6), and property was 'an inviolable and sacred right' (Article 17).[67]

These three examples are characteristic of part of the genre. We should note that the leaders were not always military heroes (although some such examples can be found); rather, there are a grieving widow, an elected civic official and an elder statesman, wise, respected, but too old and weak to serve at the front. Nor was the format always that of leader echoed by the others present. The equality of men and the unity of the republican cause were conveyed sometimes in a spontaneous group oath (at least that was the literary conceit). A striking example is 'Si dans le sein de Rome il se trouvait un traître', another oath that threatens painful death to any traitors within (*Horatius Coclès*, scene vi).

In situation, in language, in topic (defence of country and liberty against enemies from without and within), these operatic oaths, whether in works with contemporary settings (a new departure for the Opéra) or in those with traditional classical ones, have the strong imprint of the Revolutionary model.

FURTHER OPERATIC CONSEQUENCES OF REVOLUTIONARY RHETORIC

Literary reflections of current concerns in the librettos are numerous and pervasive. What were the musical consequences? In considering the operas piece by piece from a historical and analytical point of view, we could note that much of the music is derivative, closely following models from the reign of Louis XVI. There are many choruses indebted to the precedents of Gluck and Salieri and *airs* in a Piccinnian or Sacchinian mould. In addition, works by these four composers still dominated the repertory. But merely to go through the scores looking for strikingly new features misses the main point.

Although the composers of the 1793–4 repertory invented few forms and procedures, their operas do not sound overall like those of the previous generation. In works with contemporary settings composers responded to the themes of heroism and duty to country with symbols easily recognized by their audiences. The *chanson* and *hymne* are the most obvious; favourites such as the *Marseillaise* and *Ah! ça ira* could be quoted, and new ones were written in similar forms and styles. Though

---

67 B. Benoît, *Les grandes dates de la Révolution française* (Paris, 1988), pp. 93–4, reprints the Declaration.

Ex. 1   Excerpt from Candeille's *La patrie reconnaissante*, i: the opening of the *Marche lugubre* for the *Cérémonie funèbre*, F-Po A.346, pp. 127–8

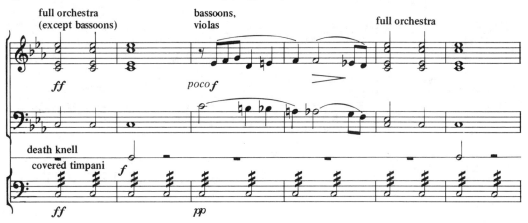

not many in number, they were frequent enough to contribute to a new tone – popular, often heroic and specifically French – and, according to critics and police informants, spectators reacted positively, as I have shown elsewhere. Yet, the works with more traditional classical settings, taken as a whole, also seem unlike their predecessors in spite of clear examples of imitation in individual pieces.

For operas in both groups it is a question of balance and emphasis quite different from the *ancien régime* conception. The martial spirit is often reflected in more numerous marches and sections in march-like style, even when not suggested by the text or dramatic action (as in the opening scenes of *Toute la Grèce*, where the music accompanying patriots hard at work establishes the general atmosphere). Gluck and his contemporaries used marches too, but in a much more restricted way: to accompany soldiers leaving for battle, to allow solemn entrances of priests and priestesses, and so on. One further powerful symbol was imported into some works of 1793–4 from the exterior: namely the funeral march. Gossec's *Marche lugubre* of 1790 and similar works inspired Candeille's (Ex. 1). The addition to the standard Opéra orchestra of the serpent, the death knell and, on stage, the military field drum signals the genre. The covered timpani and slow full chords, *ff*, alternating with softer passages where the winds are often prominent are also familiar features. (Gluck's 'O Diane, sois-nous propice!' from *Alceste* (Act 4 scene ii) is typical of earlier procedures: homophonic in style, the chorus accompanied simply and the orchestra dominated by strings and supported by woodwinds.)

The military themes prompted composers to write broadly spanned, fanfare-like melodies, and, of course, the brass with vigorous dotted rhythms figure in the accompaniment. In Méhul's hands Horace's

Ex. 2 Excerpt from Méhul's *Horatius Coclès*, scene i: passage for Horace in the air 'Montrer la tendresse d'un père'

(By this dagger, which before our eyes Lucretia's blood and a great man's arm have hallowed, ...)

determination to oppose tyranny comes across effectively (Ex. 2). Here the traditional depiction of heroism in melody, rhythm and orchestration is intensified by a harmonic surprise – significantly, on the word 'sang'. In several other operas (such as *Toulon soumis* and *Le siège de Thionville*) less skilful musicians have overused the clichés without any compensating variation for interest. But, while often aesthetically unsuccessful, these works are set apart from operas of the 1770s and 1780s by the thorough-going presence of elements which were previously found only occasionally and in more limited contexts.

Another part of the response to subject (and a reflection of current views) is the dearth of major scenes for women. There are no female soloists at all in *Horatius Coclès* and *Le siège de Thionville*; the only one

Ex. 3   Excerpt from Méreaux's *Fabius*, Act 2 scene i: air and chorus, 'Hélas! Si nos malheurs sont grands', *F-Po* A.350, ii, pp. 12–16 [the voices are doubled by woodwinds and strings]

(Alas! If our misfortunes are great, the fine sentiments that patriotism inspires are even more powerful.)

in *Miltiade à Marathon* portrays a young man;[68] and the few present in the other works play secondary roles that seldom receive extended musical emphasis. One looks in vain for figures comparable to Gluck's Alceste and Iphigenia or Piccinni's Dido. Even the donation of gifts usually results in only a brief female chorus in the Gluckian tradition. Example 3 shows the opening of Méreaux's in *Fabius*. After a striking leap of an augmented fourth, harmonized by an unprepared augmented sixth chord (a new gesture), to emphasize 'hélas!', the vocal lines move quite smoothly, mostly in thirds, and the tonal definition of C is clear (tending to C minor when their misfortunes are recalled, and ending in C major as confidence in the ultimate victory of right is expressed).

---

68 At least one critic found this (a traditional operatic practice) absurd: 'mais nous croyons que ce rôle seroit plus intéressant, joué par un jeune homme; car une voix de femme, quelque belle

Further differences in degree can be found in the use of spectacle. Impressive staging was part of the heritage of the Opéra. In *Toute la Grèce* Beffroy de Rigny merely extended accepted procedures in scene iv; the stage directions in the libretto read:

Elles entrent sur la scène de tous les côtés, mais avec ordre et lentement, de sort qu'il n'en arrive que deux à-la-fois. On lit sur l'enseigne de la première Phalange: Athènes, vive la République! *sur la deuxième,* Lacédémone, La Liberté ou la mort; *sur la troisième,* Corinthe, ordre et discipline; *sur la quatrième,* Thèbes, obéissance aux loix; *sur la cinquième,* Argos, respect à l'Eternel; *sur la sixième,* Dodone, sûreté, propriété; *sur la septième,* Lemnos, honneur aux beaux arts; *sur la huitième,* Delphes, haine aux tyrans; *sur la neuvième,* Mégare, moeurs et fraternité; *sur la dixième,* Marathon, bon exemple à nos enfants; *sur la onzième,* Délos, l'union fait la force; et enfin, *sur la douzième,* Etolie, courage, Républicains!

[Twelve phalanxes] come on stage from all sides, but slowly and with decorum, so that only two arrive at a time. On the banner of the first phalanx, Athens, is the motto: *Long live the Republic!*; on the second, Lacedonia, *Liberty or death*; on the third, Corinth, *Order and discipline*; on the fourth, Thebes, *Obedience to the laws*; on the fifth, Argos, *Respect for the Eternal Being*; on the sixth, Dodona, *Security, property*; on the seventh, Limnos, *Respect for the fine arts*; on the eighth, Delphi, *Hatred of tyrants*; on the ninth, Megara, *Morals and brotherhood*; on the tenth, Marathon, *A good example for our children*; on the eleventh, Delos, *Strength in unity*; and finally, on the twelfth, Aitolia, *Courage, Republicans!*

Many of the slogans were entirely in accord with current French views (although a few, like Dodona's, indicate the librettist's reluctance to accept the Jacobin extreme). The costumes and scenic effect were much admired and cited as impressive in every review.[69]

Other authors sought to deviate from accepted Opéra norms. In some works, such as *Toulon soumis* and *Le siège de Thionville*, spectacle is placed at the dramatic centre – hitherto a procedure more common in contemporary works for the Opéra-Comique or the boulevard theatres. Scenes v and vi of *Toulon soumis* take place at night, and to the sound of canons we see patrols of English soldiers, the city in the background in flames, and finally a house, downstage, igniting. A woman holding a child is trapped. The craven English ignore her cries for help, but a convict, who has escaped in the confusion, risks his life and freedom to save them. Meanwhile the English are being driven back; townspeople flee; the courageous convict now pursues an enemy officer. All of this action is in pantomime; much of the music is instrumental, but offstage

---

qu'elle soit, est un peu ridicule dans un Héros couvert du casque & de l'armure d'*Achille* (*Affiches, annonces et avis divers,* 17 brumaire an II/7 November 1793, p. 4723).

69 See, for example, the *Journal de Paris national,* 18 nivôse an II/7 January 1794, p. 1500; *Affiches, annonces et avis divers,* 23 nivôse an II/12 January 1794, p. 5670; and the *Journal des spectacles,* 18 nivôse an II/7 January 1794, pp. 1501–5, which mentioned, however, that a bigger stage would have permitted a better effect.

choruses, of inhabitants, and later of the English, bemoan their fate in scene v, and in scene vi the evil enemy general tries to persuade the innocent and patriotic Adèle to leave with him. The arrival of the French, including Adèle's lover, to the strains of *Ah! ça ira*, foils his plans. What is new at the Opéra is the division of action, the deliberate confusion of events, the multiplicity of characters (some, like the woman and child, appear and disappear quickly as part of a stage effect; others, like the convict, have a dramatically crucial role), the importance of relating the story through gesture and the playing down of a traditional sense of coherence where events follow a logical progression.[70]

As marches, spectacle, and (as we shall see below) choruses took more extensive roles, in many operas the number and length of solo airs correspondingly decreased. The older, more conservative Méreaux kept closest to the Gluck-Piccinni heritage in *Fabius*, but the younger, more innovative Méhul did not hesitate to find a musical equivalent for 'fraternité'. In *Horatius Coclès* the little music for soloists, apart from recitative to advance the plot, is for the most part in the form of duos and trios, not solos. Bouquier and Moline took another tack: there are still quite a few solos (as well as choruses) in *La réunion du dix août*, but, except for the largely spoken roles of the President of the National Convention and the *fête* organizer, individual characters appear in only one of the five acts (and for massing in the finale). Thus, they assume the role of chorus leader rather than star.[71]

In addition to its traditional function to convey narrative, recitative was often the choice for emotionally charged situations that a decade earlier would have called for an impressive *air* and formed an important part of the structuring of climax usually ending in a chorus of collective action. In scene iv of *La patrie reconnaissante* the general's widow sings a short lyrical plea, 'A mes désirs daignez vous rendre', but the main musical weight is on her long lament, flexibly treated in a variety of recitative styles, and the scene culminates in her exhortation to her fellow citizens, 'Français, vengez-moi, vengez-vous' and their promise, 'Ils expireront sous nous coups'. As the stage directions indicate, Beaurepaire's young son 'draws his sword and runs to join the citizens

---

70 Not all critics liked this innovation at what had been the most dignified theatre in France. The *Abréviateur universel* (20 ventôse an II/10 March 1794, p. 1735) and the *Affiches, annonces et avis divers* (16 ventôse an II/6 March 1794, p. 6475) praised it, but the more conservative reviewer for the *Journal de Paris national* (20 ventôse an II/10 March 1794, p. 1756) found it too confusing and illogical. He was even more scathing about *spectacle* in *Le siège de Thionville*: 'Ce genre de Pièce destiné plus particulièrement pour la Pantomime réussit rarement, lorsque des scènes un peu étendues en font partie: elles jettent du froid dans l'âme des Spectateurs, & c'est sans doute à ce défaut qu'il faut attribuer le peu de succès du siège en lui-même' (16 June 1793, p. 670).
71 They are so described in the *Journal des théâtres et des fêtes nationales*, 5 vendémiaire an III/ 26 September 1794, p. 321.

who are swearing to avenge his father's death' (scene iv). The conclusion of this scene was the most applauded in the opera, which was otherwise found weak and unworthy of its subject.[72] In *Le siège de Thionville*, after Wimpfen *fils*'s suicide, the mayor eulogized him: 'Model for the French, he died for his country. She had his vows, he fulfilled his duty' ('Modèle des Français, il meurt pour sa Patrie./Elle avait ses sermens, son devoir est rempli'). Even his father regrets only his not being able to sacrifice himself for his son; expressions of grief would be unbecoming in a republican commander (Act 2 scene ix). This entire passage is in recitative, which again lends musical emphasis by contrast to what follows: the chorus, led by Wimpfen *père* swears vengeance.

A further indication of the change in attitude to the relative import-ance of soloists and ensembles lies in the fact that more often airs were cut substantially or entirely. In *Le siège de Thionville* the enemy Waldek lost his 'La résistance est vaine' (Act 2 scene vii). While the desire to deprive a villain of musical emphasis may have contributed in this case, the young hero, Wimpfen *fils*, also saw his 'Du plus affreux trépas' (Act 2 scene iv) severely reduced. While Gluck and other late *ancien régime* composers integrated the chorus into the drama very effectively (the opening of *Iphigénie en Tauride* is particularly striking), they never allowed it to become the foreground phenomenon for a whole opera that it frequently is here. For them the genre remained a soloist-dominated one.

Authors in the 1790s, too, were conscious of the shift in emphasis to the sovereignty of the people and the musical consequences for the chorus. Careful to cite classical precedents, one librettist wrote:

Dans cet Acte, comme dans les Tragédies des Anciens, le Choeur tient le premier rang, parce que les principaux personnages n'étant que les représentans, les mandataires du Peuple, c'est à celui-ci à dominer, tout se rapportant à lui. Aussi ne pourroit-on supprimer aucun des Choeurs, sans nuire à l'action, tandis que l'on a pu retrancher, de l'Iphigénie en Aulide le Choeur, Chantons, célébrons notre Reine, sans que cela ait fait le moindre tort à l'ensemble de ce bel ouvrage.[73]

In this work, as in the tragedies of the ancients, the chorus is in the forefront, because the principal characters being only the representatives or the proxies of the People, it is the people who must dominate, for everything relates to them. Thus, [in this opera,] one could not cut a single chorus without harming the dramatic action, whereas one was able to delete the chorus 'Chantez, célébrez votre reine' from *Iphigénie en Aulide* without damaging in the least that fine work.

One could in fact argue for the deletion of a chorus or two from *Fabius*.

---

72 *Journal de Paris national*, 5 February 1793, p. 144: 'tout ce morceau a porté dans l'âme des Spectateurs le plus grand enthousiasme & a reçu des applaudissemens universels'.

73 J. M. Barouillet, *dit* Martin, in the original 1792 publication of *Fabius* (it was extensively revised before setting), Preface, p. iii.

Furthermore, it should be noted that Barouillet's Gluck example is from a *divertissement*. Even more important, during the first season Legros (singing Achilles) encouraged the audience to consider this chorus as a compliment for Marie Antoinette, and they were not slow to take up his suggestion. It became a tradition at the Opéra to sing it whenever the queen attended. Even when she was not present its performance often prompted pro-royalist demonstrations. In 1790 Lainez, responding to an invitation from the boxes, announced that all the French should love their queen and insisted on repeating it, in spite of opposition from the all-male *parterre* (the cheapest seats). The result was a near riot, and at a later performance the singer was forced to apologize to the *parterre* – a sign of the impending crisis which identified the queen with the enemy Austria.[74]

But what I want to stress here is the intention of the *Fabius* librettist to highlight the people; he and his colleagues saw the increase in choral writing as the necessary result of this philosophical and political decision – very much a reflection of its time and place.

Finding a distinctive musical translation for the collective oath was the greatest musical innovation in these operas, although there were antecedents. Before 1789 collective oaths were rare: Salieri's *Les Horaces* (1786) did not have a scene paralleling David's painting; rather, the librettist N. F. Guillard followed closely his main source, Corneille's play. He did, however, have the younger Horace, the only son present, swear 'Either Rome will be free, or I shall no longer exist' ('Ou Rome sera libre, ou je ne serai plus'), in recitative without particular emphasis (Act 2 scene ii). In *Les Danaïdes* (1784) the daughters agree to fulfil their father's wishes to kill their husbands on their wedding day in a choral dance around Eumenides's altar ('Oui, qu'aux flambeaux des Euménides', Act 2 scene i), almost in the fashion of a witches' sabbath, rather than in a formal oath. There are three clear instances where the text is a collective oath: one in Philidor's *Ernelinde* (1767),[75] another in Piccinni's *Didon* (the conclusion to the finale, 1783) and the third in Gossec's incidental music for Racine's *Athalie* (1785). All were known to the Parisians of the 1790s: *Didon* was still in repertory, and both the Philidor and Gossec choruses were used in the Revolutionary *fêtes*.[76]

In Philidor's 'Jurez sur vos glaives sanglants' (Ex. 4) the leader, Sandomir, exhorts his followers to take up arms in Ernelinde's defence and swear by Mars; they do so, echoing his words. Musically the composer adopted a dignified hymn-like style in Eb major (a conventional key choice for quasi-religious pieces). The alternation of soloist

74 Bartlet, 'From *Académie Royale to Opéra National*'.
75 I am grateful to Professor Julian Rushton for drawing this example to my attention.
76 See C. Pierre, *Les hymnes et chansons de la Révolution* (Paris, 1904), nos. 71 (Philidor) and 107 (Gossec).

Ex. 4   Excerpt from 'Jurez sur vos glaives sanglants', from Philidor's *Ernelinde*, Act 1 scene iii [the orchestra largely doubles the voices]

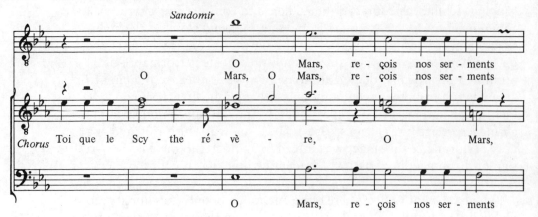

(Thou whom Scythia reveres, O Mars, accept our vows.)

and homophonic chorus in the opening section gradually dissolves into a simple contrapuntal texture (another eighteenth-century symbol for the hymn) towards the end, as all repeat their invocation to the god.[77]

The *Didon* example is hardly surprising; the legend as transmitted by Virgil in the *Aeneid* requires that the Carthaginians swear eternal hatred of the descendants of Aeneas and his followers. Example 5 shows its opening. It is not an independent chorus, but rather only the concluding section (given almost completely here). The first phrase is forceful, insistent; the contrast between its mostly unison writing and the two- or three-note chords of 'haine, fureur, guerre éternelle' is effective, but the orchestral accompaniment is full both times. In the phrase setting the key words, 'nous le jurons', the declamatory impact takes second place to harmonic emphasis on dominant, tonic and subdominant; the scales in parallel thirds between the *haute-contre* and tenor are trite. These features make the passage virtually indistinguishable from Piccinni's usual writing for male chorus.

Gossec, too, chose Eb major and, after beginning forcefully with a line for the men (mostly in unison), made use of a contrapuntal texture in the chorus, supported by the orchestra with some flourishes for emphasis (Ex. 6). Only at the first major cadence do all voices coincide. The words here contain the moral, what the people swear to do: 'put Joas back on the throne'. Significantly, however, it is not the first time that this text has been sung; rather, the homophonic repetition is a conventional way of ending the passage.

---

77 Philidor's *Thémistocle*, Act 1 scene v, offers another, much shorter example: 'Vengeons l'affront de Salamine' is a two-line, seven-bar oath chorus set in homophonic chords with a strongly cadential function. It is little more than a choral exclamation.

Ex. 5 Opening of the concluding section of the finale of Piccinni's *Didon*: chorus, 'A cette race criminelle' [there follow six more bars of chorus with a largely cadential function and six bars of orchestral conclusion]

(To this criminal race, hatred, rage, eternal war, we swear it by this pyre!)

Ex. 6 Gossec, incidental music for *Athalie*: the opening of 'Oui, nous jurons ici pour nous', Act 4 scene iii, *F-Po* Rés. F.1125, pp. 199–202

(*Women*: Swear for your own sake, for all your brothers,
Men: Yes, we swear here for ourselves, for all our brothers,
Both: to return Joas to the throne of his forebears.)

In conclusion, these three examples, while clearly oaths in text and dramatic function, do not share a common musical type. Rather, each composer sought to write a forceful piece in a style which cannot be distinguished from much of his other choral writing.

A more important musical model for Revolutionary composers was Gluck, and in this case specifically 'Poursuivons jusqu'au trépas' (*Armide*, Act 1 scene iv). After the four soloists have a phrase in unison,

Ex. 6 (cont).

the chorus enters with the passage in Ex. 7. The text does not entirely
conform to the oath-chorus type, in spite of the second line: rather, as
the first indicates, it belongs to another, the action chorus, as Armide's
followers decide to pursue, even to the end, the enemy Renaud. Several
musical symbols point to the importance of this example for composers
of the 1790s: the strong opening phrase in octaves for the chorus (not
just a cadential conclusion, common in Gluck, as Julian Rushton has
noted, and often imitated by his successors), supported by an only
slightly decorated version of the line, with *marcato* markings (▾) in the
orchestra; a contrast in texture to underline the switch from the action of
the first line to the wish of the second; syllabic setting of the words; and a
dissonance (here a diminished triad) to underline the important word,

Ex. 7   Gluck, *Armide*, Act 1 scene iv: the opening of the ensemble 'Poursuivons jusqu'au trépas'

(Let us pursue to the death the enemy who insults you! May he not escape our vengeance.)

'vengeance'. The combination of musical aspects noted here is unique in a late *ancien régime* work still in repertory. It was taken over by the composers of the 1790s.

   While the idea may have originated in the Gluck chorus, his successors extended the symbols and sometimes introduced others, similar in spirit, for additional intensity. The choruses are often far longer than the older composer's, but what is more important is that Revolutionary musicians applied the combination only in oath choruses or others closely related to them. Thus, changes in texture matched to the text, together with a declamatory syllabic style *and* strategic placement of dissonance defined the oath musically, just as 'Nous le jurons', 'Nous faisons le serment' or 'Que' plus the subjunctive signalled it by words.

Examples 8 to 15 are by no means all from the 1793–4 repertory; the first two, both in 1793 operas, have the musical characteristics without the clear textual clues, but the dramatic context implies an oath. Rather than pointing out in detail the three characteristics mentioned above (which are obvious in the passages cited), I shall show how the effect of these is reinforced and extended by some additional features. In Ex. 8, for instance, after the shout 'Vive la République!' and assertive C major chords in the orchestra, the chromatic lines in unison ending on the leading note introduce tonal tension, which pushes forward towards the resolution on 'du tyran'. As for the text, in spite of the indicative here, it expresses a wish, not a reality, for at this point in the work Thionville is in dire straits. The words of Ex. 9 follow the 'Poursuivons jusqu'au trépas' pattern. Méreaux deliberately simplified the vocal writing in the first phrase, and in the second took the dissonance level one step further (an incomplete diminished seventh chord over D, the tonal centre of the passage) in comparison to Gluck. In Ex. 10 'jurons' is emphasized by the use of dissonance, and the Carthaginians' blood by the choral unison. In Ex. 11 the contrast in texture occurs between soloist and chorus, and 'jurons' is underlined by the syncopated figure occasionally found in Gluck and his contemporaries and that was a mannerism used to indicate tension in works of the 1790s. Soloist and chorus in Ex. 12(a) show their unity of purpose by singing the same line (the piece opens with another Gluckian reference – this one to the Thessalians' chorus, 'Pleure, ô patrie', in *Alceste*: Ex. 12(b)). In Ex. 13 the doubling of the soprano and *haute-contre*, resulting in a three-part choral texture for four written lines, is a technique imported into opera from the music for the Revolutionary *fête*. The close spacing of the three lower (male) lines and the gap between soprano and *haute-contre* in Ex. 14 reflect another *fête*-like texture and intensify the contrast made by the octave passage that follows; the octaves themselves again underline the object of the curse, in this case the one who 'would wish to usurp supreme power' (which now belongs to the people). Méhul's *Horatius Coclès* provides the most impressive example (Ex. 15). Here dynamics as well (*pp* in the first two phrases, *ff* in the third) allow the vow, 'qu'il meure', to shock with a musical violence matching the words. In addition, the composer used the most extreme dissonance in his chordal vocabulary – a diminished seventh chord over a dominant pedal – and the rhythmic tension figure we saw in Ex. 11.

In contemporary reviews choruses, particularly the oath choruses, were cited for their effect more often than choruses generally had been in the previous decades. Sometimes lengthy quotations from their texts

Ex. 8   L. E. Jadin, *Le siège de Thionville*, Act 1 scene vii: opening of the chorus 'Nous n'avons plus de roi', *F-Po* A.349, i, pp. 303, 306–8

(Long live the Republic! We no longer have a king; we no longer have a master. The tyrant's reign is over.)

were printed.[78] But that was not enough: the didactic purpose of theatre

78 For example, the *Journal des spectacles* (12 August 1793, p. 334) on *Fabius*: 'Plusieurs morceaux cependant ont été applaudis & méritoient de l'être. De ce nombre sont le serment qui fait le peuple romain à Paul-Emile, de sauver la patrie & de respecter la vie des hommes & les propriétés'; the *Journal de Paris national* (18 nivôse an II/7 January 1794, p. 1500) on *Toute la Grèce*: 'Le serment qu'ils font au moment du départ, de mourir ou revenir vainqueurs, a produit le plus grand effet' (the *Journal des spectacles* of the same date, pp. 1502–3, also praised this chorus highly and published the text); the *Journal de Paris national* (19 brumaire an II/9 November 1793, p. 1260) on *Miltiade à Marathon*: 'Le public a sur-tout vivement applaudi le choeur qui termine le 2ᵉ Acte, & par lequel les Grecs jurent la mort du traître qui parlera d'un

Ex. 9 Méreaux, *Fabius*, Act 1 scene ii: excerpt from the ensemble 'Allez, courez aux armes', *F-Po* A.350, i, pp. 219–22 [the accompaniment of woodwinds and strings largely doubles the voices]

(Run to take up arms! And do not lay them down until Asdrubal and his accomplices have atoned by their deaths [for their treacheries and murders].)

was truly achieved only if the audience responded favourably. Thus comments such as the following were highest praise:

> L'enthousiasme donné par le Musicien à ses Acteurs, passe tout entier dans l'âme des Spectateurs.[79]

The enthusiasm imparted by the musician to his actors was entirely transmitted to the spectators' souls.

and

> Les Spectateurs étoient à fois témoins & Acteurs eux-mêmes; & lorsque les Guerriers Grecs qui sont sur la Scène jurent de vaincre pour la Patrie, les Guerriers

Roi' and (5 February 1793, p. 144) on *La patrie reconnaissante*: 'le choeur pathétique & brûlant qui, après avoir pleuré avec elle [the widow of Beaurepaire], jure de venger & Beaurepaire & la Patrie, tout ce morceau a porté dans l'âme des Spectateurs le plus grand enthousiasme & a reçu des applaudissemens universels'. This last review is otherwise negative.

79 *Journal de Paris national*, 16 June 1793, p. 670, on the première of *Le siège de Thionville*.

Ex. 10 Méreaux, *Fabius*, Act 3 scene i: the opening of the chorus 'Oui, nous jurons sur cette épée', *F-Po* A.350, iii, pp. 108–11 [the accompaniment of woodwinds and strings supports the voice]

(Swear on this sword! Yes, we swear on this sword still damp with Carthaginian blood, in the name of the sovereign people [to set aside all plotting].)

François qui sont dans la Salle répètent tous avec le Spartiate: *Ce qu'ils ont dit, nous le ferons*.[80]

The spectators were themselves at one and the same time witnesses and actors [i.e. active participants]; and when the Greek warriors on stage swore to conquer for their country's sake [at the end of *Toute la Grèce*], the French soldiers in the audience reacted by declaring 'What they have sworn, we shall do'.

While the wish to advertise their patriotic orthodoxy may have influenced some journalists, it was the job of the agents of the secret police to spy on the 'esprit public' (the public's mood), and one measure of that was audience reaction (appropriate or inappropriate). They, too, reported enthusiasm for Revolutionary sentiments at the Opéra in 1793–4. (Public reaction was different when *Miltiade à Marathon* and

80 *Affiches, annonces et avis divers*, 23 nivôse an II/12 January 1794, p. 5671, on *Toute la Grèce*.

Ex. 11   Méreaux, *Fabius*, Act 1 scene ii: excerpt from the ensemble 'Non, vous levant à ma voix', *F-Po* A.350, i, pp. 209–10

(Swear at the price of your lives to save our country! We swear it!)

Horatius Coclès were revived during the Directory, 1797–9.)[81] One illustration will suffice: concerning a performance of *Le siège de Thionville*, one agent reported:

A ces mots la salle déchirée de bravos a été confondue dans un seul et même applaudissement, si fort qu'on eût dit que les toits allaient se soulever pour le laisser arriver jusqu'aux cieux.[82]

At these words the bravos roared in the theatre, and there was a single, united applause so strong that one might have thought that the roof would be raised to allow it to reach the heavens.

81 Some examples for *Horatius Coclès* are cited in Bartlet, *Etienne Nicolas Méhul*, pp. 334–7 and 1584–7.
82 *Tableaux de la Révolution française*, ii:66 (quoting Perrière).

Ex. 12   J.-B. Lemoyne, *Miltiade à Marathon*, Act 2 scene iii: two excerpts from the ensemble 'C'en est donc fait, nous n'avons plus d'espoir', *F-Po* A.350, ii, pp. 102–5 and 113–14 [after the first excerpt the chorus repeats Callimaque's line in octaves to a repetition of the orchestral accompaniment where the winds sustain and the strings have more rhythmically active lines; in the second excerpt the instruments largely double the voices]

a)

(a) (Ah! rather would death end our misfortunes!)
(b) (It has happened. Weep, unfortunate country! We no longer have any hope.)

Ex. 13 Lemoyne, *Toute la Grèce, ou Ce que peut la liberté*, scene vi: excerpt from the ensemble 'Non, nous voulons tous', *F-Po* A.354a, pp. 344–6

(No! We all want him to prevail or to perish [in the attempt]!)

What was the legacy of the new Opéra repertory of 1793–4? It would be foolhardy to claim direct and strong influence. The only work to be performed after 1800 was the ballet *Le jugement de Pâris*, whose scenario could have just as easily been written during the late *ancien régime* or the Empire. Only two works (*Miltiade à Marathon* and *Horatius Coclès*) were revived – and these still during the Revolution under considerable government pressure. The rest perished during the Thermidorian Reaction with the change in political regime, so closely

Ex. 14   B. Porta, *La réunion du dix août, ou L'inauguration de la République*, Act 3 scene i: opening of the chorus 'Oui, nous jurons de réduire en poussière', *F-Po* A.357a, pp. 408–11 [full orchestra supports the voices]

(Yes, we swear to reduce to dust, to exterminate without warning the presumptuous, the foolhardy, who would wish to usurp supreme power.)

did they mirror the discredited ideals of the Terror. Few were published or performed elsewhere. Even well-intentioned critics, while praising the patriotic sentiments promoted, expressed concern over mediocrity in several cases, and they were right to do so.[83]

83 See, for example, the *Journal de Paris national*, 20 ventôse an II/10 March 1794, p. 1756, on *Toulon soumis*:

> En rendant justice aux moyens de l'Opéra pour traiter ce sujet, on conviendra plus difficilement que l'exécution y ait répondu.

and the *Journal des spectacles*, 12 August 1793, on *Fabius*:

> La musique de Fabius est d'une teinte trop uniforme & n'est pas assez déclamatoire. L'ouverture ne nous paroît point analogue au sujet. Au lieu de nous peindre ces élans tumultueux d'un grand peuple qui ne veut pas qu'on lui arrache la liberté, elle ne nous fait entendre qu'un fragment de marche & un menuet gracieux qui n'annoncent point du tout ce qui va se passer.

Ex. 15 Méhul, *Horatius Coclès*, scene vi: opening of the chorus 'Si dans le sein de Rome il se trouvait un traître'

(If in Rome's midst there is a traitor who grieves for the kings and wants a master, may he die a painful death.)

Still, some of the authors remained active as librettists, composers or teachers. The oath chorus had a continuing tradition throughout the Consulate and Empire; examples include 'Que tout frémisse' in Spontini's *Fernand Cortez* (Act 3 scene ii, 1809) and Berton's 'Nous jurons tous', the finale of *L'oriflamme* (1815). From operas like Spontini's it was transmitted as a model. Even Rossini in *Guillaume Tell* (1829) was aware of it and used it effectively in the concluding section of the second-act finale ('Si parmi nous il est un traître'). After the experiments of 1793–4 the chorus as prime agent in the action was a possible alternative. As filtered through the later serious operas by Cherubini, Le Sueur, Spontini, Méhul and Catel, ultimately the reconsideration of the chorus's roles proved one of many sources for nineteenth-century *grand opéra*.

APPENDIX
New works at the Opéra, 1793–4
(those performed during the Terror are marked *)

F-Pn – Paris, Bibliothèque Nationale
F-Po – Paris, Bibliothèque-Musée de l'Opéra

Pièces de circonstance with contemporary settings

Le triomphe de la République, ou Le camp de Grand-Pré
> *Divertissement lyrique* in 1 act by Marie-Joseph Chénier, set by François-Joseph Gossec
> Première: 27 January 1793; 10 performances, the last on 26 February 1793
> Major MS sources: F-Po A.345a–b, Rés.98 (1–2) [autograph], A.345c, Recueils XLIII (1–6), XLIV (2–3)
> Printed full score: *Le triomphe de la République, ou Le camp de Grand Pré, divertissement lyrique en un acte représenté à l'Opéra le 27 janvier l'an 2ᵉ de la République française, une et indivisible, paroles du Cⁿ. Chénier, les ballets du Cⁿ. Gardel* (Paris, Mozin, [1794])

La patrie reconnaissante, ou L'apothéose de Beaurepaire
> *Opéra héroïque* in 1 act by Jean-Joseph Leboeuf, set by Pierre Joseph Candeille
> Première: 3 February 1793; 3 performances, the last on 15 February 1793
> Major MS source: F-Po A.346

* *Le siège de Thionville*
> *Drame lyrique* in 2 acts by N. F. Guillaume Saulnier and Dutilh, set by Louis Emmanuel Jadin
> Première: 14 June 1793; 24 performances, the last on 12 Messidor An II/ 30 June 1794
> Major MS source: F-Po A.349 (I–II)

Toulon soumis
> *Fait historique (opéra)* in 1 act by Antoine Fabre d'Olivet, set by Jean-Baptiste Rochefort
> Première: 14 Ventôse An II/4 March 1794; 17 performances, the last on 4 Thermidor An II/22 July 1794
> Major MS sources: *F-Po* Rés.A.356a [autograph], *F-Pn* Vm.2936

La réunion du dix août, ou L'inauguration de la République française
> *Sans-culottide dramatique* in 5 acts (dedicated to the Convention Nationale) by Gabriel Bouquier and Pierre-Louis Moline, set by Bernardo Porta
> Première: 16 Germinal An II/5 April 1794; 35 performances, the last on 2 Pluviôse An III/21 January 1795
> Major MS sources: *F-Po* A.357a–b, Recueils XXXV (24–5), LVI (12), LXXV (7–12)

La rosière républicaine, ou La fête de la vertu
> *Opéra* in 1 act by Pierre Sylvain Maréchal, set by André-Ernest-Modeste Grétry
> Première (planned for 11 Nivôse An II/31 December 1793, but banned): 16 Fructidor An II/2 September 1794; 7 performances, the last on 8 Brumaire An III/29 October 1794
> Major MS sources: *F-Po* Rés.105 [autograph of the overture originally written for *Cécile et Ermancé, ou Les deux couvents*], A.353b, Recueils XL (10–22), LIII (15), *F-Pn* D.5048

Pièces de circonstance with classical settings

*Fabius
> *Tragédie lyrique* in 3 acts by Marie-Joseph Désiré Martin Barouillet, set by Nicolas-Jean Le Froid de Méreaux
> Première: 9 August 1793; 16 performances, the last on 15 Pluviôse An II/6 February 1794
> Major MS sources: *F-Pn* MS 2348 [autograph], *F-Po* A.350 (I–III)

*Miltiade à Marathon
> *Opéra* in 2 acts by Nicolas François Guillard set by Jean-Baptiste Lemoyne
> Première: 15 Brumaire An II/5 November 1793; 54 performances on the initial run, the last on 18 Floréal An III/7 May 1795, and 12 on the revival, 30 Frimaire An VI – 24 Thermidor An VII/20 December 1797 – 11 August 1799
> Major MS source: *F-Po* A.351 (I–II)

*Toute la Grèce, ou Ce que peut la liberté
> *Tableau patriotique* in 1 act by Louis Abel Beffroy de Rigny, *dit* Cousin Jacques, set by J.-B. Lemoyne
> Première: 16 Nivôse An II/5 January 1794; 30 performances, the last on 6 Thermidor An II/24 July 1794
> Major MS sources: *F-Po* A.354a–b

*Horatius Coclès
  Opéra in 1 act by Antoine Vincent Arnault set by Etienne-Nicolas Méhul
  Première: 30 Pluviôse An II/18 February 1794; 18 performances on the initial
    run, the last on 8 Brumaire An III/29 October 1794, and 9 on the revival,
    26 Brumaire – 2 Pluviôse An VI/16 November 1797 – 21 January 1798
  Major MS sources: F-Po A.355a, Recueil LXVII (16)
  Printed full score: Horatius Coclès, acte lyrique, paroles du Citoyen Arnault,
    représenté pour la première fois sur le Théâtre Nationale [sic] de l'Opéra
    le décadi 30 pluviôse (Paris, les Citoyens Cousineau père et fils, [1794])

Denys le tyran, maître d'école à Corinthe
  Opéra bouffon in 1 act by Maréchal, set by Grétry
  Première: 6 Fructidor An II/23 August 1794; 10 performances, the last on
    6 Frimaire An III/26 November 1794
  Major MS sources: F-Po A.358a–b, Recueils XXXII (18–19), XL (1–9), F-Pn
    D.5030

Other works

*Le jugement de Pâris
  Ballet pantomine in 3 acts, choreography by Pierre Gabriel Gardel, set by
    Méhul
  Première: 6 March 1793; 54 performances by the end of 1794, more than
    200 by 26 November 1825
  Major MS sources: F-Po A.347 (I–III), Recueils XXXIV (15), LI (1–10), LIII
    (11)

*Le mariage de Figaro
  Comédie lyrique in 5 (later 4) acts by Pierre Augustin Caron de Beaumarchais
    as arranged by François Notaris (who translated the musical numbers),
    set by Wolfgang Amadeus Mozart
  Première at the Opéra: 20 March 1793; 6 performances, the last on
    1 September 1793
  Major MS sources: F-Po A.348 (I–IV), Recueil XLVIII (7–11), F-Pn L.10.675
    (1–4)

*Les muses, ou Le triomphe d'Apollon
  Ballet anacréontique in 1 act, choreography by Auguste Hus père, set by
    Louis-Charles Ragué
  Première: 12 December 1793; 4 performances, the last on 16 December 1793

DAVID GALLIVER

Léonore, ou L'amour conjugal: a celebrated offspring of the Revolution

Towards the end of his life Jean-Nicolas Bouilly, Chevalier de la Légion d'Honneur and respected *doyen* of the Parisian literary fraternity, published his memoirs of a long career as a man of letters. Looking back some thirty years, he wrote of the now distant days of the Revolution, which he had spent in the Touraine, his homeland, where, amid other commitments, he had written his play *Léonore, ou L'amour conjugal*. The plot had been based on a real event which had taken place in the Touraine, and in which he had played a part. Exemplifying a wife's devotion to her husband and his rescue from unjust imprisonment through her heroism, the play would later serve Beethoven in *Fidelio*, and thus secure Bouilly's name for posterity. Comparative studies of its various versions have already been undertaken by scholars; this essay considers its genesis and offers a prologue to that celebrated libretto.

By the beginning of 1791 the twenty-eight-year-old Bouilly had already achieved a promising reputation in the Parisian theatre. At the outset of his career he had practised in the capital as a lawyer, but had soon relinquished the bar in order to further his ambition of becoming a writer for the theatre. In 1790 his four-act *comédie mêlée de chants* entitled *Pierre le grand*, with music by Grétry, had been well received at the Théâtre-Italien. Some months later a short play, *Jean-Jacques Rousseau à ses derniers moments*, had been something of a popular success. The young author had been received in audience by Queen Marie Antoinette and had gained *entrée* to the literary salon of Madame de Staël.[1] Most recently the composer Etienne Méhul, whose *Euphrosine* had just taken Paris by storm, had agreed to collaborate with Bouilly in *La jeunesse d'Henri Quatre*, which the *sociétaires* of the Théâtre-Italien had already approved for future production.[2]

But early that same year Bouilly, who had only just met Méhul and

1 D. Galliver, 'The Career of Jean-Nicolas Bouilly, Auteur Dramatique', in *Studies in the Eighteenth Century*, vi (Williamsburg, Virginia, 1987), pp. 141ff.
2 M. E. C. Bartlet, 'Etienne Méhul and the Opéra during the French Revolution, Consulate, and Empire' (Ph.D. diss. University of Chicago, 1982), pp. 244ff.

could scarcely have had time to deliver the text of his play to his new colleague, suddenly forsook the Parisian scene and returned to his native Tours. This seemingly precipitate departure was no doubt occasioned principally by his desire to escape the inevitable holocaust now threatening Paris, exacerbated probably by his sense of personal loss at the death, a few weeks earlier, of the young Antoinette Grétry, to whom he was greatly attached and may have been betrothed. By February 1791 Bouilly was back home in Tours, applying himself to affairs of a very different kind.

Politically Bouilly's standpoint hitherto had been that of a moderate radical. Schooled by his stepfather in the liberal traditions of Rousseau and Montesquieu, his views had been consolidated during his sojourn in Paris through his friendship with the young Antoine-Pierre Barnave, colleague of Mirabeau.[3] *Pierre le grand* had constellated Bouilly's liberal ideals: underlining the equality of all men, rich and poor, high-born and lowly, at the same time it supported the existing order, with a monarch (albeit a humane one) at its head. It was thus not really surprising that, when visiting his home town the previous year, Bouilly had joined the Société des Amis de la Constitution, newly formed by citizens and merchants of Tours anxious to preserve stability.[4] After returning home permanently, Bouilly began to play an active part in the affairs of the Amis, his legal qualifications securing his immediate appointment as one of the *secrétaires*; and in the municipal elections held at the end of 1791 he was appointed one of the administrators of the District of Tours.[5] The man of letters had thus, for the moment, become once again a man of law, thereby achieving security and employment for the difficult years ahead.

By 1792 the activities of the previously conservative Amis had evolved in an overtly anti-clerical and anti-aristocratic direction. There is no record of Bouilly having played any significant role in this at that time, although in his official capacity he must have condoned the secularization of one of Tours's renowned monasteries, the Abbaye St Julien, and its conversion to a military barracks. Nonetheless, he still maintained in public his liberal principles and support for the monarch, going as far as to propose to the Amis in March 1792 that the National Assembly should be asked to conscript eight men from each *département* to serve as a royal bodyguard and prevent any attack on the king. Not surprisingly, Bouilly's motion lapsed.[6]

---

3 J.-N. Bouilly, *Mes récapitulations* (Paris, 1837), i, pp. 172ff.
4 *Régistre des citoyens admis dans la Société Régenerée ... an 2 de la République* (Archives d'Indre-et-Loire).
5 'Déliberations du Conseil Général du Département, vol. L74 (26 juillet 1790 – 15 décembre 1791)', *Inventaire sommaire*, ser. L, Archives Départmentales d'Indre et Loire, Tours.
6 A. Philippon, 'La deuxième Commission Militaire, Tours, novembre 1793 – mai 1794', *Bulletin de la Société Archéologique de Touraine*, xxxiv (1966), p. 445.

In Paris, meanwhile, events were moving towards a climax. The royal palace was stormed in August 1792 and the king and royal family imprisoned; in September the new Republic was proclaimed. In Tours public unrest developed, with shortage of food causing bread riots and other disturbances. The following year a serious royalist uprising in the neighbouring Vendée brought an increased military presence. Citizens were conscripted to help fight the insurgents and repressive measures were taken against those suspected of being opponents of the new regime. As one inhabitant wrote,

Tout le monde ici est dans l'épouvante et le désespoir. Il est peu de familles qui ne comptent un ou plusieurs de leurs membres parmi les personnes jetées en prison comme suspects, et menacées d'être conduites à la guillotine. Libre aujourd'hui, il suffira de la fausse dénonciation d'un misérable, pour que demain on soit en prison.[7]

Everyone lives in fear and despair. There are few families which do not count one or more members among those thrown into prison as suspects, under threat of the guillotine. Free today, the false accusation of a wretch is enough for him to be imprisoned tomorrow.

Under the new administration Bouilly's career had meanwhile advanced considerably. Promoted *commissaire* of the Tribunal Criminel in September 1792, in November he had been appointed a judge of the tribunal.[8] On 10 August 1793, when the Festival of the Unity and Indivisibility of the Republic was celebrated at a public ceremony in Tours, it was recorded that

Un tombereau a conduit jusqu'à la place de justice une couronne, un sceptre, un cordon bleu, les portraits de tous les rois de France, un recueil des armoires de la ci-devant noblesse ... on est ensuite arrivé sur la place de Justice où était préparé un bûcher. Le citoyen Bouilly, juge du Tribunal du district de Tours, monté sur le char de la Liberté, au pied de la déesse, a ... devoué à l'exécration les rois et la royauté, la féodalité barbare, l'aristocratie et ses préjugés, et précipitant sur le bûcher les restes de ces divers genres de Tyrannie, il a voté de même la destruction de quiconque oseroit tenter de devenir le dominateur ou l'oppresseur des ses concitoyens.[9]

A tumbril containing a crown, a sceptre, a blue sash, the portraits of former kings of France and a number of coats-of-arms of the aristocracy was drawn to the Place de Justice ... where a bonfire had been prepared. Citizen Bouilly, judge of the court of the district of Tours, standing on the Chariot of Liberty at the feet of the Goddess ... execrated all kings and royalty, the barbarity of feudalism and the antiquated code of the aristocracy, and hurled into the flames the vestiges of these various forms of

7 J.-X. Carré de Busserole, *Souvenirs de la Révolution dans le Département d'Indre-et-Loire* (Tours, 1864), pp. 205–6.
8 'Permanence du Conseil: procès verbaux des assemblées, vols. L78 (19 juillet – 11 novembre 1792) and L79 (12 novembre 1792 – 3 mai 1793)', *Inventaire sommaire*, ser. L, Archives Départmentales d'Indre et Loire, Tours.
9 Philippon, 'La deuxième Commission Militaire', pp. 446ff.

tyranny, threatening the death penalty to anyone who dared attempt to dominate or oppress his fellow citizens.

Had, then, the erstwhile liberal and supporter of the king changed sides? Was Bouilly now a henchman of the new regime? If his own words are to be believed, the true situation was exactly the opposite. His identification with the Revolutionary administration was in fact only a cloak for his real activities. Behind the scenes he was totally engaged in saving his home town and its citizens from the ravages of assassins. He recalled proudly,

Plus le danger devenait imminent, plus je m'y dévouais avec courage et résolution, Ni les conseils d'amis prudens, ni les menaces des puissans du jour, ni surtout les larmes de mon excellente mère qui n'avait plus que moi pour soutien, ne pouvait arrêter l'élan de mon ame, tempérer l'exaltation de mon dévoument à la cause sacrée des nombreuses familles dont j'étais environné.[10]

The more immediate the danger, the more courageously and resolutely I applied myself. Neither the warnings of prudent friends nor the threats of the authorities – not even the tears of my excellent mother, who had only myself as support – could arrest the fervour of my spirit or temper my devotion to the sacred cause of the numerous families around me.

The evidence in support of these brave assertions, however, is extremely tenuous. Bouilly's claim to have been one of the ten leading citizens of Tours who had banded together to ensure the safety of leading families under suspicion remains so far unsubstantiated. There is one known case, however, which, although it rests partly on his own testimony, might be considered as giving some support to his claim; and it is this case which leads us directly to *Léonore, ou L'amour conjugal*.

Among the many letters of denunication which arrived on his desk, Bouilly had noticed one by an agent of the police in Paris, a certain Héron, denouncing as royalists the wealthy Parisian family Mercier, who had recently purchased La Plaine, an extensive property situated at Fondettes, close to the Loire near Tours. The husband, a former chief magistrate of Paris, was now in his sixties, but his wife was much younger. Madame Mercier confided to Bouilly, that, when she and her husband had been living in Paris, Héron, who owed money to her husband, had conceived a great passion for her; but she had refused his amorous advances and, in consequence, 'full of resentment against an honest woman, who had been more true to herself in remaining faithful to her duty than by surrendering to a vile intriguer, he now sought vengeance by contriving her execution' ('plein de ressentiment contre une honnête femme qui avait trouvé plus naturel de rester fidèle à ses devoirs, que de s'abandonner à un vil intrigant, celui-ci cherchait à s'en

10 Bouilly, *Mes récapitulations*, ii, p. 63.

venger, en lui faisant couper la tête').[11] Using his official position, Bouilly was able to place the Merciers under the protection of his friends, discredit Héron with the Parisian authorities and free the family from suspicion.

In consequence of all this Bouilly became a frequent visitor to the Merciers' home.

Dès que la nuit couvrait de son ombre tutélaire les belles rives de la Loire, je les parcourais en secret, et j'arrivais au bout d'une heure de marche, au délicieux séjour de La Plaine, où je me délaissais des travaux de la journée; où je racontais ce que j'avais fait . . . pour adoucir le sort des prisonniers, et calmer la terreur des innocens accusés.[12]

As soon as night had cast its protective cloak over the fair banks of the Loire, I passed along them secretly and, after an hour's walk, arrived at the delightful residence of La Plaine. Here I could abandon the cares of the day, and I would relate what I had been doing . . . to alleviate the sufferings of the prisoners and to calm the fears of the innocent accused.

Bouilly's audience included several of the elegant and attractive women of high birth whom he admired so greatly. Elisabeth Mercier was still young and 'in the full bloom of her beauty, endowed with the most entrancing grace and wit, of which she offered a rare and captivating combination' ('dans tout l'éclat de la beauté; ce qui chez elle ne pouvait être comparé qu'à la grace la plus ravissante, à l'esprit le plus fin dont elle offrait le rare et séduisant assemblage').[13] There were also two visitors from Paris, Elisabeth Mercier's aunt, Marie Louise Langlois, who had been present at one of the performances of *Pierre le grand* in Paris and was interested in the young writer, and her daughter from a previous marriage, Eugénie Rével, whose striking blond hair and expressive eyes reminded Bouilly of his beloved Antoinette Grétry. Before this company Bouilly could assume once again his role as man of letters. Despite his arduous administrative duties, he had found time to write a new play; now, at the regular gatherings at La Plaine, where 'in order to distract ourselves from the storm of the Terror we had recourse to the consolation offered by the arts' ('pour nous distraire des orages de la terreur, nous recourions au prestige consolant des arts'),[14] he gave it a first reading.

The play was *Léonore, ou L'amour conjugal*. It was based on 'a sublime deed of heroism and devotion by one of the ladies of the Touraine, whose noble efforts I had the happiness of assisting' ('trait sublime d'héroïsme et de dévouement d'une des dames de la Touraine, dont j'avais eu le bonheur de seconder les généreux efforts').[15] Thus it was, apparently, a true drama of the Revolution, conceived and born

---

11 Ibid., pp. 67ff.   12 Ibid.   13 Ibid.   14 Ibid.   15 Ibid., p. 81.

during a period of great turmoil and based on a real event. But what that event was, and who the participants were, Bouilly was never to reveal. No record of occurrences in the Touraine during the Revolution has been found to support his statement; the lines cited above, written thirty years or so afterwards, remain the only testimony to the origins of the plot.

Might Bouilly's heroine perhaps have been Elisabeth Mercier? Her husband Nicolas-Jean Mercier, *conseiller du roi en l'hôtel de ville de Paris*, and former *échevin* of that city, had purchased La Plaine in September 1792.[16] Bouilly's close friendship with the family must have begun about this time, and Elisabeth Mercier, then thirty-one years of age, was to remain his 'dearest and most worthy friend' ('ma plus aimable et ma plus digne amie')[17] until her death thirty years later. Any act of bravery in which she could have been instrumental in saving her husband must necessarily have taken place in Paris during the early part of the Revolution. By then her husband would have ceased to be an *échevin* of the city, although he may have continued in some of his judicial functions. As one who held office as far back as the reign of Louis XV, he must have come under suspicion as a royal sympathizer, but it seems he had escaped imprisonment. No obvious parallel with the plot of *Léonore, ou L'amour conjugal* appears likely.

According to Bouilly's narrative, however, there was one significant figure associated with the Mercier family, both in Paris and in Tours: the infamous Louis-Julien-Simon Héron, notorious police agent of the Committee of Public Safety.[18] In putting herself in danger by resisting Héron's attempts to seduce her, Elisabeth Mercier had remained faithful to her marriage vows. Bouilly's stage heroine would preserve the same ideals:

> Exécrable Pizarro! Je saurais déjouer tes complots et braver ton barbarie!
> O toi mon unique espérance,
> Toi qui venges le juste et frappes le méchant,
> Sauve à fois, Dieu tout-puissant,
> L'Amour, l'Hymen, et l'innocence.[19]

Hateful Pizarro! I can thwart your intentions and defy your cruelty! O all-powerful God, my only hope, who avenges the righteous and puts down the wicked, preserve at once my Love, my marriage and my innocence.

Did Bouilly perhaps convolute two quite separate events: Elisabeth Mercier's heroism in defying Héron in Paris and the perils which would

---

16 'L'inventaire après décès d'Elisabeth Louise Bocher du 13 novembre 1822, devant M. Bidault, notaire à Tours', *Minutes notariales*, Archives d'Indre et Loire, Tours.
17 Bouilly, *Mes récapitulations*, ii, p. 82.
18 J.-X. Carré de Busserole, *Curieuse histoire d'un procureur de la Commune de Tours, 1793–1796* (Tours, 1888), pp. 56–7.
19 J.-N. Bouilly, *Léonore, ou L'amour conjugal* (Paris, an VII/1798–9), Act 1 scene viii (p. 22).

later beset the Mercier family in Tours, and which Bouilly himself would help to avert? Even if they were true, however (and both episodes rely entirely upon Bouilly's testimony), the obvious discrepancies between the two situations would seem to relegate any direct comparison between Elisabeth Mercier and Léonore to the realms of fantasy.

But fantasy was very much Bouilly's stock-in-trade. As a writer he had never set great store by following the letter of history. In *Pierre le grand* he had accommodated facts reported by Voltaire in the interests of dramatic effect, and in *Jean-Jacques Rousseau à ses derniers moments* his lack of veracity had occasioned some indignant correspondence in *Le moniteur*.[20] What was all-important for Bouilly was the presentation 'of natural scenes, at all times more striking and durable than those which, overladen with literary ornament and riches of history, lack the felicitous disposition of character and harmony of colour which form the fundamental marks of a great work' ('des tableaux naturels, toujours plus frappans et plus durables que ceux qui, surchargés d'ornemens littéraires, de richesses historiques, sont dénués de cet heureux agencement des figures, de cette harmonie des couleurs qui forment le mérite fondamental d'une grande composition').[21]

This tendency to confuse fact and fantasy was characteristic of his whole personality. As the poet and dramatist Ernest Legouvé wrote,

Il mettait de l'imagination en tout et partout. Les actes les plus ordinaries de la vie, les événements les plus simples, se transformaient pour lui en scènes, en dialogues, qui bientôt passaient dans sa tête à l'état de réalités. Il croyait tout ce qu'il s'imaginait.[22]

In everything and everywhere he used his imagination. The most normal action, the most simple of events, transformed themselves for him into scenes and dialogues which soon assumed in his mind the state of reality. He believed everything which he imagined.

Legouvé, who had been Bouilly's ward, affectionately recalled a characteristic incident from a later period in his guardian's life:

J'entre un matin chez lui. – "T'ai-je raconté, me dit-il, la rencontre que j'ai fait l'autre semaine au musée du Louvre? – Non. – C'était le lundi, jour où le public n'est pas admis. Le conservateur, avec qui je suis lié, m'avait amené devant un tableau de maître, acquis depuis quelques jours. Tout à coup une porte s'ouvre, et je vois entrer … qui? Le roi Louis XVIII! On le poussait dans une petite voiture roulante. Je me hâte de m'esquiver; mais l'aide de camp de service m'ayant reconnu, me nomma au roi, qui me fit de la main et de la tête le plus gracieux salut. – Cela ne m'étonne pas", dis-je; et je pars. Huit jours après je reviens. – "T'ai-je raconté, me dit-il, ma rencontre et ma conversation avec Louis XVIII, au musée du Louvre? – Votre rencontre, oui; mais non votre conversation. – Elle a été courte, mais assez curieuse.

20 *Le moniteur*, 11 January 1791.   21 Bouilly, *Mes récapitulations*, ii, pp. 33–4.
22 E. Legouvé, *Soixante ans de souvenirs* (Paris, 1886), p. 92.

L'aide de camp m'ayant nommé a lui, le roi me fit signe de m'approcher, et me dit un mot bienveillant sur *L'abbé de l'épée*,[23] Moi, qui sait son goût pour Horace, je lui ripostai par un vers de son poète favori, qui se trouvait une allusion assez délicate à son goût pour les arts. Il sourit, et je m'éloignai avec un salut respectueux." Quelques jours plus tard, je le trouve dans son cabinet, avec le sourire sur les lèvres. – "T'ai-je raconté, me dit-il, ma conversation avec Louis XVIII? – Quelques mots à peine. – Oh! nous nous sommes dit des choses ... très intéressantes. Une citation d'Horace a engagé la partie. Puis, tu comprends bien qu'on n'a pas toujours un roi pour interlocuteur, et ma foi ... le vieux libéral s'est lancé. Et je lui ai adroitement glissé quelques vérités qu'il n'est pas habitué à entendre! Il a répondu! ... J'ai répondu à mon tour!" Et là-dessus le voilà qui me raconte tout un dialogue, avec répliques, ripostes, interruptions; sur quoi, sa femme entrant et écoutant: – "Mon Dieu! Bouilly, lui dit-elle, que tu es donc cachotier! Tu ne m'as jamais dit un mot de cette conversation. – Par une bien bonne raison, répondit-il en éclatant de rire, c'est que je l'ai arrangée ce matin, dans mon lit, en rêvassant, et que je viens de faire la scène pour Ernest."[24]

I visited him one morning. 'Did I tell you', he said, 'of the meeting I had the other week at the Louvre?' 'No.' 'It was Monday, when the public is not admitted. The curator, a friend of mine, was showing me a valuable painting which he had recently acquired, when suddenly the door opened, and who should enter but King Louis XVIII. He was being wheeled along in a little carriage. I hastened to withdraw, but the aide-de-camp, who recognized me, told the king who I was, and he acknowledged me most graciously with a movement of his hand and head.' 'That doesn't surprise me', I said, and took my leave. A week later I returned. 'Did I tell you', said Bouilly, 'of my meeting and conversation with Louis XVIII at the Louvre?' 'Your meeting, certainly, but not your conversation.' 'It was short, but interesting. The aide-de-camp presented me to the king. The latter beckoned me to approach, and said something generous about *L'abbé de l'épée*. Knowing of his liking for Horace, I responded with a line of his favourite poet, containing a tasteful allusion to his love for the arts. He smiled, and I left with a respectful bow.' A few days later I found Bouilly once again in his room, with a smile hovering on his lips. 'Did I tell you about my conversation with Louis XVIII?' 'Only a few words.' 'Ah, we had a most interesting dialogue, A quotation from Horace set him off. Now, of course, one doesn't always have the opportunity to talk with a king, and – my word! – the old Liberal was awoken in me. I skilfully let slip a few home truths such as he doesn't usually hear. He responded ... I answered.' Thereupon Bouilly recounted an entire conversation, with answers, responses and interjections. Suddenly his wife appeared on the scene, and heard what he was saying: 'Good gracious, Bouilly, what a dark horse you are! You never told me anything of this conversation.' 'Of course not', he replied, exploding with laughter. 'I dreamt it all up in bed this morning, concocting a scenario for Ernest!'

Knowing of our subject's propensities, and lacking other evidence, one may well suspect that the plot of *Léonore, ou L'amour conjugal* did

---

23 Bouilly's play, *L'abée de l'épée*, first performed in 1799 at the Théâtre de la République, was instrumental in securing the release from prison of the celebrated *abbé* Sicard, director of the Institut des Sourds Muets in Paris. See Galliver, 'The Career of Jean-Nicolas Bouilly', pp. 147–8.
24 E. Legouvé, *Soixante ans de souvenirs*, pp. 92–3.

not originate from any single historical event, but was rather an imaginative synthesis of Bouilly's own experiences and fantasies. Background material was certainly at hand amid the turmoil and violence of Revolutionary Touraine. The setting itself, 'une prison d'état', might have been one of the great châteaux – Loches, Amboise or Chinon – which at that time were crammed with prisoners, many of them innocent suspects. There were prototypes for the characters, too. Pizarro might have been modelled on Héron, or perhaps on the unbalanced Gabriel-Jérome Sénar, whom Bouilly had come across in the course of his administrative duties;[25] similarly, it has been suggested already that the inspiration for the character of Léonore might have come from Elisabeth Mercier, 'cette femme adorable'[26] who mirrored so strikingly Bouilly's ideal of womanhood.[27]

Uncertainty regarding the origins of the plot itself extends also to Bouilly's report of the first reading. Did this in fact ever take place at La Plaine in the summer of 1793, or was this yet another fantasy? It will be recalled that, according to Bouilly, Elisabeth Mercier's cousin, Eugénie Rével, had been among the company at La Plaine. When reading his play, the author recalled,

Elle produisit un effet très remarquable sur tous mes auditeurs; mais aucun d'eux ne me parut sentir aussi vivement le noble élan de mon héroïne, que la belle Eugénie. Ses regards attachés sur le miens, semblaient me dire qu'elle ne serait pas moins dévouée à son époux, que ne l'était Léonore; et je crus entendre en ce moment l'ombre d'Antoinette Grétry me dire tout bas: 'Voilà celle qui seule peut me remplacer dans ton coeur'.[28]

It produced a most remarkable effect on all my listeners; but none seemed to feel so deeply the noble impulses of my heroine as did the beautiful Eugénie. Her eyes, fixed on mine, seemed to say that she would not be less devoted to her husband than Léonore had been; and at that moment I thought I heard the voice of Antoinette Grétry whisper, 'Here is the one who alone can replace me in your heart'.

A few months later, in November 1793, Eugénie Rével and Jean-Nicolas Bouilly were married.

The previous month Bouilly had received professional promotion, with an appointment as public prosecutor and shortly afterwards membership of the Commission Militaire, newly set up to search out and punish the ringleaders of anti-Revolutionary disturbances in Tours; three months later he became president of the Commission.[29] Compromises and delaying tactics would no longer suffice. Between February

25 J.-X. Carré de Busserole, *Dictionnaire d'Indre-Loire* (Tours, 1878), iii, pp. 42ff.
26 Bouilly, *Mes récapitulations*, ii, p. 82.
27 'L'amour conjugal doit être le premier trésor qui existe sur terre' (Bouilly, *Léonore*, Act 1 scene iii (p. 11)).
28 Bouilly, *Mes récapitulations*, ii, pp. 81–2.
29 *Régistres d'état civil* (Archives d'Indre-et-Loire).

and May 1794 Bouilly signed the death warrants for some five convicted anti-Revolutionaries, at least one of these cases being a cruel miscarriage of justice. After his death fellow Tourangeaux would quote them as evidence of Bouilly's pusillanimity.[30] In fairness to Bouilly, however, there are mitigating circumstances. No doubt still a liberal at heart, opposed to the oppressive tyranny around him, Bouilly must have been fearful that any action on his part suggesting sympathy with opponents of the regime would have resulted not only in his own arrest but also in that of his new wife and her relatives at La Plaine. In his favour it can be said that the decline in the number of death sentences carried out by the Commission Militaire during Bouilly's term of office suggests that he at least did what he could to restore a spirit of justice.[31] It may be said that at the outset of the Revolution Bouilly had resolved to play a dramatic role, involving disguise, danger and faith in lofty principles, such as he had created for his stage characters in *Pierre le grand*. But now any self-assumed role as champion of the oppressed could no longer be sustained under the disguise of an exemplary officer of the Revolution. Providentially for Bouilly, the ultimate crisis was averted by a *deus ex machina*. On 9 Thermidor/27 July 1794 came the fall of Robespierre, ending an epoch 'when fearsome anarchy had broken every family tie, torn down all limits of good sense and reason, vilified every heart and intimidated every conscience' ('où l'exécrable anarchie avait brisé tous les liens, rompu tous les digues et du bon sens et de la raison, avili tous les coeurs, épouvanté toutes les consciences').[32]

The man of law was able once again to be a man of letters. It seems likely that it was this period, in the immediate aftermath of the Terror, rather than the eighteen months or so before it, that saw the birth of *Léonore, ou L'amour conjugal*. Making preparations for a return to Paris and the theatre, Bouilly would have been eager (as always) to seize on a topical and popular theme. Tales of the bravery displayed by wives in rescuing their husbands from prison during the Terror were coming into vogue,[33] and preoccupation with such a theme, giving it an original twist from his own experiences and imagination, might have enabled Bouilly to suppress the somewhat less glorious memories of his own recent activities. But there is another factor: Bouilly's subsequent dedication of the play to his wife. This dedication would not appear in the published libretto, but only in a volume of collected poems which appeared towards the end of the author's life. It includes the line 'Tu fus mon guide et mon original'.[34] In 1793 Eugénie Rével could not have

---

30 See, for example, Carré de Busserole, *Souvenirs de la Révolution*, pp. 235ff.
31 Philippon, *La deuxième Commission Militaire*, p. 465.
32 Bouilly, *Mes récapitulations*, ii, p. 59.
33 D. Galliver, 'Fidelio – Fact or Fantasy?' *Studies in Music*, xv (1981), p. 90.
34 J.-N. Bouilly, *Le vieux glaneur, ou de tout un peu* (Paris, n.d.), p. 187.

served as a historical model for Léonore, but to have been named subsequently as the author's inspiration for what they both knew to be an imaginary plot would no doubt have been acceptable to a young wife, who in 1794 would already be sharing in her husband's work and ambitions.

There are, of course, other possible explanations of the various factors; what is virtually certain is that when, some time in 1795, the Bouilly family returned to Paris the libretto of *Léonore, ou L'amour conjugal* was completed.[35] Bouilly had secured an advisory post in the Committee of Public Instruction, and this would provide financial support pending his re-establishment in the theatre.[36] In February 1796 his one-act comedy, *La famille américaine*, opened at the Opéra-Comique, followed in September by a short play, *René Descartes*, at the Théâtre de la République. These minor successes were, however, over-shadowed by a major disaster. *La jeunesse d'Henri Quatre*, with Méhul's music, had been put aside during the Revolution, but now reappeared as *Le jeune Henri*, suitably purged of royalist overtones and adapted to current republican sentiments. Its première in May 1797 was, except for the overture, a total failure. 'It would be impossible to write anything worse' ('Nous croyons qu'il est impossible de faire un ouvrage plus mauvais') wrote the *Courrier des spectacles* (2 May 1797). Although the lightweight *Mort de Turenne* at the Variété the following month was well received, this was only a *pantomime dialoguée*. Bouilly must have been anxious to redeem his reputation.

The opportunity to do so was close at hand. Soon after his return to Paris Bouilly had become a founder-member of the Société Philotechnique, formed by politicians and men of letters 'to oppose the ravages of vandalism ... and bad taste' ('pour s'opposer aux ravages du vandalisme ... et du mauvais goût').[37] By 1797 the composer and singer Pierre Gaveaux had become a fellow member, and it may have been in the prestigious surroundings of the Louvre, where the society was permitted to hold its meetings, that Bouilly persuaded Gaveaux to cooperate with him in a new production, *Léonore, ou L'amour conjugal*. His choice of collaborator was not fortuitous. Gaveaux was a well-known composer; in 1792 his *L'amour filial* had been an enormous success, suggesting perhaps to Bouilly the analogous subtitle of his own play. Moreover, Gaveaux's long association with the Théâtre Feydeau would assist the acceptance of the play by that theatre; Bouilly no doubt hesitated to approach its rival, the Opéra-Comique, so soon after his recent *débâcle*

---

35 The title page of the original MS includes some lines which Bouilly later crossed out. These are difficult to decipher, but one word, 'Tours', is clear.
36 Bouilly, *Mes récapitulations*, ii, pp. 121ff.
37 Depping, 'Notice sur les premiers temps de la Société Philotechnique', *Annuaires de la Société Philotechnique, 1840* (Paris, 1840), p. 7.

there. Gaveaux would not only compose the music for *Léonore*, but also undertake the role of Florestan. All appeared set for a complete success.

Léonore, ou L'amour conjugal duly opened at the Feydeau on 19 February 1798. Bouilly had made it known that this *fait historique* was related to 'an event which occurred in France some years ago' ('un événement arrivé en France il y a quelques années'),[38] thus ensuring its topical appeal. It was received with acclaim. 'For a long time there has not been in any theatre so complete and universal a success' ('on n'a vu depuis longtemps sur aucun théâtre un succès aussi complet, et aussi universel') wrote *Le journal de Paris* (22 February 1798). For the first time Bouilly was recognized as a writer able not only to edify and entertain, but also to create gripping dramatic tension. The dungeon scene, it was agreed, was strikingly effective: 'Nothing could have been more heartrending or arresting' ('Rien n'est plus déchirant, et rien, en même temps, ne fixe davantage l'attention du spectateur') asserted the *Courrier des spectacles* (20 February 1798). Adverse comment was only slight, directed at tedious passages in the first act and lack of a dénouement for the character of Marceline – a criticism which has persisted. Much praise was given to Gaveaux's music, but this was not (as had been the case when Grétry was Bouilly's collaborator) such as to overshadow the merits of the libretto. *Léonore* became part of the regular repertory at the Feydeau, and remained so for some years. Its favourable reception appears to have been the catalyst that enabled Bouilly to forsake the secure but confining corridors of the Committee of Public Instruction and to devote himself again totally to the world of letters.[39]

The last performance of *Léonore* in Paris took place in 1806. By then it had been eclipsed by Bouilly's spectacular successes with *Les deux journées* and *L'abbé de l'épée*. Twenty years later, when *Fidelio* was first played in Paris, the original play had been forgotten. Bouilly's star in the theatre had also waned, and he was chiefly occupied with moral tales for children and young women. But for this *vieux conteur*, now taking up his pen to embark upon his memoirs, the recollection of La Plaine and that far-off summer of 1793 was still green. Knowing our author, it is not surprising that he may have added dramatic impact to his story by introducing a fictitious historical event as the basis of his play, and by romanticizing its first reading in that evocative setting where his destiny had been so deeply involved. For his constant preoccupation was to present 'an ever-increasing dramatic interest ... a scenario to captivate the heart and entrance the spirit' ('un intérêt toujours croissant ... formant un ensemble qui captivait le coeur et charmait l'imagination').[40] He was above all a man of the theatre.

38 *Courrier des spectacles*, 20 February 1798.   39 Bouilly, *Mes récapitulations*, ii, p. 136.
40 Ibid., p. 21.

DAVID CHARLTON

On redefinitions of 'rescue opera'

The term 'rescue opera' is suffering from a kind of automatic, self-perpetuating existence typical of the age of reproducing machines. As one result, it seems likely to mislead non-specialists into assuming that the musical theatre of the French Revolution was all of one general type, very loosely defined in various ways cited in Appendix 1, below. Such an assumption would be entirely wrong. Further, the crude generality of the phrase 'rescue opera' plays false on three levels the musical theatre that it purports to represent. Firstly, it is unable to distinguish between works of contrasting moral purpose and very different dramatic styles. Secondly, it imposes the blanket concept of 'rescue' but cannot define any other moral actions involved, and does not imply them. Thirdly, it ignores eighteenth-century perceptions of its own theatre. Perhaps these things would matter less if present definitions of 'rescue opera' were wholly accurate in themselves. But no single definition in Appendix 1 (they date from between 1940 and 1987) can be said to be so; they all, variously, fail to account for certain operas and tendencies. This is not to say that the better definitions are entirely unhelpful, or unsympathetic towards the repertory. There are indubitable concerns here with 'personal loyalty' (Grout); 'secular idealism of the age' (Dean); destruction of tyranny (Dent, and Headington) and associations with 'real-life situations' (Rosenthal and Warrack, also Grout). But these operas do not all display such things and, as we said, they exhibit enormous variations. Moreover, there is much of interest to be observed about them that finds no mention in the given definitions.

Thirty years ago R. Morgan Longyear published 'Notes on the Rescue Opera'.[1] This began with the salutary reminder that the term was essentially a twentieth-century invention, totally absent from Hugo Riemann's *Opern-Handbuch* (1887; 2nd edition, 1893) and his *Musik-Lexikon* (first issued in 1882), although it appears it was German in

---

1 R. M. Longyear, 'Notes on the Rescue Opera', *The Musical Quarterly*, xlv (1959), pp. 49–66.

origin.[2] In *Die Oper von Gluck bis Wagner* (Ulm, 1913, p. 281) by Karl M. Klob, Longyear located the phrase 'sogenannte Rettungs- oder Befreiungsstück'. By 1927 Dyneley Hussey had written, 'The type of plot [of *Léonore* and *Les deux journées*] was in vogue at the time, and the Germans, with their genius for categorisation, have invented the word *Rettungsstück* (Rescue-piece) as a label for it'.[3] Unfortunately, Longyear's article proceeds to a series of discussions predicated on five 'literary traits' that are not sufficiently comprehensive, and that raise distracting points about both genre designation and the supposed absent influence of Gothic horror. After that, there is a discussion of musical style that attempts to find 'musical traits that separate the rescue opera from the earlier varieties of *opéra comique*'. As the present article is not about music itself, it will not be appropriate to address musical style here, nor fruitful to take issue in detail with Longyear's assumptions and conclusions.[4] But I shall mention Longyear's helpful observations in due course.

Before proposing an alternative system of dramaturgical analysis, it is essential to review selected factors that the eighteenth and early nineteenth centuries saw as affecting the subject matter of this repertory. These are not intended to help establish dramaturgical criteria as such, but to establish a counterbalancing number of concepts to set against the notion of 'rescue'. Obviously, a complete exegesis of the myriad political and social references that exist in the librettos would occupy a great deal more space than we have to hand. And a complete account of the works listed in Appendix 2 would be yet longer.

It is convenient to begin with an overview provided by the most intelligent librettist, dramatist and critic of the period, François-Benoît Hoffman (1760–1828), author of *Phèdre*, *Euphrosine*, *Médée* etc. In an undated review-article, Hoffman traced an evolution of taste under the late *ancien régime* that had led to certain changes of priority on the stage.[5] Originally the all-powerful *opéra comique* audience arbitrated upon new works by applying a standard set of traditional literary values;

---

2 Longyear reports that it is also absent from G. Fink, *Wesen und Geschichte der Oper* (Leipzig, 1838) and M. Dietz, *Geschichte des musikalischen Dramas in Frankreich* (Vienna, 1885).

3 (Located by Longyear.) The citation continues, 'The characters of *Leonore* are ordinary men and women ... in everything except their intense pre-occupation with goodness or villainy. Indeed there is no essential difference between the story of Florestan's rescue by Leonore, and the thousands of popular rescues of innocent men effected, in the nick of time, by virtuous young women, who are, however, usually unmarried until the end of the film.'

4 Contentious ones would include: 'Comic elements are almost entirely eliminated', which is considered in due course; identification of Marmontel as a purveyor of 'pièces à mouchoir'; construction of 'rescue opera as a musico-literary form'; and the assumption that all dialogue operas of the earlier 1790s can be taken together as a musical-stylistic group for comparison, using the idea of rescue as a point of reference.

5 'Théâtre de l'Opéra-Comique, ou Recueil des pièces restées à ce théâtre', in *Oeuvres de F.-B. Hoffman* [ed. L. Castel] (Paris, 1829), ix, pp. 509–42.

this was natural not least because at the Parisian Comédie-Italienne (its home) spoken plays of distinction (by Marivaux, for example) alternated in the repertory with *opéras comiques*. Gradually, however, the composition of the standing *parterre* changed,[6] and lower-class citizens (see below) frequented the theatres during the 1780s. The section of the company giving spoken plays was finally pensioned off in 1790.[7] Hoffman saw this new audience as more interested in 'physical action' than 'moral action', and 'brusque, rapid movement' than 'the effect of accumulating tableaux'.

Comme les gens qui n'apportent au théâtre que des yeux et des oreilles sont infiniment plus nombreux que ceux qui y viennent avec du goût et de l'esprit, les romans dialogués, les pièces à processions, à prisons et à fracas, attirèrent bientôt la foule du peuple.[8]

Since people who take to the theatre only their eyes and ears are infinitely more numerous than those who go there with taste and intelligence, dialogued novels and shows dedicated to processions, prisons and *fracas* soon drew them in crowds.

Hoffman was especially interested in the influence of Michel-Jean Sedaine (1719–97), the great librettist of crucial works like *Richard Coeur-de-lion*. He appreciated Sedaine's theatrical abilities, but also considered that he relied excessively on 'physical motivating forces' in his later work:

Il a vu qu'une prison intéressait le peuple, il a montré deux actes de prison dans le *Déserteur*, une autre prison dans le *Comte d'Albert*, puis un château-prison dans *Barbe-Bleue*, puis une tour-prison dans *Richard Coeur-de-Lion*, puis deux prisons dans *Aucassin et Nicolette*.[9]

He saw that prisons interested people, he showed two prison acts in *Le déserteur*, another prison in *Le Comte d'Albert*, then a castle-prison in *Raoul Barbe-bleue*, then a tower prison in *Richard Coeur-de-lion*, then two prisons in *Aucassin et Nicolette*.

Thus for Hoffman (who himself contributed to the 'prison' genre in *Léon, ou Le château de Monténéro*) an implied decadence in dialogue operas was in the first place founded on merely physical excitement, such as escaping from a tower (*Aucassin*) or obtaining a last-minute reprieve, the heroine battling through crowds (*Le déserteur*); or a siege (*Richard*). In the second place, it involved an outright pandering to low taste in giving the public prison scenes, construed as part of the same tendency towards 'physical motivating forces, of themselves far more potent [than

---

6 For a general account, see D. Charlton, *Grétry and the Growth of Opéra-Comique* (Cambridge, 1986), Chapter 1, and the 'Historical Introduction' to C. D. Brenner, *The Théâtre Italien: its Repertory, 1716–1793* (Berkeley and Los Angeles, 1961), pp. 1–35.

7 Brenner, *The Théâtre Italien*, p. 34.   8 Hoffman, 'Théâtre de l'Opéra-Comique', p. 536.

9 Ibid., p. 529. For datings of operas, see Appendix 2, p. 188.

others] on the common people' ('toujours des ressorts physiques, et par cela même, bien plus puissans sur le vulgaire des spectateurs').[10] For such works, 'rescue' as the corollary of 'imprisonment' would certainly have been recognized as a criterion, and equally condemned, by Hoffman. Even though Sedaine's librettos are cleverer than the above rhetoric implies, and never duplicate themselves, we are correct to identify his work with stage actions intimately connected, in the plot, with the righting of a perceived injustice. It is no accident that his final success was *Guillaume Tell*; at the same time we are quite wrong to see him as a purveyor of mere melodramas. Sedaine's worth to his contemporaries was expressed in his election to the Académie Française in 1786.

When we attempt to define the 'new' audiences of the 1780s, it seems clear that the bourgeois backbone of commercial, manufacturing and professional people was, at least by 1787, mixed in the *parterre* with a majority of those to become known as *sans-culottes*: traders, craftsmen, labourers and so on.[11] Their presence is identified in a report of two rowdy evenings in December 1787, the first at the Comédie-Française, the second at the Comédie-Italienne. On the 18th a version of Sheridan's *The Rivals* was forced off the stage in Act 3, and on the 26th Grétry's new work, *Le prisonnier anglais*, libretto by François-Georges Fouques, called Desfontaines, was also put an early end to.

On le croiroit à la manière indécente & grossière, à l'habitude barbare que nos Parterres contractent depuis quelque temps, & au ton [d']irrévérence avec lequel ils écoutent, accueillent ou repoussent arbitrairement les ouvrages ... la liberté qu'on accorde aux spectateurs dégénère souvent en une licence répréhensible, & qu'il est à craindre qu'une trop longue indulgence n'accoutume une jeunesse indisciplinée, sans principes, & sans éducation, à des excès ...

Il se trouve toujours des gens honnêtes dans nos Parterres, mais c'est le petit nombre, principalement dans les Parterres debout. Des Artisans de la plus basse classe, des Perruquiers, des Coiffeurs de femme, des gens sans aveu; voilà ce qui les compose le plus ordinairement; voilà les Juges des talens.[12]

One would think [the public had become artistic executioners], judging from the indecent, coarse, barbaric habit that the *parterres* acquired some time ago, and from the irreverent tone with which they hear, welcome, or arbitrarily reject works ... the liberty that has been granted to the spectators often degenerates into reprehensible licence [among] undisciplined, unprincipled and uneducated youth ...

There are always honest people in our *parterres*, but they are in the minority, especially when standing is customary [i.e. at the Comédie-Italienne]. Artisans of

10 Ibid., p. 529. Hoffman saw Sedaine as the father of the nineteenth-century *mélodrame*, as practised by Pixérécourt.
11 See the definitions in G. Rudé, *The Crowd in the French Revolution* (Oxford, 1959; 2nd edn, 1972), p. 12.
12 'Comédies Françoise et Italienne', *Mercure de France*, 5 January 1788, p. 39.

the lowest class, wigmakers, ladies' hairdressers, disreputable people; those are the ones who usually make up [the *parterres*]; those are the judges of talents.

'Realism is the keynote of the genuine rescue opera', said Longyear,[13] and that is obviously what 1780s audiences liked, if by 'realism' one means 'audience self-identification': the historical reality of medieval subjects like *Richard Coeur-de-lion* or *Raoul Barbe-bleue* was a matter of taste. But 'reality' at this time signified more than a physical approach to dramaturgy and moral content. It went together with exploitation of contemporary characters, both higher and lower in class (as in *Le Comte d'Albert*);[14] with allusions in librettos to that unification of classes ardently desired by many French people (as will be seen in *Raoul, Sire de Créqui*); with a taste for spectacular stage pictures and effects; and eventually, after 1789, 'realism' broke free in dramatized versions of recent history itself. None of these elements, however, was the exclusive legacy of operas with 'rescue' episodes. They were part and parcel of the 'group psychology', the 'group fantasy' of their age. The degree to which a general impulse was felt towards portrayal of the whole of society in a sympathetic and unifying light is nowhere clearer than in the formulation of the Comte de Lacépède. In his drily methodical *La poétique de la musique* (1785) he waxed surprisingly lyrical on the composer's need to subsume all 'poor and suffering humanity' (as he called it) in *comédie-lyrique*:

… qu'il parcoure les diverses classes de la société, elles peuvent toutes devenir le sujet de ses tableaux … qu'il ne dédaigne pas la cabane du pauvre & du malheureux …qu'il aprenne à goûter le plaisir de la pitié bienfaisante & consolatrice: qu'il mêle ses pleurs à ceux de ces victimes innocentes du sort …[15]

Let [the musician] range over the various classes of society, they may all become the subject of his pictures … let him not disdain the hut of the poor and unfortunate … let him learn to taste the pleasure of beneficial and consoling pity: let him mingle his tears with those of such innocent victims of fate.

Such 'victims' were not portrayed, however, as actual prisoners before 1789.

Through the survival of Bouilly's libretto, *Léonore*, in its incarnation as *Fidelio*, the idea seems to have arisen that there existed a 'rescue' type of opera which has (at least by implication) a certain exclusive relationship to reality through its portrayal of actual events: 'Some rescue operas were based on contemporary real-life incidents'; 'Many of the stories, arising out of the Revolution, were supposedly based on fact'; 'the

13 Longyear, 'Notes on the Rescue Opera', p. 53.
14 The imprisoned Count d'Albert is helped to escape by a street porter, who has himself earlier been rescued by the count from serious assault.
15 B. G. E. M. de Lacépède, *La poétique de la musique* (Paris, 1785, reprinted 1970), ii, 285–6.

French Revolution and the closer involvement of opera with real-life situations'.[16] (Bouilly's *Léonore* does no more than call itself, as others of a different type had been called, a *'fait historique'*. The tale of its supposed prototype action appeared only in the author's *Mes récapitulations* and, as David Galliver has shown elsewhere in the present volume, is wide open to doubt.)

A moment's reflection will remind us of the wider ramifications of this question, and of its importance for the historical opera of the nineteenth century. Those 'rescue' works that enjoyed a perceived privileged relation to historical fact were merely part of a growing body of historically-based librettos identifiable before 1789, which spoke by analogy to the national political situation of the *ancien régime*. Some were seen at the Opéra: *Ernelinde* (1767, revived 1773), *Péronne sauvée* (1783) and *Arvire et Evélina* (1788).[17] Others were seen at the Comédie-Italienne: *Henri IV* (1774), *Les mariages samnites* (1776) and *Richard Coeur-de-lion* (1784).[18] Even domestic subject matter, however, was sometimes taken from the 'real' world, but for the same purpose of reflecting moral imperatives on the France of the 1770s and 1780s.

If the above works aimed at a national message, others partook of a tradition of 'humanity' operas, originating in the moral reform of *opéra comique* before 1750. Their moral lesson was in time directed towards the ruling classes, particularly in their attitude to humbler individuals: an example is Marmontel's *Silvain* (1769), which took the poaching laws as its realistic mainspring. Another was the popular vaudeville comedy *Les solitaires de Normandie* (1788), showing a local duchess, in a fable believed to have been taken from actual life, who takes on responsibility for a destitute, homeless family on her land.[19] Fables were also used to show the humbler classes capable of setting an example to a ruling individual: Monvel's *Julie* or Desfontaines's *Le droit du seigneur*.[20] In the case of Monvel's *Les trois fermiers* (1777) the libretto was explicitly based on an incident reported in the *Ephémérides du citoyen*, vol. 2 (1769), in which the farmers and peasants of a landowner in

16 W. Dean in *The New Grove Dictionary of Music and Musicians*, ed. S. Sadie (London, 1980), xv, p. 755; G. Martin, *The Opera Companion* (London, 1962), p. 188; and H. Rosenthal and J. Warrack, *The Concise Oxford Dictionary of Opera* (Oxford, 1964; 2nd edn, 1979), p. 413.
17 *Ernelinde* (Poinsinet, rev. Sedaine, set by Philidor), based on Scandinavian history; *Péronne sauvée* (Sauvigny, set by Dezède), based on the siege of Péronne in 1536; *Arvire et Evélina* (Guillard, set by Sacchini), based on the Roman occupation of Anglesey as recounted in William Mason's *Caractacus*.
18 *Henri IV* (Rosoi, set by J. P. A. Martini), complete with historically derived dialogues; *Les mariages samnites* (Rozoy, set by Grétry), based on Roman (fictionalized) history; *Richard Coeur-de-lion* (Sedaine, set by Grétry), based on events around the year 1194.
19 See *Mercure de France*, 26 January 1788, pp. 183–5: 'L'Anecdote qui a donné lieu à cet Opéra comique, est connue depuis long-temps. Madame de Sillery l'a célébrée dans un ouvrage qui a été beaucoup lu & beaucoup loué'.
20 *Julie* (1772), set by Dezède; *Le droit du seigneur* (1784), set by J. P. A. Martini. These are discussed briefly in Charlton, *Grétry*, pp. 223–4 and 281–3.

Lower Brittany joined together to raise 300,000 *écus* to prevent his estates being sold to financiers and presented him with eight fine horses so his wife could appear at church 'd'une manière convenable'.[21] Monvel's object was to 'honour humanity' in an 'ennobling' spectacle – that is, to raise all classes to one level.

All these musical stage works displayed a material (as well as moral) dilemma, in some cases taken from life, that was 'rescued' by humane action. The evolutionary line to *Léonore* was uninterrupted. And even after 1789 it was not just the 'rescue', of whatever sort, that sustained plots taken from life. Life itself became theatrical art in versions of ceremonials or bellicose events, like *Le siège de Thionville* and *Le nouveau d'Assas*.[22] Anti-Terror works existed just as 'factually' as pro-Terror ones. Thus, F.-B. Hoffman's *Le brigand*, produced in July 1795 with music by Kreutzer, although placed in seventeenth-century Scotland, 'deceived no-one': 'its brigand is the prototype of the proconsuls of the Reign of Terror, and one of the most fervent apostles of the god Marat' ('son brigand est le prototype des proconsuls du règne de la terreur, et l'un des plus fervens apôtres du dieu Marat').[23] Conscious of the pervasive presence of social comment in librettos, writers like Longyear and Dean have identified 'rescue' operas with pervasive expressions of this sort: 'Almost all . . . contain passages that indicate the social protest of the times' and 'It . . . often carried a social message'.[24] Others, more circumspect, are more correct to refer instead to vagaries like '[the assurance] that freedom would always triumph over tyranny' (see Headington and others, in Appendix 1). Many operas using 'rescue' episodes seem, nevertheless, basically outside the politically 'humanitarian' and socially realistic tradition: *Eliza*; the two *Paul et Virginie* works; the two *La caverne* works; and the two chief 'Gothic horror' works, Dalayrac's *Camille* and his *Léon*. These are all set in variously fantastic or exotic *milieux*, and their relation to contemporary politics ranges from the non-existent to the temporary. In the latter case, for example in Méhul's *La caverne*, after the *banditti* have been rooted out of their lair, the closing vaudeville referred to the end of the Terror and the need for general toleration: 'Mes amis, ne détruisons pas'.[25] But the source of the fable, as everyone would have known, was Alain-René Lesage's picaresque novel *Gil Blas* (1715–35).

---

21 Untitled introduction to *Les trois fermiers* (Paris, 1777).
22 *Le siège de Thionville* (Saulnier and Dutilh, set by L. Jadin), Opéra, 2 June 1793; *Le nouveau d'Assas* (Dejaure, set by H.-M. Berton), Comédie-Italienne, 15 October 1790.
23 'Avertissement' (by ? L. Castel) in *Oeuvres de F.-B. Hoffman*, ii, pp. 3–4.
24 Longyear, 'Notes on the Rescue Opera', p. 52; Dean, in *The New Grove* xv, p. 755.
25 This unpublished opera is discussed, and the libretto pieced together, in M. E. C. Bartlet, 'Etienne Nicolas Méhul and Opera during the French Revolution, Consulate and Empire' diss., Chicago University, 1982), pp. 1797–8.

We shall shortly discuss the concept of imprisonment, that ubiquitous state referred to by Hoffman. A key element of its popularity was, doubtless, a wide social repugnance for the exercise of arbitrary power. But another was surely the rise of the Gothic fantasy. The *Bibliothèque bleue* of popular literary tradition had probably never forsaken medieval tales, and in 1765 *The Castle of Otranto* by Horace Walpole was first issued in London. It was rapidly followed by a French translation in 1767, with a new edition in 1774.[26] This story, as is well known, defined many characteristics of the new genre, such as the late medieval setting in its oppressive castle and dungeons; its central figure of the all-powerful tyrant (Manfred), with his nefarious designs on the virginal Isabella; its supernatural strokes and fateful warnings and its final resolution in Manfred's acceptance of religion and atonement. Walpole also deliberately injected humour, in the form of the naive servant Bianca, and justified this by reference to Shakespeare's example, specifically opposing the ideas of Voltaire.[27] Bianca's lines such as, 'Oh, dear lady, I would not speak to a ghost for the world'[28] find their echo in England in, for example, a 1799 adaptation of Dalayrac's *Camille*: 'You don't mind a ghost or two, do you?'[29] This line is spoken to the comic servant Mousic, adapted from the equivalent character of Fabio in *Camille*. The same blend of horror with verbal humour occurs in *Léon*, where a comic valet (Longino) enters in Act 2; he wants to hear a song about ghosts, and is also a classic coward. Longyear mentions the comic intrigue in Act 2 of Cherubini's *Lodoiska*, but misses the wider significance of the comic servant Varbel in the same opera, declaring that 'Comic elements are almost entirely eliminated from the libretto [of 'rescue operas']'; later, he rejects both 'the idea of the supernatural' and 'Gothic horror' from the same repertory.[30] This is surely to fly in the face of evidence. Even as early as 1769 Sedaine's *Le déserteur* (glancing at Shakespeare) had worked up prolonged juxtaposition of the comic within its prison scenes, mixing reactions of sentiment and mirth. This is the opera that Longyear himself understandably classified as 'the ancestor of the rescue opera' (p. 50). Gothic influence, escape from a tower and humorous detail were first memorably staged in Sedaine's *Aucassin et Nicolette* (1779), whose comic shep-

26 *Le château d'Otrante*, translated by M[arc-Antoine] E[idous] (Amsterdam 'et se trouve à Paris', 1767).
27 'Preface to the Second Edition', in *Three Gothic Novels*, ed. P. Fairclough (Harmondsworth, 1968), pp. 44–7.
28 Ibid., p. 76.
29 *The Captive of Spillburg … as performed at the Theatre Royal, Drury Lane* (London, 1799), Act 1 scene ii.
30 Longyear, 'Notes on the Rescue Opera', pp. 50 and 54.

herd appears in the closing act.[31] And *Aucassin*'s successor in style and ambition, *Richard Coeur-de-lion*, is far from excluding humour, particularly in its first act.

During the 1780s the Gothic influence spread even more notably in all the arts.[32] The dark towers beginning to find representation on the stage were being drawn from life, engraved and published in the *Voyage pittoresque de la France*.[33] Striking prefigurations of Gothic horror in French opera were seen, again mingled with the comic, in Paisiello's *La frascatana*, produced at the Opéra by a visiting company in 1779. The main female character, Violante, is abducted by her tutor Don Fabrizio and taken at night to a 'lofty, ruinous tower ... with a door that shuts by a large bolt', adjacent to his own house.[34] He shuts her inside; her lover, the shepherd Nardone, endeavours to scare Fabrizio by echoing his words. When the French parody of *La frascatana* was seen in 1780 at Strasbourg and then throughout France (as *L'Infante de Zamora*) the adapter, Framery, retained all three elements: the nocturnal tower, the imprisonment and the scaring tactic.[35] In her book *Le roman terrifiant* Alice M. Killen mentions *Camille* as part of the tendency towards 'des thèmes lugubres', if not 'le genre "noir"'; but she counts *Léon* as 'une imitation assez prononcée' of Anne Radcliffe's *The Mysteries of Udolpho*, as was supposed at the time in the press.[36]

Extremely important as a link between the age of *Aucassin* and the burgeoning of 'dark tower' operas ten years later were Gothic melodramas. *Pierre de Provence* (1781) gave as its source 'un trait Historique *véritable* et *remarquable* de la très-illustre *Bibliothèque bleue*'.[37] The staging at the Ambigu-Comique included in scene ii Maguelonne appearing at a grilled window of a tower, bewailing her fate. In 1791 Cherubini's heroine similarly appeared in the first finale of *Lodoiska*. The year 1782 saw the Ambigu company's production of *Dorothée*, in which this medieval heroine is rescued from the clutches of a lustful

---

31 Medieval subject-matter in opera was never far removed from the supernatural, as in *tragédies lyriques* like Lully's *Roland*, even if the later *ancien régime* tendency was to remove the supernatural.

32 For music, see G. Cucuel, 'Le Moyen Age dans les opéras-comiques du XVIIIᵉ siècle', *Revue du dix-huitième siècle*, ii (1914), pp. 56–71; and T. Gérold, 'Le réveil en France, au XVIIIᵉ siècle, de l'intérêt pour la musique profane du moyen âge', in *Mélanges de musicologie offerts à M. Lionel de la Laurencie* (Paris, 1933), pp. 223–34.

33 First volume issued in 1784, as *Description générale et particulière de la France*, ed. J. B. de La Borde and J. E. Guettard.

34 As described in the King's Theatre translation, *La frascatana: a Comic Opera* (London, 1778), Act 2 scene v.

35 *L'infante de Zamora, comédie en quatre actes, mêlée d'ariettes* (Paris and Strasbourg, 1781), pp. 63–72: 'Le théâtre change & représente une forêt obscure; dans le fond on voit une vieille tour, au pied de laquelle est la porte d'un souterrein', etc.

36 A. M. Killen, *Le roman terrifiant, ou roman noir de Walpole à Anne Radcliffe et son influence sur la littérature française jusqu'en 1840* (Paris, 1923), pp. 107 and 117.

37 *Pierre de Provence et la belle Maguelonne* (Paris, 1781), p. v.

mayor who has imprisoned her and then almost succeeded in burning her at the stake.[38] Such works epitomized Hoffman's quality of 'physical action' at the expense of 'moral action': in the sense that they reduced a fable to its lowest common denominator – rescue – leaving the moral to look after itself, one might be tempted to see them as history's truest 'rescue operas', albeit works lacking singers.

It is now convenient to take stock of the collected definitions in Appendix 1 and to identify which of their aspects seem most valid. Dent's prescription is singularly narrow, and potentially therefore most accurate. Because it does not account for operas such as Les deux journées and Eliza (which have nothing to do with tyrants or prisons) no-one else has accepted it. Grout's ideas isolate an important quality we have not discussed so far: 'suspense', or 'a new spirit of urgency'. The importance of this is obvious when one compares most works of the 1790s with neo-classical precedents such as Orphée or Alceste (that is, rescues from the underworld, the last-named, especially, concentrating upon Revolution-period qualities like 'humanity', 'conjugal devotion' and 'exemplary loyalty'), or with Baroque precedents like Alcina (which is centred on Ruggiero's rescue from Alcina's enchantment, and indeed from her island as a whole).[39] But can we assert that 'suspense' is a quality characteristic of no other type of opera in the 1790s? Clearly not, when we consider Guillaume Tell or Médée. Yet it is a better criterion than those merely specifying a rescue 'at the last [moment]', for this quite excludes several important works (Raoul, Sire de Créqui; Les deux journées) and borderline examples like Méhul's La caverne.[40] 'Suspense' was certainly a far more universal demand; it had been a quality essential to Le déserteur, and is apt to almost every work in Appendix 2.

The criterion of individual heroism, frequently advanced in definitions, is often present. Yet it does not adequately define those many cases where rescue is effected by an armed group. The latter convey a different stage morality, even if the assault has been instigated by a principal character, as Blondel instigates the siege that resolves Richard Coeur-de-lion. The group is bound primarily to express physical action, whereas individuals effecting a release are bound to convey a greater moral conviction, which their physical efforts symbolize. The epitome of

38 Dorothée, pantomime à spectacle (Paris, 1782). Even this violent melodrama, in which the mayor himself is beaten and finally thrown on the flames, has a historical tendency, and possibly a political subtext, being set in Orléans at the time of Joan of Arc.

39 Rosenthal and Warrack's definition of a 'rescue opera' in the Concise Oxford Dictionary of Opera would appear to include Handel's Alcina within its ambit (see Appendix 1); other definitions do not reach back so far in time.

40 See C. Headington and others (Appendix 1): 'the imprisoned hero or heroine is rescued at the last'. Raoul is released in the central act; in Les deux journées there is a deus ex machina in the form of a message carried in by Mikéli in Act 3 scene x; and in Méhul's La caverne the principals are rescued in the central act (see Bartlet, 'Etienne Nicolas Méhul', p. 1797).

what we might therefore call the 'moral rescue' is undoubtedly the story of Mikéli, the water-carrier in *Les deux journées*, who uses his cunning much more than his muscles.[41] The epitome of the 'physical rescue' is seen in Cherubini's and Kreutzer's *Lodoiska* operas, each of which ends with a spectacular scene of destruction effected by an army of Tartars, who have only a generalized connection with the relevant tyrant, and a secondary connection with the eponymous heroine. Individual heroism is lost in the mêlée, or subsumed within it.

It is nevertheless possible that, in the sense in which a fictionalized army represents mass heroism, some operas analogically portray the heroism of the French people: something akin to what Winton Dean terms 'the secular idealism of the age'. After all, the whole point of *Les rigueurs du cloître* is that the convent is invaded by a detachment of the National Guard itself, whose officer justifies its action in the name of 'humanity' and of 'the law', which now (in Revolutionary France) give back its inhabitants to 'nature' and 'society'.[42] The words of the final chorus express the true moral thrust of *Les rigueurs* and of certain later operas showing rescue from affliction within dark towers:

> O liberté! déesse de la France
> Plutôt mourir que de vivre sans toi,
> Du despotisme étouffer la puissance,
> N'obéir jamais qú'à la loi …[43]

(Oh Liberty! Goddess of France, death is preferable to life without you; to snuff out despotic power, obedient only to the law …)

That is, they ought morally to be called 'Liberty' or 'Liberation', or even 'Bastille' operas. Just as models of the Bastille were carried in certain public festivals of the 1790s as symbols of the feudal past that had given way to liberty, so, too, operas of release from unjust detention (the latter manifest as the result of exertion of arbitrary power) express in fictionalized forms the actions of 14 July 1789.[44] Even before that date, the Bastille was an object regarded as redolent of a Gothically feudal past. When the writer and propagandist L.-S. Mercier envisaged the year 2440 in a Utopian book issued in 1770 (afterwards banned), he envisaged a demolished Bastille along with other marks of rational progress.[45] 'Rumour and pamphleteers [says a recent historian] had for

41 He constructs a secret compartment in his water-cart for Count Armand, but the process of construction is not dramatized.
42 On this opera, see K. Pendle, '*A bas les couvents!* Anticlerical Sentiment in French Opera of the 1790s', *The Music Review*, xlii (1981), pp. 22–45.
43 J. Fiévée, *Les rigueurs du cloître* ([Paris], n.d.), pp. 41–2.
44 On the festivals and their meanings, see M. Ozouf, *Festivals and the French Revolution*, trans. A. Sheridan (Cambridge, Massachusetts, and London, 1988); a model Bastille is referred to on p. 70. An obvious operatic 'Bastille' incident is the freeing of prisoners in Act 1 of Méhul's *Doria, ou La tyrannie détruite*; see Bartlet, 'Etienne Nicolas Méhul', p. 1796.
45 J. A. Leith, *The Idea of Art as Propaganda in France, 1750–1799* (Toronto, 1965), pp. 88–90.

years been disseminating a picture of its dungeons packed with wretched state prisoners ... The significance of the fall of the Bastille lies in its symbolic value.'[46]

At the same time, it is important to grant that an individual opera featuring a rescue of some sort, even one containing individual heroism, can display a concluding moral that does not concern itself simply (if at all) with 'liberté', the Terror or tyrannical injustice. Instead, it may build on such things, as though established conventions, to say something else. Hoffman's Gothic-influenced *Léon*, for example, uses a recurring chanson that closes with the homily that applies generally to the work:

> La bonne ou mauvaise action
> A tôt ou tard sa récompense.

The good or bad act is recompensed sooner or later.

Another of the opera's recurrent notions is the deceptive relation between appearance and reality. Similarly coherent is Bouilly's moral throughout *Les deux journées*, again associated with recurring musical material in a chanson: 'Un bienfait n'est jamais perdu' ('A good turn is never wasted'). These two operas make various allusions to the hope afforded by religion, even if their stress concerns (in Bouilly's words) 'the service of humanity'. Marsollier's libretto for *Léhéman* (1801) was on one level perceived at the time as a 'demi-Richard', that is, an epigone of *Richard Coeur-de-lion*;[47] but it too developed the larger-scale moral refrain, this time in a *romance* of hope called later by C. M. von Weber 'a comforting star', in that it periodically encourages the eventually successful Hungarians against the Austrians.[48] By now, the accoutrements of a rescue, and the sophisticated handling of this recurring *romance* theme, are techniques cladding what is a plot taken from history, comparable as such with the works mentioned earlier in notes 17 and 18: the revolt of Prince Rákóczi II of Transylvania in 1703–11 against Leopold I of Austria. Clearly, a work such as this must be accepted as containing many different resonances, including religious hope, and to have taken up the challenge laid down in Sedaine's *Richard* of a historical *opéra comique* in which rescue was not the most important aspect. For, in fact, Sedaine never originally intended the siege as his dénouement, and conceived *Richard* as a kind of Orpheus

46 A. Cobban, *A History of Modern France* (3rd edn, Harmondsworth, 1963), i, pp. 149–50.

47 'Spectacles', in the *Gazette nationale ou Le moniteur universel*, no. 132, 12 pluviôse an X, p. 529: 'une espèce de drame à spectacle dans lequel le citoyen Marsollier a imité Sedaine, ses effets pantomimes et ses coups de théâtre ... C'est ... si l'on veut, un *demi-Richard*'.

48 Weber's review is translated in *Carl Maria von Weber: Writings on Music*, ed. J. Warrack (Cambridge, 1981), pp. 82–4. Further notes on *Léhéman* are in D. Charlton, 'Motif and Recollection in Four Operas of Dalayrac', *Soundings*, vii (1978), pp. 38–61.

opera, in which the rescuing means was as important as the historically necessary end.[49]

In view of the many differences we have identified in the 'rescue' works so far mentioned, it is necessary to advance ideas towards a new theoretical framework. This rests on three main supports, which I shall treat as separate categories of opera: (1) 'tyrant' operas, (2) 'exemplary action' operas and (3) 'judgment' operas. It goes without saying that some operas partake of characteristics from more than one of these categories. A fourth category is also desirable, containing relevant works by Sedaine, whose inner and moral designs stand apart from, as well as antecedent to, most of the others; this must be explored elsewhere, however. It must be said that, for present purposes, analysis of given genre labels – whether works were called 'comédie', 'fait historique', 'pantomime', 'opéra', 'comédie héroïque', 'drame mêlé d'ariettes' or 'drame lyrique' – is beside the point. Examples of all these are to be found in Appendix 2.

The phrase 'arbitrary power' is actually employed in Bouilly's *Léonore* when Pizare opens the warning letter in Act 1:

Pizare: ... les prisons d'état que vous commandez, renferment plusieurs victimes du pouvoir arbitraire

Pizare: (quoting the letter): ... the state prisons that you command contain several victims of arbitrary power

and this was taken over into the German libretto for Beethoven: 'die Staatsgefängnisse, denen Sie vorstehen, mehrere Opfer willkürlicher Gewalt enthalten'. Almost all so-called rescue operas involve victims of arbitrary power, whether or not this is portrayed in terms of detention. Physical detention was a ubiquitous emblem of such power; hatred of summary justice was keenly felt in eighteenth-century France, where the *lettre de cachet* existed as the unchallengeable arm of monarchy by divine right. Structurally, however, it is useful to isolate 'tyrant operas', defined as works in which the tyrant, or exerciser of arbitrary power, is represented, and works where no such person plays a part. The latter will form Type 2.

When arbitrary exercise of power was overcome through defeat of its exerciser, this figure became the embodiment of everything morally repugnant, the obverse of liberty and justice. Either justice or vengeance was required to act against a tyrant at the close of such operas. These Type 1 works are first cousins to *Don Giovanni*, partly because they present an explicit moral resolution to the issue of arbitrary

---

49 In fact, the siege was not part of the work for its first fourteen months of life, and constituted only its third version. See Charlton, *Grétry*, especially pp. 241 and 248–50.

power.[50] Tyrant figures are male, except for one, and detain their victims out of different motives, often greed, lust or jealousy. Post-1789 examples might graft political references onto these plots. Kreutzer's *Lodoiska* explains the rift between Lodoiska's father and her lover (Lovinski) by the fact that Lovinski voted in Warsaw for Poniatowski as king, the latter being 'un homme vertueux', whereas her father obviously held the opposing political view, never specified (see Act 1 scene iii). But these issues are minor compared to the treachery of Boleslas and his defeat by the Tartars. In *Léonore* Florestan has been victimized for exposing Pizare's 'crimes', 'abuse of authority' and 'outrages'.[51] But the rest is vague. Type 1 works take to one extreme the duty-love syndrome of classical French drama and equivalent *opere serie*: the leading male character, who is in a position of power and is forced into doing the right thing in the end, or else is overcome with force and delivered to justice. Sometimes he is punished by his own conscience, in the tradition of Walpole's Manfred, Prince of Otranto, who finally abdicates. Coradin, in Méhul's and Hoffman's *Euphrosine*, is a rather similar character who repents in the end, as do the Gil Blas and Roland of *La caverne* in Le Sueur's setting. A related 'model' of correction and repentance is perceptible in the case of Alberti, the sadistic jealous husband in Dalayrac's *Camille*.[52] Medieval feuding lies behind the abductions in *Léon*, in which opera the tyrant is finally entrusted – however unconvincingly, in context – to 'la justice seule' that shall decide his fate. Dourlinski, in Cherubini's *Lodoiska*, is finally destined for lifelong imprisonment himself. All these tyrants have a certain developed relationship with their victims; when the latter are women, rape is inevitably the implicit objective (this, too, stems from *Otranto*). These aspects, with the widespread presence of jealousy, also betray the connection with the operatic past. In the case of Sedaine's *Raoul Barbe-bleue*, of course, murder rather than rape is the danger that is averted; this opera was a turning-point in respect of the mortal vengeance wreaked upon Raoul, and in respect of its concluding sentiments, which define Raoul as a monster (musically and dramatically) and freedom from him as a general or social benefit as much as a private one:

> Choeur général: Ce tyran exécrable,
> Ce monstre abominable
> Expire sous vos coups,
> Et sa mort nous venge tous.

---

50 Included in Type 1 would be *Aucassin et Nicolette*, *Raoul Barbe-bleue*, both versions of *La caverne*, both of *Lodoiska*, *Léon*, Méhul's *Euphrosine* and *Camille*.
51 J. N. Bouilly, *Léonore, ou L'amour conjugal* (Paris, an VII), pp. 24 and 29.
52 As the character Laurette reports, 'La pitié l'a emporté. Qu'elle [i.e. Camille] vive, s'est-il écrié . . .'. But Alberti yields only under pressure of an order from the King of Naples, as well as on the part of his nephew Lorédan.

(This execrable tyrant, this abominable monster dies by your hand, and his death avenges us all.)

Social benefit, naturally, was the moral objective behind *Les rigueurs du cloître* too; though the tyrant figure was an openly venal abbess, her institution as a whole is the object of ethical attack, and collectively obliged to 'repent' by being abolished.[53]

The tendency of Type 1 works is to conclude with the 'physical rescue' rather than the 'moral rescue', as discussed earlier. Type 2, or 'exemplary action' operas, tend to stress the role of individual action; perhaps they echo the role of the saviour in a Christian sense. They also exclude the tyrant figure as such, though one may exist in the imaginative background.[54] Victims in these works fall into misfortune for various reasons, ranging from a misdemeanour for which they are arraigned (Count d'Albert, for duelling), to political opposition (Count Armand, the *parlement* representative in *Les deux journées*) and individual *force majeure* (King Richard, Raoul de Créqui). Their extrication therefore also illustrates a mixture of moral purpose, but one usually centred on some individual concept of humanity. They typically express the interdependence of individuals. In *Le Comte d'Albert*, for example, Sedaine explained in his libretto how he modified the moral in La Fontaine's source fable of the lion and the rat to show interdependence of great and small, common people with those of higher birth. (*Richard Coeur-de-lion*, however, remained simply an example of devoted friendship.) Exemplary acts of charity or friendship were commonplace as subjects of paintings, of course; and the emerging fashion for oath-taking scenes could be related to the same issues. Raoul de Créqui, in Dalayrac's work, has been incarcerated by a boorish enemy who is never seen; his release and full restoration are celebrations of humanely justified loyalty between a lord and his people, and of the pure humanity of all young people, which is seen as exemplary. (Raoul is released by the bravery and humanity of the children of his own gaoler.) Créqui's starving son, Craon, says to these same children in Act 1 scene ii, 'misfortune teaches me that we are all equal' ('le malheur m'apprend que nous sommes égaux'), thus enunciating a certain levelling-down of high- to low-born. In Grétry's opera Count d'Albert is finally welcomed home by his dependent families into a state of ideal social equilibrium.

53 Needless to say, the victim, Lucile, has been committed to the convent by a corrupt man, never seen. Lucile's counterpart in Diderot's *La religieuse* (1760, published 1796) is subjected to quasi-rape by the prioress; and in de Sade's *Justine* (1792) the victim's rapes, by religious and other tyrants, form the centre of attention. Karin Pendle's 'A bas les couvents!' analyses other relevant fictions.
54 Main Type 2 works are *Le déserteur*, *Le Comte d'Albert*, *Le prisonnier anglais*, *Raoul, Sire de Créqui*, *Les deux journées* and *Richard Coeur-de-lion*.

'Tyrant' operas particularly expressed the destruction of the old, and of injustice; 'exemplary action' operas particularly expressed the shape of the new: unity and fraternity.

Bouilly's *Léonore*, viewed from such perspectives, had the best of both worlds. Its structural significance is that it neatly combined tendencies of plot from Types 1 and 2: Pizare's downfall and Léonore's exemplary action. This gave it an exceptional force, as did the choice of a wife as rescuer of her husband. The only notable precedent for this was *Le Comte d'Albert*, where the countess is helped by Antoine (the street-porter) in staging a tableau to cover her husband's escape, and thereby puts her safety at some risk. Le Sueur's *La caverne* includes a husband in disguise, seeking his captured wife, but the plot is not otherwise comparable.

Léonore also developed another characteristic further than had been done in these operas: the portrayal of suffering. Whereas Type 1 operas did not much dwell on the human suffering of its victims, Type 2 operas could use such suffering to increase the effect of the counterbalancing act of humanity. Since 1769 performances of *Le déserteur* had shown the prolonged desperation of Alexis under his sentence of death. In *Raoul, Sire de Créqui* new stress on physical details made injustice bite all the harder: Raoul's chamber (which is seen) has no adequate roof, causing him to sleep on wet ground; he is close-chained, long-bearded, fed small amounts of black bread only, and 'must have all the appearance of the most profound misery'.[55] Some years later Bouilly's Florestan suffered yet more terribly: he explains himself,

ces vêtemens pourris par l'humidité de ce cachot, forment sur mon corps une glace mortelle ... si vous saviez ce que je souffre! ... Par pitié, une seule goutte d'eau, pour rafraîchir un peu mes entrailles brûlantes ...[56]

Rotten from the dampness in this cell, my clothes are forming a deathly coat of ice on my body ... if you knew what I am suffering! ... For pity's sake, a single drop of water, to refresh my burning entrails a little ...

By the time of Bouilly's *Les deux journées*, however, the concept of suffering had shifted from the physical to the psychological. Rejecting the convention of the imprisoning space (except for its vestigial appearance as the water barrel), he left his refugees 'on the run', forcing them to use their wits to survive, and interacting with Mikéli throughout Acts 1 and 2 instead of being united superficially with this artisan and representative of the common people. Armand and his wife, after all, are not shown as paternalistic landowners, but representatives themselves,

---

55 J.-M. Boutet de Monvel, *Raoul, Sire de Créqui* (Paris, 1791), Act 2 scenes i–iii. Raoul's aria in scene iii, recounting a dream about his wife, may have inspired Florestan's aria in *Léonore*.
56 J.-N. Bouilly, *Léonore, ou L'amour conjugal*, p. 30.

hunted by agents of Mazarin.[57] Thus the specificity of political reference
and its social lessons took the 'humanitarian' libretto further than ever
before. In fact, like *Léhéman* a year later, it can be regarded as an
evolutionary stage in the emergent historical opera in France, using
'rescue' conventions for wider dramatic ends. Its avowed seventeenth-
century historical basis is more significant, in short, than the rumour that
it was based on an incident in the 1790s.[58] And Mikéli in fact helps the
couple to 'rescue themselves' by his example.

'Rescue' operas of Types 1 and 2 thus, perhaps, developed con-
tingently and led to the nineteenth century by making their victims into
specifically historical representatives of social groups or classes. But
Type 3 operas partook essentially neither of history, nor of the Gothic
prison, nor of ostentatious 'humanity'. The operas concerned are
nevertheless important: the two *Paul et Virginie* works (Favières and
Kreutzer, 1791; Dubreuil and Le Sueur, 1794), *Mélidore et Phrosine*
(Arnault and Méhul, 1794) and *Eliza* (1794) by Saint-Cyr and Cherubini. Bernadin de Saint-Pierre's novel, *Paul et Virginie* (1788), reaches its
tragic climax in the storm that destroys Virginie as she is starting
unwillingly on her sea journey towards a decadent Europe from the idyll
in Mauritius. The operas both rescue her, but take over the storm as the
essential focus.[59] A near-tragic storm in *Mélidore* resolves the emotional
triangle between Phrosine, her lover (Mélidore) and her obsessive
brother Jule. In *Eliza* the painter Florindo, imagining himself crossed in
love, seeks death in the heights of the St Bernard pass. During a storm an
avalanche is precipitated, but Florindo is saved. These operas stand
apart in their depiction of Nature both as visible scenery and as the
means of intervention in human affairs. Visible nature is heightened
through exoticism, whether of equatorial heat or glacial cold, but the
effect is no different in context from Mrs Radcliffe's descriptions, for
example, of Gascony and the Pyrenees in *The Mysteries of Udolpho*
(1794). This is a Nature potentially symbolizing the immanent presence
of God; and Radcliffe's novels 'were adapted for the stage [in France]
almost as soon as they were translated into French'.[60] In Saint-Pierre the
reader is left in no doubt that the storm brings retribution not only to the
immediate cast of characters but also, by extension, to a corrupt

57 Armand is described as 'président à mortier du parlement de Paris'; the action is set in 1647; he
has dared to accuse Mazarin in the queen's presence, even to threaten him with the law, 's'il ne
cessait de dévaster la France'.
58 Some continuities in the French historical opera are explored in D. Charlton, 'The Dramaturgy
of *Grand Opéra*: Some Origins', in *Atti del XIV congresso della Società Internazionale di
Musicologia*.
59 Kreutzer's storm is an especially remarkable design, 415 bars in length and very closely
controlled in tonal movement.
60 Killen, *Le roman terrifiant*, p. 109; the first group dates from 1798, both plays and melodramas.

civilization. In *Mélidore* the storm ends the incestuous passions of Jule. Coleridge wrote in 1798 of 'the beauty of the inanimate impregnated, as with a living soul, by the presence of Life'.[61] And we might recall the rapid development in contemporary Germany of *Naturphilosophie* in the hands of Schelling.

Because in these four operas the storms express a destructive power so far beyond the capability of man to match, the issue of 'rescue' perforce takes second place to that of providential mercy. They are 'physical rescues', but their humanity is instinctively achieved, rather than standing as a moral example. *Eliza*, so obviously a non-political opera, may seem unique among its peers. But its conjunction of (seemingly) doomed love and natural catastrophe points in its way – as indeed do the other operas – towards the suicide of Fenella and the climactic eruption of Vesuvius (an eruption that is construed as divine vengeance) in the 'first' French *grand opéra*, *La muette de Portici* (1828) by Scribe and Auber. Once again, because the rescue is not the most important aspect of the work, a redefinition must withdraw *Rettungsstück* as a guiding concept from Type 3 works, and see them, too, rather as a forward-looking stage in the art of the libretto. Authentic 'rescue-pieces', in the form of melodramas on the Boulevard du crime, naturally continued to serve François-Benoît Hoffman's despised 'people who take to the theatre only their eyes and their ears'. The very fact that Hoffman contributed the libretto of *Léon* (a 'tyrant' work) can only be explained by the fact that he himself saw in the genres represented in our Types 1 and 2 the potential for some intelligence of treatment, and 'moral action' at the expense of 'physical action'. In other words, we ought also to distinguish the moral purpose of these *opéras comiques*, even if categories like 'tyrant', 'exemplary action' and 'judgment' be rejected. The dramaturgical dialogue between popular and traditional vogues, so necessary in the 1780s and 90s, must not be taken for an isolated, freakish cul-de-sac.

APPENDIX I
Some definitions

(i) **Edward J. Dent, *Opera* (Harmondsworth, 1940; new edn, 1945), p. 49:**
a type of libretto in which the hero or heroine is shut up in prison by a villainous tyrant; the wife or husband attempts to set the prisoner free, but generally makes the situation far worse, and the invariable happy end is brought about by the sudden entry of a chorus of soldiers who arrest the tyrant.

61 Letter to his brother, 10 March 1798, cited in W. Wordsworth and S. T. Coleridge, *Lyrical Ballads*, ed. R. L. Brett and A. R. Jones (London and New York, 1963; 2nd edn, revised, 1965), p. xxi.

(ii) **George Martin, *The Opera Companion* (London, 1962), p. 188:**

A term used to describe a type of French opera that was very popular during and after the French Revolution. In it one paragon of virtue saves another after overcoming the most fearful trials and tribulations. Many of the stories, arising out of the Revolution, were supposedly based on fact. The most famous example is Beethoven's *Fidelio* (1805).

(iii) **Donald Jay Grout, *A Short History of Opera* (New York, 1947; 2nd edn, 1965), pp. 259, 300 and 304:**

The rescue plot was a favorite in operas of the late eighteenth and early nineteenth centuries, blending the emotions of suspense, personal loyalty and triumph of virtue over evil in an effective dramatic pattern, familiar to us still through Beethoven's *Fidelio*.

Thus *Les Deux Journées*, for example, is filled with outbursts of the most exemplary sentiments of loyalty, kindness, and general devotion to the ideals of "humanity," with which the "good" characters of the libretto are fully identified. This infusion into the libretto of a new spirit of urgency, of direct concern with the sentiments and the fate of recognizably "real" people ... called for a new kind of musical expression.

(iv) **Harold Rosenthal and John Warrack, *The Concise Oxford Dictionary of Opera* (Oxford, 1964; 2nd edn, 1979), p. 413:**

The name given to an opera in which an essential part of the plot turns on the rescue of the hero or heroine from prison or some other threatening situation. Examples are to be found at various times in the 18th century, but it developed into a recognizable genre with the French Revolution and the closer involvement of opera with real-life situations, often highly dramatic.

(v) **Winton Dean, in *The New Grove Dictionary of Music and Musicians* ed. S. Sadie (London, 1980), xv, p. 755:**

The name given to a type of opera (more strictly *opéra comique*), very popular in France during the years after the 1789 Revolution, in which the hero or heroine is delivered at the last moment either from the cruelty of a tyrant, or from some great natural catastrophe (or both), not by a *deus ex machina* but by heroic human endeavour. It reflected the secular idealism of the age and often carried a social message. The genre was anticipated before the Revolution in Grétry's *Richard Coeur-de-lion* (1784), but its earliest true representative is Berton's *Les rigueurs du cloître* (1790) ...

(vi) **Christopher Headington, Roy Westbrook and Terry Barfoot, *Opera: a History* (London, 1987), pp. 114–15:**

Camille is also an example of a 'rescue opera', a type of plot in which the imprisoned or endangered hero or heroine is rescued at the last by a lover, spouse, or other agent. It was not new to *opéra comique*, for both Monsigny's *Le déserteur* and Grétry's *Richard Coeur-de-lion* have this theme, and a resolution by a *deus ex machina* was almost as old as opera itself. But during the Revolution, and particularly during the Terror of 1793–94, the theme touched the lives of many more people. It also gave an opportunity to express popular ideals of the period such as fidelity, selfless heroism, and married love, and to assure the spectator that freedom would always triumph over tyranny.

APPENDIX 2
Chronological list of relevant stage works

1769 *Le déserteur* (Sedaine and Monsigny)

1774 *La frascatana* (Livigni and Paisiello)

1779 *Aucassin et Nicolette* (Sedaine and Grétry)

1781 *Pierre de Provence et la belle Maguelonne* (Arnould)

1782 *Dorothée* (attrib. Audinot and Arnould)

1784 *Richard Coeur-de-lion* (Sedaine and Grétry)

1786 *Le Comte d'Albert* (Sedaine and Grétry)

1787 *Le prisonnier anglais* (Desfontaines and Grétry)

1788 *Les solitaires de Normandie* (Barré and de Piis)

1789 *Raoul Barbe-bleue* (Sedaine and Grétry); *Raoul, Sire de Créqui* (Monvel and Dalayrac)

1790 *Les rigueurs du cloître* (Fiévée and Berton); *Euphrosine, ou Le tyran corrigé* (Hoffman and Méhul)

1791 *Paul et Virginie* (Favières and Kreutzer); *Camille, ou Le souterrein* (Marsollier and Dalayrac); *Lodoiska* (Fillette-Loraux and Cherubini); *Lodoiska* (Dejaure and Kreutzer)

1793 *La caverne* (Palat-Dercy and Le Sueur)

1794 *Paul et Virginie* (Dubreuil and Le Sueur); *Eliza, ou Le voyage aux glaciers du Mont St-Bernard* (Saint-Cyr and Cherubini); *Mélidore et Phrosine* (A. V. Arnault and Méhul)

1795 *Le brigand* (Hoffman and Kreutzer); *La caverne* (Forgeot and Méhul)

1798 *Léonore, ou L'amour conjugal* (Bouilly and Gaveaux); *Léon, ou Le château de Monténéro* (Hoffman and Dalayrac)

1800 *Les deux journées, ou Le porteur d'eau* (Bouilly and Cherubini)

1801 *Léhéman, ou Le tour de Neustadt* (Marsollier and Dalayrac)

MUSIC AND THE NEW POLITICS

CYNTHIA M. GESSELE

The Conservatoire de Musique and national music education in France, 1795–1801

On 3 August 1795 the French Conservatoire de Musique was established by decree of the National Convention. The Conservatoire's enduring legacy was the centralization of musical training in Paris and the standardization of teaching methods in France. The Conservatoire's decision to concentrate on its pedagogical programme, rather than on a national programme of music education, can be related to proposals for music education set forth by Jean-Baptiste Leclerc and Bernard Sarrette. These proposals indicate how *ancien-régime* traditions of music theory, music education and musical style converged with the Conservatoire's monopoly on the composition and performance of music at the *fêtes nationales*. The gradual reduction in the number and importance of festivals after 1795, however, weakened the Conservatoire's monopoly. Its adoption of Charles-Simon Catel's *Traité d'harmonie* as its didactic harmony method in 1801 reflects how the administration of the Conservatoire hoped to remain in control of musical style through its pedagogical programme.

Before discussing the Conservatoire during the Revolutionary period, it is useful to examine several themes that came to light in the musical discourse of the late eighteenth century. One is the connection of music theory and musical style; a second is the notion of a music school as both academy and conservatory; and a third is the control of performance and genre conventions by a central educational institution. These themes, brought forward in the *ancien régime*, are important to an understanding of the forces that determined the Conservatoire's programme of education and the interdependency of the Conservatoire and the national festivals.

The cornerstone of French music theory in the eighteenth century was the system proposed by Jean-Philippe Rameau. The unifying principle of Rameau's system was its foundation upon the physical properties of a sonorous body (*corps sonore*), such as a vibrating string. According to Rameau, any chord in common practice was ultimately related to 'the chord' formed by the fundamental sound and the first overtones (the octave, perfect fifth and major third) emitted by the sonorous body. Inversions of chords were treated as analogous to their original tertian or fundamental form. The succession of fundamental notes (or roots) of chords formed the notes of the *basse fondamentale*, or fundamental bass. Rameau then promulgated rules for successions of chords in terms of the intervals between successive notes in the fundamental bass, the most important interval being the perfect fifth.

Although many theorists in the second half of the eighteenth century rejected Rameau's proofs of the 'scientific' foundation for his system of fundamental bass, they generally accepted his premises that the fundamental bass represented the lowest notes of tertian chords, and that chord inversions related to a fundamental chord. Later theorists also tried to complete Rameau's work through revision or reinterpretation of his basic tenets and to reconcile the speculative and practical principles of his system in didactic methods for accompaniment and composition.[1]

According to Rameau, the practical importance of the fundamental bass was that it provided an understanding of accompaniment, the eighteenth-century term for basso continuo realization. Accompaniment, in turn, provided a foundation for compositional practice. In Rameau's conception fundamental bass was intended for the continuo player as a performance aid that made sense of continuo figures in a tonally relational way. The performer would acquire an understanding of basic and natural progressions of harmony through the relationship of basso continuo chords to the generating chords of the fundamental bass. Although the fundamental bass was not a requisite addition to a performer's score, it could be represented on an extra staff below the basso continuo line. Thus the fundamental bass staff graphically depicts the basic progression of consonant fundamental chords (tonics) and dissonant fundamental chords (dominants). It follows that fundamental bass is also an analytical system that describes the harmonic content of a work of music.[2] It is an additional, non-performed representation of both vertical and linear elements of harmony.

In Rameau's second treatise of 1726, the *Nouveau système de musique théorique*, he devoted the final chapters to continuo practice and addressed the difficulties of figuring basses and understanding continuo figures. In this treatise Rameau provided fundamental bass analyses of an operatic monologue by Lully and passages from a set of sonatas by

1 One of the best-known and most popular examples is Jean le Rond d'Alembert's *Eléments de musique, théorique et pratique, suivant les principes de M. Rameau* (Paris, 1752; reprinted New York, 1966). This work was reprinted in 1759; a revised edition of 1762 was also reprinted in 1766, 1772 and 1779.
2 See A. R. Keiler, 'Music as Metalanguage: Rameau's Fundamental Bass', in *Music Theory Special Topics*, ed. R. Browne (New York, 1981), pp. 83–100; and M.-E. Duchez, 'Valeur épistémologique de la théorie de la basse fondamentale de Jean-Philippe Rameau: connaissance

Corelli. Rameau concluded that Lully was the musician, above all others, who observed the laws of harmony. The music of Corelli, on the other hand, was filled with errors in the continuo figures that led the performer astray from the true path of the fundamental bass. Although Rameau insisted that he was not condemning Corelli's works, only his figures, he had only praise for his French compatriot.[3]

Rameau's opposition of Corelli and Lully provides an example of how a system of harmonic theory could be called into a comparison of musical styles. Vitriolic polemics in which the merits and deficiencies of French operatic style were weighed against Italian operatic style erupted sporadically throughout the eighteenth century. The controversies of Le Cerf de la Viéville and François Raguenet in the 1700s, of the Lullistes and Ramistes in the 1740s, of the Bouffonistes in the 1750s, and of the Gluckistes and Piccinnistes in the 1770s demonstrate a consuming passion for debates centred on this tenuous comparison. One of the most uncompromising pronouncements to arise from these battles was that of Jean-Jacques Rousseau. Rousseau came to the conclusion in his *Lettre sur la musique française* (1753) that France had no music to call its own.[4]

After a lapse of many years, a fundamental bass theorist responded directly to Rousseau's pronouncement and offered his *Recherches sur la théorie de la musique* (1769). The author, Jamard, declared that the 'problem' with French music was not the music, but the theory. Jamard's reasoning was simple: melody was the product of harmony in fundamental bass theory, and if this theory was true, and was studied by French composers, then French music was necessarily superior to Italian. He realized, however, that this argument was contradicted by reality. Every day Italian composers who '[did] not have even the slightest idea of these [harmonic] principles' ('n'ont pas même la plus légère idée de ces principes') were presenting melodious works on French stages to public acclaim.[5] Jamard's resolution of the problem was to redesign fundamental bass theory by offering an improved unifying principle based upon propositions garnered from geometry.[6]

Reviewers of Jamard's treatise, in both the *Journal encyclopédique*

scientifique et représentation de la musique', *Studies on Voltaire and the Eighteenth Century*, ccxlv (1986), pp. 91–130.

3 J.-P. Rameau, *Nouveau système de musique théorique, où l'on découvre le principe de toutes les règles nécessaires à la pratique, pour servir d'introduction au Traité de l'harmonie* (Paris, 1726), pp. 41, 79–90 and 94–106.

4 Rousseau's final sentence in the *Lettre* seems to settle the matter: 'D'où je conclus que les Français n'ont point de Musique et n'en peuvent avoir; ou que si jamais ils en ont une, ce sera tant pis pour eux'. The complete text is reprinted in *La Querelle des Bouffons: texte des pamphlets avec introduction, commentaire et index*, ed. D. Launay (Geneva, 1973), pp. 669–764.

5 Jamard, *Recherches sur la théorie de la musique* (Paris and Rouen, 1769), p. iii.

6 Jamard based his unifying principle on the work of Charles-Louis-Denis Ballière de Laisement and his generating principles upon that of Jean le Rond d'Alembert.

and the *Journal de musique*, passed over his speculative propositions and focussed on the equation of music theory and musical style.[7] Likewise, a reviewer in the *Mercure de France* restated Jamard's view:

La découverte de la basse fondamentale et les préceptes de cette théorie ne nous ont pas donné une musique; les Italiens, sans s'astreindre à l'observation d'aucune règle, en ont une, parce qu'ils ne consultent que l'oreille et qu'ils ne suivent que les mouvements du coeur. *Les principes sont donc de trop*; et il ne sont sans doute *de trop* que parce qu'ils *ne sont point les vrais principes de l'harmonie* ...[8]

The discovery of fundamental bass and the precepts of this theory have not given us a music. The Italians, who do not feel compelled to observe any rules, have one because they consult only the ear and follow only the impulses of the heart. Therefore, *the principles are de trop*, and doubtless they are *de trop* only because they *are not the true principles of harmony* ...

The contemporary response to Jamard's system is but one example of how the system of fundamental bass, in any guise, was increasingly seen as untenable in its relationship to practice.

One of the most prolific and vocal critics of fundamental bass was Anton Bemetzrieder. Beginning with an accompaniment treatise published in 1771, Bemetzrieder presented a harmonic theory that rejected the underlying organizing principles of fundamental bass.[9] Nevertheless, he had to assume the contemporary and general acceptance of Rameau's concepts of the tertian generation of chords and of chord inversion, as well as much of Rameau's terminology. Like many Ramist fundamental bass methods, Bemetzrieder took accompaniment practice as the basis for teaching rudimentary principles of harmony.

Unlike Rameau, Bemetzrieder did not use accompaniment practice as the foundation for his didactic composition method. Instead, he posited an analytical methodology that applied to existing works. Bemetzrieder called his analytical signifier of chord progressions the *basse générale*. *Basse générale* 'analysis' involved the reduction of the melodic and harmonic elements of a musical phrase to a series of simple basso continuo chords. Fundamental bass interpreters, on the other hand, often labelled rhythmically discrete harmonies by individual fundamental bass chords, resulting in detailed, localized descriptions of the underlying harmonic content of a passage.[10]

---

7 *Journal encyclopédique*, iii/1 (April 1770), pp. 48–55; *Journal de musique* (May 1770), pp. 67–8.
8 *Mercure de France* (June 1770), p. 113. The italicized text, as given in the *Mercure* article, indicates direct quotations from Jamard's preface.
9 A. Bemetzrieder, *Leçons de clavecin, et principes d'harmonie* (Paris, 1771; reprinted New York, 1966).
10 See, for example, P.-J. Roussier, *Traité des accords et de leur successions: selon le système de la basse-fondamentale; pour servir de principes d'harmonie à ceux qui étudient la composition ou l'accompagnement du clavecin: avec une méthode d'accompagnement* (Paris, 1764; reprinted

Although the *basse générale* resulted in a largely reductive analysis, whereas the fundamental bass resulted in a basically descriptive analysis, the goal of each methodology was to validate a composition's integrity. Bemetzrieder took the prescriptive content of fundamental bass to be its greatest liability:

... il y en a qui condamnent toute succession d'accords dont la marche ne quadre pas avec la basse fondamentale, quoiqu'ils satisfassent l'oreille et qu'ils impriment à l'âme la sensation que le sujet demande.[11]

... there are those who condemn any succession of chords in which the progression does not square up with the fundamental bass, even if [the chords] satisfy one's ear and produce in one's soul the impression that the subject demands.

Bemetzrieder's comment on Rameau's system suggests that he was offering a system of harmonic theory that related to and described musical style, but that did not limit a composer's creativity.

In his later works Bemetzrieder addressed the issue of the relationship of music education and musical style. His views on this issue cannot be dissociated from the continuing opera battles of the late eighteenth century. In the mid-1770s the new camps of the Gluckistes and Piccinnistes (and Sacchinistes) began calling for the establishment of a formal vocal school as a means of rescuing French opera from what was seen as its decline. Critics of the privileged Académie Royale de Musique and its ineffectual school, the Ecole du Magasin, felt that French opera would be improved by the creation of a vocal school modelled on Italian conservatories.[12] Other writers saw the need not just for the reform of vocal training, but for the introduction of a complete pedagogical programme for music. Claude-Philibert Coquéau, a Piccinniste, noted that Italian conservatories trained generations of composers:

Je crois que vous oubliez une des principales causes des progrès de la musique en Italie, les conservatoires et l'excellente méthode qu'on y professe. A l'aide de cet établissement utile, les travaux des hommes de génie ne furent pas perdus avec eux.

Geneva, 1972) and *L'harmonie pratique, ou Exemples pour le Traité des accords* (Paris, 1775); P.-H. Azaïs, *Méthode de musique sur un nouveau plan à l'usage des élèves de l'Ecole Royale Militaire* (Paris, [1776]); and J.-J. Rodolphe, *Théorie d'accompagnement et de composition, à l'usage des élèves de l'Ecole Royale de Musique, contenant l'origine des accords, divisée en deux classes, l'harmonie naturelle, et l'harmonie composée; la basse fondamentale de chaque accord, et des leçons de pratique* (Paris, [1785]).

11 A. Bemetzrieder, *Lettre de M. Bemetzrieder, à MM. *** musiciens de profession: ou Réponse à quelques objections qu'on a faites à sa méthode-pratique, sa théorie et son ouvrage sur l'harmonie* (Paris, 1771), p. 15.

12 In a 1774 brochure, *Dialogues sur la musique, par Mlle de Villers, adressés à son amie* (Paris, 1774), Clemence de Villers called for the establishment of a French conservatory of vocal training. According to de Villers, the school would encourage French vocal technique and would contribute to the amelioration of French opera in general. Reviews of the brochure applauded the proposal for a French conservatory as necessary to the 'progress' of music in France. See the *Mercure de France*, i (January 1775), pp. 159–63: and *L'année littéraire*, ii (1775), pp. 58–63.

Ils purent transmettre à leurs élèves une étincelle du feu qui les embrasait et la carte qui les avait guidés leur route.[13]

I think that you forget one of the principal reasons for the progress of music in Italy – the conservatories and the excellent method taught there. Because of this useful institution, the works of men of genius did not die with them. They were able to pass on to their students a spark from the fire that set them alight, and the map that has guided them on their path.

Bemetzrieder, who called himself a *Toutiste*, also saw the problem as one of music education in France.[14] In his 1776 *Traité de musique* he suggested that the Académie de Musique should take on the administration of a school that trained composers, as well as vocalists.[15] Two years later Bemetzrieder had decided that the Académie was not really an 'academy' in any sense of the word, and proposed an alternative music academy in his *Réflexions sur les leçons de musique*.[16] Bemetzrieder first presented a letter which he claimed was addressed to him by a reader of his *Traité*:

Cette manière de réunir des Maîtres pour perfectionner la méthode des leçons de Musique et pour fixer le bon goût, me paraît très-nécessaire. Les progrès des Arts, chez une Nation, dépendent beaucoup de l'enseignement: c'est par l'établissement de ses Conservatoires que l'Ecole de Naples est devenue la première de l'Italie.[17]

This means of bringing teachers together [in an academy] to improve the method of music lessons and to determine good taste seems absolutely necessary. The progress of the arts within a nation depends largely upon teaching. This is how, by the establishment of its conservatories, the Naples school has become pre-eminent in Italy.

In the ideal academy teachers would educate future generations of composers as well as the general public, using Bemetzrieder's system of theory. Thus the academy's educative function and the improvement of French musical style depended upon the adoption of Bemetzrieder's pedagogical method.

In a new edition of the *Réflexions* (1781) Bemetzrieder gave a more specific proposal for a music academy and set out a unified stylistic

---

13 Anon. [Claude-Philibert Coquéau], *Entretiens sur l'état actuel de l'Opéra de Paris* (Amsterdam and Paris, 1779), p. 125; reprinted in *Querelle des Gluckistes et des Piccinnistes: texte des pamphlets avec introduction, commentaires et index*, ed. F. Lesure (Geneva, 1984), ii, pp. 368–540.

14 See A. Bemetzrieder, *Le tolérantisme musical* (Paris, 1779), p. 8; reprinted in *Querelle des Gluckistes*, ii, pp. 337–66.

15 A. Bemetzrieder, *Traité de musique, concernant les tons, les harmonies, les accords et le discours musical* (Paris, 1776).

16 A. Bemetzrieder, *Réflexions sur les leçons de musique: méthode pour enseigner la lecture musicale, l'accompagnement, l'exécution et les éléments de la composition* (Amsterdam and Paris, 1778), p. i.

17 Ibid., p. 5.

strategy. The academy was to comprise a college of teachers who trained performers and composers and an academic society of composers, men of letters and amateurs who would essentially control the performance of works at the Opéra.[18] Thus the academy, guided by Bemetzrieder's theory and didactic method, would reign over the musical life of Paris from the basics of elementary music education to the details of stage productions.

The unified stylistic strategy proposed by Bemetzrieder can be seen as a response to another issue raised at the time: that of 'national music'. In a letter to the *Mercure* in Feburary 1773 Gluck introduced his opera *Iphigénie en Aulide* and disclosed that his vision was 'to produce music that is suited to every nation and to abolish the absurd distinctions of national musics [or styles]'. (' … j'envisage de produire une musique propre à toutes les nations, et de faire disparaître la ridicule distinction des musiques nationales').[19] In the newly rekindled battles, the tenuous comparison of French and Italian musics (in the plural) was often set aside in attempts to define the novel concept of a single 'national music'. Writers from both camps echoed the call for a 'national' style. J.-B.-A. Suard, an adamant Gluckiste, credited his idol with having given France 'a truly national music'.[20] Jean François Marmontel, a Piccinniste, insisted that French composers should instil a 'national' taste for musical style in the public.[21]

National music was to be a new, reformed and synthetic style and would be encouraged through a public music education system. Thus the call for conservatories by the opera polemicists and the call for a music academy by Bemetzrieder were mandates for an institution that would engender a musical ideology and pedagogical method which, in turn, would promote a 'national' style of opera. The answer to these demands came in 1784 with the creation of the Ecole Royale de Chant.

The establishment of the school was applauded in the *Correspondance littéraire*, but it was also suggested that a more academic institution was necessary. Like Bemetzrieder's academy, the improved school would educate the general public and composers, as well as singers:

18 The academic society would examine and revise old operas, re-adjust modern operas that had not been successful, parody the operas of the Comédie-Italienne for the Académie de Musique, choose subjects for operas, survey new works in all the arts and elect associates from contemporary musicians and poets. A. Bemetzrieder, *Méthode et réflexions sur les leçons de musique, nouvelle édition* (Paris, 1781), pp. 6–7.

19 'Lettre de M. le Chevalier Gluck à l'auteur du Mercure de France', *Mercure de France*, February 1773; reprinted in *Mémoires pour servir à l'histoire de la révolution opérée dans la musique par M. le chevalier Gluck*, ed. [Gaspard Michel, *dit* Leblond] (Paris, 1781), pp. 8–10.

20 Anon. [J.-B.-A. Suard], 'Réponse de l'anonyme de Vaugirard, à M. le Chevalier Gluck', in *Mémoires pour servir*, pp. 282–313, specifically p. 283.

21 Anon. [J. F. Marmontel], 'Essai sur les révolutions de la musique en France', in *Mémoires pour servir*, pp. 153–90, specifically pp. 188–9.

L'on pensait encore avec raison que le moyen le plus sûr de faire fleurir en France un art ... c'était de créer une chaire où les principes de cet art enchanteur fussent professés publiquement, et d'établir en même temps des maîtres de composition qui apprissent l'application des principes aux jeunes élèves.[22]

It is still rightly thought that the surest means of encouraging the blossoming of an art [music] in France ... is to create a chair where the principles of this enchanting art would be taught publicly, and at the same time to appoint teachers of composition who would teach the application of these principles to young students.

A 'chair' of music, resembling the respected chairs of the other French academies, would institutionalize musical style through a unified system of theory and education.[23] Nevertheless, the enforcement of a complete stylistic strategy, such as that proposed by Bemetzrieder, could occur only if performance genres and forces were also controlled. The Ecole Royale de Chant was not an administrative body, nor was it connected to the Académie de Musique and its school, the Ecole du Magasin. Therefore the administration of the Ecole de Chant had no control over the performance of operas in the French capital.

The Ecole Royale de Chant continued in existence through the tumultuous events of 1789–95. In a plan for the reorganization of the school drawn up in 1791, its director, François-Joseph Gossec, placed the enforcement of musical and political nationalism within the domain of a music academy:

Les musiciens étrangers, sans s'attacher à notre patrie, corrompront notre langue et dénatureront notre goût. ... Les oreilles délicates en seront d'abord blessées, mais le long usage forcera ceux qui ont le goût le plus difficile à s'y accoutumer. ...

Il est donc avantageux, ou pour mieux dire nécessaire, que nous ayons une musique vraiment nationale, et pour y parvenir avec succès, nous avons besoin d'une Académie de musique.[24]

Foreign musicians, without attachment to our nation, will corrupt our language and pervert our taste. ... Our delicate ears will at first be offended, but continued usage will force even those with the most decided taste to grow accustomed to [their music] ...

It is therefore advantageous – or, better stated, necessary – that we have a truly national music, and to arrive successfully at this point we need an Academy of Music.

Gossec's academy was to be an outgrowth of the Ecole Royale de Chant, but surely part of his concern was the growing importance of another music school.

22 *Correspondance littéraire, philosophique et critique par Grimm, Diderot, Raynal, Meister, etc.*, ed. M. Tourneux, (Paris, 1877–82), xiii (February 1784), p. 483.
23 The idea of a 'chair' of music was also raised by Jean-Benjamin de La Borde in his *Essai sur la musique ancienne et moderne* (Paris, 1780; reprinted New York, 1978), iii, p. 680.
24 C. Pierre, *Le Conservatoire National de Musique et de Déclamation* (Paris, 1900), p. 46.

Indeed, by 1791 an instrumental music school was taking shape. The musicians of the National Guard, who were assembled on 14 July 1789 by Bernard Sarrette, formed the nucleus of the Ecole de Musique de la Garde Nationale in 1792. In 1793 the school was renamed the Institut de Musique and it came under the jurisdiction of the National Convention and its Committee of Public Instruction. The school was no longer a city-sponsored band but was truly a national institution.[25]

The students and faculty of these two schools made up the main body of trained musical performers at the national festivals, the mass-educative rituals of the Revolution. The students of the Ecole de Chant and of the Institut were trained almost exclusively for participation in the Revolutionary festivals.[26] Ultimately, through the collaboration of Gossec and Sarrette, the Institut de Musique also gained a monopoly of the new genres of music composed for the festivals.[27]

In the 1794 plan of Sarrette and Gossec for the internal organization of the Institut, the *maître de musique* (Gossec) would compose and direct music for the national festivals; four adjunct composers would assist him in these tasks. Any composer could submit his work to a jury of Institut members, but the composition would become 'national property' if it were selected and performed at a public festival. The work would then be deposited in the library of the Conservatoire and be printed for national distribution by the Conservatoire's publishing enterprise, the Magasin de Musique.[28]

In July 1795 Marie-Joseph Chénier went to the National Convention to seek its ratification of a new school that would be formed by the union of the Ecole de Chant and the Institut. France and its music – that is, the music of the armies and of the national festivals – were at last to reign victorious:

Si donc cet art est utile, s'il est moral, si même il est nécessaire pour les armées, pour les fêtes nationales, et, ce qui comprend tout, pour la splendeur de la République, hâtez-vous, Représentants, de lui assurer un asile. ... L'Allemagne et l'orgueilleuse

25 C. Pierre, *B. Sarrette et les origines du Conservatoire National de Musique et de Déclamation* (Paris, 1895), p. 44.
26 In 1795 the professors of the vocal school stressed the patriotic utility of their students: 'Les fêtes nationales s'embellissent par les chants de leurs élèves, et il est peu de pièces patriotiques dans lesquelles ils ne soient admis pour en faire une des principaux ornements' (Pierre, *Le Conservatoire*, pp. 58–9). Performance at the national festivals and civic ceremonies was mandatory for the students of the instrumental school, who were also expected to act as musical corps in the armies of the French nation (ibid., pp. 83–6).
27 In 1794 the Institut was called upon to answer for its monopolistic control of the festivals (see Pierre, *B. Sarrette*, pp. 103–9).
28 Five members of the jury of nine composers would be chosen from the Institut's faculty; four would be nominated by the applying composer. In other words, the Institut still held the majority (Pierre, *Le Conservatoire*, pp. 108–10). This project would have countermanded the decrees of 19 July 1793 that had given authors property rights over 'd'écrits de tout genre, des compositeurs de musique, des peintres et des dessinateurs'. See *Procès-verbaux du Comité*

Italie, vaincues en tout le reste par la France, mais longtemps victorieuses en ce genre seul, ont enfin trouvé une rivale.[29]

Therefore, if this art [of music] is useful, if it is moral, and moreover if it is necessary to the armies, to the national festivals and, in the broadest sense, to the splendour of the republic, make haste, Representatives, to assure it a safe haven. . . . Germany and vainglorious Italy, vanquished in all other arts by France, but long a victor in this genre alone, have at last met a rival.

The festivals were instituted as a primary duty of the newly created Conservatoire. Following the outline proposed by Gossec and Sarrette in 1794, the Conservatoire regulations drawn up in 1796 stated that no music could be performed at a national festival without the express approval of the Conservatoire's inspectors and the executive government.[30] The importance of music in the national festivals offered an unusual opportunity for consolidation of the Conservatoire's power. Now within the Revolutionary context, the music academy could be the supreme enforcer of a 'national' musical style.

Sarrette's address at the opening of the Conservatoire in October 1796 indicates how he envisaged the integration of musical style, education and the national festivals:

Le règlement ne doit pas se borner à organiser les institutions indispensables à l'étude de la théorie générale de la musique; il faut aussi qu'il fournisse à la pratique les moyens de transmettre les leçons utiles de l'expérience; . . . il faut que, par une exécution complète dans des exercises solennels, le musicien puisse entendre et faire connaître aux amis des arts les productions qui honorent le sien. . . .

Ces productions, en imprimant le sentiment du beau, exciteront l'émulation des jeunes compositeurs; elles aideront au développement de leur génie, et feront naître des ouvrages dignes d'illustrer l'Ecole qui s'établit.[31]

The regulations must not be restricted to the organization of institutions indispensable to a study of the general theory of music; they must also furnish the practical study of music with the means of transmitting useful lessons of experience. . . . By means of a technique perfected in special exercises, the musician must be able to understand, and to make known to lovers of the arts, the works that do credit to his own.

These works, as they instil a conception of beauty, will stimulate young composers to emulate them; they will help in the development of their genius, and will bring into being works worthy of doing honour to the school that is established.

Sarrette's primary concern was the musically educative aspects of the festivals. At about the same time as this address, he presented some form of a plan for a national system of music education.[32] The issue of music

---

d'Instruction publique de la Convention nationale, ed. J. Guillaume (Paris, 1891–1907), ii, pp. 80–2.

29 Pierre, Le Conservatoire, p. 122.   30 Ibid., p. 225.   31 Pierre, B. Sarrette, p. 187.
32 There is no record of Sarrette's first plan. We can only surmise its contents from his 1796 address (given in Pierre, B. Sarrette, pp. 182–7).

schools outside Paris was first raised in 1793 with the founding of the Institut de Musique, but was not considered by the Committee of Public Instruction.[33] In February 1795 Sarrette and Gossec asked the National Convention to consider the establishment of music schools in the large communes to replace the education previously attended to by the *maîtrises*, the music schools connected to major cathedrals, which had been suppressed in 1792.[34] Again the request must have been put aside, as no mention of departmental schools is made in the 1795 decree that established the Conservatoire.

In 1796 the publicly educative aspects of the festivals and the formation of a national system of music schools were taken up Jean-Baptiste Leclerc, a member of the Council of Five Hundred. Leclerc published an ideological plan for national music education entitled *Essai sur la propagation de la musique en France, sa conservation, et ses rapports avec le gouvernement*.[35] Leclerc proposed a complete stylistic and pedagogical strategy that resembled Bemetzrieder's 1781 proposal. He first stressed that the opportunity for the enforcement of 'a national music' had arrived and that the central government should make use of the propitious moment. Leclerc felt that the state needed to provide the public with a system of celebrations that would engage the citizenry in the same ways that opera engaged the audiences of the *ancien régime* and, furthermore, would substitute for religious ceremony. The *genre hymnique* and the Theophilanthropic cult were these substitutes.[36]

The *genre hymnique* described music that was to be composed in simple forms with simple harmonizations and would promote the unification of the limited performance abilities and comprehension of

33 Ibid., p. 43.

34 Pierre, *Le Conservatoire*, pp. 114–15. In 1796 Sarrette estimated that 500 *maîtrises* existed before the Revolution (Pierre, *B. Sarrette*, p. 185). For studies of individual centres, see: M.-T. Bouquet, *Musique et musiciens à Annecy: les maîtrises, 1630–1789*, xvi, *La vie musicale en France sous les rois Bourbons* (Annecy, 1970), J.-A. Clerval, *L'ancienne maîtrise de Notre-Dame de Chartres du Ve siècle à la Révolution* (Paris, 1899); A. Collette, *Histoire de la maîtrise de Rouen* (Rouen, 1891); D. Launay, 'L'enseignement de la composition dans les maîtrises, en France, aux XVIe et XVIIe siècles, *Revue de musicologie*, lxviii (1982), pp. 79–90; and B. Lavillat, *L'enseignement à Besançon au XVIIIe siècle* (Paris, 1977).

35 J.-B. Leclerc, *Essai sur la propagation de la musique en France, sa conservation, et ses rapports avec le gouvernement* (Paris, prairial an IV/May–June 1796). In the *Essai* Leclerc states that he had presented his plan to the Committee of Public Instruction in the previous year. No formal record of such a presentation is contained in the *procès-verbaux* of the Committee of Public Instruction. Leclerc's initial plan was integrated into Claude-François Daunou's plan of 1795 for the organization of national education. Leclerc, however, may have shown his plan to Daunou as early as 1794 (see *Procès-verbaux*, iv, p. 964, note 2).

36 Leclerc was a close associate of Louis-Marie de La Révellière-Lépeaux, M.-J. Chénier and Claude-François Daunou, the Directory's committed advocates of Theophilanthropism. See J. Godechot, *Les institutions de la France sous la Révolution et l'Empire* (2nd edn, Paris, 1968), pp. 532–5, and M. Ozouf, *La fête révolutionnaire, 1789–1799* (Paris, 1976; English translation by A. Sheridan as *Festivals and the French Revolution*, Cambridge, 1988). The cult and the festivals are discussed on pp. 270–71 of the English edition.

the people in small villages with the more grandiose expressions of civic sentiment in populous cities. Leclerc was actually classifying all existing Revolutionary festival music into the *genre hymnique*. In effect, he was describing within his own taxonomy what had become standard practice in the festivals. Nevertheless, he would not admit the music of the church or theatre in his classification, and he even felt that most purely instrumental music should be discouraged.

Popular acceptance of the state-approved and propagated *genre hymnique* would depend upon the creation of a musical style that would fit into the everyday life of every citizen – that is, simple tunes that resembled popular songs. As a substitute for religious education and institutions, Leclerc suggested that music schools be established in each major city where a state functionary (resembling a priest) would oversee elementary music education and the performances of the festivals. As for music education on more advanced levels, he concluded that compositional training, which could be provided only at the level of the central Conservatoire also needed to be regulated.

Leclerc's answer was a didactic method which rested upon the principles of fundamental bass. To enforce stylistic simplicity in the *genre hymnique* he insisted that the harmony of an earlier period should be adopted:

... quant à l'harmonie, nous croyons qu'il sera nécessaire de rétrograder de quelques années. Comme il importe de la circonscrire dans des bornes dont elle ne s'écarte jamais, if faut chercher l'époque où sa pratique s'accordait le plus avec une théorie simple et en quelque sorte législative. Le système de la basse fondamentale, malgré ses imperfections, est celui qui remplira le mieux cet objet; et nous l'adoptons d'autant plus volontiers, qu'il unit la fécondité à la sagesse, et qu'il offre à l'homme de génie des ressources suffisantes pour produire tous les effets qu'il est raisonnable d'attendre de la musique.[37]

... as for harmony, we think it will be necessary to turn the clock back a few years. As it is important to keep it within limits that it should never exceed, we must look for the epoch when its practice best agreed with a simple and somewhat legislative theory. The system of fundamental bass, despite its imperfections, is the one that best meets this objective, and we adopt it the more willingly because it unites fecundity with wisdom, and because it offers the man of genius sufficient resources to produce all the effects that can reasonably be expected from music.

Leclerc saw the system of fundamental bass as prescriptive, and thereby the ideal pedagogical system for the monopoly of genre he proposed. Leclerc's vision of the Conservatoire was essentially like Bemetzrieder's plan for a music academy that controlled operatic production. In Leclerc's plan the medium of public contact that was controlled by a central institution was the national festival, while Bemetzrieder's analy-

37 Leclerc, *Essai sur la propogation*, pp. 35–6.

tical method was replaced by Rameau's fundamental bass as the didactic method for compositional training.

Leclerc revised his plan and presented it repeatedly to the Council of Five Hundred in the following years.[38] His plan related to the system of *écoles spéciales*, secondary schools for advanced training in the arts and sciences. These schools were part of the general system of national education, in which the faculties were appointed by the executive Directory.[39] Leclerc's plan also served as the basis for another proposal, by Jean-Marie Heurtault-Lamerville, which was presented in 1799 upon the demand of the executive government for further reductions in the expenses of the Conservatoire. Following Heurtault-Lamerville's plan, reductions in the number of faculty and a reorganization of the Paris Conservatoire were completed in March 1800, but the establishment of departmental schools was put aside.[40]

Perhaps to counter the plans being drawn up from outside the Conservatoire, Sarrette offered his own plan for a national education system in May 1801. Sarrette's plan suggested four degrees of schools that, unlike the *écoles spéciales*, would be controlled exclusively by the Paris Conservatoire.[41] Sarrette's observations appended to the proposal point to the sovereignty of the French school and how 'national music', originally incarnated in the music of the festivals, would be affirmed and carried on by the Conservatoire's composers and pedagogical programme:

... le Conservatoire de musique et les établissements proposés peuvent nous rendre entièrement indépendants; déjà plusieurs de nos artistes, parvenus au dernier degré de perfection, relèvent l'école française de l'état d'avilissement dans lequel elle était

38 J. A. Leith, in 'Music as an Ideological Weapon in the French Revolution', *Canadian Historical Association: Papers Presented at the Annual Meeting*, 1966, p. 137, note 40, mentions Leclerc's successive presentations in 1796, 1797 and 1798. Leclerc's 1798 plan is reprinted in Pierre, *Le Conservatoire*, pp. 334–41.

39 In 1795 Claude-François Daunou had proposed a system of *écoles spéciales* situated in the departments that would offer secondary education in the arts and sciences. Daunou's plan was the basis for the sweeping education reform decree of 3 Brumaire An IV/25 October 1795 (see F. Ponteil, *Histoire de l'enseignement en France: les grandes étapes, 1789–1964* (Paris, 1966), pp. 77–86). A decree of 1 May 1802 instituted the *écoles spéciales* and gave the right of appointment of their first faculties to the National Institute of Sciences and Arts; thereafter the First Consul was to fill vacancies (see L. Aucoc, *Institut de France: lois, statuts et réglements concernant les anciennes académies et l'Institut, de 1635 à 1899* (Paris, 1899), pp. 64–5).

40 Pierre, *Le Conservatoire*, pp. 341–4 and 137–8. Lack of financing for schools outside Paris and the élitism of the Conservatoire have been suggested as reasons for the neglect of national music education by Jean Mongrédien in *La musique en France des Lumières au Romantisme (1789–1830)* (Paris, 1986) and B. Brévan in *Les changements de la vie musicale parisienne de 1774 à 1799* (Paris, 1980). Mongrédien (pp. 31–3) also discusses the abortive attempts in the early nineteenth century to establish schools outside Paris. Although two *écoles succursales* were established in Lille and Toulouse in 1826, a national system of musical education was not effectively instituted until 1884.

41 Sarrette had also offered a plan at the same time as a revision of Leclerc's 1798 plan was presented (Pierre, *Le Conservatoire*, p. 338; the complete text of Sarrette's 1801 plan is reprinted on pp. 344–8).

tombée. Que sera-ce lorsque, par suite d'un système complet d'enseignement, nous pourrons atteindre cette extrême perfection dans toutes les parties de l'art musical ... [?][42]

... the Conservatoire de Musique and the proposed institutions [departmental schools] can make us entirely independent [of foreign musicians]. Already several of our artists, having attained the last degree of perfection, are raising the French school out of the state of degradation into which it had fallen. What will it be like when, through a complete system of education, we will be able to attain the utmost perfection in every area of musical art ...[?]

Furthermore, Sarrette emphasized the commercial aspects of the school and showed that the Conservatoire's original focus on the festivals and instrumental training had shifted towards the theatre and vocal training. In sum, the monopoly of genre was to be replaced by a monopoly on the manufacture of musical instruments and on training in performance and composition.

Both Leclerc's and Sarrette's plans extended the teaching of music to all parts of the nation and proposed an admission system that included students from all *départements*. The two plans, however, differed in their particular conceptions of the role and function of the Paris Conservatoire within society. While Leclerc's plan stressed the more abstract issue of civic and moral education of the masses through Revolutionary music, Sarrette's stressed the reality of how the Conservatoire would control the works and style of Revolutionary music inside and outside Paris.[43]

A comparison of the 1796 regulations and the 1800 regulations of the Conservatoire is enlightening. The 1796 regulations first give detailed rules for the execution of the festivals and then turn to the Conservatoire's educational programme. In the 1800 regulations the educational programme is first addressed at length, while the Conservatoire's role at the festivals is only briefly treated. In addition, the 1800 regulations emphasize the utility of the Conservatoire in training performers and composers for service outside the realm of the national festivals and armies.[44]

This change reflects the transformation between 1795 and 1800 of the very nature and importance of the festivals. The *fêtes nationales* were considered an integral part of the moral and political education of French citizens, but the interweaving of religious and patriotic ceremony

---

42 Pierre, *Le Conservatoire*, p. 347.
43 Neither Leclerc's nor Sarrette's plan was ever instituted. The general education decrees of 1802 did create a system of *écoles spéciales* for specific secondary training in law, medicine, geography, drafting and other vocational studies. The original project included eight music schools that were never put into place. See Godechot, *Les institutions de la France*, pp. 745–6.
44 Pierre, *Le Conservatoire*, p. 230.

and symbolism undermined their politically educative impact.[45] After 1795 the festivals continued to be celebrated, but were increasingly formalized and lost much of their original spontaneity.[46] By 1798 the attendance of the citizenry and participation in the festivals had to be enforced by law, and by December 1799 the government formally sanctioned only two festivals.[47] Thus, by 1800 the festivals were virtually extinct.[48] Furthermore, beginning in 1795 the production of the Revolutionary genres of songs and hymns fell off dramatically,[49] and the Magasin de Musique, which was originally designated to print and distribute Revolutionary musical works, turned to printing stage, chamber and sacred works in the late 1790s.[50]

With such a transformation of the Conservatoire's mission, national style and national education once again became an issue of didactic method and of academic control of education. During its early years the Conservatoire held a monopoly on the music of the festivals and the armies, and on the ceremonial music of the legislative bodies. With the decline in the number and importance of the festivals, the opportunity for the establishment of an academy like Bemetzrieder's, in which a central musical school controlled education, performance and genre, had passed. What was left was an enforcement of musical style through music theory: a reversion to Jamard's view that the 'problem' with French music was French theory.

The problem of a standardized programme of music education for Conservatoire students had also been neglected. Despite the Institut's 1794 decree for the creation of elementary textbooks, in 1796 no such standardized texts existed.[51] The crystallization of the Conservatoire's

45 After the almost spontaneous Festival of the Federation on 14 July 1790 the formalization of the national festivals began with the 1791 constitution, in which the guarantee of public education and the institutionalization of the national festivals are presented in adjacent articles. Robespierre's calendar of national festivals, instituted in 1794, set forth a plan for festivals that remained intact in some form until 1799. See *Procès-verbaux*, iii, pp. 305–12; and Ozouf, *La fête révolutionnaire*, especially Chapter 10.

46 For a discussion of the festivals after 1795, see A. Durey, *L'instruction publique et la Révolution* (Paris, 1882; reprinted Evreux, 1975), pp. 309–35; and J. Tiersot, *Les fêtes et les chants de la Révolution française* (Paris 1908), pp. 211–40.

47 Godechot, *Les institutions de la France*, pp. 533–5 and 709–10.

48 The constitution of An III/1795 reaffirmed the connection of general education and the festivals. The constitution of An VIII/1799, however, made no mention of either.

49 C. Pierre, *Hymnes et chansons de la Révolution: aperçu général et catalogue* (Paris, 1904), p. 34. By Pierre's accounting, in 1789 116 hymns and songs were produced; in 1790, 261; in 1791, 308; in 1792, 325; in 1793, 590; in 1794, 701; in 1795, 137; in 1796, 126; in 1797, 147; in 1798, 77; in 1799, 90; and in 1800, 25.

50 C. Pierre, *Le Magasin de Musique à l'usage des fêtes nationales et du Conservatoire* (Paris, 1895), *passim*.

51 Pierre, *Le Conservatoire*, p. 96. The National Convention had decided in 1794 that religiously orientated textbooks were to be replaced with new 'republican' texts approved by the Committee of Public Instruction (see *Procès-verbaux*, i, pp. 84–104). The Institut's decree of August 1794 is clearly a response to the general decree by the National Convention. For discussion of the contents and ideology of the elementary texts, see L. Grimaud, *Histoire de la*

pedagogical programme did not begin in earnest until 1799. By May of that year a commission was established to write a textbook of elementary principles,[52] and in December 1800 a commission was appointed to approve a treatise on harmony. In early May 1801 the General Assembly of the Conservatoire approved Catel's *Traité d'harmonie* and its publication was announced in December.[53]

Only after May 1801, when the rudimentary principles and the harmony treatise were approved, did Sarrette offer a well-considered plan for national music education. The Conservatoire's adoption of Catel's treatise as its method for teaching fundamentals of harmony marks the institutionalization of a system of music theory as the basis for compositional pedagogy. The report on Catel's treatise bears witness to the heated debates over the systems presented, and emphasizes the rejection of Rameau's system of fundamental bass.[54] Catel's system apparently fulfilled, more satisfactorily than fundamental bass, the original 1794 intentions of the Institut regarding its didactic system: internal control, simplicity, practicality and uniformity of method.[55]

liberté d'enseignement en France (2nd edn, Grenoble, 1944), ii, pp. 171–6; J. A. Leith, 'French Republican Pedagogy in the Year II', *Canadian Journal of History*, iii (1968), pp. 52–67; and J.-F. Chassaing, 'Les manuels de l'enseignement primaire de la Révolution et les idées révolutionnaires', in *Le mouvement de réforme de l'enseignement en France, 1760–1798*, ed. J. Morange and J.-F. Chassaing (Paris, 1974), pp. 97–140.

52 The completed work was promulgated as the basic Conservatoire text in June 1800: *Principes élémentaires de musique arrêtés par les membres du Conservatoire de Musique pour servir à l'étude dans cet établissement suivis par des solfèges* (Paris, an VIII/1799–1800). The contributors were Henri-Joseph Agus, Charles-Simon Catel, Luigi Cherubini, François-Joseph Gossec, Honoré-François-Marie Langlé, Jean-François Le Sueur, Etienne-Nicolas Méhul and Henri-Jean Rigel.

53 C.-S. Catel, *Traité d'harmonie par Catel, membre du Conservatoire de Musique, adopté par le Conservatoire pour servir à l'étude dans cet établissement* (Paris, an X/1801).

54 Catel, *Traité*, Preface:
   La commission, après avoir consulté les meilleurs ouvrages qui traitent de l'Harmonie, pour s'appuyer sur des autorités respectables, ou pour combattre des erreurs que le temps a consacrées, et que le temps doit détruire, à entendu l'exposé de trois systèmes nouveaux soumis à son examen.
   Les deux premiers, entièrement opposés dans leurs principes théoriques, ont fait naîtres des discussions vives et utiles, mais dont le résultat, en prouvant les connaissances des membres de la commission, n'atteignit cependant le but proposé. Le système de Rameau fut successivement attaqué et defendu. Les suffrages qu'il obtint ne ramènerent point ses adversaires qui combattirent encore cette théorie dans ses développements incomplets, en rendant toutefois justice à ce qu'elle offre de vrai et d'imposant dans la création et la génération de la grande famille des accords.

55 Report of the General Assembly of the National Institute of Music, 12 Fructidor An II/29 August 1794, printed in the preface to the *Principes élémentaires*:
   L'Institut considérant, que la précision et la simplicité des principes élémentaires sont la base constitutive d'une bonne école; que ces principes, en même temps qu'ils doivent tendre à agrandir le cercle des connaissances, doivent être dégagés des sophismes systématiques consacrés par l'usage; arrête:
   1° Les artistes de l'Institut s'occuperont de la formation des ouvrages élémentaires pour l'étude de la musique, du chant, de l'harmonie, de la composition et de toutes les parties instrumentales.

In the first instance Catel's treatise demonstrates the success of the pedagogical system of the Conservatoire and its predecessors. Catel's career began at the Ecole de Chant in 1784, but was nurtured by the Revolution. As a member of the Ecole de Musique de la Garde Nationale and of the Institut, he became one of the principal composers of military and festival music.[56] The rejection of Rameau's system was not simply a rejection of fundamental bass, but was also a repudiation of the *ancien régime* and the endorsement of the new generation of Revolutionary musicians and theorists who held internal control of the Conservatoire.

Secondly, Catel's system exemplifies simplicity. The *Traité* is a tersely written work. In only seventy pages Catel summarized contemporary harmonic practice. The unifying principle of the *corps sonore* and the mathematical manipulations used by Rameau to justify his system were the most often misunderstood, disputed and revised aspects of his theory. In contrast to Rameau's hierarchy of propositions, in Catel's system the *corps sonore* serves only as a conceptual basis for chord generation by thirds; the source does not rule the system. There are no digressions for rationalizations of chord generation, only simple descriptions of eight chords from which all others arise through suspensions, retardations or passing notes.[57]

Thirdly, Catel's system is eminently practical. Chords are classified into two groups: simple and composite. Simple, or natural, harmony (i.e. chords) needs no preparation; it is the source of all composite, or artificial, harmony – those chords that require preparation. This division resolves theoretical as well as practical problems. Chords that contain ninths, elevenths, thirteenths or augmented and diminished intervals created interminable dilemmas for continuo and fundamental bass theorists. Catel described these problematic chords as products of passing-note 'alteration' of chord notes or as products of the 'prolongation' of non-chord notes over simple chords. Dissonance resolution in composite chords is essentially contrapuntal and one needs only to suppress (or reduce out) the non-chord notes of composite harmonies in order to understand the progression of simple chords and the linear treatment of the individual voices. Catel specifically stated that his work was a preliminary course in composition that gave students 'the first

---

2° Il est établi une commission spécialement chargée de la rédaction des principes élémentaires de musique. Cette commission est formée de compositeurs.

56 Catel's contributions were praised in the *Journal des spectacles* in 1793 and he was described as a product of the inspiring opportunities afforded by the National Guard musical corps (in Pierre, *B. Sarrette*, pp. 50–51). For Catel's biography see J. Carlez, *Catel: étude biographique et critique* (Caen, 1894); F. Hellouin and J. Picard, *Un musicien oublié; Catel de l'Institut Royale de France (1773–1830)* (Paris, 1910); and F.-J. Fétis, H.-M. Berton and P.-M.-F. de Sales Baillot, 'Hommage à la mémoire de Catel', *Revue musicale*, x (1830), pp. 105–17.

57 The natural chords include major, minor and diminished triads; dominant, diminished and half-diminished seventh chords; and major and minor ninth chords.

notions of counterpoint' without recourse to traditional accompaniment methods.[58]

Fourthly, Catel's system could provide the basis for uniformity of method for compositional training. Leclerc advocated the system of fundamental bass as a prescriptive, didactic system. Catel's system could be taken as a prescriptive method if one considered the relationship of all chords to simple harmonies as the preferred basis of a musical composition. Indeed, this was the message of Bemetzrieder, who felt that his system, because it enforced simplicity in accompaniment, performance and composition, would supply a complete didactic method.[59]

Here I must return to Bemetzrieder's theory. A striking example of the prescriptive nature of his system was given in the *Journal de Paris* dated 19 October 1778. In that issue Bemetzrieder published a brief passage of basso continuo figured only by major and minor triads. He then supplied a forty-three-bar melody with accompaniment which expanded the bass line into a simple composition. This process was to be a model for composers. Bemetzrieder saw his system as a means of enforcing harmonic simplicity. Leclerc hoped fundamental bass would similarly limit the harmonic content of the *genre hymnique*. Likewise, Catel's system implies the same harmonic simplicity.

Nevertheless, Bemetzrieder's system could be applied generally as an analytical method. In fact, Bemetzrieder supplied several harmonic analyses of pieces from the operatic repertory, in the *Traité de musique*.[60] Similarly, Catel provided a way of understanding existing compositions through an analytical methodology that is *not* limiting (despite the implied prescriptive foundation of his system upon the class of simple chords). Catel's system allows for a flexible interpretation of linear and vertical elements through the concepts of alteration and prolongation, and therefore can also be seen as broadly analytical. A flexible analytical system was necessary to discuss and to explain even the Revolutionary genres of 'national music', which had only their performance situations in common. Thus, the techniques and individual styles of composers such as Gossec, Le Sueur, Méhul and Cherubini could be analysed within a consistent framework of harmonic termin-

58 Catel, *Traite*, 'Avant-propos': 'Je me suis donc proposé dans cet ouvrage d'enseigner l'harmonie en donnant les premières notions du contre-point ...'

59 The implied simplicity of harmony has been connected to Rameau's system because of its generation from the perfect triad (i.e. the first overtones of the harmonic series). See Mongrédien, *La musique*, pp. 40–41, and J.-L. Jam, 'Fonction des hymnes révolutionnaires', in *Les fêtes de la Révolution: colloque de Clermont-Ferrand (juin 1974)*, ed. J. Erhard and P. Viallaneix (Paris, 1977), pp. 433–42 and 450.

60 Bemetzrieder analysed the recitative 'Respirons un moment' and the aria 'O toi qui ne peut m'entendre' from François-André Philidor's *Tom Jones, comédie lyrique en trois actes* (Paris, [1766]), and a duet, 'Des simples jeux de son enfance', from J.-J. Rodolphe's *L'aveugle de Palmyre, comédie pastorale en deux actes en vers* (Paris, [1768]) in the *Traité de musique*, pp. 232–52 and plates 56–76.

ology, and the compositional techniques of the masters of national music could be communicated to aspiring student composers.

Finally, Catel's system could embrace all musical forms and compositional styles. The *Traité d'harmonie* provided a standardized didactic method that would keep pace with the transformed situation of the Conservatoire within musical life and with the resurgence of the church and theatre as prospective domains for composers' efforts.

At the Conservatoire's inception its monopoly extended only over the festivals. The control of the Opéra was not part of Sarrette's original design. Indeed, in 1797 he refused to put the direction of the Opéra under the administration of the Conservatoire.[61] By 1801, however, the Conservatoire was involved in a struggle centred on the scheduling of performances of Catel's first opera and an opera by Le Sueur. Throughout 1801 and 1802 Le Sueur and his supporters attacked Sarrette and the Conservatoire. Le Sueur saw the Conservatoire as an ideal institution for the regeneration of French opera and supported an elementary education system provided by the *maîtrises*. It is of some importance that Le Sueur was an advocate of the system of fundamental bass and a personal adversary of Catel.[62]

The Conservatoire was thus confronted by a challenge both to Sarrette's plan for national schools and to its newly adopted harmony method. Seeing the loss of the monopoly of the festivals, Sarrette and the Conservatoire turned towards pedagogical method, national education and musical commerce. In effect, the institution lost control of a genre, but not of the education of performers and composers. The fear of diluting the Conservatoire's central authority led to the neglect of national systems of education in favour of building a central institution and pedagogical method that might fulfil a goal of promulgating a French national music. This goal, first articulated in the *ancien régime* by opera polemicists, found its opportunity in the Revolutionary period through the Conservatoire's control of the national festivals. Still, the importance of operatic production was not to be swept away by the brief period of the Revolutionary festivals. The preface to Choron and Fayolle's *Dictionnaire historique des musiciens* (1810) indicates that the goal of 'national music' was not achieved; the same questions raised by the Gluckistes and Piccinnistes were voiced once again:

Si les Italiens ont été inventeurs dans toutes les parties de l'art musical, s'ils les ont perfectionnées presque toutes, et que les Allemands aient mené au même point celles que les premiers avaient laissées imparfaites, qu'ont donc fait les Français? se

---

61 Pierre, *B. Sarrette*, pp. 140–41.
62 See Mongrédien, *La musique*, pp. 23–5, and *Jean-François Le Sueur: contribution à l'étude d'un demi-siècle de musique française (1780–1830)* (Bern, 1980), i, pp. 458–76. In his memoirs Berlioz attested to Le Sueur's didactic method, which relied on the system of fundamental bass;

demandera-t-on, et quels droits ont-ils à figurer comme école à suite des peuples qui semblent avoir tout achevé?[63]

If the Italians were the innovators in all areas of musical art and perfected almost everything, and if the Germans brought to perfection what the Italians had left imperfect, one wonders what the French have done, and what right they have to be represented as a school after these people who seem to have accomplished everything?

Choron's answer was the superiority of the *drame-lyrique* and of French instrumental performance. As for music education, he recommended the applied method books of the Conservatoire and Catel's treatise on harmony. Choron hoped that further amelioration of the Conservatoire's pedagogical methods, previously held back in their development by the system of fundamental bass, would ensure a general superiority of the French school in all areas of music. The Conservatoire did remain the focal point of musical training in France, but the foundation and maintenance of a distinct musical style through the association of music theory and music education was perhaps an unattainable goal. The creation of the Conservatoire during the Revolutionary period, however, laid the groundwork for a pedagogical system that would be enforced by a powerful and centralized institution of music education.

see *Memoirs of Hector Berlioz*, trans. and ed. R. Holmes, E. Holmes and E. Newman (New York, 1932), pp. 24–5.

63 *Dictionnaire historique des musiciens, artistes et amateurs, morts ou vivants*, ed. A.-E. Choron and J. Fayolle (Paris, 1810; reprinted Hildesheim, 1971), p. lxxvii.

French Revolutionary perspectives on Chabanon's *De la musique* of 1785

Any study of the changes that took place in French musical thought during the period of the French Revolution must consider whether traditional views were sustained as elements of stability, or new ideas were greeted as harbingers of a progressive musical outlook. As an approach to this question, this essay will consider the main concepts in the culminating work of Michel-Paul-Guy de Chabanon (1730–92)[1] and the ways in which his ideas were utilized or modified by seven authors of the Revolutionary period: Vigué, Le Sueur, Lefébure, Saint-Ange, Framery, Leclerc and Olivier.

Chabanon's thought in *De la musique considérée en elle-même*[2] reflects the interests of a distinguished man of letters and academician who was also a composer of sonatas[3] and a respected amateur violinist.[4] Chabanon played in instrumental groups, including the Concert des Amateurs under Gossec's direction, and this provided a firm pragmatic basis for his theoretical speculations. Described in the *Encyclopédie méthodique* as an 'elegant and learned author who could have become renowned also as a teacher of music' (élégant et savant écrivain, qui,

---

1 For full bibliography, see R. Cotte, 'Chabanon, Michel-Paul-Guy de', in *The New Grove Dictionary of Music and Musicians*, ed. S. Sadie (London, 1980), iv, pp. 95–6; and A. Sorel-Nitzberg, 'Chabanon, Michel, Paul, Guy de', in *Die Musik in Geschichte und Gegenwart*, ed. F. Blume (Kassel, 1952), ii, cols. 996–1004. Recent scholarship is listed separately below. Brief mention of Chabanon is also made in B. S. Brook, *La symphonie française dans la seconde moitié du XVIIIe siècle* (Paris, 1962), i, pp. 333–4; G. Snyders, *Le goût musical en France aux XVIIe et XVIIIe siècles* (Paris, 1968), pp. 171–6; and W. Weber, 'Learned and General Musical Taste in Eighteenth-Century France', *Past and Present: a Journal of Historical Studies*, lxxxix (1980), pp. 58–85, especially p. 79.

2 Anon. [M.-P.-G. de Chabanon], *De la musique considérée en elle-même et dans ses rapports avec la parole, les langues, la poésie, et le théâtre* (Paris, 1785). All English translations are by this author.

3 Anon. [M.-P.-G. de Chabanon], *Trois sonates pour clavecin ou forte piano avec accompagnement de violon* (Paris, n.d.). This author thanks M. Erick Haspot of the Department of Music, Bibliothèque Nationale, Paris, for kindly providing photocopies of these works. See also Mr de Chabanon, *Sonate pour le clavecin ou le piano-forte* (Paris, 1785).

4 The *Tablettes de renommée des musiciens: auteurs, compositeurs, virtuoses, amateurs et maîtres de musique vocale et instrumentale, les plus connus en chaque genre* (Paris, 1785; reprinted Geneva, 1971), p. Ai, describes him as an 'amateur' and 'excellent Violon'.

même comme professeur de musique, auroit pu se faire encore un grand renom'),[5] Chabanon published his augmented and revised major work on musical aesthetics in 1785; the first part had originally appeared in 1779 as *Observations sur la musique et principalement sur la métaphysique de l'art*.[6] The author's involvement in musical and literary affairs allowed him to question the prerogatives automatically assumed by men of letters on musical issues, to encourage professional musicians (whom he praised) to learn more about other fields, and to promote greater association between the two groups.[7]

The major achievement of Chabanon's *De la musique* is its recognition of music as a separate and independent art that differed both from verbal language and from other arts esteemed in the French critical tradition for their ability to imitate nature. Chabanon was able to encompass in his ideas both vocal and instrumental music, and his treatment of 'la musique considérée en elle-même' needs to be emphasized. He asserted that music, in contrast to painting, pleased independently of imitation through a direct appeal to the senses. As an art which organized tones in a manner agreeable to the ear, its first obligation was not to paint but to sing: 'peindre n'est que le second de ses devoirs, chanter est le premier'. Except in the theatre, the single advantage of vocal over instrumental music was that the text helped 'demi-connoisseurs' and the ignorant to determine the character of the music. But he also affirmed that 'the more one possesses a trained and sensitive ear and is gifted with musical instinct, the more easily one dispenses with words' ('plus on a l'oreille exercée, sensible, & douée de l'instinct musical, plus on se passe aisément de paroles').[8]

Chabanon decried the common French practice of calling only vocal music 'singing'; was it not a strange restriction of the term 'melody'? Citing his admiration for symphonies like those that had been performed at the Concert des Amateurs, he defended instrumental music from its many detractors by connecting its attractive features to song.[9] Contradicting Rousseau's assertion that the merit of song was to resemble verbal discourse,[10] Chabanon held that song had originated earlier than speech and, in addition, that the processes of song were entirely different from those of language. As an example of this disparity he noted that simple recitative most resembled the spoken word but was the least expressive of all musical styles. Music, as song, followed separate

---

5 N. E. Framery and P. L. Guinguené, eds., *Encyclopédie méthodique: Musique* (Paris, 1791), i, p. ix.
6 Anon. [M.-P.-G. de Chabanon], *Observations sur la musique et principalement sur la métaphysique de l'art* (Paris, 1779). See also *Musical Aesthetics: a Historical Reader*, ed. E. A. Lippman (New York, 1986–8), i, pp. 257–8 and 295–318.
7 Anon. [Chabanon], *De la musique*, pp. 22–4.   8 Ibid., pp. 62–6.   9 Ibid., pp. 33–5.
10 Ibid., pp. 73–7.

processes that did not depend on the pronunciation of words in speech. These included perceptible interval and key relationships and the harmonic coexistence of tones.

Chabanon explained that words were conventional signs for other objects, whereas tones comprised song itself. The position of tones in a musical phrase was fixed and could not be changed, while the order of words in a sentence could be altered. Musical tones lacked intrinsic signification; only in relation to each other and through musical procedures resulting in contrast, as well as through appropriate performance, did they acquire meaning. Chabanon accounted for differences in instrumental expressivity with his theory of four general musical characters: 'tendre, gracieuse, gaie, vive'. He equated these with the terms 'largo', 'andante', 'allegro' and 'presto' respectively.[11]

Affirming the intrinsic importance of melody, rhythm and harmony as musical elements, Chabanon acknowledged the traditional sovereignty of melody, but as a strong supporter of Rameau's theories he insisted that harmony was an essential component. It had an important role in symphonic music and in operatic works such as those of Gluck, in which the vocal line did not always predominate but engaged in diverse dramatic exchanges with the orchestral material. Chabanon was most ready to justify that kind of harmony which engendered easy and natural melody.[12]

As an advocate of new artistic ideals stressing sensuous beauty more than an appeal to reason, Chabanon believed that all the arts shared the primary goal of pleasing, but he made subtle distinctions regarding music. He considered music, in his view a universal language of tones based on natural principles, to be the most popular of the arts, and one that appealed to a wide audience, but he recognized that a more complex type of music required study and reflection as well as careful listening. This was the kind of music that satisfied the sophisticated taste of musicians, and he asserted that 'the work that pleases musicians will please the public sooner or later, if no cause extraneous to the music opposes it' ('l'ouvrage qui plaît aux Musiciens, plaîra tôt ou tard au Public, si aucune cause étrangère à la Musique ne s'y oppose').[13]

Modern scholars disagree about the nature of Chabanon's innovative thought. Rémy Saisselin argues that, although it did not actually postulate the autonomy of music, it did introduce a new emphasis on interior sentiment and destroyed the old formulation uniting the arts by an imitative principle.[14] Roger Cotte, however, considers that Chabanon's works, culminating in *De la musique*, mark 'one of the earliest

11 Ibid., pp. 166–8 and 145–57.   12 Ibid., pp. 184–94.
13 Ibid., pp. 367–87, especially p. 385.
14 R. G. Saisselin, *The Rule of Reason and the Ruses of the Heart: a Philosophical Dictionary of Classical French Criticism, Critics, and Aesthetic Issues* (Cleveland, 1970), pp. 230–32.

attempts at an autonomous aesthetic of the art';[15] Ivo Supičič regards Chabanon as formalism's 'first proponent in eighteenth-century musical aesthetics';[16] and Maria Rika Maniates recognizes 'his gallant attempt to justify a theory of inherent expressivity in absolute music', while judging that his treatment of the expression of individual emotions in instrumental music remained problematic.[17] Notwithstanding its limitations, Chabanon's treatise explored new terrain in its attempt to expand the meaning of song more comprehensively, for instrumental as well as vocal music. In the framework of the flourishing symphonic and operatic activity in the Paris of the *ancien régime*, it confronted issues that might have challenged other musical thinkers to build on its insights in the closing years of the eighteenth century.

The first notice of Chabanon's work appeared in 1785 in *Réflexions sur la musique, ou Recherches sur la cause des effets qu'elle produit*, thought to be by a certain Vigué.[18] The substance of this essay had been presented earlier, in 1776, at a private gathering in the home of Count Bernard Germain Etienne de Lacépède, author of the important *La poétique de la musique*.[19] When Vigué finally published it he added a preface responding to Chabanon's *De la musique*, which had recently appeared. The author claimed that he had gone further than Chabanon in denying to music an imitative character. He disagreed with Chabanon's definition of melody, which he considered vague, but severely limited his own discussion of music by emphasizing the importance of vocal melody and its connection to arbitrary rules.[20] Vigué thus disregarded the totality of Chabanon's more inclusive approach to music, in which melody was but one of several essential elements.

The composer Jean-François Le Sueur wrote the *Suite de l'essai sur la musique sacrée et imitative*[21] as one of five essays published in 1786–7

---

15 Cotte, 'Chabanon, Michel-Paul-Guy de', *The New Grove*, iv, p. 96.

16 I. Supičič, 'Expression and Meaning in Music', *International Review of the Aesthetics and Sociology of Music*, ii (1971), pp. 193–211, esp. p. 198.

17 M. R. Maniates, '"Sonate, que me veux-tu?": the Enigma of French Musical Aesthetics in the 18th Century', *Current Musicology*, ix (1969), pp. 117–40, esp. p. 131.

18 'M. V****' [Vigué], *Réflexions sur la musique, ou Recherches sur la cause des effets qu'elle produit* (Amsterdam and Paris, 1785). This is listed in *Répertoire international des sources musicales: écrits imprimés concernant la musique*, B-VI$^{1-2}$ (Munich and Duisburg, 1971), ii, p. 862 under the name 'Vigué' (in brackets), without further identification.

19 B. G. E. M. de la Ville-sur-Illon de Lacépède, *La poétique de la musique* (Paris, 1785). For further information about this work, see O. Frishberg Saloman, 'La Cépède's *La poétique de la musique* and Le Sueur', *Acta musicologica*, xlvii (1975), pp. 144–54.

20 Anon. [Vigué], *Réflexions sur la musique*, pp. vi–xi, 31–3 and 50.

21 J. F. Le Sueur, *Suite de l'essai sur la musique sacrée et imitative, où l'on donne le plan d'une musique propre à la fête de Pâque* [sic] (Paris, 1787). For recent scholarship and further bibliography on Le Sueur, see J. Mongrédien, *Jean-François Le Sueur: contribution à l'étude d'un demi-siècle de musique française (1780–1830)* (Berne, 1980), and 'Le Sueur, Jean-François' in *The New Grove*, x, pp. 694–7; M. Herman, 'The Sacred Music of Jean François Le Sueur: a Musical and Biographical Source Study' (diss., University of Michigan, 1964);

to explain his ideas about dramatic sacred music for soloists, chorus and orchestra, which he, as *maître de chapelle*, had composed for performance at Notre Dame. Le Sueur described the importance of expressing sentiments and dramatic situations connected to the observance of specific religious feastdays. These goals were to be accomplished through the combination of original and traditional music associated with a particular feast, carefully selected texts and explicative brochures to be distributed at the performances. In the *Suite de l'essai* he expressed sentiments similar to Chabanon's about the importance of writing song that would be pleasing to the ear. Significantly, Le Sueur chose to link his discussion of the unity of subject and style, which would contribute to the coherence of the musical whole in the last part of his motet for Easter, with Chabanon's concern for the structural unity of musical pieces. Naming only Chabanon and Lacépède as particularly informed about the poetics of music, the composer expressed the hope that they and other knowledgeable listeners would perceive the construction of the piece as he intended it. Le Sueur explained that he had carefully planned the final section around a central musical point and it was his wish that those cognizant of the crucial relationship of the parts to the whole would connect them appropriately.

Si les Chabanons, les la Cépède, & ceux qui, comme eux, sentent la poétique de la Musique, y voient que le Compositeur a eu l'intention que tous les grouppes particuliers fissent d'abord ressortir ce qui les entoure, & finissent par former un grouppe total; s'ils y découvrent qu'il a eu le dessein de faire graduer les sensations des assistans, jusqu'au moment où la Musique arrive au centre; s'ils y découvrent qu'il a voulu que les Auditeurs apperçussent, de ce point central, toutes les parties de l'ouvrage, qui se réuniront alors pour leur faire éprouver à-la-fois, les différens mouvemens qu'elles leur auront fait sentir en détail, il aura rempli son objet.[22]

If the Chabanons, the Lacépèdes and those who, like them, are aware of the poetics of music, see that the composer has intended that all the separate sections should at first set off the one next to them, and end by forming a single complete section; if they discover that he planned that the feelings of the audience should be engaged gradually up to the middle of the piece; and if they find that he wanted the listeners to perceive, from this central point, all the parts of the work, which will then be brought together so that the audience can experience at one and the same time the different emotions they will have been made to feel in detail – then he will have fulfilled his aim.

In associating his aims for dramatic religious music with Chabanon in this single positive reference, the young composer sought to identify himself with the distinguished older aesthetician's recently expressed views regarding the importance of structural cohesion in musical works.

O. Frishberg Saloman, 'The Orchestra in Le Sueur's Musical Aesthetics', *The Musical Quarterly*, lx (1974), pp. 616–25, and 'La Cépède's *La poétique de la musique*'.
22 Le Sueur, *Suite de l'essai*, pp. 65–6.

It should be noted, however, that Le Sueur remained committed to a concept of imitative music whose fundamental expressive aim could be achieved only through dramatic music with text, as both his writings and his music suggest. Chabanon, in contrast, had considered the separation of instrumental music from an imitative principle in 1779 and more fully in 1785. Consequently, although Le Sueur enriched French musical thought through an emphasis on the distinctive, necessary and indispensable function of active instrumental lines in dramatic music written for the theatre or the church, he did not pursue the ramifications of Chabanon's more progressive views regarding independent instrumental music by composing symphonies or sonatas.

Louis-François Henri Lefébure's *Bévues, erreurs et méprises de différents auteurs célèbres, en matières musicales* (Paris, 1789) took issue with Chabanon as someone who undervalued musical expression.[23] Lefébure, a musician, author and government official, cited Chabanon's view that separate musical tones possessed no intrinsic signification, no sense, no expression, in contrast to the distinctive properties of syllables and words in verbal language[24] – an argument fundamental to Chabanon's assertion that independent processes shaped music, in contrast to language, and that they produced variety through the interaction of specifically musical elements, including melody, rhythm, harmony and dynamics. Lefébure insisted that, on the contrary, there were marked differences between tones. He contended that through their pitch and duration tones comprised expressive song. In considering the power of music Lefébure, unlike Chabanon, rejected as primary reasons for its effect the development of motifs, rhythmic changes and consonance–dissonance treatment. Instead he asserted that its chief domain was the expression of varied sentiments. Lefébure agreed with Chabanon's enlightened position in recommending that the dated theory of imitation be discarded as the main principle of all the arts and that harmony be recognized as essential, rather than subsidiary, in music.[25] Ultimately, however, he overlooked a fundamental innovative aspect of Chabanon's thesis by limiting his own discussion to opera. In so doing he emphasized the connection of vocal music to the definite meanings of text rather than confronting the issue raised by Chabanon: that instrumental music can move the listener through entirely musical procedures in situations independent of words.

Michel de Chabanon died in 1792, and during the following years of the Terror there is no evidence of his work's influence. In 1795, however, his *Tableau de quelques circonstances de ma vie* was published post-

---

23 For biographical information about Lefébure, see *Baker's Biographical Dictionary of Musicians*, ed. N. Slonimsky, 7th edn (New York, 1984), p. 1326.
24 Lefébure, *Bévues, erreurs et méprises*, pp. 86–111.   25 Ibid., pp. 75–80.

humously in accordance with his wishes.[26] Its appearance may have renewed interest in his work. The hope that it would do so was stated by the *Tableau*'s editor, the poet and translator Ange-François Fariau de Saint-Ange, who had been Chabanon's friend during the last six years of his life. Saint-Ange's preface, loyal and warm in remembrance of Chabanon, reveals his horror of events occurring in the years between Chabanon's death and the book's appearance. His point of view was characteristic of someone who had enjoyed royal protection before the Revolution, found himself suddenly without resources and only gradually regained employment, in Saint-Ange's case as a teacher of grammar and literature.[27]

The *Tableau* revealed incidents in Chabanon's life in which music had been an important background element. An outstanding event in Chabanon's youth was his attendance at a concert given by Jean-Marie Leclair *l'aîné* at the Concert Spirituel; it had been memorable to a boy with violinistic ability because of Leclair's instrumental mastery and as a first encounter with concert music. Incidents recounted by Chabanon about his adult years reflect the role of music in bringing him into social contact with individuals through his performances as orchestral leader or violinist at private gatherings.[28] Chabanon reaffirmed in this work the later eighteenth-century position asserted in *De la musique*: that the arts, particularly music, affect the senses first and reason later.[29]

The following year, 1796, brought publication of the *Avis aux poëtes lyriques* by Nicolas Etienne Framery. Framery's call for elegant simplicity from musicians and poets rang with renewed vigour in its application to a genre which had recently acquired particular significance in French society: civic hymns.[30] In building his case for the importance of simplicity in melody and text, Framery invoked Chabanon's name to disagree with his assertion that symmetry in versification and in music was not always essential. Chabanon had actually introduced this idea after stressing the natural human instinct and taste for symmetrical arrangement; he had then suggested that musical prerogatives, rather than poetic rules, might warrant exceptions to customary practice.[31] Disregarding the context of Chabanon's remarks, Framery proposed as

---

26 M.-P.-G. de Chabanon, *Tableau de quelques circonstances de ma vie, Précis de ma liaison avec mon frère Maugris: ouvrages posthumes de Chabanon*, ed. A.-F. F. de Saint-Ange (Paris, an III/1795), Preface, p. ix.

27 Biographical information about Saint-Ange is available in *Grand dictionnaire universel du XIXe siècle français, historique, géographique, mythologique, bibliographique, littéraire, artistique, scientifique, etc.*, ed. P. Larousse (Paris, 1866–79; reprinted Geneva and Paris, 1982), xiv/1, p. 57.

28 Chabanon, *Tableau de quelques circonstances*, pp. 12 and 27.   29 Ibid., p. 172.

30 N. E. Framery, *Avis aux poëtes lyriques, ou De la nécessité du rhythme et de la césure dans les hymnes ou odes destinés à la musique* (Paris, an IV/1796), especially pp. 26–35. For information about Framery, see *Baker's Biographical Dictionary*, p. 754.

31 Chabanon, *De la musique*, pp. 251–8.

necessary the use of rhyme in poetry and greater adherence to symmetry in both music and verse. He insisted on the advantages of these traits to the French language and as practical requirements in civic hymns. Their value, he suggested, would be to adorn national festivals and 'through the charms of melody, to plant in the memory of the people patriotic sentiments, examples of virtues and maxims of philosophy and reason' ('pour pénétrer dans la mémoire du peuple, pour y fixer, par les charmes de la mélodie, les sentimens patriotiques, les exemples des vertus, les maximes de la philosophie et de la raison').[32]

Deriding a searching for effect through complicated music whose varied instrumental components might overwhelm the vocal part and challenge the memory of the participants, Framery exhorted the musician of the Revolution to associate himself with it in perpetuity by composing easy vocal melody with agreeable refrains geared to the range of the musically untrained. This *Avis*, printed by order of the Committee of Public Instruction, heralded simple functional music with text performed by a mass of citizens in the service of patriotic goals, rather than complicated instrumental music.

Jean-Baptiste Leclerc was elected to the Convention; he was imprisoned under the Terror and subsequently served as a member of the Council of Five Hundred and assisted in the creation of the Conservatoire de Musique.[33] In 1796 he published an *Essai sur la propagation de la musique en France* in which he attacked the vagueness of music without text.[34] Leclerc lamented that orchestras, despite their best efforts, were unable to imitate perfectly the sounds of nature and noted that they sometimes managed to create illusion with the assistance of decorations or a poetic text. Citing the title of Chabanon's work without naming the author, he stated that he had learned from it that music imitated imperfectly and expressed only generalities:

La symphonie n'exprime non plus que les généralités, telles que le calme ou l'agitation, la joie ou la douleur. Dans toutes les subdivisions, elle a besoin d'un interprète. J'ai retrouvé cette idée dans un écrit sur la musique considérée en elle-même et dans ses rapports.[35]

The symphony expresses no more than generalities, such as calmness or agitation, joy or sorrow. For finer shades of expression it requires an interpreter. I found this idea in a written work on music considered in itself and in its relations [to other things].

Leclerc added that if ten people were asked the meaning of a symphony by Haydn, ten different replies would be given.

32 N. E. Framery, *Avis aux poëtes lyriques*, p. 29.
33 For biographical information about Leclerc, see *Le petit Robert: dictionnaire universel des noms propres*, new revised edition ed. A. Rey (Paris, 1987), p. 1040.
34 J.-B. Leclerc, *Essai sur la propagation de la musique en France, sa conservation, et ses rapports avec le gouvernement* (Paris, an IV), especially pp. 22–3.
35 Ibid., pp. 62–3, note 19.

Having dispensed with purely instrumental music as inarticulate and thus incapable of either imitation or expression, Leclerc advocated as a functional objective that national music should become more inspirational. He proposed that henceforth instrumental music be made inseparable from poetic text to assure its meaning. This would encompass the prohibition of marches for the National Guard and dance tunes in public festivals unless they had been originally composed to words with a moral or political purpose.

Leclerc thus distorted Chabanon's attempt to explain the significance of purely instrumental music and subverted it to formulate a negative statement about its indefinite, and thus non-utilitarian, status. Leclerc's complaints against recent increases in the size of orchestras and the freedom of orchestral writing stemmed from his conviction that a revolution in morals could best be accomplished through simple melody allied to pure texts.[36] The adoption of a repertory of hymns and songs with appropriate sentiments would assure the re-establishment of the balance between human passions and strengthen the necessary association of music with civic virtue.

A similar concern pervaded citizen Gabriel-Raimond-Jean de Dieu-François d'Olivier's *L'esprit d'Orphée, ou De l'influence respective de la musique, de la morale et de la législation*, published in Paris in three volumes (1798, 1802 and 1804). Olivier, a lawyer writer and judge,[37] issued many writings of which this alone was devoted to music. In the introduction, framed as a dream, the ghost of Orpheus charges the author to seek ways in which music influences customs and morals. Consistent with that mission, Olivier stresses the capacity of music, beyond other arts, to express and direct human passions, as well as to inspire a love of moral virtue.[38] Therefore, whether in opera or in religious music, Olivier emphasizes the significant connection of music to text. He also urges attention to appropriate text setting for the achievement of characteristic expression in music for the theatre.

That Olivier failed to consider symphonic music is not surprising in view of the work's aim. His two overt references to the 'ingénieux académicien' noted agreement with Chabanon's preference for the social company of musicians and cited his knowledgeable discussion of the close links between music and dance among the arts.[39]

The role of vocal melody as a vehicle for the expression of sentiments was of central interest to authors of French Revolutionary writings on music. They echoed several of Chabanon's traditional interests in

---

36 Ibid., pp. 24 and 30–33.
37 Biographical information about Olivier is in *Grand dictionnaire universel du XIXe siècle*, xi/2, p. 1315.
38 G.-R.-J. de D.-F. d'Olivier, *L'esprit d'Orphée*, i, pp. 39–88.   39 Ibid., iii, pp. 23 and 53.

structural unity, in pleasing melody and in the potential appeal of music to a wider audience, without recognizing the larger implications of his thought regarding 'la musique considérée en elle-même'.[40] The documents provide evidence that the writers supported the composition of vocal music with text because it could help to instil civic virtue and love of country.

Revolutionary authors turned from the vagueness of instrumental music, as some mistakenly believed Chabanon had described it, to promote the communication and reinforcement of clear political and social messages through easily sung melodies with memorable refrains. When they utilized Chabanon's idea that musical tones were not in themselves 'expressive', they dissociated it from its original intellectual context and shaped it to justify their championship of patriotic, educational or inspirational goals. They also favoured a pragmatic approach that challenged Chabanon's progressive interest in the purely musical processes inherent in instrumental music and disregarded the vital contemporaneous composition and performance of symphonies concertantes and virtuoso concertos. They shared instead a prevailing enthusiasm for music with text, often joined to spectacle, as an effective means of celebrating the nation's ideals during an eventful era.

40 For further information about Chabanon's early musical thought, see O. Frishberg Saloman, 'Chabanon and Chastellux on Music and Language, 1764–1773', *International Review of the Aesthetics and Sociology of Music*, xx/2 (1989), pp. 109–20.

This essay was written with the support of a Fellowship Award granted by Baruch College of The City University of New York. The author wishes to thank particularly Dean Norman Fainstein of the School of Liberal Arts and Sciences, Baruch College, CUNY.

Marie-Joseph Chénier and François-Joseph Gossec: two artists in the service of Revolutionary propaganda

La Révolution peut être comparée à un grand drame lyrique paroles de Marie-Joseph Chénier, musique de Gossec ...

The Revolution may be likened to a great lyric drama with words by Marie-Joseph Chénier and music by Gossec.

This famous statement of Challamel's is one of those simplistic formulas on which the mythology of the Revolution has fed for almost two centuries. In fact, even nowadays, lacking precise knowledge of the function of poetry and music in Revolutionary festivals, historiography is usually content with Rouget de Lisle's colourful and evocative *Marseillaise*, the *Chant du départ* of Méhul and Chénier, and perhaps Gossec's *Marche lugubre*. Thus music and poetry are consigned in historical discourse to a subsidiary role, and patriotic songs are seen merely as decorative features of Revolutionary celebrations. As for the role of Chénier and Gossec, it is clear that this was not as fundamentally important as Challamel claimed, although no one would dispute that these two, the one with forty-four scores and the other with thirty poems, were the most active providers of such material for civic festivals. Furthermore, among the works they wrote for various events, twelve resulted from a mutual collaboration which, given their radically different personalities, one would not have expected.[1]

A MAN OF THE PAST

In 1789 François-Joseph Gossec was fifty-five years old. Although an esteemed composer and a respected teacher, Gossec was a failure as an artist – or at least he himself thought he was. In actual fact, although his career was not at a complete standstill, his justifiable hopes and expectations had not been realized. His reserved character, lack of

---

[1] This study is based on the corpus of Revolutionary hymns by Chénier and Gossec included in the following publications of Constant Pierre: *Musique des fêtes et cérémonies de la Révolution française* (Paris, 1899) and *Les hymnes et les chansons de la Révolution* (Paris, 1904).

determination, and above all his uncommonly bad luck had all combined as obstacles to his success. He was a talented symphonist, but could not claim to be on an equal footing with his contemporary Joseph Haydn, whose most ardent admirer in France he nevertheless remained. However, his name was often associated with that of the Austrian composer on Parisian concert bills, in published anthologies of symphonies,[2] and in the estimation of informed amateurs and professional musicians such as Grétry, who wrote in his *Mémoires*, 'Whatever Fontenelle said, we know what a good sonata wants of us, and above all a symphony of Haydn or Gossec' ('Quoiqu'en ait dit Fontenelle, nous savons ce que nous veut une bonne sonate, et surtout une symphonie de Haydn ou de Gossec').[3]

In reality, the considerable reserve, indeed suspicion, of the French public towards instrumental music (to which Grétry alluded indirectly) prevented Gossec from displaying that talent to which his entire symphonic production from op. 3 (1756) to the Symphony in seventeen parts (1809) bears witness. The Revolution saw no end to this ostracism; on the contrary, the theorists of the festivals showed themselves more than reticent towards instrumental music, which they condemned, in the name of neo-Platonicism, as harmful, idle and useless to the point of insignificance.[4] Doubtless Gossec was soon aware that the climate was unfavourable towards his particular genius, since as early as 1765 he decided to write *opéras comiques*, which were then enjoying great popularity. After a few moderate successes, he gave up in 1767 following the failure of *Le double déguisement*. Two years later Grétry's star began to rise, with *Le huron*, on a long and brilliant career which robbed Gossec of any hopes of staging a come-back. In 1773 Gossec, together with Simon Leduc and Pierre Gaviniès, became a director of the Concert Spirituel, but he did not abandon the lyric stage, which he now set out to conquer through the prestigious medium of the *tragédie lyrique*. On 22 February 1774 the Parisian première of *Sabinus* took place; it was a success. Alas, two months later, almost to the day, Gluck produced his *Iphigénie en Aulide*, relegating Gossec's work to second rank. The disappointment, four years later, of seeing the libretto of *Iphigénie en Tauride* slip through his hands and into those of that same Gluck made him abandon for ever any hope of success. It was therefore a bitter and disillusioned man who in 1784 accepted the post of director of the Ecole Royale de Chant et de Déclamation after Piccinni had declined it. The following letter, written by Gossec in 1778, shows in what frame of mind he found himself at the age of forty-four, with still half a century to live:

2 E.g. *Trois symphonies ... composées par Mrs Gossec, Haydn et Bach* (Paris, 1777).
3 A.-E.-M. Grétry, *Mémoires, ou Essais sur la musique* (Paris, 1812), i, p. 78.
4 J.-B. Leclerc, *Essai sur la propagation de la musique en France* (Paris, [1796]), p. 22.

Recevez mes remerciements, Monsieur, de ce que vous voulez bien m'assigner dans la partie dramatique, une place immédiatement au-dessous de M. Gluck. Vous me flattez et vous n'êtes pas sincère. Je ne pense pas comme vous; je suis trop petit pour atteindre si haut. Je n'ai pas même l'espoir de produire un ouvrage sur la scène, tant que M. Gluck la tiendra; *Sabinus* fut éclipsé par lui; *Iphigénie en Tauride* m'est enlevée par lui; *Thésée*, fixé à l'hiver prochain, sera renvoyé à deux ans par lui. Dans deux ans, M. Piccini ou M. Gluck me rejetteront en 3ème année, d'autant qu'il est tout naturel de leur laisser les honneurs de la scène.... En attendant mes cheveux blanchissent, mes espérances s'évanouissent et mon courage s'éteint. Tout pour moi n'est que motif de dégoût.[5]

I am grateful to you, Monsieur, for allotting me a place immediately below M. Gluck in the realm of dramatic art. You flatter me, and you do not speak frankly. I do not agree; I am too small to reach so high. I cannot even hope to produce a work on the stage as long as M. Gluck holds it; *Sabinus* was overshadowed by him; *Iphigénie en Tauride* is taken off the stage because of him; *Thésée*, fixed for next winter, will be postponed for two years by him. In two years' time M. Piccinni or M. Gluck will cast me aside for a third year, all the more since it is quite natural to allow them the honours of the stage.... While I wait my hair grows white, my hopes vanish and my courage is dampened. Everything for me is only a cause for disgust.

Some ten years later, when the Revolution was beginning and when none of his works was any longer in the repertory of the Concert Spirituel (with the single exception of the motet *O salutaris hostia*), Gossec had ceased to expect anything much from life. He was a man of the past.

A MAN OF THE FUTURE

In 1789 Marie-Joseph Chénier, although no more than twenty-five years of age, was already, if not a celebrity, at least well-known to a good number of his contemporaries. Thanks to his mother's practice of holding regular salons, he had made many acquaintances in the artistic and literary circles of the capital. In this way he became friendly with Charles Palissot de Montenoy, who encouraged him to take up a career as a dramatist. After trying first with *Edgar* (1785) and *Azémire* (1786), he wrote *Charles IX*, a historical and moralistic tragedy in the tradition of Voltaire's *Mahomet*; he admired Voltaire and secretly hoped to succeed him in the theatre. On 2 September 1788 *Charles IX* was unanimously accepted for performance at the Comédie-Française, but the censor banned it because it was critical not only of intolerance but also of the authority of the monarch and the Church. Chénier made every effort to get the ban lifted: in January 1789, with Palissot's help, he secured permission for a private performance in the presence of the Duke

5 J. Tiersot, ed., *Lettres de musiciens écrites en français du XVème au XXème siècle* (Turin, c. 1924), pp. 200–1.

of Orleans. The result was not what he had hoped for: the future Philippe-Egalité was uneasy about this anti-aristocratic pamphlet. In justifiable despair Chénier appealed to public opinion: on 15 June he published a pamphlet entitled *De la liberté du théâtre en France*, in which he called for an end to censorship. In September he returned to the attack with another text, *La dénonciation des inquisiteurs de la pensée*, which appeared simultaneously with his *Courtes réflexions sur l'état civil des comédiens*, in which he claimed for actors the right to be chosen as officers in the National Guard. Liberty and the Rights of Man were then the order of the day; *Charles IX* became a symbol, and its author made his entry into politics. The events of July 1789 could only favour his cause. On 19 August at the Théâtre Français the public demanded *Charles IX*; the historic days of October confirmed his triumph, and the piece was performed on 4 November. On that day there was a huge audience; Talma had his first success, and among the spectators Mirabeau was to be seen, as well as several deputies from the National Assembly, including the future stars of the Club des Cordeliers, Camille Desmoulins and George Jacques Danton. Danton declared: 'Si *Figaro* a tué la noblesse, *Charles IX* tuera la royauté' ('If *Figaro* killed the nobility, *Charles IX* will kill the monarchy'). The republican party had just recognized one of its spokesmen, and Marie-Joseph Chénier had started on his career as a politically committed poet.

HOW SHOULD THE REVOLUTION BE CELEBRATED?

From the end of the year 1789 the idea of commemorating the taking of the Bastille was in everyone's mind. The increasing number of regional federations, or rallies of National Guards, led certain Parisian politicians, among them Jean-Silvain Bailly, to propose a national Festival of the Federation. This festival, to be held on 14 July 1790, would be the occasion for a big official event and would conclude (following the tradition of the *ancien régime*) with a thanksgiving mass. The brilliance that the authorities wished to impart to the celebration, but also the difficulties of performing in the open air, required the composition of a new *Te Deum* which would be suitable to the festival, both ideologically and in practical terms. Gossec was naturally entrusted with this task. In fact, in 1790 there was no other French composer of church music with a reputation equal to his. His motets and his grand oratorios, such as *La nativité* (1774), which had been in the repertory of the Concert Spirituel for ten years, were still fresh in the memory. As for his *Grande messe des morts*, this had been regularly performed ever since it was composed in 1760; Parisians were able to hear it again in August 1789, performed by members of the Académie Royale de Musique on the occasion of a funeral service for those from the Saint Martin-des-Champs district who had died during the storming of the Bastille.[6] Besides, Gossec's position as director of the Ecole Royale de Chant et de Déclamation made him the only establishment musician who was not directly in the service of the king or of the Church – an essential qualification in the circumstances.[7]

The work was finished on 9 July.[8] If it is not to be compared with that of 1779, this is not because the 1790 *Te Deum* brings any innovatory qualities to Gossec's work (except for the extensive use of wind instruments). One would look in vain for any boldness of style here, and the setting of the liturgical text for male voices in three parts belongs to the tradition of the *a cappella* motet that *O salutaris hostia* had brought back into fashion. Also one can recognize numerous 'borrowings', such as the Pastorale that Gossec does not notate, but whose insertion he indicates after the verse 'Tu Patris sempiternus es Filius'; this is, in all probability, taken from *La nativité*. Or again there is the instrumental piece that illustrates the verse 'Judex crederis esse venturus' and recalls exactly the introduction to 'Mors stupebit' in the *Grande messe des morts*. In fact, Gossec's originality is shown mainly in the way he breaks up the Ambrosian hymn and sets the different verses: the phrases of text are sung homophonically, alternating in an unusual way with instrumental interludes of an expressive or dance-like character. The mood of each interlude is determined by the verse that precedes it: the recalling of Christ's birth prompts a musical evocation of the adoration of the shepherds, and apocalyptic trumpets conjure up the Last Judgment. This is all very ordinary. On the other hand, Gossec shows more originality when he chooses to illustrate verses in praise of the Lord (such as the 'Sanctus' and the 'Laudamus') with the passepied and the rigaudon, dances of a decidedly folk-like character, which serve well to express and prolong a feeling of joy. Thus the *Te Deum* of 1790 bears witness to Gossec's efforts to write the kind of music that conformed to the spirit of this Festival of the Federation, from which no one should feel excluded. If the clergy and the nobility, as well as the bourgeoisie and the 'petit peuple', could not actually join in the singing of this unusual work, at least all the sensibilities of the nation could vibrate in listening to it.

The spirit of the Federation, which Gossec sought to capture in his *Te*

6 The organizers no doubt considered commissioning Giroust or Le Sueur; but the latter, after being dismissed from the *maîtrise* of Notre Dame, Paris, had retired to Sucy-sur-Marne, while the former, *Surintendant de la Musique du Roi* since 1782, was no doubt too 'compromised' with the court.
7 The Ecole Royale de Chant et de Déclamation was never opposed by the Revolution. After Louis XVI had announced on 1 July 1791 that he would no longer be responsible for the salaries of the teachers at the Ecole, the National Assembly decided on 26 September to take charge. The Ecole became 'public' in May 1792 and continued in existence until the formation of the Conservatoire in August 1795.
8 The date appears on the autograph manuscript in the Bibliothèque Nationale, Paris (Cons.Ms.1.430). This work, which was never repeated after 14 July 1790, was revived by

Deum, bestowed on that hymn a new significance which broke with tradition. But well before this 'regeneration' of the *Te Deum* had been revealed to the audience on 14 July 1790, opposition had been expressed towards a canticle too often associated with the misdeeds of kings and tyrants. In a letter dated 24 June on the subject of the *Te Deum*, an anonymous correspondent to the *Chronique de Paris* wrote, 'Ah! ce n'est pas là l'hymne du 14 juillet' ('Ah, this is not the hymn for 14 July!'). He went on to propose the writing of a work suitable for the occasion, and nominated a possible author:

... je demande un hymne français qui ne soit qu'au-dessus du *Te Deum*. Certes, nos jeunes poètes ne doivent pas craindre de se mesurer avec Saint Augustin. Pourquoi l'auteur de *Charles IX* n'entrerait-il pas en lice? Ce jeune poète n'est pas tout à fait un prodige; mais l'évêque d'Afrique n'est pas un Horace.

... I ask for a French hymn which can only be better than the *Te Deum*. Indeed, our young poets should not be afraid to measure themselves against St Augustine. Why shouldn't the author of *Charles IX* enter the lists? This young poet is by no means a prodigy, but the Bishop of Africa is no Horace.

Marie-Joseph Chénier was not slow to respond to this entreaty. In a letter dated 10 July in the *Chronique de Paris* he wrote:

J'ai vu hier dans votre journal, messieurs, l'invitation que me fait un ennemi du Te Deum, de composer un hymne pour la fête du 14 juillet. J'avais eu cette pensée depuis longtemps, et l'ouvrage est fait depuis plusieurs jours.

Yesterday I saw in your paper, sir, the invitation made to me by an opponent of the *Te Deum* to write a hymn for the festival of 14 July. I have had this idea for a long time, and the work was completed several days ago.

This hymn, later set to music by Gossec, was not given at the Federation of 1790,[9] but despite this the names of Gossec and Chénier were henceforth united. In fact they were almost the only collaborators at the first civic festivals: in 1791 and 1792 half of the patriotic hymns were written by Chénier and three-quarters of them were composed by Gossec. This near monopoly eventually gave rise to protests. On 30 August 1792 one might have read in a Paris newspaper: 'Plusieurs jeunes artistes se plaignent que, dans toutes les fêtes nationales, les hymnes sont exclusivement musique de Gossec et paroles de M. Chénier ...'[10] ('Many young artists are complaining that at all the national festivals the music of the hymns is invariably by Gossec and the words by M. Chénier ...'). The situation was to change later and other composers were to

J.-L. Jam and given a second performance at the bicentenary celebrations at Riom, near Clermont-Ferrand, on 25 June 1989, under the direction of Georges Guillot.
9 On the history of the *Chant du 14 juillet* by Chénier and Gossec, see Pierre, *Les hymnes et les chansons*, pp. 197–205.
10 *Affiches, annonces et avis divers*, no. 30.

make their contribution to the production of hymns, in particular Méhul from 1793 and Cherubini from 1794.

IN SEARCH OF A NEW LITURGY

The Federation had disclosed the need for some adjustments, or even a thorough overhaul, of the old Catholic liturgy. The Civil Constitution of the Clergy, debated at length from spring 1790 and put into effect in August 1791, made final the break between the traditional Church and the nation, which from that date required a special ritual capable of expressing, celebrating, but above all inspiring, its own values. The new-born Republic expected, therefore, that a new liturgy would ensure a widespread and clear diffusion of its ideological message among large crowds assembled in the open air, whose liberal participation was desired no matter what part of the country they happened to be in. The Revolutionary hymn was the preferred instrument of this liturgy. It was above all a question of reinforcing the stresses of the words with musical accents in order to make the discourse audible to the citizens assembled at these festivals, the ideal model for which Rousseau had conjured up in his *Lettre sur les spectacles*. Rousseau elsewhere remarked that, if other European languages were 'muted in tone' and 'cannot be heard in the open air' ('ne peuvent se faire entendre en plein air'),[11] French in particular could not in any way be classed with the 'languages favourable to liberty' ('langues favorables à la liberté'), which he defined thus: 'They are resonant languages, prosodic and harmonious, the sense of which can be distinguished at a great distance' ('Ce sont les langues sonores, prosodiques, harmonieuses dont on distingue le discours fort loin').[12]

Thus the eternal problem of the relation between poetic stress and musical accent was raised once again. Revolutionary propaganda was putting back on the agenda (though for reasons completely unconnected with aesthetics) the old objective of a perfect union of music and poetry.[13] For this to succeed, poet and musician must agree to rigorous discipline, to concessions on both sides and perhaps even to heroic renunciations. In matters of technique a close collaboration was certainly desirable. At least in the case of the simplest piece (the hymn in rondo form) the musician would have to respect the poetic stresses of the refrain and first couplet, while the poet, for his part, would have to see

---

11 J.-J. Rousseau, *Du contrat social* (1762) iii, Chapter 15, 'Des députés' (Garnier edition (Paris, 1966), p. 303).

12 J.-J. Rousseau, *Essai sur l'origine des langues*, Chapter 20: 'Rapport des langues au Gouvernement' (Ducros edition (Bordeaux, 1969), p. 199).

13 On this point, see J.-L. Jam, 'Framery, un théoricien des hymnes révolutionnaires', in *Région, Nation, Europe: unité et diversité des processus sociaux et culturels de la Révolution française* (Besançon, 1988), pp. 265–72.

that his verses scanned regularly. In fact, for the hymn to be an effective piece of propaganda both artists had to subordinate their interests to those of the state. Gossec and Chénier shared this conviction, but in very different ways.

MAÎTRE GOSSEC

From the point of view of effective propaganda, the music that Gossec wrote for Chénier's hymns turns out to be altogether disappointing. His compositions are not very successful at lending weight to the accents of the text. While other composers manage to observe 87% of the stresses in the regular strophes and 95% of those in the refrains, Gossec manages an average of only 74%, which makes him the least skilful of Chénier's collaborators.[14] What is more, he never achieves that simplicity of style which would allow the common people to join in: his melodies, although plain, never attain the true economy of folksong. Diachronic study, moreover, shows no indication of a desire to limit ornamentation, which for the period 1795–9 is four times as extensive as it is in the melodies of Méhul.[15] In other respects his writing remains that of a 'symphonist', more concerned with harmonic and contrapuntal structures than mindful of the constraints placed on music destined for untrained voices.[16] Thus in Gossec's hymns the voices, treated in a concertante manner, are frequently interrupted by difficult instrumental sections which cannot be cut, making performances of these works impossible except at Parisian festivals or those of large provincial cities. Theorists such as Leclerc had, however, insisted on this point: 'Take away the overture from the *Chant du départ* and simplify its accompaniment, and there will not be a single village with a National Guard where you will not be able to have it performed' ('Otez au *Chant du départ* son ouverture, et simplifiez son accompagnement, alors il n'y aura pas de village ayant une garde national où on ne puisse le faire exécuter').[17]

In short, the hymns of Gossec are in most cases more like motets than folksongs. And yet it is obvious that he made a great effort to adapt when, in 1794, he made a popular version of the *Hymne à l'Etre Suprême*, paying particular attention to the propagandist rules. This was reproduced in the well-known *Receuil des époques* intended for all

14 Composers setting Chénier's verses respect their prosody to the following extent: from 1789 to 1792, 82%; from 1792 to 1794, 96%; from 1794 to 1799, 85% (95% in the refrains).
15 With Gossec, the number of notes exceeds the number of syllables by 12%; with Méhul, the excess is on average 3% (1% in the refrains).
16 For examples of contrapuntal writing, see *Hymne à la liberté*, bars 35 etc.; *Choeur à la liberté*, bars 26, 42, 78 etc.; *Serment républicain*, bars, 9, 34–6, 62 and 80–81. For vocal difficulties (sustained notes), see *Hymne à la liberté*, bars 64–6, and *Choeur à la liberté*, bars 44–5, 54–68 and 80–81. For performing difficulties, see *Serment républicain*, bars 17, 50, 92 etc.
17 Leclerc, *Essai sur la propagation de la musique*, p. 52.

citizens, and especially for 'those in rural communes' ('ceux des communes rurales').[18] Apart from this, the only work he produced that satisfied the rules of the propagandists was the *Hymne à Jean-Jacques Rousseau* (1794). This piece adopts the couplet-refrain form and presents a continuous melody with little ornamentation, relatively conjunct and respecting about 54% of the stresses in the text. Nevertheless, the circumstances in which it was written, and which Gossec himself reminds us of in a letter to Coupigny, makes us wonder whether this relative perfection came about by design or by chance.

Citoyen mon collaborateur,
Je suis malade d'une fluxion aux dents qui me tient depuis 8 jours et qui m'oblige d'avoir la tête enveloppée de linge et de coton, et de garder par conséquent la maison; malgré cela il m'a fallu composer la fête pour J. J. Rousseau qui aura lieu décadi prochain au jardin national et de là, au Panthéon. Pour cette fête il m'a fallu passer encore trois nuits et cela provient de ce que les poètes sont toujours en retard ainsi que les arrêtés et les ordres des autorités constituées.[19]

Citizen collaborator,
I have been ill with a toothache for a week, which obliges me to have my head bandaged up and to remain indoors. In spite of this I've had to write music for the *fête* for J. J. Rousseau which is to take place next *décadi* at the Jardin national [the Tuileries Gardens] and after that at the Panthéon. I have already had to spend three nights on this *fête*, and this is because poets are always late, as also are the decrees and orders of the licensed authorities.

This letter is interesting for the evidence it contains about Gossec's participation in the system of festivals and in public musical life during the Revolutionary decade. One can sense, behind the reproaches he aims at poets and at the authorities (Chénier, the author of the *Hymne à J. J. Rousseau*, belonged to both categories), that same lassitude that we have noticed since 1778. Furthermore, a few lines later in the same letter Gossec becomes more explicit. On the subject of a Revolutionary opera, *La prise de Toulon*, which he failed to get performed, he wrote:

L'Opéra ne m'a point renvoyé ma musique, mais je l'ai redemandée, ce qui revient au même. J'aime mieux renoncer que d'être ballotté; il est dans mes principes que partout où je trouve de la résistance et des difficultés, je me retire. Je n'aime point les débats ni les démarches.... N'y pensons plus. Dans la circonstance où je me trouve en ce moment où l'organisation de l'Institut est sur le tapis, où je suis chargé de faire des ouvrages élémentaires, je ne puis donner d'autres soins qu'à ceux que mon devoir m'impose.

The Opéra has never returned my music, but I've asked to have it back, which

---

18 The musical stresses of the 'popular' version respect all the stresses in the text, against 83% in the original version. The 'popular' version is entirely syllabic, while in the original version the number of notes exceeds the number of syllables by 10%.
19 Letter of 17 Vendémiaire An III/8 October 1794, in *Lettres des musiciens*, p. 216.

amounts to the same thing. I prefer to forego something myself than to be tossed aside. It's one of my principles that whenever I meet opposition and objections I withdraw. I never like disputes or canvassing.... Let's not think any more about it. In my present circumstances, with the organization of the Institute under discussion and when I am required to do elementary work, I can't make any more effort beyond that which duty requires.

From this we see that Gossec did not really concern himself with the Revolutionary adventure, for which he no doubt felt neither sympathy nor antipathy. Employed by the state since 1784, he had done no more than respond to the demands of his employer, even when the character of that employer had drastically changed. At each request from the authorities he had fulfilled his duties without enthusiasm, and his hymns never reach the proportions of those by his younger colleagues such as Méhul, Lesueur and Cherubini. Also, he was always ready to 'borrow' from other works: his *O salutaris* became in 1794 a *Hymne à la liberté*, and one of the *Intermèdes pour la tragédie d'Athalie* which he had composed for Racine's play in 1785 was transformed in 1795 into the *Serment républicain*. While some musicians – Monsigny and Grétry for example – took refuge in a discreet or even reproachful retirement and others, like Piccinni, chose to leave the country, Gossec carried on, quite unruffled, as a competent and conscientious pedagogue. His output of hymns, a duty he could not avoid, formed an activity only marginal to his academic and administrative work. It cannot possibly have had the importance attributed to it by Challamel.[20] The Revolution must at least have given Gossec a last opportunity to remind people, with his *Marche lugubre*, what a great symphonist he could have become if only the French public had wished it.

CITIZEN CHÉNIER

By contrast, the contribution of Chénier to the liturgical repertory of the 'fêtes civiques' shows a genuine political involvement. Chénier was an author elected by the public in 1789, the quasi-official poet of Revolutionary festivals from 1790, and while continuing his work in the theatre he gradually became an active participant in the Revolution. In July 1792 he was made a member of the central committee of the Paris Commune, and in this capacity he was able to make two speeches at the Legislative Assembly, one of which called for the dethronement of the king. A few weeks later he was one of the principal figures in the events of 10 August, when the Tuileries were seized and the monarchy overthrown, and this won him a seat in the Convention. Nevertheless,

---

20 In 1790 Gossec produced 100% of the hymns; in 1791, 50%; in 1792, 60%; in 1793, 40%; in 1794, 13%; in 1795, 20%; in 1796, 28%; in 1797 and 1798, none, and in 1799, 14% (figures based on C. Pierre).

and despite voting for the king's execution, Chénier was always considered to be a moderate, and even by some people a 'counter-revolutionary in disguise'. Dismissed from the Committee of Public Instruction in October 1793, and under suspicion during the spring of 1794, he nevertheless became again, after Thermidor, one of those chiefly responsible for civic celebrations and for those of the Decadist cults. In Chénier's view the hymn was above all the indispensable instrument of propaganda, which it was advisable to make as efficient as possible. However, an examination of his output of hymns shows a certain lack of rigour in applying the rule of 'prosodic conformity': that the placing of the poetic stresses should remain constant in each stanza so that they will match the musical stresses in a strophic setting.

No doubt the metrical disparity of some of the hymns made it difficult to put this rule into practice, but even in hymns in which each line had the same metre the stresses of the first strophe are never entirely respected in the subsequent ones. In the best case (the *Hymne du IX Thermidor*) about 63% of the stresses in the first strophe are matched in the rest of the text, but elsewhere the prosodic conformity can amount to as little as 19%. Generally speaking, fewer than 50% of the stresses in the opening strophe are matched in subsequent ones. Chénier was not the only one to be negligent in this respect; indeed, it was at the request of 'some distinguished composers, persuaded of their usefulness' ('quelques compositeurs distingués, pénétrés du sentiment de leur utilité') that Framery published in October 1795 his *Avis aux poètes lyriques*, in which he attempted to convince them of 'the necessity of [regular] metre and caesura in hymns or odes intended for musical setting' (la nécessité du rhythme et de la césure dans les hymnes ou odes destinés à la musique').[21] This work, which takes up the theories of François Jean de Chastellux (while at the same time impoverishing them), did not have the hoped-for effect: the poets' negligence continued to worsen, especially as the increasing use of the rondo-type hymn allowed them to evade, in some measure, the delicate problem of prosodic conformity, which, as far as the refrain type was concerned, depended entirely on the skill and goodwill of the musician. The refrain, being essentially repetitive, encouraged memorizing and therefore served for effective propaganda. Poets, Chénier in particular, devoted their attention to the strophes intended as refrains, providing short lines, sometimes elliptical, often symmetrical and always independent from each other in meaning. The refrains of Revolutionary hymns were the favourite place for such phrases as 'gloire au peuple français!', 'Vive la République!' and 'Périssent les rois!' (*Le chant des victoires*); 'Sachons vaincre ou sachons

---

21 N. E. Framery, *Avis aux poètes lyriques, ou de la nécessité du rhythme et de la césure dans les hymnes ou odes destinés à la musique* (Paris, brumaire an IV/1796). On Framery's theories, see Jam, 'Framery, un théoricien'.

périr!' (*Le chant du départ*); 'La victoire a conquis la paix!' (*Le chant du retour*); 'Plus d'assassins, plus de rois!' (*Hymne des vingt-deux*); and 'Sans préjugés et sans maîtres!' (*Hymne à la République*). All things considered, Chénier seems to have been scarcely aware of the problem of audibility in the hymns; on the other hand, he was concerned with their intelligibility to the extent of changing noticeably his usual practices.

Poetic language, leaving aside its musical dimensions of metre, assonance and rhyme, is characterized mainly by the use it makes of *figures* (modifications to the natural order or meaning of words). It is through these *figures* that 'discourse, in the expression of ideas and feelings, distances itself more or less from what would have been expression plain and simple' ('le discours, dans l'expression des idées et des sentiments, s'éloigne plus ou moins de ce qui eût été l'expression simple et commune'); it is these that 'give the language greater nobility and dignity' ('donnent au langage plus de noblesse et plus de dignité). This definition of *figures* given by Fontanier[22] makes clear the incompatibility of poetic language and republican discourse, whose prime virtue was to be readily understood. In point of fact, a diachronic study of Chénier's hymns shows a sharp and continuous decline in its use of figures. We notice a spectacular drop in the number of expressions with unusual or varied meanings, and also in allusions which presuppose a certain culture in the listener. In fact, inversion also would have been completely abandoned were it not for the metrical flexibility it brings to the verse. But as well as *figures* such as these, which detract from the clarity (and therefore from the effectiveness) of the discourse, there are others which, by contrast, possess remarkable propagandist virtues, either because of their construction (for example, antithesis), or because of their memory-jogging qualities (for example, repetition) or simply because of their rhetorical power (for example, the interrogative). Thus antithesis, indisputably the most propagandist of figures, is thrice as common at the end of the Revolutionary decade as it was at the beginning. And yet the writing of hymns is characterized as a whole by a 'de-poetizing', evident, for example, in the steadily decreasing use of epithets, transferred epithets (*épithètes antéposés*) and present participles. Was it propagandist requirements that freed Chénier from certain constraints of classical poetry several years before Lamartine's revolutionary *Méditations* (1820) and the stylistic audacities of Victor Hugo? Certain lines of Chénier's hymns seem undeniably to resonate in sympathy with those of the poet of *La légende des siècles* (1859–83).

But antithesis, the favourite tool of Revolutionary polemic, which reduces a complex reality to a simple choice between two alternatives, will serve quite different ends in the work of the author of *Verso de la*

22 P. Fontanier, *Les figures du discours* (Paris, 1968).

page to reveal what he called 'that obscure law of progress in mourning, of success in failure and of haven in shipwreck' ('cette obscure loi du progrès dans le deuil/Du succès dans la chute et du port dans l'écueil'). No doubt the violent and contrasting images of chaos, tempest and volcano, and indeed all the poetic imagery of boiling, springing up and spurting forth are to be found in the Revolutionary hymns of Chénier before becoming the very substance of Hugo's language; but their meaning is by no means the same. The relationship between the two poets would be even more tenuous if we tried to base it on structural parallels rather than on symbolic or thematic ones. Certainly the hymns of Chénier bear witness on occasion to the efforts he made to invent a special language bringing together free verse and rhymed eloquence.[23] These endeavours could have led him to a rhythmic, or even poetic, prose, but the aesthetic principles of strict classicism prevented him from advancing further towards the new poetic horizons that he could only dimly perceive.[24] As for his political convictions, they did not extend to the sacrifice of rhyme and metre, the only elements of traditional versification spared in the 'de-poetization' necessitated by the propagandist message.

OLD VERSES AND NEW THOUGHTS

Although this essay appears in a musicological publication, its coverage of the subject would be incomplete if it failed to summarize the actual message of Chénier's hymns. In fact, Revolutionary hymns, by their very nature and function, demand a rounded study which evaluates not only the effectiveness of the music and the text but also the meaning of the ideological message they were intended to put across.

Completely dominated as they were by those in power, the hymns of the years 1791–9 engage in a protean discourse whose varying tones reveal the successive trends of the Revolution. A statistical and chronological study of the vocabulary used in Chénier's hymns faithfully mirrors the political constants and variables of the Revolutionary decade. If we divide this decade into three periods in the traditional way (14 July 1789 – 10 August 1792; 10 August 1792 – 9 Thermidor An II; and 9 Thermidor An II – 18 Brumaire An VIII), it is possible, by examining the specific vocabulary of each period, to characterize their particular ideologies.[25]

---

23 See the *Serment républicain* and the *Hymne guerrier* of January 1795.
24 Chénier, who translated the *Ars poetica* of Horace and the *Poetics* of Aristotle, was himself the author of an *art poétique* in verse entitled *Les principes des arts*, in which he declared his opposition to poetic prose.
25 By 'specific vocabulary of each period' we mean the terms used *exclusively* in one or other of the three periods.

The first period is distinguished by a grandiloquent celebration of the victorious struggle of the Enlightenment against the obscurantism of the *ancien régime*. The texts of these hymns deal chiefly with two themes: anticlericalism and the abolition of privilege. Although they touch on the downfall of the monarchy, no reference is made to the various crises connected with this that bedevilled the new regime (the flight to Varennes, the Declaration of Pillnitz and conflicts between the king and the Assembly).[26] This ignoring of current events during the first period is hardly affected by the mention of Voltaire's ashes being transferred to the Panthéon (on 11 July 1791) or by a discreet allusion to Benjamin Franklin; can one talk of current events when one of these men had been dead for a year and the other for thirteen, and when both were already regarded as legendary and symbolic figures?

The second period, by contrast, did not disregard topical events, although it retained only a minute fragment of all that went on at the time in the world of politics and events. Revolutionary hymn texts now focussed entirely on the war. Faced with danger from without, it was essential to inspire and reassure the nation. The hymns of this period deal explicitly with the English enemy, whose weakness, cowardice, pride and especially treachery they are quick to point out. At the same time they describe in dynamic terms the combined forces of the people, humankind and natural elements which guarantee eventual victory for the Revolution. All this was, of course, intended to urge the patriots along the sacrificial path in the wake of the martyrs of Liberty. It was also a matter of legitimizing an administration whose power was both severe and necessary.[27]

Finally, the third period is particularly interesting because it assigns the propagandists a more delicate task than they had been faced with during the previous periods. In fact, it was no longer a question of extolling the founding fathers of the Revolution or of spurring the nation into action against an external foe who was only too real, but of warning against a two-fold menace which threatened to imperil the country from within. To the criminal iniquity of kings must now be added the bloodthirsty rage of tyrants of the people. More than the restoration of the monarchy, it is a return to anarchy, with its scaffolds and catacombs,

26 Terms specific to the first period:
    (siècles) trompés / (prêtres) menteurs / mensonges / divinité / divin;
    Providence / Eternité / cantique / fanatisme / détrôner / privilèges;
    joug (des Grands et des Rois) / vigilant / découvrir.
27 Terms specific to the second period:
    guerrier / se lever / se soulever / s'avancer / poursuivre / renverser;
    abattre / anéantir / volcans / allumer / foudroyer / perfide / pervers;
    punique / orgueilleux / impuissant / lâche / infame / Angleterre / Capet;
    Bara / Viala / efforts / gémir / blessures / expirant / cadavre / larmes;
    gouverner / conduire / guider.

that the hymns of the third period depict. But if the dismal evocation of the Terror and its victims helped to protect France from a return of the assassins, it also perpetuated the sad memory of dissensions. It was appropriate, then, during this period to call for national reconciliation, and to invite the citizens 'to a feast of forgetting' ('au festin de l'oubli'). Through the voices of the victims themselves, the hymns preached clemency and forgiveness. The uncompromising idols of yesterday, the goddesses Reason and Equality, gave place to a 'touchante et sainte Humanité'. In fact, all things considered, the intention of the new Republic was to place itself under the patronage of Cybele, goddess of plenty.[28]

THE REPUBLICAN PARNASSUS

The way that the content of hymns was adapted to the ideological changes of the Revolution thus demonstrates *a posteriori* the chief function of poetry and music in Revolutionary festivals. Being a licensed medium of propaganda, the texts were obliged to use only those poetic forms that would guarantee intelligibility. They must also be suitable for a type of music which would make them audible to large gatherings in the open air. Gossec and Chénier, brought together by chance, tried to respond to these formidable constraints and devoted themselves to serving the Revolution, the one from political conviction and the other from professional conscience. The result was a number of works which in the end satisfy neither aesthetic taste nor propagandist efficiency, but for which Gossec and Chénier should still be remembered. More than in any other sphere, myth (nourished on sayings like Challamel's) has displaced historical fact and cast a shadow over two artists whose works were by no means without merit. Neglected by historians of literature and music, Chénier and Gossec have not succeeded in matching the glory enjoyed in the Parnassus of the Revolution by Rouget de Lisle, who – a further humiliation for them – was 'neither a poet nor a musician by profession' ('ni poète, ni musicien de profession').[29] Some will view this as an injustice, others as a deserved rebuke. But in the final reckoning, is it not fitting that Gossec and Chénier were in the end engulfed in the legend of the Revolution whose first intermediaries they were?

Translation by Beryl Boyd

28 Terms specific to the third period:
   tyrans populaires / anarchie / anarchique / fureur / terreur / échafauds / hécatombes / haïr / usurpateur / tombe / tombeaux / mort;
   ténèbres / sombres / tocsin / funèbres / cyprès / attrister / martyrs;
   souvenir / pardonner / clémence / unir / oubli / cimenter / garder / sénat;
   avenir / demain / léguer / descendants / dot / aspirer / Cybèle / florissant / prospère / croître.
29 N. E. Framery, *Avis aux poêtes lyriques*, pp. 30–31.

The sung constitutions of 1792:
an essay on propaganda in the Revolutionary
song

To sing the articles of a constitution seems to us today an absurd undertaking. Our conception of what song is does, of course, include its serving to comment on social and political phenomena or on moral attitudes, but it is contrary to the essential brevity and lyrical quality of a song for it to transmit legal texts of considerable length. The writing of song cycles that the setting of constitutions to music necessarily leads to was, moreover, something quite new when the earliest sung constitutions came into existence – an innovation predating the rise of the cycle in the realm of the art song in Germany, which began with Beethoven's *An die ferne Geliebte*, op. 98, 1815–16.[1] The sung constitutions of the Revolutionary period can be understood only in the context of the new culture in which songs, almanacs[2] and illustrated pamphlets[3] all played a part in the education of both young people and adults, as well as in propaganda for various political groups. The constitutions, then, were publicized or criticized not only through a politicized press, among which broadsheets are to be numbered, but also through sung constitutions. The best known and, during the whole of the Revolutionary period, the most popular almanac to serve the dissemination of a constitution was that of Collot d'Herbois,[4] which appeared in 1792 – the same year as the first of the *constitutions en vaudevilles*. The author defended the constitution of 1791 in twelve dialogues. Catechisms and songs are recognized as means of educating

---

1 Cf L. E. Peake, 'Liederkreis', in *The New Grove Dictionary of Music and Musicians*, ed. S. Sadie (London, 1980), x, p. 847. In Germany also demands for material for song cycles were satisfied by parodies of known tunes. Publications with the name *Liederkreis* appeared from 1812, e.g. F. A. Tiedge, *Das Echo oder Alexis und Ida: ein Zyklus von Liedern* (Halle, 1812).
2 Cf J.-J. Tatin, 'Politische Reflexion und Heldenkult in den Almanachen zwischen 1760 und 1793' and L. Andriès, 'Die Almanache des Jahres II', in *Die Französische Revolution als Bruch des gesellschaftlichen Bewußtseins*, ed. R. Koselleck and R. Reichardt (Munich, 1988), pp. 270–85 and 286–304.
3 Cf the important study by K. Herding and R. Reichardt, *Die Bildpublizistik der Französischen Revolution* (Frankfurt, 1989).
4 *Etrennes pour les citoyens-soldats et les soldats-citoyens ... accompagnées des entretiens du père Gérard* (Paris, 1792); cf Tatin, 'Politische Reflexion', p. 279.

the lower classes, while the song itself was valued as the most suitable and effective instrument for propaganda and for influencing the masses, especially country people.[5] The song and the hymn therefore belong to the most strongly politicized genres of the Revolution. Songs which served to publicize or criticize the constitution form an additional instrument to the politicized press and the catechisms of the Revolution, which aimed at democratizing information.

Sung constitutions, which were current from 1792 onwards, reflect on the texts of constitutional documents and the hopes of the people, as well as on their criticisms of particular articles that legislate on their rights and duties. They are both a public art form and a type of political publicity of unprecedented independence and with a new social significance. As art for the masses, political songs in general and sung constitutions in particular represent one of the most effective means of stirring the emotions and political awareness of the 'petit peuple'. For this reason they must be studied if the character and trends of the popular movement of the Revolution are to be understood. Like the illustrated prints, the folk theatre, the pamphlets and the political newsheets, they represent an essential part of a carefully considered publicity campaign. Their importance lies not only in the reproduction and broadcasting of facts and events, but much more in the forming of attitudes and opinions on political and social issues.

As with the illustrated pamphlets,[6] publication in pairs is to be observed. The sung constitution (1792) of the ultra-royalist François Marchant, which violently attacks the constitution of 1791 and voices numerous criticisms which people made at the time, is answered by an anonymous author, probably a Jacobin, who vehemently defends the constitution and its operation. This author may with good reason be named 'Anti-Marchant', since he directs ironic or sarcastic criticism towards Marchant's *La constitution en vaudevilles*:

> Le prince atteint de félonie
> Sera condamné justement
> A copier, toute sa vie,
> Les vaudevilles de Marchant.[*]

[*]C'est le nom de l'esclave bel esprit qui a rimaillé la constitution française en vaudevilles tudesques. [No. 106][7]

A prince overtaken by felony will rightly be condemned to copy, all his life, the vaudevilles of Marchant.[*]
[*]The name of the witty drudge who has rhymed the French constitution in Teutonic vaudevilles.

5 Cf Andriès, 'Die Almanache', p. 286.
6 See Herding and Reichardt, *Die Bildpublizistik*, pp. 7–15.
7 Numbers refer to the entries in Appendix 1. According to no. 107, the king's civil list served to finance the vaudevilles of Meude-Monpas and Marchant.

In the 'Epilogue' (no. 131) he again opposes the songs of Marchant and urges the fair townswomen: 'Donnez-lui sur les doigts'. The anonymous author deals on the one hand with the constitution, and on the other with the attitudes propagated in François Marchant's sung constitution.

As can be seen from the bibliography of *constitutions en vaudevilles* (Appendix 4, below), there appeared a series of publications between 1792 and 1799 which made use of a similar title.[8] The authors often hid their identity under amusing signatures which inevitably arouse the reader's curiosity, such as 'par un législateur de boudoirs'[9] or 'œuvre posthume d'un homme qui n'est pas mort' (this is, in fact, Villiers, who had been writing and versifying for some time). Constitution songs found their way into theatre pieces, and especially into scenes enacted at festivals. They were also disseminated outside France in German reprints, for example in Johann Friedrich Reichardt's *Frankreich im Jahre* ... or in *London und Paris*, a periodical which appeared in Goethe's Weimar.[10]

The first to publish a *constitution en vaudevilles* was François Marchant (1761–93). According to Constant Pierre, the Revolution prevented Marchant from following his career as a cleric. He therefore became a journalist, and in 1793 founded the *Chronique du manège*,[11] a journal in prose and verse closely connected in ideology to the *Actes des Apôtres* of Girey-Dupré. He published also *Les sabbats jacobites* (1791–2), from which he took several songs for the second part of *La constitution en vaudevilles*. In the *Bienfaits de l'Assemblée Nationale*, and again in the *Folies nationales pour servir de suite à La constitution en vaudevilles*, published in 1792 by the Libraires Royalistes, he made devastating criticisms of both prominent and little-known Jacobins.[12] According to Pierre, Marchant fled entirely penniless to his native city of Cambrai, where he died on 27 December 1793.[13] In view of his strong support for the royalist cause, it seems probable that it was for political rather than for financial reasons that he sought safety in a flight from Paris.

If a petition by Thomas Rousseau is to be believed,[14] 20,000 copies of Marchant's *Constitution en vaudevilles* were sold. Even if this figure is

8 Cf H. Schneider, 'Les constitutions chantées de l'an VIII', in *Le tambour et la harpe: oeuvres pratiques et manifestations musicales sous la Révolution, 1788–1800*, ed. J.-R. Julien and J. Mongrédien (Paris, 1991), pp. 147–78.

9 Marchant mentions 'un boudoir' as one of the possible places to perform his songs (see the 'Avertissement', p. 34).

10 The original of the *Constitution en vaudevilles* by Desrosier, from which extracts are quoted in *London und Paris*, has not so far been discovered.

11 C. Pierre, *Les hymnes et chansons de la Révolution* (Paris, 1904), p. 78.

12 The *Folies nationales*, missing from Pierre's bibliography, will not be fully covered in the discussion that follows, since it does not relate directly to the Constitution.

13 Pierre, *Les hymnes et chansons*, p. 78.

14 Thomas Rousseau was shocked to learn that '20,000 exemplaires de l'infâme et abominable *Constitution en vaudevilles*' had been sold; see Pierre, *Les hymnes et chansons*, p. 7.

only an approximate one, it underlines the exceptional success of this collection in the 'song-war' between royalty and the early achievements of the Revolution. Robert Brécy, who mentions new editions under different titles, such as *Etrennes au beau sexe, ou La constitution française mise en chansons*,[15] describes *La constitution en vaudevilles* wholly incorrectly as a 'pamphlet contre les droits de l'homme'.[16] Pierre places *La constitution française en chansons* of Anti-Marchant earlier than that of Marchant himself, despite the fact (mentioned above) that the numerous references it makes to Marchant's show it to be a later publication. In order to engage in the debate about the new constitution, to supply arguments for those who supported him and to convince, or at least to influence, the waverers, Marchant, like Collot d'Herbois, brought out his work immediately after the adoption of the constitutional Act by the National Assembly on 3 September and its acceptance by the king, who swore to it on the 13th.[17]

Of the sung constitutions listed in Appendix 4, only two are furnished with a preface. Marchant states in his 'Epitre dedicatoire' addressed to the *émigrés*, 'one cannot do without a constitution; you will prefer one that brings you glee to one that makes you flee, one which you will be able to sing while you wait for the day when you can return to France' ('on ne peut se passer de constitution, vous préférerez encore la constitution qui fait rire à celle qui fait fuir, et que même vous pourrez la chanter en attendant le jour ou vous rentrerez en France'). Following a calendar of the type commonly printed in almanacs, listing the saints' days for the whole year, is a preface ('Avertissement') which repeats all the commonplaces usually to be found in the corresponding sections of collections of *cantiques* and catechisms with music. The constitution is sung 'à la portée de tout le monde', that is for everyone, including the two-thirds of the French population who are illiterate and who, by singing and amusing themselves, will at the same time receive instruction.[18] Nor does the author miss the opportunity for the usual complaint against the 'chansons bachiques' and 'romances langoureuses' which he contrasts with his own much superior songs. In ironic phrases he expresses his opposition to the constitution:

... il est vrai qu'on chante ce qui ne vaut pas la peine d'être lu ... et si, par un de ces évènemens que la sagesse humaine ne peut prévoir, la constitution française

---

15 R. Brécy, *La Révolution en chantant* (Paris, 1988), p. 84. Unfortunately Brécy gives no precise references.
16 Ibid., p. 84. On pp. 85–6 Brécy reproduces nos. 1, 2, 6, 10, 11, 17, 57 and 58 (see Appendix 1, below).
17 Cf J. Godechot, *Les constitutions de la France depuis 1789* (Paris, 1970), pp. 30–31.
18 'J'ai tâché de réunir l'agréable à l'utile le plus qu'il m'a été possible'; '[ils] s'instruiront en s'amusant' ('Avertissement', p. 34).

devenoit un ouvrage inutile, la mienne pourrait se chanter, tandis que celle de l'assemblée nationale ne trouveroit pas un lecteur'.[19]

... it is true that one sings things that are not worth reading ... and if, by reason of one of those events that human wisdom cannot predict, the French constitution became a useless piece of work, mine could still be sung, while that of the National Assembly would not find a single reader.

Like other *chansonniers* of the Revolution,[20] he announces the presentation of his work 'à ma section' [which he fails to identify], 'where I hope it will take the place of a patriotic gift or a tangible contribution from me' ('où j'espère qu'elle me tiendra lieu de don patriotique et de contribution mobilière').[21]

Altogether different is the viewpoint of Anti-Marchant, as is apparent from his definition of the constitution:

C'est un bon manteau que la nation s'est mise sur les épaules, pour être à l'abri du vent & de la grêle. Ce manteau a des taches. N'importe; tel qu'il est, il vaut encore mieux s'en servir que d'aller tout nud, & montrer son derrière, comme nous le faisons depuis plus de mille ans.[22]

It is a good cloak that the nation has put round its shoulders to shelter it from the wind and the hail. This cloak bears some stains. No matter, it's much better to use it, just as it is, than to go about completely naked and show one's backside, as we have been doing for more than a thousand years.

Anti-Marchant addresses himself to the 'honnêtes gens' or 'français aimables', and we may conclude from the content of the work and the political stance of the author that these are to be understood as the supporters of the 1791 constitution, and in particular the lower classes. The preface, in which he outlines his aims, is again based on a commonplace in which the influence of the political song is clearly apparent:

> Chantez, chantez, amusez-vous,
> Amusez-vous, Français aimables,
> Puisque dans vos jeux les plus doux
> Vous êtes encore redoutables:
> Vous faites plus par vos chansons,
> Que d'autres avec leurs canons.[23]

19 Ibid., pp. 33–5.
20 For example, *Chansons patriotiques par le citoyen Piis, Paris, An deuxième*, 'Avertissement': 'puissent-ils [ces vaudevilles républicains] être agréés par plusieurs sections comme ils l'ont été par celle des Tuileries ... Puissent-ils enfin, circuler dans ces communes agricoles au sein desquelles je tiens à honneur d'habiter, et être substitués insensiblement à ces noels grossiers dont les berçait le fanatisme'.
21 'Avertissement', p. 35.   22 *La constitution française en chansons*, p. 104.
23 In a note he cites as an example the song *Ça ira*.

Sing and amuse yourselves, kind French people, since in your gentlest pastimes you are still formidable; you do more with your songs than others do with their cannons.

THE 'CONSTITUTIONS CHANTÉES' AS CYCLES OF POLITICAL SONGS

The constitution of Marchant, like that of his critic, Anti-Marchant, is divided into two parts: in the first, articles selected from the 1791 constitution are criticized or commented on in fifty-eight songs, while the second part consists of fifteen songs on a variety of subjects. Anti-Marchant devotes forty-eight songs to the constitution and ten to other subjects, and follows these with nine poems and aphorisms, a poem on the new streetnames in Paris, a prayer to be said following the catechism, a catechism for 'grands enfants' and finally the 'Pour et contre, anecdote de la chapelle du roi au Louvre'.

Marchant's concentration on the text of the constitution, headed by the 'Déclaration des droits de l'homme', the 'Réflexion morale et philosophique ... sur la constitution française' and the two songs *Les droits de l'homme* and *de la femme*, mark out his work as a cycle. Admittedly, it ends with a loose succession of further songs ('chansons républicaines, nationales, civiques'), a 'vaudeville constitutionel' and a 'vaudeville patriotique', but this only emphasizes more clearly the unity of the main part of the publication, to which additional songs have been joined in a loose sequence. In comparison, the cyclic conception of Anti-Marchant's *La constitution française en chansons* is strengthened by the 'Préface' and the 'Epilogue', especially as there are no sung items following the latter. But as a whole it is clearly a multi-faceted publication, in the sense that the author includes not only songs opposing royalist propaganda, but also a catechism, aphorisms and a pamphlet against Marie Antoinette.[24]

Appendix 2, below, gives an overall view of the articles in the 1791 constitution that are commented on in our two sung constitutions. In comparison with the two *constitutions chantées* published in 1799, in which practically all ninety-five articles are criticized or summarized in a cycle of songs, we are dealing here with a relatively small selection from the voluminous first constitution of the Revolution – forty-seven articles in the case of Marchant, forty-six in the case of Anti-Marchant (who includes also some decrees). A quantitative evaluation of the attitudes adopted by the two authors shows the almost total opposition of Marchant to all the political changes made during the Revolution: he opposes 68% of the clauses and is neutral in the case of 23%, while he is in favour of only 8.5%. Against this stands Anti-Marchant, with his

---

24 Cf Appendix 1.

approval of 78.3% of the provisions; he takes an aggressive stance against 19.6% of clauses, in which without exception the rights of the king are enshrined (an unfortunate provision for the new political order in his view, since these should have been annulled from the very beginning of the Republic). Anti-Marchant deals, of course, with most of the articles that his opponent had covered, but he omits those concerned with the functioning of new political systems (the obligation to swear allegiance on entry into the National Assembly, the power of the legislature in comparison with the executive, free adjudication in legal disputes, admission of the bourgeoisie into officer ranks of the army previously reserved for the nobility), with the role of the monarchy (the indivisibility of the monarchy, the 'degrading' of the king to the rank of citizen after his abdication, controls on the free movement of the 'prince royal', appointment of ministers by the king, the king's image on the currency) and with foreign policy (the renunciation of conquest). There follow other songs concerning certain decrees not contained in the 1791 constitution.[25] They provide for the following regulations: the taking of oaths of allegiance to the constitution by the king's officers ('officiers de ligne'), the establishing of a permanent supervisory committee, proclamation of the immunity of the king, the possible lawful prosecution of the king after his abdication, the accountability of ministers and finally, the king's right of veto. The songs of Anti-Marchant express his deep-rooted mistrust of all those who represent the *ancien régime* and of the king in particular, a distrust which he explains as springing from the latter's deplorable activities against the new constitution.

THE POLITICAL ATTITUDES OF MARCHANT AND ANTI-MARCHANT

The political thinking of François Marchant was based on a view of mankind diametrically opposed to that of his adversaries. According to Marchant the common people are not good, but stupid, uncultured, depraved and corrupt.[26] In addition, they understand nothing about politics and cannot even cope with the simplest problems of everyday life (no. 2; see Ex. 1(b)). Marchant's complaints about the granting of equal rank to all men[27]

---

25 Cf W. Schmale, 'Recht und Verfassung: von der alten Monarchie zur Republik', in *Die Französische Revolution*, ed. R. Reichardt (Freiburg and Würzburg, 1989), pp. 132–3.
26 In no. 37 he speaks of the 'classe la plus vile'.
27 'Tous sont égaux, Laquais et Maîtres, / Ducs et barbiers, catins et prêtres / Aux Jacobins' (no. 71).

The sung constitutions of 1792

Ex. 1 (a) Tous les hommes sont bons

a) Tous les hommes sont bons

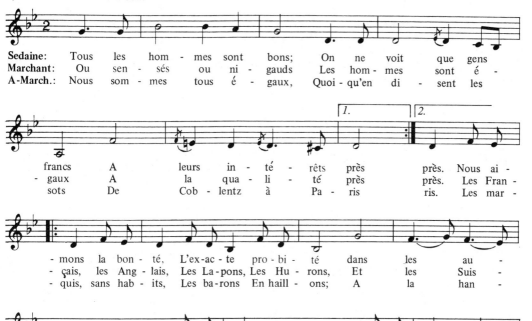

Sedaine: Tous les hom - mes sont bons; On ne voit que gens
Marchant: Ou sen - sés ou ni - gauds Les hom - mes sont é -
A-March.: Nous som - mes tous é - gaux, Quoi - qu'en di - sent les

francs   A   leurs in - té - rêts près   près. Nous ai -
- gaux   A   la qua - li - té près   près. Les Fran -
sots   De   Cob - lentz à Pa - ris   ris. Les mar -

- mons la bon - té, L'ex -ac - te pro - bi - té dans les au -
- çais, les Ang - lais, Les La -pons, Les Hu - rons, Et les Suis -
- quis, sans hab - its, Les ba -rons En haill - ons; A la han -

- tres. Fai - re le bien est si doux, Pour ne rendre heu -reux que nous et
- ses, Ont les mê -mes pas - si - ons, Mê - mes in - cli - na - tions, Mê -
- che De nos deux premiers par - ens, Prê-tres, no - bles et ma - nans Chac -

les   nô -   tres. Nous ai - tres.
- mes   vi -   ces. Les Fran - ces.
- un   tran -   che. Les mar - che.

SEDAINE: All men are good; one sees only upright people, except when it comes to their own interests. We like goodness and strict probity in others. To engage in good works is pleasant only when it is a case of making ourselves and our own ones happy.

MARCHANT: Whether sensible or simpletons, all men are equal, except in quality. The French, the English, the Laps, the Huronians and the Swiss all have the same passions, and even the same inclinations and vices.

ANTI-MARCHANT: We are all equal, whatever fools may say from Coblenz to Paris. The marquises without their clothes, the barons in rags, priests, nobles and peasants, each cut to size beside our first two parents.

243

and the abolition of the nobility give further insight into his thoughts:

> Comme en tout ce que nous faisons
> On ne voit ni grandeur ni noblesse,
> Pour cause nous abolissons
> Un ordre dont l'éclat nous blesse. [No. 3]

As in everything we do there can be seen neither grandeur nor nobility, we abolish for that reason a class of society which wounds us with its brilliance.

Ex. 1   (b) Vive le vin

b) Vive le vin

Vi - ve le vin, vi - ve l'a - mour, A - mant et bu - veur tour à
Ils sont tous in - dis - tinc - te - ment Fils d'un pa - pa, d'une ma -
Sur la bé - quille à Bar - na - bas, Cha - cun de nous tous i - ci

tour, Je nar - gue la mé - lan - cho - li - e: Ja - mais les
- man. Peu - pler et cul - ti - ver la ter - re, Voi - là quel
bas A des droits se - lon sa me - su - re. Sans pré - fé -

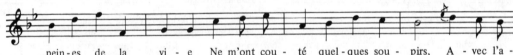

pein - es de la vi - e Ne m'ont cou - té quel - ques sou - pirs, A - vec l'a -
est leur min - ist - è - re; Mais tous n'ont pas l'heureux ta - lent De pou-voir
- ren - ce, la na - tu - re, Qui veille à tous ce qu'il nous faut, Donne à cha-

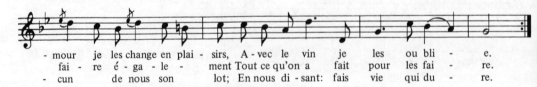

- mour je les change en plai - sirs, A - vec le vin je les ou bli - e.
fai - re é - ga - le - ment Tout ce qu'on a fait pour les fai - re.
- cun de nous son lot; En nous di - sant: fais vie qui du - re.

MONSIGNY: Long live wine, long live love; lover and drinker by turns, I shrug off melancholy. Life's troubles have never cost me a sigh; with love I change them into pleasures, with wine I forget them.

MARCHANT: They are all without distinction the sons of a father and a mother. To populate and cultivate the earth, that is their duty; but not everyone has the happy talent to do equally well all that has been done to create them

ANTI-MARCHANT: On Barnabas's crutch each of us here on earth has rights according to his standing. Nature looks after everything we need and gives each of us his share, without favour, saying, 'Make a life that lasts'.

Against this stands Anti-Marchant's humanistic view of mankind, which is encouraging towards the 'petit peuple' (no. 75; see Ex. 1(a)).

The Jacobins are the resolute enemies of Marchant, for whom he would have liked to retain the proscribed sash of the order, the 'cordon gris', since it 'could well decorate the neck of Gorsas and several others' ('Pourra for bien orner le cou/De Gorsas et de plusieurs autres').[28] Other songs refer to the Jacobins in such abusive terms as 'cuistres' (no. 42), 'mutins' and 'gredins' (no. 33) or as hypocrites and cowards (no. 62) and as out-and-out schemers:

> Pour ameuter la classe la plus vile,
> Les jacobins impudemment sauront
> Attribuer à la liste civile
> Tous les forfaits qu'en secret ils payeront. [No. 37]

To assemble a mob from the lowest and basest of the people, the Jacobins will shamelessly charge to the civil list all the underhand payments they will make.

Disapproving and contemptuous criticism of the Jacobins, and of certain well-known figures among them,[29] finds expression also in outspoken lampoons such as the *Confession d'un jacobite à Madame Nation* (no. 62), in which the 'Jacobite' confesses all his misdeeds in reply to the routine questioning of the nation: 'What else have you done, dear Jacobite? Tell me quickly' ('Qu'as-tu fait de plus, cher Jacobite?/ Réponds-moi bien vite'). There is present here, incidentally, through the use of the quasi-responsorial *Air de la confession*, a close semantic connection between melody, *timbre*[30] and parody text. It is just such witty songs in dialogue form that account for the popularity of Marchant's publication.[31]

Marchant's opinion of the 1791 constitution and of the political developments that followed it may be briefly summarized in three points. Firstly, he criticized the removal of the privileges enjoyed by the aristocracy. For him only the royal family and the aristocracy were capable of providing France with political and cultural leadership. He disapproved of the prejudice directed against the nobility as a whole, without any discrimination between one person and another, and regretted the mistrust shown towards them by all the new institutions.

28 No. 4. Antoine Joseph Gorsas was the editor of the *Courrier*.
29 Pétion in no. 21, Robespierre in nos. 61 and 65, Gorsas, Menou, Lameth and Chabroud in no. 61 etc.
30 The term 'timbre' is used for the line of verse that identifies the melody of the vaudeville. To indicate to the singer which melody to use one simply specifies the *timbre* (e.g.: 'Air, *Il n'y a qu'un pas du mal au bien*') instead of showing the tune in musical notation.
31 Another example is no. 66, in which each of the eight strophes sung by the Jacobin Voidel is contradicted in the last line, sung by 'Truth'; e.g. 'M. *Voidel*: Dans ce pays agité / J'ai semé la discorde, / Mais aussi, sans vanité, / De lui j'ai bien mérité ... *La vérité*: La corde, la corde, la corde'.

Secondly, he considered it important to expose the contradictions of the new order, and those that existed between the laws newly drafted under the constitution and their practical application. He commented on freedom of movement with allusions to the actual danger of travelling, on the equality of men with what he saw as the increasing abasement of the nobility. Beside freedom of religious observance he placed the discrimination shown towards the Catholic church; he contrasted the recognition of the monarchy contained in the constitution with the efforts being made to replace it with a republic; and against the immunity enjoyed by the deputies he placed the violation of their wives. This last discrepancy he expressed through a play on the double meaning of the word 'violation'. He was at one with Anti-Marchant in saying that if women were debarred from the crown and the regency they could daily exercise power through the bed. The legislation on property rights provides a good example of how Marchant attempted to expose inconsistencies in order to drive home his views:

> Les biens et les propriétés
> En tous lieux seront respectés:
> Si les chasseurs de Robespierre
> Brûlaient un châtel élégant
> Nous dirions au propriétaire:
> Nous vous plaignons sincèrement.
>
> Les biens et les propriétés
> En tous lieux seront respectés:
> Mais nous prendrons sans nul scrupule
> Tous les biens du clergé romain,
> Nous prendrons même la cellule
> De la nonne et du capucin. [No. 17]

Wealth and property will everywhere be respected. If Robespierre's men burnt down an elegant château we would say to the proprietor, 'We are really sorry for you'.
Wealth and property will everywhere be respected, but we shall seize all the belongings of the Roman clergy without scruple; we shall even take the cells of nuns and Capuchins.

Finally, Marchant summarized some paragraphs of the new constitution without making known his own attitude towards them. Obviously he considered it his task to inform, as well as to struggle against the political developments taking place. If, however, he reproduces, say, Article 8 (Titre III, Chapter 2, according to which the king would become an ordinary citizen after his abdication) without making his views known about it, there can be no doubt, given his royalist sympathies, that he was not in agreement with it. With his song on the abolition of religious vows he associated himself with what in 1792 was a broad consensus:

> Les gentilles nonnains
> Fuyant leur monastère
> Avec les capucins
> Présent pourront faire
> L'amour
> La nuit et le jour. [No. 5]

The gentle nuns, fleeing from their monasteries with the Capuchins, will now be able to make love night and day.

The new division of the kingdom into *départements*, which he approved of, was also accepted by the people as a whole.

As far as Anti-Marchant is concerned, it is clear from his 'Petit catechisme à l'usage des grands enfants'[32] that he was most likely a Jacobin. His description of the 'club des Jacobins' is warmly approving: 'It is the forge of the National Assembly. It is an anvil on which one strikes the hot metal. It is the furnace of patriotism, that warms the whole of France' ('C'est la forge de l'Assemblé nationale. C'est une enclume où l'on bat chaud. C'est le fourneau du patriotisme, qui chauffe toute la France').[33] For him the aristocracy and the clergy were the true villains,[34] and he warned that they were ready to overturn the new system and to restore the former absolutist regime. He commented in the following way on the 'Décret sur la distribution du pouvoir législatif & du pouvoir exécutif':

> Gardons-nous que le nom de roi
> Dans les plateaux de nos balances,
> L'emporte d'un grain sur la loi,
> Ah! surveillons ces deux puissances
> C'est au pouvoir législatif
> A poser de courtes lisières
> A ce pouvoir exécutif
> Qui jamais ne dormira guère. [No. 93]

Let us beware lest the name of king tips the balance [of justice] away from the law, even in the least degree. Let us keep an eye on these two powers. The legislative power must place short reins on executive power, which will hardly ever sleep.

Here the author is clearly reacting to Marchant's warnings (see Ex. 2, below). As well as strongly supporting the new rights of all citizens, he gives a good deal of specific advice. On the question of electing the 'citoyen actif' to the National Assembly, he warns about over-active, scheming deputies. Regarding the permanence of the National Assembly, he says:

---

32 *La constitution française en chansons*, pp. 101–20.   33 Ibid., p. 114.
34 He uses strong words for the aristocracy: 'C'est une bête rampante, qui a les oreilles d'un âne et la tête d'un singe ... Cet animal léchoit le derrière aux rois, & donnoit des coups de pied dans le ventre du peuple' (ibid., pp. 102–3).

> ... Il ne faut qu'un mauvais moment
> Car la cour jetteroit des pierres
> Dans nos jadins sans cadenats,
> Tenons tout prêts les reverbères
> Pour éclairer les scélérats. [No. 95]

It takes only a single bad moment for the court to throw stones into our unlocked gardens; let us keep our lamps ready to shine on the villains.

Similar appeals to erect barriers against the court are repeated in song no. 96, the *timbre* of which clearly contributes to the meaning (see Ex. 2, below). The *assignats* (promissory notes issued by the Revolutionary government), the introduction of which Marchant had vehemently criticized,[35] were less of a problem for Anti-Marchant.[36] In order to underline the didactic intention of the reply to his opponent's warnings, Anti-Marchant used the *timbre* 'Nous sommes précepteurs d'amour':

> Mais rien n'ira, si nous laissons
> La clef du trésor à nos princes:
> Citoyens, tenez les cordons
> De nos bourses déjà si minces. [No. 99]

But nothing will work out right if we leave the key of the treasure chest with our princes. Citizens, hold on to our purse-strings, since our purses are already quite empty.

There are also many witty satirical songs aimed at the frequent solemn exhortations from officials, especially those in the speeches of ministers:

> De la guerre ou de la marine
> Quand vient un ministre au sénat,
> Pour, avec sa voix pateline
> Se blanchir de quelqu'attentat:
> Avant d'entendre sa doctrine,
> Sur son passage il seroit bon
> De placer une guillotine,
> Ou si mieux l'on aime un cordon. [No. 121]

When a minister of war, or of the navy, comes to the senate to clear himself of some outrage in a wheedling voice, it would be well, before hearing his testimony, to place in his way a guillotine or, if preferred, a rope.

Anti-Marchant also threatens the *émigrés*, whom he sees as the most hated representatives of the *ancien régime* and the most implacable enemies of the Revolution:

---

35 No. 17: 'Croit-on payer ceux qu'on opprime / En leur donnant des assignats?'; no. 22: 'Qu'on juge enfin avec doux murmure, / Les Députés par-tout seront reçus, / Si parmi nous chaque législature / En assignats convertit les écus'; see also nos. 59 and 71.

36 A critical remark on the assignats is found in no. 126: 'Nous n'avons pas beaucoup d'argent; / Du papier est notre comptant; / C'est ce qui nous désole.'

> Vous en voulez des bayonettes;
> Eh bien! vous en aurez, messieurs,
> Messieurs les joueurs de roulettes,
> Pour vous guérir de vos vapeurs, et des engins, & du canon;
> Ces arguments (ultima ratio populorum) sont sans répliques,
> Pour inoculer la raison. [No. 121]

You wish for some bayonets; then you shall have some, gentlemen roulette players, to cure your vapours, and some missiles, and some cannon. There is no reply to these arguments (*ultima ratio populorum*) when it comes to making people see sense.

One of the few things on which both authors are in agreement is their firm hostility towards England. Marchant, however, finds the foreign enemies of France of greater importance than does Anti-Marchant, for whom the native opponents of the Revolution present the greatest threat.[37] With his outspoken anti-clericalism, Anti-Marchant takes up a theme which was very much in the air in 1791–2:

> A l'honnête homme il ne faut pas de prêtres
> Son sanctuaire est au fond de son coeur.
> Qu'ils étaient sots nos tant dévots ancêtres
> De s'égorger pour quelque sainte erreur. [No. 83][38]

The honest man needs no priest; his sanctuary is in the depths of his heart. What fools our devout forebears were to punish themselves for some blessed error.

Altogether he knew, as his use of *timbres* shows, how to combat Marchant's attacks on the 1791 constitution. Even if his arguments are sometimes coarse and his expression of them often vulgar (though with good reason), he appears altogether more convincing than Marchant.

THE ROLE OF THE *TIMBRES* AND THE MUSIC

The authors of song collections intended for political propaganda and the instruction of the people did not as a rule set their texts to music, but parodied well-known melodies (*timbres*). This widespread practice presupposed some knowledge of at least several hundred melodies on the part of the public. But a hundred years later, when the technique had fallen into disuse and was little understood, even Constant Pierre supposed that the melodies served merely to make the memorizing of the

---

37 Marchant: 'Renoncez à l'anglomanie; / Elle a fait d'un peuple léger / Un peuple près à s'égorger' (no. 60); 'On veut que l'anglomanie / Bientôt nous ayons la manie / Aux jacobins' (no. 71). Anti-Marchant: 'La dédaigneuse Angleterre / Ne nous croyoit que galans' (no. 127).
38 Other examples include no. 128 (sung to O filii, o filiae), 12th strophe: 'Du peuple le clergé fera / A peu près tout ce qu'il voudra / Tant que le peuple chantera / Alleluya'; *Epitaphe à Jésus Christ*, p. 87; and no. 130, in which the pope is represented as a drunkard.

texts quicker and easier.[39] Nevertheless, research shows that the melodies, their character and expression, and the words associated with them (the most frequently parodied *timbres* could have several texts) play an important, and often even a key, role in the understanding of songs or vaudevilles.[40]

This is also the case with the two sung constitutions under consideration here. Appendix 3, below, provides a survey of the sixty-nine *timbres* used in them, forty-three (62.3%) of which date from the period before 1780 and twenty-six (37.7%) of which are contemporary. Most of the *timbres* derive from the *opéra comique* or from the dramatic vaudeville; only three derive certainly from elsewhere,[41] while the origin of four other melodies is not yet known.[42] If we add a piece from Salieri's successful opera *Tarare* (1787) to the large corpus of popular theatre music, then 91.3% of the *timbres* are drawn from the stage, traditionally the most important musical source for vaudevilles criticizing contemporary society. This again underlines the special role that *opéra comique* played as mediator between the élite and the common people, between the literary culture of the educated classes and the semi-oral culture of the 'petit peuple'. The *timbre* (that is, the original text of the melody)[43] was used by the song-writers to give their songs an additional layer of meaning. For the same reason lines from the original version, especially refrains, were often retained, or were incorporated into the new text with only slight alterations. A revealing example of this is the *timbre* 'A la façon de Barbari', in which the three lines of the original that are preserved in the parody (shown below in italics) persuade one not to take the matter seriously. In other words, Marchant is demonstrating that he is not disposed to respect the new constitution:

39 Pierre, *Les hymnes et chansons*, pp. 46–7: 'Certes la musique sert à fixer les paroles, à donner du charme à l'ensemble, à retenir l'attention des auditeurs; mais c'est surtout pour les avantages qu'elle leur procure au point de vue de la transmission de leur oeuvre que les chansonniers la considèrent.'

40 See H. Schneider, 'Der Formen- und Funktionswandel in den Chansons und Hymnen der Französischen Revolution', in *Die Französische Revolution als Bruch*, pp. 321–78; R. Reichardt and H. Schneider, 'Chanson et musique populaire face à l'histoire à la fin de l'ancien régime', *Dix-huitième siècle*, xvii (1986), pp. 117–42; and H. Schneider, 'Les mélodies des chansons de Béranger', in *La chanson française et son histoire*, ed. D. Rieger (Tübingen, 1988), pp. 111–48. In a dissertation completed in 1989, Thomas Betzwieser showed also that as far as exoticism, for example, was concerned, eighteenth-century *opéra comique* provided a small number of vaudevilles which were re-used again and again, with the result that their meaning is certain; see his *Exotismus und 'Türkenoper' in der französischen Musik von Lully bis Grétry: Untersuchungen zu einem ästhetischen Phänomen des Ancien Régime* (Heidelberg, 1989).

41 Appendix 3, nos. 12 and 61; no. 32 is from Salieri's opera *Tarare*.

42 Nos, 15, 35, 36 and 43.

43 There are also several 'faux-timbres', in which a parody text replaces the original *timbre*, either because it is particularly well-known or topical, or because it serves as a more appropriate connection between the meaning of the *timbre* and that of the parody text.

Original text	Parody text
Les Anglais ont voulu, dit-on	Des autres constitutions
Reprendre la Grenade	La nôtre est le modèle;
Au vaillant amiral Biron	On l'admire chez les hurons,
Qui parassait malade.	Tant elle paroît belle.
Chacun avait l'air d'un dragon,	Qu'elle a bon air, bonnes façons!
La fari dondaine, la fari dondon,	*La fari dondaine, la fari dondon,*
Il avait du courage aussi,	Je lui serai fidèle aussi,
Biribi,	Dieu merci,
A la façon de Barbari,	*A la façon de Barbari,*
Mon ami.	*Mon ami.* [No. 16]

It is said that the English wished to retake Granada from the valiant Admiral Biron, who seemed to be ill. Each had the appearance of a dragoon, *La fari dondaine, la fari dondon,* and courage as well, Biribi, *in the Barbary style, my friend.*

Our constitution is the model for others; it is admired by the Huronians, so fine is it. It looks good, it has style! *La fari dondaine, la fari dondon,* I will be faithful to it also, thank God, *in the Barbary style, my friend.*

The aria 'Ne perdons jamais l'espérance' from Monsigny's *Le roy et le fermier* (1762), known by the *timbre* 'Il n'est qu'un pas du mal au bien', was particularly suitable for parody because of its refrain text. Anti-Marchant used it to counter the hope expressed by his opponent, using the same *timbre*, that Louis XVI would dismiss the 1200 new 'kings' (Ex. 2).

As well as including lines straight from the original verses, authors also used more refined techniques. The song 'La rente apaganère accordée aux fils puinés du roi' was sung to the *timbre* 'Chantez, dansez, amusez-vous' by Grétry. By his choice of *timbre* Anti-Marchant underlines the idea that princes can dance and enjoy themselves, since they receive an income without having to work to earn their livelihood. In the song quoted in Ex. 1(a) Marchant's parody develops the first line of Monsigny's original aria *ad absurdum*, while his opponent restores and incorporates its original meaning. Both authors avail themselves of the cheerful character of the drinking-song, which in *Le déserteur* was sung along with 'Tous les hommes sont bons'.

The *timbre* 'Monsieur le Prévôt des Marchant' was traditionally used when it was a question of financial or economic matters. Our two authors also draw on the presence of a traditional 'inner meaning' in the song 'L'inviolabilité des propriétés' (nos. 17 and 90). In 'L'exercice du pouvoir législatif' Marchant avails himself of an appropriate refrain from the *timbre* 'Je connais un berger discret':

> Nos sages sénateurs auront
> De nos loix la fabrique,
> Et ce sont eux seuls qui pourront

Taxer l'impôt unique.
Il feront mieux. Car ils feront
Et la paix et la guerre,
[*Refrain*] Et le roi, lors qu'ils agiront,
Les regardera faire.

Our wise senators will be responsible for making our laws, and only they will be able to raise the single tax. They will do better, for they will make both peace and war, [*refrain*] and when they act the king will look on.

During the Revolutionary period writers occasionally justified their choice of *timbre*. Anti-Marchant, for example, explained that 'I have chosen this drinking-song for preference, since in the primary and electoral assemblies there are as many drunkards as there are drinkers' ('On a choisi cet air bachique de préférence, parce que dans les

Ex. 2 Il n'est qu'un pas du mal au bien

SEDAINE: Let us never give up hope. The storm destroys our forests, but
                 it brings peace, and your happiness starts from there. One
                 must not be surprised at anything; it is only a single step from
                 evil to good.

MARCHANT: But if, regaining his throne and soon reclaiming his rights,
                 Louis removed the crown and sceptre from our twelve
                 hundred kings, I would not be surprised at anything; it is only
                 a single step from evil to good.

ANTI-MARCHANT: We must stem the frothy torrent from the courts. The courts
                 know more than one trick, and have played some on us. Even
                 with the most trustworthy king, it is only a single step from
                 good to evil.

assemblées primaires et électorales, il y a autant d'ivrognes que de buveurs').[44] For this reason he used for the decree regarding the 'assemblées primaires et électorales' the *timbre* 'Aussitôt que la lumière':

> Il est plus d'une mâchoire
> Dans un corps électoral.
> Peuple, il y va de ta gloire
> Crains surtout de choisir mal.
> Citoyens, parmi les merles,
> Contre un blanc le reste est noir,
> Et pour découvrir des perles
> Dans un fumier, faut bien voir. [No. 98]

There is more than one jaw in an electoral body. People, you are staking your pride; be careful, above all, not to choose badly. Citizens, among the crows there is only one white one; the rest are black. And to find pearls in a dunghill you have to look very carefully.

This example is most instructive, since it suggests a possible line of inquiry in the task of establishing the relevance of the *timbre* to the meaning of the songs. Here the *timbre* identifies the particular shortcoming that certain deputies were accused of.

In no fewer than twenty-two songs, each dealing with a particular article of the constitution, both our authors use the same *timbre*.[45] The large number of *timbres* used in common to voice opposite political standpoints underlines the function played by the *timbres* as conveyors of meaning in an affirmative, dissociative, ironic or other sense. Why Rousseau's 'Je l'ai planté' was chosen for the songs dealing with the swearing of oaths is not altogether clear, but the relationship of Anti-Marchant to Marchant is obvious in nos. 2 and 76 (see Ex. 3).

It must be admitted that in numerous cases the use of a particular *timbre* remains puzzling, but little attention has so far been given to this question, which is an important one, not only for the kinds of songs we are dealing with here but also for the popular theatre and sung poetry as a whole. There are many discoveries still to be made in this area. It cannot, for example, be a coincidence that twenty-six of the *timbres* that appear in the corpus of texts at present under discussion were used again in the constitutions of 1799.[46] If we hope to analyse and understand the

---

44 *La constitution française en chansons*, p. 30.
45 In the following list the twenty-two songs are identified (in parentheses) by the numbering used in Appendix 1, the other numbers refer to the *timbres* listed in Appendix 3: 1 (4 and 74, 51 and 110); 2 (11 and 84); 3 (16 and 89); 10 (41 and 110, 42 and 111); 25 (8 and 82); 28 (23 and 96); 31 (26 and 88); 38 (18 and 91); 40 (12 and 85); 46 (17 and 90); 50 (63 and 131); 51 (20 and 93); 52 (70 and 126); 54 (14 and 89); 55 (13 and 86); 57 (19 and 92); 61 (36 and 107); 62 (52 and 120); 65 (12 and 94); and 67 (2 and 76). In addition, there are three songs that deal with similar problems and use the same *timbre*: 27 (49 and 118); 43 (29 and 100); and 51 (55 and 101).
46 See my article cited in note 8, above. The *timbres* in question are listed in Appendix 3 as nos. 1, 3, 6, 7, 8, 9, 10, 11, 16, 18, 19, 20, 22, 23, 26, 30, 31, 32, 40, 42, 46, 47, 51, 60, 62 and 64.

Ex. 3   Je l'ai planté, je l'ai vu naître

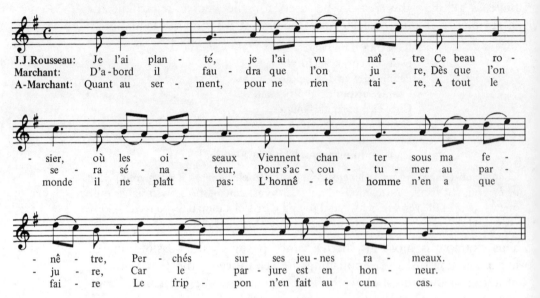

J.J.Rousseau: Je l'ai plan - té, je l'ai vu naî - tre Ce beau ro-
Marchant: D'a - bord il fau - dra que l'on ju - re, Dès que l'on
A-Marchant: Quant au ser - ment, pour ne rien tai - re, A tout le

- sier, où les oi - seaux Viennent chan - ter sous ma fe-
se - ra sé - na - teur, Pour s'ac - cou - tu - mer au par-
monde il ne plaît pas: L'honnê - te homme n'en a que

- nê - tre, Per - chés sur ses jeu - nes ra - meaux.
- ju - re, Car le par - jure est en hon - neur.
fai - re Le frip - pon n'en fait au - cun cas.

genres that make use of *timbres*, we shall have finally to identify and study the way inner meanings were incorporated in them at various levels. As well as studying the 'chanson' and the 'mélodie', one could direct attention to other categories of song; hints of possible starting-points for further exploration are offered by the publications them-selves,[47] leading to a systematic analysis of song genres in general.[48]

The question of whom these songs were intended for, and where and when they were sung, has already been answered indirectly, at least in part. In addition, our two authors give some indications of the places and the people involved. According to Marchant's preface, the sung constitutions were performed publicly in his 'section', as well as in private surroundings, 'dans un cercle ou dans un boudoir'.[49] It is certain also that through the 'colporteurs', referred to emphatically by Anti-Marchant as 'the mouthpieces of the Revolution, the trumpets of Judgment Day for the priests and the aristocrats' ('porte-voix de la révolution, les trompettes du jugement des calotins & des aristo-

47 Anti-Marchant, for example, uses the term 'air aristocratique' for the *timbre* 'Paris est au roi' ('Air de la Camargo', after a contredanse from around 1750). In this case a systematic investigation might be made of all the melodies or *timbres* associated with specific political groupings. On this see S. Wallon, 'La chanson des rues contre-révolutionnaire en France de 1790 à 1795', in *Vibrations. Orphée phrygien. Les musiques de la Révolution*, ed. J.-R. Julien and J.-C. Klein (Paris, 1989).

48 Important are ballad-like narrative songs, often with very many strophes, which are designated 'romance historique' (nos. 122 and 124), 'chanson diplomatique' (no. 64) or 'chanson nationale' (nos. 69 and 72, on the 'Expédition de Vincennes').

49 *La constitution en vaudevilles*, p. 34.

crates'),[50] the songs of our two authors were spread to provincial cities and to country districts.

The sung constitutions we have examined constitute an important part of the conflict between royalists and supporters of the new regime, a conflict which the constitution of 1791 had placed on a low level. The wide diffusion of Marchant's song collection is shown by the large number that were printed. The numbers for Anti-Marchant's collection are unfortunately not known, but his catechism, mentioned above, indicates that his 'constitution chantée' was in use in pedagogical circles. The sung constitutions must be seen as part of a strong didactic movement during the Revolutionary period, and in the context of other methods of propaganda and education intended for the people. The exercise of power through the people could be achieved only if the populace were directed and enlightened, and if new social values and principles were procured for them. To this end people worked with great pride, skill and energy, and popular music played an important role. The character of the songs as a whole is mainly polemical, those of Anti-Marchant being anti-feudal and anti-monarchical, but combative for the new political order.

Analysis of these song collections and the references to them in Constant Pierre's catalogue lays bare the methodological deficiency of that standard work. For the most part, Pierre took into his catalogue only a few pieces from printed collections of political songs: in the case of those considered here, only twenty-two of the 131 songs. He also omitted numerous *timbres* and failed to provide references for many of those he did include, with the result that one can no longer rely on Pierre alone for reliable statistics concerning the use of *timbres* during the Revolutionary period.

Translation by the editor

---

50 *La constitution française en chansons*, pp. 114–15: 'Sans eux & les piques du faubourg Saint-Antoine, nous ne serions pas si grands garçons.'

APPENDIX I
The songs in the *constitutions chantées* of Marchant and 'Anti-Marchant'

(A) La constitution en vaudevilles (1792) by François Marchant

Title	Content	Timbre
Declaration des droits de l'homme et du citoyen [Art.1]:		
1 Ou sensés ou nigauds	All men are equal, whether enlightened or stupid, even in their vices	Tous les hommes sont bons (du Déserteur)
2 Ils sont tous indistinctement	Men should populate and cultivate the earth; many are unfit for this	Vive le vin, vive l'amour
Abolition de la noblesse [constitution française]:		
3 Comme en tout ce que nous faisons	Nothing we do has greatness or nobility; we do away with the nobility, since we find its splendour distasteful	Air de la Croisée
Abolition des cordons rouges, bleus etc. [constitution française]:		
4 Nous réformons tous les cordons	The gray sash remains, since Gorsas and others will soon be hung on it	Accompagné de plusieurs autres
Abolition des voeux religieux [constitution française]:		
5 Les gentilles nonnains	The nuns may now make love day and night with the Capuchins	La nuit et le jour
Admission de tous les citoyens aux places et emplois quelconque [Titre I.1]:		
6 Les citoyens par leur serment civique	All who have sworn the citizens' oath may take up any appointment	Triste raison, j'abjure ton empire
7 Nous allons la France infecter	France is spoilt by the lack of opportunities for employment	On compterait les diamants
Punition égale pour tous les délits sans aucune distinction [Titre I.3]:		
8 De notre autorité divine	Crimes by the clergy will be punished by the guillotine	En jupon court, en blanc corset
9 Il n'est pas besoin de témoins	Aristocrats will be tried without witnesses, but twenty will be needed to condemn a democrat	Nous sommes précepteurs d'amour
Exercice libre de toutes les religions [Titre I.3]:		
10 Tous les cultes seront permis	All religions may be observed, except for Catholicism	Ce fut par la faute du sort
Pleine liberté à tout homme d'aller, de partir, sans pouvoir être arreté [Titre I.3]:		
11 Notre divin aéropage	You may leave the country with your girl; somewhere you will then be deprived of your freedom and your passport	Ah, que je sens d'impatience (d'Azémia)
Liberté à tout homme de parler, d'écrire et d'imprimer ses pensées [Titre I.3]:		
12 A présent dans cet empire	Freedom to express opinions; slanderers will be arrested	Les trembleurs

Division du royaume [Titre II.1]:

13	Comme on devoit tout restaurer	At present eighty-three *départements* cost less to govern than the former thirty-three regions into which the country was divided	Philis demande son portrait

Suite de l'article précedent. Qualités requises pour être citoyen français, et comment on en perd le titre [Titre II.2]:

14	De plus nous avons	Institutions of the state; one is born French; foreigners must comply with the citizens' oath (*serment civique*); foreigners will be members of the Jacobin societies; one is no longer a citizen if one lives abroad or wears a sash	Paris est au roi

Forme du serment civique [Titre II, Art.5]:

15	Je crains, je respecte et j'estime	I love my nation and the law ...	Réveillez-vous belle endormie
16	Des autres constitutions	Our constitution is the model for all others; it is admired by the uncivilized; I shall be true to it *à la façon de Barbari*	A la façon de Barbari

Inviolabilité des propriétés [Titre I.3]:

17	Les biens et les propriétes	Property will be respected; but what has been destroyed through Robespierre is lost; church assets will be confiscated without compensation; settlement will be made with *assignats* [promissory notes]	Monsieur le prévôt des marchands

La souveraineté dévolue au peuple [Titre III, Art.1]:

18	Nous conserverons le roi	We keep the king, but the people make the laws; they retain the highest power and the diadem	Le saint craignant de pécher
19	De ce peuple devenu roi	One values the power of the people; if it hangs or robs you, and you want to know the reason, it replies: 'my will is my law'	Qu'en voulez-vous dire

Distribution du pouvoir législatif et du pouvoir exécutif [Titre III, Art.2]:

20	Si du pouvoir législatif	The people have the legislative power; Louis XVI is king in name only	On compterait les diamants

Le gouvernement reconnue monarchique [Titre III, Art.4]:

21	Cet état jadis monarchique	Despite Louis XVI, the state is already a republic if Pétion has his way	Tu croyais en aimant Colette (du Mari retrouvé)

Permanence de l'Assemblée Nationale [Titre I, Art. 1]:

22	Notre sénate qui changea tout en France	Through its decree of permanence the Assembly raises its claim to eternity; dissatisfaction with the *assignats*	Mon honneur dit que je serais coupable (des Amours d'été)
23	Mais si, remontant sur son trône	It would not be surprising if the king took all the power away again from the 1200 potentates	Il n'est qu'un pas du mal au bien (du Roi et le Fermier)

Qualités requises pour être député [Section II, Art.2]:

| 24 | Du sublime aréopage | A deputy can also become uncivilized if he is active | Que ne suis-je la fougère |

Tenue et régime des assemblées primaires et électorales [Section V, Art.6]:

| 25 | Quand il faudra remonter le sénat | All the reformers come together in a splendid room; after this farce they go their separate ways | En quatre mots je vais conter ça (des Amours d'été) |

Obligation de prêter le serment en entrant à l'Assemblée Nationale [Section V, Art.6]:

| 26 | D'abord il faudra que l'on jure | As a deputy one must first swear, in order to adjust to the current mode for perjury | Je l'ai planté, je l'ai vu naître |
| 27 | Nous le dirons publiquement | Criticism of the mode for oath-taking | Nous sommes précepteurs d'amour |

Inviolabilité des députés [Section V, Art.7]:

| 28 | Sénateurs respectables | Deputies remain forever inviolate; their wives shall, for shame of it, take care to be no longer violated | Tous les bourgeois de Châtres |

Indivisibilité de la royauté, et délégation d'icelle à la famille régnante [Chap.II, Art.1]:

| 29 | Nous n'aurons qu'un roi | One king will govern and carry out the laws | Ma pantoufle est trop étroite |

Exclusion perpétuelle des femmes à la couronne de France [Chap.II, Art.4]:

| 30 | Les femmes jamais | Women will not rule in France; but they have power at their disposal through the bed | Ma pantoufle est trop étroite |

Nécessité de jurer pour être roi de France [Chap.II, Art.4]:

| 31 | D'après notre moderne code | Oaths are in fashion; the king must swear them in order to retain confidence | Du serin qui te fait envie |

Le refus de jurer regardé comme abdication [Chap.II, Art.5]:

| 32 | Du haut en bas | Unless he swears, the king forfeits his position | Du haut en bas |

Déposition du monarque lorsqu'il se mettra à la tête d'une armée contre la nation [Chap.II, Art.6]:

| 33 | S'il veut faire la guerre | If he makes war on the Jacobins or on insurrectionists, or advances into the country with the help of foreign troops, he will be deposed | Apprenez qu'une belle (du Printemps) |

Déposition du monarque lorsqu'après être sorti du royaume, il n'y rentrera pas après une proclamation du corps législatif [Chap.II, Art.7]:

| 34 | Pour suivre en tout point l'ordonnance | If the king wishes to take the waters at a spa, he risks losing his throne | Amusez-vous, jeunes fillettes |

Entrée du monarque dans la classe des simples citoyens après son abdication expresse et légale [Chap.II, Art.8]:

35	Privé par nous du pouvoir monarchique	After his abdication he will become an ordinary citizen	Vous l'ordonnez je me ferai connaître

Liste civile accordée au monarque par la nation [Chap.II, Art.10]:

36	Pour l'agréable et l'utile	The king's civil list leaves Warville, Desmoulins and Carra squealing	Romance de Daphné
37	Pour ameuter la classe la plus vile	In order to stir up the lowly mobs the Jacobins will attribute all their misdeeds to the civil list	Les folies d'Espagne

Minorité du roi jusqu'à l'âge de 18 ans accomplis, et nomination d'un régent pendant cette minorité [Section II, Art.1]:

38	Tant que le roi sera chez sa nourrice	The regent is accountable to the National Assembly	Les folies d'Espagne

Les femmes exclues de la régence [Section II, Art.2]:

39	Aucune citoyenne	I much regret the ineligibility of the queen to be regent	de Malbrougk

Le nom du Dauphin changé en Prince Royal. Ni lui, ni la reine-mère, ni le régent peuvent sortir de la France sans perdre tous leurs droits [Section III, Art.1]:

40	Grâce à notre manie étrange	The decreed change of name, and the prohibition on leaving the country	Je suis né natif de Ferrare

Rente apanagère accordée par la nation aux fils puinés du roi, lorsqu'ils auront 26 ans accomplis, ou lors de leur mariage [Section III, Art.8]:

41	Du roi tous les autres enfants	Since no inheritance is due to the children of the king, we grant them a dowry	Chantez, dansez, amusez-vous

Nomination des ministres accordée au roi et leur responsabilité [Section IV, Art.1]:

42	Par bonté nous laissons au roi	Ministers will be appointed by the king, but will receive their orders from the Jacobins; the latter are punished by their stupidity	Chantez, dansez, amusez-vous

Exercise du pouvoir législatif [Chap.III, Section I]:

43	Nos sages sénateurs auront	Laws now enable deputies to exercise power (i.e. taxes, war, peace etc.)	Je connais un berger discret

Da la sanction royale [Chap.III, Section III]:

44	Il faut que le roi sanctionne	For the good of the nation, the king must ratify decrees; the veto belongs to him only if he makes no use of it	L'amour sans aucune contrainte

Relation du corps législatif avec le roi [Section IV]:

45	Le pouvoir dit exécutif	The executive may intervene in the National Assembly just in order to laugh	Le petit mot pour rire

De l'exercice du pouvoir exécutif [Chap.IV]:

46	Le roi sera le roi de France	As compensation for the loss of power, the king's head may adorn the currency	Avec les jeux dans le village

Le pouvoir exécutif tenu d'envoyer les lois faites par l'Assemblée Nationale aux corps administratifs et aux tribunaux [Chap.IV, Section I]:

| 47 | Nous ne voulons pas que le roi | The king must make known the laws everywhere | De la p'tit poste de Paris |

Droit accordé au roi de signer avec toutes les puissances étrangères tous les traités de paix, de commerce et d'alliance [Chap.IV]:

| 48 | Le roi ne pourra jamais faire | The king may merely sign treaties | De tous les capucins du monde |

La justice rendue gratuitement [Chap.V, Art.2]:

| 49 | Quoique maintenant la justice | Beware of the capriciousness of justice | Faut attendre avec patience |

Etablissement des jurés par toute la France [Chap.V, Art.7]:

| 50 | Des jurés l'on établira | Jurors pass judgment on intentions, not on deeds | Mon père je deviens devant vous |

Etablissement d'un tribunal de cassation [Chap.V, Art.19]:

| 51 | Nous allons avoir à présent | The Court of Appeal will declare only other judgments invalid | Accompagné de plusieurs autres |

Etablissement d'une haute cour nationale [Chap.V, Art.23]:

| 52 | Notre sénat installe | In Orleans a national High Court will be established to try criminals and innocent aristocrats | Tous les bourgeois de Chartres |

De la force publique [Titre IV, Art.1]:

| 53 | Nos vausseaux et nos régiments | The soldiers now take the ranks of the officers they have dismissed | De Joconde |

Etat actuel de nos armées [Titre IV, Art.2]:

| 54 | Si chez nous chaque régiment | There are foreign threats and desertions, but also the heroes of Gonesse | Du curé de Pomponne |

Renonciation de la nation française à toutes sortes de conquêtes [Titre IV]:

| 55 | Nous ne voulons plus conquérir | We are disgusted with fighting, murder etc., and wish to do nothing to defend the colonies | On compterait les diamants |

Réflexion morale et philosophique faite sur la constitution française:

| 56 | A cette Targinette là | All citizens welcome 'Targinette', the constitution; if she perishes, it is no loss | Colinette au bois s'en alla (de Nicomède dans la lune) |

Les droits de l'homme, vaudeville constitutionnel:

| 57 | Par le dieu d'amour inspiré | The rights of man bring dissension, disorder, injustice and threats from foreign powers; they serve as a pretext for all kinds of folly | De la croisée |

Les droits de la femme, vaudeville constitutionel:

| 58 | Pour mieux faire admirer ma voix | Women should influence men through love; the Assembly changes their rights, so that there will soon be women with twenty husbands each year, who knows the rights of women? | Je connais un berger discret, ou Philis demande son portrait[51] |

Les exploits de Jacobins:

| 59 | Honneur au sénat clémentin | The Assembly takes a quarter of one's belongings for itself, and soon all the rest of a citizen's goods. The Jacobins should not talk so much and make so many proposals; soon we shall be rich with *assignats* | Accompagné de plusieurs autres |

Le règne de la folie:

| 60 | Oui, croyez-moi, mes chers amis | Folly reigns in French history; typically a king was held captive in his castle; the anglomania that drove us to self-destruction has been given up | Regards vifs et joli maintien (de Sargines) |

Les ah, eh, hi, oh, hu, ou Les cinq exclamations jacobites:

| 61 | Messieurs, allons bien vite | Robespierre and Menou praise Marat; from Avignon or Arles Lameth and others speak in the Jacobins' Assembly; if Gorsa talks about his incorruptibility, no-one laughs; even criminals can make friends through the pleasures of the table; the Jacobins would like to let the Assembly fall | Dans Paris la grand'ville |

Confession d'un Jacobite, à Madame la Nation:

| 62 | Je viens devant vous R (dialogue) | I behave like a robber, and am praised for it; I cause mayhem in the taverns, but never pay; in battle I take to my heels; I play the hypocrite, but am valued in the Assembly; I fail to mobilise the élite against the court | Air de la confession |

Couplets aux français:

| 63 | De l'aimable folie | Frenchmen, give up your dismal anglomania and be cheerful again; all your recent achievements are worth less than one of your traditional songs | O ma tendre musette |

---

51 Given as 'Du joli réservoir d'amour' in the new edition of Marchant's constitution, *Poésies révolutionnaires* ... (see Appendix 4), p. 94, and in Pierre, *Les hymnes et chansons*, no. 545**.

Chanson diplomatique en l'honneur de M. Carra, écrivain patriote:

64	Oh! c'est un bien grand homme	An ironic portrait of the writer and orator Carra; his commentary on Seneca; his translation from the English of the history of Greece; his newspaper earned him a post as deputy; he wanted to be bishop of Calvados; he was thrashed in the Tuileries gardens; with his slanders he will end up on the gallows	Oui noir, mais pas si diable

Les dix-huit francs, vaudeville constitutionnel:

65	Pour les 18 francs qu'on lui donne	The deputies can stir up a lot of trouble for their 18F; Robespierre, for example, insulted the king	Chansons, chansons

Promenade civique de l'incomparable M. Voidel au bois de Boulogne [prose introduction]:

66	J'ai de l'esprit et du goût (dialogue)	Voidel reports on his deeds, which the nymph ('Truth') exposes as lies	Jardinier, ne vois-tu pas

Chanson républicaine:

67	Un soir disait Condorcet	Condorcet wishes to introduce the republic; Danton will take the place of the king; ingratitude of the republicans towards their leaders; in the republic even the women are common property	Le saint craignant de pécher

Couplets civiques:

68	Nous jouissons d'un sort plus doux	Return to cheerfulness, enjoy life	On compterait les diamants

L'expédition de Vincennes, ou Relation exacte et véritable de l'enterprise de vingt mille brigands, soudoyés par le sénat clémentin, pour aller détruire, le 28 février, le donjon et le château de Vincennes. Chanson nationale:

69	La troupe des brigands s'en alla	The large crowd marched towards Vincennes, robbing and burning down; La Fayette brought it to an end	Colinette au bois s'en alla (de Nicomède dans la lune)

Chanson civique:

70	Le français si charmant jadis	No joy any longer in France; Orleans forsakes Albion; no longer any good authors; Marat writes: that prevents him doing worse things; the defenders of the Bastille will defeat foreign enemies; daily flood of pamphlets in Paris	On doit 60 mille francs

Les Jacobins et les Capucins, vaudeville patriotique:

71	Il est deux partis dans la France	Jacobins wish to copy the Roman republic, the Capuchins to sustain the monarchy; the people are with the Jacobins, against anglomania; I remain a Capuchin	Chansons, chansons

Les chemises à Gorsas, ou L'arrestation de Mesdames, tantes du roi, à Arnay-le-duc [prose introduction]:

| 72 | Donnez-nous les chemises à Gorsas | Give back Gorsas' shirts; Adelaide says, seek them from the magistrates; the ladies are detained for ten days; what freedom! | Rendez-moi mon écuelle de bois |

Chanson nationale dédiée au bon peuple:

| 73 | O vous qu'au pillage on excite | You people, roused to plunder, you are cheated by the Jacobins; they wish to win you over in order to gain power | Vous qui d'amoureuse aventure (de Renaud d'Ast) |

(B) La constitution française en chansons (1792) by 'Anti-Marchant'

	Title	*Content*	*Timbre*
74	Préface: Chantez, amusez-vous	Sing and enjoy yourselves; your songs are worth more than cannons	Chantez, dansez, amusez-vous

Déclaration des droits de l'homme et du citoyen [Art.1]:

| 75 | Nous sommes tous égaux | All men are equal, whatever the nobleman says | Tous les hommes sont bons |
| 76 | Sur la béquille de Barnabas | Nature has provided all men with their heritage, which they must make something of | Vive le vin, vive l'amour |

Constitution française [Art.1], *Décret sur l'abolition de la noblesse:*

| 77 | O ma chère noblesse | The nobleman would sooner lose his life than his title to nobility | O ma tendre musette |
| 78 | Ainsi, dans un châtel antique | To console the unfortunate lord of the castle, one says, 'The law is taking from you what the rats would have gnawed away' | Un jour me demandait Hortense |

Décret portant suppression des cordons noirs, rouges et bleus:

| 79 | Marquis et ducs, comtes, barons | Do not make a fuss about your decorations and honours; you will have to hang yourself one day with their sashes | Accompagné de plusieurs autres |

Décret sur l'abolition des voeux religieux:

| 80 | Sortez, dansez, amusez-vous | Nuns, rejoice in your freedom; we celebrate mass in silence | Allez (= Chantez), dansez, amusez-vous |

Décret sur l'admission de tous les citoyens aux places & emplois quelquonques [Titre, I.1]:

| 81 | Au temps passé nature avait beau faire | Hitherto talent counted for nothing without a noble background; today it is talent alone which is the deciding factor | Dans nos hameaux la paix et l'innocence |

Décret portant punition égale pour tous les délits, sans aucune distinction [Titre, I.3]:

| 82 | Thémis qui sous l'ancien régime | Thémis hitherto showed respect for a coat-of-arms; now crimes are punished without regard for the person | En jupon court, en blanc corset |

Décret: Exercice libre de toutes les religions [Titre I]:

83 A l'honnête homme il ne faut pas de prêtres | Holiness lies in the hearts of men; error of religious wars | O Mahomet, ton paradis des femmes

Décret donnant pleine liberté à tout homme d'aller & venir, sans pouvoir être arrêté [Titre I]:

84 Un émigrant, ceinture pleine | Emigrants quote the decree, but they must change their gold into currency at the border | Ah! que je sens d'impatience (d'Azémia)

Décret accordant liberté de parler, d'écrire & d'imprimer [Titre I]:

85 La censure et la police | Hitherto the police kept an eye on what was said or written; today one can express opinions freely on walls or anywhere else | Air des trembleurs

Décret sur la division du royaume en quatre-vingt-trois départments [Titre II, Art.1]:

86 Les uns aux autres inconnus | Hitherto French people were divided by their belonging to different provinces, and by prejudice; now all are equal, also before the law | Philis demande son portrait

Décret qui désigne les qualités requises pour être citoyen français [Titre II, Art.2]:

87 Eh! n'avions-nous pas | Hitherto one's reputation depended on one's breeding; any foreigner may become a citizen if he is a good man | Paris est au roi (air aristocratique)

Décret qui exige le serment civique [Titre II, Art.2]:

88 Quant au serment, pour ne rien taire | The oath is not taken seriously by everyone | Je l'ai planté, je l'ai vu naître

Décret qui soumet au serment les officiers de ligne:

89 Peut-on compter sur le serment? | Do not trust the oath of a king's officer | A la façon de Barbari, mon ami

Décret sur le droit de propriété [Titre ?I]:

90 Charbonnier est maître chez lui | Not until to-day was the charcoal-burner the master in his own home; before now the tax-farmer and the clergyman took everything | Monsieur le prévôt des marchands

Décret qui ôte la souveraineté au roi:

91 Aristocrates, pourquoi | What agitation among the nobility about removing the sovereignty of the king, who always misused his power | Le saint craignant de pécher

Décret qui rend la souveraineté à la nation [Titre III, Art.1]:

92 Enfin donc, dame nation | The stricken nation is sovereign | Qu'en voulez-vous dire

Décret sur la distribution du pouvoir législatif et du pouvoir exécutif [Titre III, Art.2 and 3]:

93 Gardons-nous que le nom de roi | The legislature must keep the executive and the king on short reins | On compterait les diamants

Décret qui reconnaît le gouvernement français monarchique [Titre III, Art.4]:

| 94 | L'état, déclaré monarchique | Declared a monarchy, the state is pleasing to the Bourbons; but woe to the Republic if it gets into their clutches | Tu croyais en aimant Colette |

Décret qui déclare l'Assemblée Nationale permanente [Titre III, Chap.I, Art.1]:

| 95 | Citoyens, c'est un parti sage | The Assembly will meet permanently; be ready to be on the alert in front of the court | Du serin qui te fait envie |

Décret portant établissement d'un comité permanent de surveillance:

| 96 | Il faut opposer une digue | Beware of court intrigues | Il n'est qu'un pas du mal au bien (du Roi et le fermier) |

Décret qui déclare les qualités requises pour être député [Section II, Art.2]:

| 97 | Selon nos décrets on peut être | Any active citizen can become a deputy, but beware of over-active schemers | Faut attendre avec patience |

Décret sur les assemblées primaires et électorales [Section II, Art.1]:

| 98 | Il est plus d'une mâchoire | Citizens, be wise electors (many deputies are drunkards) | Aussitôt que la lumière (de Me. Adam) |

Décret qui déclare l'inviolabilité de nos représentants [Section V, Art.7] *et la responsabilité des ministres* [Section IV, Art.5]:

| 99 | Tout ira tant que nous aurons | Deputies must be inviolable and ministers accountable; never give the key of the coffers to princes | Nous sommes précepteurs d'amour |

Décret qui déclare le roi inviolable [Chap.II, Art.2]:

| 100 | Défions-nous d'un roi | Beware of the inviolable king and his despotism | Ma pantoufle est trop étroite |

Décret qui exclut les femmes de la couronne [Chap.II, Art.1]:

| 101 | Nos législateurs peu galants | No woman may become queen, but she wields power through the bed | On compterait les diamants |

Décret qui exige du roi le serment civique [Chap.II, Art.4]:

| 102 | Des rois ainsi que des amants | The wind carries off the oath of the king to live and die loyal | Nous sommes précepteurs d'amour |

Décret qui déclare le refus de jurer de la part du roi, un acte d'abdication [Chap.II, Art.5]:

| 103 | Ce décret est peu nécessaire | Kings have no conscience; they swear oaths in order to retain their power | Avec les jeux dans le village |

Décret qui dépose le roi, si'il se met à la tête d'une armée contre la nation [Chap.II, Art.6]:

| 104 | Le roi faisant guerre ouverte | If the king leads an army in an uprising, he forfeits the throne; the law imposes no punishment for guerila warfare against citizens | La lumière la plus dure |

Décret qui dépose le roi, s'il sort des frontières de l'empire [Chap.II, Art.7]:

105 Sans doute rien de plus juste — If the king leaves the country he forfeits his throne — Aussitôt que la lumière

Décret portant une peine contre un roi félon, après son abdication [Chap.II, Art.7]:

106 Le prince atteint de félonie — The punishment for treachery by the king consists of his copying the vaudevilles of Marchant for the whole of his life — Je l'ai planté, je l'ai vu naître

Décret qui accorde une liste civile ou roi [Chap.II, Art.10]:

107 Certaine liste civile — The civil list serves to finance the vaudevilles of Maupas and Marchant — Romance de Daphné

Décret qui ne déclare le roi mineur que jusqu'à l'âge de 18 ans [Section II, Art.1]:

108 A dix-huit ans, par un décret étrange — At eighteen princes attain their majority, but afterwards they are always minors — Triste raison, j'abjure ton empire

Décret qui interdit la régence aux reines de France [Section II, Art.2]:

109 Aux Brunehaut, aux Frédegonde — The queen has only to bear sons; she can never be regent — Des [simples] jeux dans le village

Décret pour accorder une rente apanagère aux fils puinés du roi, à leur marriage, ou quand ils auront atteint leurs vingt-cinq années [Section III, Art.8]:

110 A tous ces princes louvetaux — Why do the princes receive such a large dowry on their marriage? — Chantez, dansez, amusezvous

Décret sur l'exercice et le rapport des deux pouvoirs, législatifs et exécutifs [Section IV]:

111 Ah! que nous serions trop heureux — How good it would be if the two powers tackled their duties together — Chantez, dansez, amusez-vous

Décret sur la responsabilité des ministres [Section IV, Art.5]:

112 De la guerre ou de la marine — Before a minister presents his lies in the Assembly, one should guillotine or hang him — Des simples jeux de son enfance (dans le village)

Décret du veto royal [Section III, Art.?1]:

113 Nous vantons notre liberté — We are wrong to feel we are men, since the king has the right of veto — Chantez, dansez, amusez-vous

Décret sur la sanction et le veto [Section III]:

114 Quand, per un décret servile — If we defend ourselves against the priests, the king interposes his veto — Air des trembleurs

Décret qui accorde au roi le droit de signer nos traités de paix, de commerce & d'alliance [Chap.IV, Section III, Art.2]:

115 Nous serons toujours en émoi — We can only call ourselves free if we make a bureaucrat of the king — Nous sommes précepteurs d'amour

Décret par lequel le pouvoir exécutif est tenu de faire parvenir les loix aux corps administratifs et aux tribunaux [Chap.IV, Section I]:

116 Eh! qu'on ne pense pas en rire — Things would happen more quickly if we made our lords the bearers of documents — Je l'ai planté, je l'ai vu naître

Décret qui, en rendant à la nation le droit de battre monnaie, laisse au roi celui de placer l'empreinte de sa figure sur nos écus [Chap.IV]:

| 117 | Ah! plût au ciel que jamais roi | It would have been good if the king's profile had no longer appeared on the currency | Nous sommes précepteurs d'amour |

Décret portant l'établissement des juges de paix [Chap.V, Art.7]:

| 118 | La justice est encore fort chère | Justice is still very expensive; make use therefore of Justices of the Peace | Faut attendre avec patience |

Décret portant l'établissement d'un tribunal de cassation [Chap. V, Art.19]:

| 119 | C'est bien au peuple assurément | We have the people to thank for the Court of Appeal, which met for the first time on 14 July | Accompagné de plusiers autres |

Décret portant établissement d'une haute cour nationale [Chap.V, Art.23]:

| 120 | Messieurs de la cour haute | My Lords in Orleans, you promised to bring bandits to justice; Lambsec still lives | Tous les bourgeois de Chartres |

Décret qui règle la force armée [Titre IV]:

121	Vous en voulez des bayonnettes	You *émigrés* would like bayonets; we have also pikes and cannons as arguments to bring you to your senses	Avec les jeux dans le village
122	Le beau Varicour, garde-du-corps, romance historique	Crime and fear now rule in Paris; march of the women on Versailles; bloodshed; the punishment of Varicour; outcry in Paris	Linval aimait Arsenne ou sur celui d'Alcimadure
123	Complainte de Marie-Antoinette, nuit du 5 au 6 octobre 1789; de notre reine infortunée	The lament of the imprisoned Marie Antoinette, who died happily since people weep for her	Complainte de Marie Stuart par Martini

Le décret de l'Assemblée Nationale qui abolit les titres de noblesse:

| 124 | Le jeune Almon, de haut lignage, romance historique | Almon was secretly in love with Suzette; his father, a nobleman, forbad their union. As his sister treacherously gave Zusette poison and she lost her child, Almon threw his patent of nobility in the fire … [Nine political poems and aphorisms] … | Air d'Emma |

Les droits de la noblesse:

125	Partout des droits de citoyen, chanson	Today everyone talks only about the rights of the citizen, but not about the former rights of the nobility	Philis demande son portrait
126	Nous n'avons pas beaucoup d'argent, chanson	The positive and the negative of the Revolution, its good and bad representatives confronted	On doit 60 mille francs
127	Au sein de nos campagnes, chanson	Let us celebrate freedom; contempt of England	L'amitié vive et pure

Déclaration des droits du clergé:

| 128 | Une charte du Saint Esprit | The appropriation and misuse of many rights by the clergy during the *ancien régime* | O filii, o filiae |

... [Epitaphe de Jésus Christ] ...

Couplet chanté par le cardinal de Bernis, à un souper qu'il donna, dans son palais à Rome à Mesdames de Polignac et Lebrun:

129 D'un vétéran de Guide et du Parnasse — All is shattered to pieces, even Bernis — Le connais-tu, ma chère Léonore

Couplet chanté par le Pape au même souper:

130 De tous les saints que l'on chaume — Noah, the tippler, is my favourite saint; he changes water into wine — Aussitôt que la lumière

131 Epilogue: Marchant sur la guimbarde — Since Marchant has practised criticism with bad verses, rap him over the knuckles — O ma tendre musette

... [Nouveaux noms donnés aux rues de paris; Inscription du drapeau des Forts-de-la-Halle; Oremus, ou Prière après le catéchisme; Petit catéchisme à l'usage des grands enfants; Le pour et contre, anecdote de la chapelle du roi – not sung] ...

APPENDIX 2

Summary of the attitudes of Marchant and 'Anti-Marchant' to the 1791 constitution

A – *against* F – *for* N – *neutral*

Reference	Subject	Attitude of Marchant	Attitude of Anti-Marchant
—	Declaration of the Rights of Man	A	F
—	Abolition of nobility's privileges	A	F
—	Abolition of sashes	A	F
—	Abolition of religious orders	A	F
Titre I. 1	Entry to all callings for each citizen	N/A	F
Titre I. 3	The same punishment for the same crime	Guillotine as penalty; equality also for nobles	F
Titre I. 3	Freedom of worship	Also for the Catholic church	F
Titre I. 3	Freedom to travel and visit	A; real danger in travelling	F; limitations on taking gold out of the country
Titre I. 3	Freedom of speech, writing and publishing	not for blasphemers	F
Titre II. 1	The unity of the state	no opinion expressed	F; no more prejudice against the provinces
Titre II. 2	Who is a French citizen	too many rights for foreigners; the *émigrés* are no longer French	F; free choice of where to live for foreigners
—	Decree that royalist officers swear an oath	—	A; mistrust of oaths
Titre II. 5	The wording of the citizens' oath	A; love of king and country	F; oath not taken seriously

Titre I. 3	Inviolability of property rights	injustice of secularization; predatory raids by Robespierre	F
—	Decree to divest the king of sovereignty	—	F
Titre III. 1	Sovereignty of the people	A; despotism of the people	F
Titre III. 2–4	Division of legislative and executive powers	A	F
Art. 4	The regime is monarchic	F; in truth, already a republic	A
Chap. I, Art. 1	The National Assembly is permanent	A; risks a *coup d'état* by the king	F
—	Decree that a permanent supervisory committee functions	—	A
Sect. II, Art. 2	Postulates on the quality of active citizens	A	F; danger of activists
Sect. IV, Art. 1	The tasks of election meetings	the National Assembly is a farce	choose good deputies
Sect. V, Art. 6	Obligation on members of the National Assembly to take the citizens' oath	A; perjury is honourable	—
Art. 7	Inviolability of deputies	A	F
Art. 5	Accountability of ministers	—	F; control by the National Assembly necessary
Chap. II, Art. 2	The person of the king is inviolable	—	A; mistrust of the king
Chap. II, Art. 1	Kingship is indivisible	A; the king is dependent on the people	—
Art. 1	Women are debarred from the throne	A; the real power of women	A; the real power of women
Art. 4	The king must swear an oath	A	F; mistrust of the king
Art. 5	Refusing the oath means abdication	no opinion expressed	A; unscrupulous kings
Art. 6	If the king leads an army against the nation, this means his abdication	A	F; guerilla warfare of the king against the people
Art. 7	If the king leaves the country and ignores a summons to return, this means his abdication	A	F
Art. 8	After his abdication the king will become an ordinary citizen	no opinion expressed	—
Art. 8	Decree ordaining the punishment of the king for treason after his abdication	—	A
Art. 10	The civil list guarantees the king's splendour	F; crimes of the Jacobins	A
Sect. II, Art. 1	During the king's minority (until he is 18) there is a regent	A	lifelong minority of the princes
Art. 2	Women are debarred from being regents	A	F
Sect. III. Art. 1	The heir to the throne is known as the 'prince royal'; he may leave the country only with the permission of the legislature and the agreement of the king	mania for using new names	—

Art. 8	The king's younger sons receive an annuity	A; it was done better formerly through inheritance	A
Sect. IV, Art 2	The king appoints and dismisses ministers	A; the reduction of his power by the Jacobins	—
Sect. IV, Art. 5	The accountability of ministers	—	F; penalties demanded
Chap. III, Sect. I	The exercise of statutary power	the deputies have too much power	—
[Sect. III]	Decree on the king's veto	—	A; no changes from former practice
Sect. III	The royal assent	A	A; veto set up in favour of the clergy
Sect. IV	Relationship of the legislative assembly to the king	executive without legislative power is disastrous	desire for good working relationship
Chap. IV	The exercise of executive power	critical of the removal of power from the king	—
Sect. I, Art. 1	The executive must dispatch laws to the administration of the courts	A	F
Sect. III, Art. 3	The king must ratify all treaties	against depriving the king of power	for the complete removal of power from the king
Chap. IV, Art. 2	The nation has the right to mint coins which portray the king	—	A
Chap. V, Art. 2	A judgment at law shall cost nothing	A; laments the uncertainty of judgments	—
Art. 7	Appointment of justices of the peace	laments the uncertainty of judgments	F; a judgment by the courts is expensive
Art. 19	Establishing of a court of appeal	no opinion expressed	F
Art. 23	Establishing of a national High Court	laments the prosecution of innocent noblemen	F; the prosecution of Lambesc demanded
Titre IV, Art. 1	Of the armed forces	disapproves of the possibility that soldiers can become officers	—
Art. 2	Disposition of the armies	condemns the lack of discipline in the army	welcomes the people's army
Titre VI	France's renunciation of conquest	A	—

SUMMARY

Attitude	Number of articles	
	Marchant	Anti-Marchant
negative:	32 (68%)	9 (19.6%)
positive:	4 (8.5%)	36 (78.3%)
neutral:	11 (23.5%)	1 (2.1%)
no attitude stated:	9	10

APPENDIX 3
List of the melodies or *timbres*

Pierre: C. Pierre, *Les hymnes et chansons de la Révolution* (Paris, 1904); the number of songs with the same timbre is indicated in parentheses ( ), the number of sources in square brackets [ ]
Capelle: P. Capelle, *La clé du caveau*, 4th edition (Paris, n.d.)

Title	No. in Appendix 1	Composer/origin	Pierre	Capelle
1. Accompagné de plusieurs autres (= Le premier de janvier)	4,51 59 79,119	P. Laujon	(7) 577*	353
2. Ah que je sens d'impatience	11,84	N.-M. Dalayrac, *Azémia* (1786)	(7)	19
3. A la façon de Barbari (= de la fari dondaine)	16,89	old melody	(14)	681
4. Amusez-vous, jeunes fillettes (Vaudeville du printemps)	34	J. P. A. Martini, *La rosière de Salency* (1769)	(1)	38
5. Apprenez qu'une belle (du Printemps)	33	?, *Le printemps*	—	—
6. Aussitôt que la lumière	98,105,130	Maître Adam, *Le meunier de Nevers* (1650)	(67)	50
7. Avec les jeux dans le village	46,103,121	Piis/Barré, *Les amours d'été* (1781)	(47)	53
8. Ce fut par la faute du sort	10	M.-A. Désaugiers *père*, *Florine* (1780)	(14)	71
9. Chansons, chansons	65 71	Valois d'Orville, *Les revenants*	514**[5] (4) 579[4]	90
10. Chantez, dansez, amusez-vous	41,42,74, 80,110, 111,113	A.-E.-M. Grétry, *La rosière de Salency* (1773)	(8)	836
11. Colinette au bois s'en alla	56 69	L.-A. Beffroy de Rigny, *Nicomède dans la lune, ou La révolution pacifique* (1790)	(6) 470**[2]	100
12. Complainte de Marie Stuart	123	Martini	236(1)	—
13. Dans nos hameaux la paix et l'innocence	81	Desbrosses	—	124
14. Dans Paris la grand'ville (= La bourbonnaise)	61	chanson, 1768	485*[3] (9)	671
15. de Emma	124	—	301(1)	—
16. de Joconde (= M. le curé n'espérez plus)	53	old song	(7)	659
17. De la confession (= Je deviens avant vous)	62	Désaugiers, Albanèse	486*[2] (1)	292
18. De la croisée (= L'autre jour je fléchissais)	3 57	Ducray-Duminil	(34) 545*	678 —
19. De la p'tit' poste de Paris (= Ah monseigneur)	47	old melody (used in *Annette et Lubin*)	(2)	16

20. Des simples jeux dans le village	109,112	J.-J. Rodolphe, *L'aveugle de Palmire* (1767)	(6)	148
21. De tous les capucins du monde	48	old melody, ?Mouret	(2)	137
22. Du curé de Pomponne (= Tant que l'homme désirera)	54	air, ronde de Collé	(5)	745
23. Du haut en bas	32	old melody	(5)	155
24. Du serin qui te fait envie	31,95	Dorat, before 1786	(26)	156
25. En jupon court, en blanc corset (= Sous un saule dans la prairie)	8,82	A. Campra	(2)	547
26. En quatre mots ja vais vous compter ça (= air des cinq voyelles)	25	old melody, used in *Les amours d'été* (1781)	—	721
27. Faut attendre avec patience	49,97,118	N. Dezède, *Les trois fermiers* (1777)	(1)	191
28. Il n'est qu'un pas du mal au bien	23,96	P.-A. Monsigny, *Le roy et le fermier* (1762)	(2)	232
29. Jardinier, ne vois-tu pas (= air des fraises)	66	old song	(5)	725
30. Je connais un berger discret (= Guillot a des yeux complaisants), or	43	old melody, used in *Les amours d'été* (1781)	(1)	201
Philis demande son portrait	58		545[*]	449
31. Je l'ai planté, je l'ai vu naître	26,88,106, 116	romance, J.-J. Rousseau	(8)	261
32. Je suis né natif de Ferrare	40	A. Salieri, *Tarare* (1787)	(32)	280
[Joli réservoir d'amour	58	—	545[**]	—][52]
33. La lumière la plus pure	104	Rodolphe, *L'aveugle de Palmire* (1767)	(3)	310
34. L'amitié vive et pure	127	Guichard, *La fête des bons gens*	(2)	315
35. L'amour sans aucune contrainte	44	—	—	—
36. La nuit et le jour	5	—	—	—
37. Le petit mot pour rire (= C'est Geneviève dont le nom)	45	Lattaignant, old melody	(2)	759
38. Le saint craignant de pécher (= Quand la mer rouge apparut)	18,91 67	old melody	(3) 536[*][4]	355
39. Les folies d'Espagne	37,38	old melody	(1)	722
40. Les trembleurs	12,85,114	J.-B. Lully, *Isis* (1677)	(11)	731
41. Linval aimait Arsène	122	J. P. A. Martini, *Romance* ou *air d'Alcimadure*	239(1)	367
42. Malbrough s'en va en guerre	39	(1709; in vogue in 1784)	(12)	662

52 See note 51.

43. Ma pantoufle est trop étroite	29,30,100	—	—	—
44. Mon honneur dit que je serais coupable (= Mon petit coeur à chaque instant soupire)	22	old melody, used in *Les amours d'été*	(4)	39
45. Mon père je deviens devant vous (= air du confiteor)	50	old song	(5)	743
46. Monsieur le prévôt des marchands	17,90	old melody, before 1642	(4)	763
47. Nous sommes précepteurs d'amour	9,27,99, 102,115, 117	old melody, before 1659 (La Garde, Vadé/Le Gat)	(3)	410
48. O filii, o filiae	128	old melody, before 1642	607[*] (18)	—
49. O Mahomet, ton paradis des femmes (= Il faut aimer, c'est la loi de Cythère)	83	Rochon de Chabannes	(1)	224
50. O ma tendre musette (= Gentille boulangère), romance	63 77 131	F.-A. D. Philidor, or J. F. de La Harpe	524[*] (13) 300	417
51. On compterait les diamants	7,20,55 68 93,101	before 1789	(31) 527[**][2]	423
52. On doit soixante mille francs	70 126	S. Champein, *Les dettes* (1787)	581[3] (4)	428
53. Oui noir, mais pas si diable	64	Grétry, *L'amitié à l'épreuve* (1770)	508[**][2] (4)	438
54. Paris est au roi (= air de la Camargo), air aristocratique	14,87	contredanse, before 1754	—	672
55. Philis demande son portrait	13 or 30, 58,86 125	E.-J.-I.-A. Albanese, old song (*Le mariage de Scarron*)	(6) 302[2]	449
56. Que ne suis-je la fougère (= D'une amante abandonnée)	24	Riboutté (1761)	(7)	490
57. Qu'en voulez-vous dire?	19,92	old song	(3)	496
58. Regards vifs et joli maintien (= air de la parole)	60	Dalayrac, *Sargines, ou L'élève de l'amour* (1788)	524[*](2)	693
59. Rendez-moi mon écumelle de bois	72	old melody	468[**][2] (6)	507
60. Réveillez-vous, belle endormie (= Philis, plus avare que tendre)	15	old melody, used in *La belle au bois dormant*	(4)	542
61. Romance de Daphné (= L'amour m'a fait la peinture)	36,107	*Lusse* (romances by Marmontel and Saint-Péravy)	(1)	700
62. Tous les bourgeois de Chartres	28,52,120	old melody	(12)	564
63. Tous les hommes sont bons	2, 75	Monsigny, *Le déserteur* (1769)	545[5] (1)606[*]	896

273

64. Triste raison, j'abjure ton empire (= Le connais-tu, ma Léonore?)	6,108,129	old melody, new text by A. Gouffé	(4)	373
65. Tu croyais en aimant Colette	21,94	old song, used in *Le mari retrouvé*	—	574
66. Un jour me demandait Hortense	78	old song	(1)	594
67. Vive le vin, vive l'amour	2,76	Monsigny, *Le déserteur* (1769)	(7)	623
68. Vous l'ordonnez, je me ferai connaître	35	Dezède, *Le barbier de Séville* (1775)	(2)	640
69. Vous qui d'amoureuse aventure (= Veillons au salut de l'empire)	73	Dalayrac, *Renaud d'Ast* (1787)	467*** [5](45)	648

APPENDIX 4
Bibliography of *constitutions chantées*

1. La féte constitutionnelle / patriotique de la France / comédie, 2 actes, en prose et vaudevilles sur la musique de Richard-Coeur-de-Lion, Rouen 1791
[*F-Pn*, MS 9259]

2. LA / CONSTITUTION / EN VAUDEVILLES / Suivie des DROITS DE L'HOMME, / DE / LA FEMME & de plusieurs autres / vaudevilles constitutionnels. / Par M. MARCHANT. / A PARIS, Chez les LIBRAIRES ROYALISTES. / 1792   [*GB-Lbl*]
Pierre cites only eighteen songs, for one of which he gives an incorrect reference: nos. 467***, 468**, 470**, 485**, 486*, 508**, 514**, 524* 524**, 527**, [536*], 545, 545*, 545**, 558* (incorrect), 577*, 579 and 581.
Two later editions: (a) POÉSIES RÉVOLUTIONNAIRES / ET / CONTRE-RÉVOLUTIONNAIRES, / OU RECUEIL, CLASSÉ PAR ÉPOQUES, / DES HYMNES, CHANTS GUERRIERS, CHANSONS RÉPUBLICAINES, ODES, SATIRES, CANTIQUES / DES MISSIONAIRES, etc., etc., / Les plus remarquables qui ont parues depuis 30 ans. / TOME PREMIER. / PARIS, / A LA LIBRAIRIE HISTORIQUE, / RUE SAINT-HONORÉ, HOTEL D'ALIGNE, N° 12, / et rue de l'Arbre-Sec, n° 26. / 1821
(b) MARCHANT / LA CONSTITUTION / EN / VAUDEVILLES / (PARIS, 1792) / Réimprimée avec une Notice / PAR / J. KERGOMARD / [vignette with OCCUPA PORTUM / IOV AVST] / PARIS / LIBRAIRIE DES BIBLIOPHILES / Rue Saint-Honoré, 338 / MDCCCLXXII

3. LA / CONSTITUTION / FRANÇAISE / EN CHANSONS. / A l'usage / DES HONNETES GENS. / Hic ficis omnium. / A PARIS, / Chez, GUEFFIER, imp.-lib, / quai des Augustins, n°. 17 / 1792   *F-Pn*
Pierre, p. 154, includes only eight songs: nos. 236, 239, 300–302, 606*, 607 and 607*

4. FOLIES / NATIONALES, / POUR SERVIR DE SUITE / A LA / CONSTITUTION / EN VAUDEVILLES. / PAR M. MARCHANT. / A PARIS. / Chez les LIBRAIRES ROYALISTES. / 1792

5. 'La Constitution de 1793 ou les Voeux accomplis, gravée avec la musique du citoyen Frère', in POÉSIES / RÉVOLUTIONNAIRES / ET / CONTRE-RÉVOLUTION-NAIRES (Paris, 1821), pp. 239–41

6. LA RÉPUBLIQUE / EN VAUDEVILLES. / PRÉCÉDÉE d'une Notice des princi- / paux évenemens de la révolution, / pour servir de Calendrier à l'an- / née 1793. / A PARIS, / Chez les Marchands de nouveautès. / 1793. [Pierre 154, no. 54; articles 1–4 concern the constitution]

7. La Constitution à Constantinople, Pièce patriotique, suivie d'un divertisse- ment et précédée d'un prologue, par Lavalée [1793]

8. LA CONSTITUTION / FRANÇAISE ET LES DROITS DE L'HOMME. / CHANSON PATRIOTIQUE. / A PARIS, / CHEZ GARNÉRY, / Libraire, n° 17. / L'AN PREMIER DE LA LIBERTÉ [melody 'Henri IV', 22 verses: 'Rendons hommage / A nos repré- sentants / A leur courage, Ainsi qu'à leurs talents; / Leur grand ouvrage / Vivra dans tous les tems.'; 8vo, 8pp, several editions]   F-Pn, Pièce 8° Ye 4311

9. LA CONSTITUTION / EN VAUDEVILLE, / OEUVRE POSTHUME / D'un homme qui n'est pas / mort [Pierre-Antoine-Jean-Baptiste de Villiers], / publiée par lui mème, ET DÉDIÉE / A Madame BUONAPARTE, / née BEAUHARNAIS. / A PARIS, / De l'imprimerie de la Constitution. / An VIII.   F-Pn, Ye 34836

10. LA / CONSTITUTION / FRANÇAISE / EN VAUDEVILLES, / Par un Législateur de Boudoirs. / SECONDE ÉDITION, / Revue, corrigée et augmentée. / Chez elle un beau désordre est un effet / de l'art. / BOILEAU, Art poétique. / A BERLIN, / Et se trouve à Paris. / AN VIII.   F-Pn

11. L'UNION VILLAGEOISE, / SCENE PATRIOTIQUE / EN PROSE ET VAUDEVILLE / Ajoutée à la suite de plusieurs pièces, sur le / Théâtre du Vaudeville, et représentée, pour / la première fois, à la suite du Prix, le vendredi / 9 Août 1793 / SECONDE EDITION / Augmentée. / [in Desfontaines's hand: 'la Vallée; Auguste / Piis et Barré, d'après Barbier'] PRIX, Dix Sols, avec la Musique. / A PARIS, CHEZ le Libraire, au Théâtre du Vaudeville, / à l'Imprimerie, rue des Droits de l'Homme, n° 44. / An deuxième [p. 3: 'fête pour l'acceptation solennelle de cette Constitution si long-tems attendue, et qui vient enfin de nous être donnée]
          F-Pn, 8° Ye Th 18646

12. Hymne sur l'acceptation de l'Acte constitutionnel du 24 Juin 1793, l'an second de la République une & indivisible des François, Chant des Marseillais [printed in R. Brécy, *La Révolution en chantant* (Paris, 1988), p. 130]

13. Couplets sur la promulgation de la Constitution de l'an III de la République française et sur la réunion de la Belgique et du Pays de Liège à la France [ibid., p. 184]

14. Lied auf die französische Constitution, 'Peuple romain si quelquefois', in J. F. Reichardt, *Frankreich im Jahre 1802* (Altona, 1802), ii, pp. 181–3

15. [12 extracts from no. 9, above], in *London und Paris*, v (Weimar, 1798), pp. 50–54; 'Nous reverrons nos guerriers' [from 'Constitution en vaudevilles de Desrosier, 10 Nivose, chez Gauthier, rue Martoly 5', a publication not so far traced], ibid., p. 55

16. [G. and G. Marty, *Dictionnaire des chansons de la Révolution* (Paris, 1988), p. 114; see Appendix 1, no. 67, of the present article]

NAPOLEON AND AFTER

The French occupation of Lucca and its effects on music

At the end of the eighteenth century, in an Italy divided under the terms of the Treaty of Aix-la-Chapelle (1748) into kingdoms, duchies, grand-duchies and republics, the Most Serene Republic of Lucca – a small territory of some 1500 square kilometres to the northwest of what is now Tuscany – still maintained its distinct physiognomy (see Fig. 1). Its republican traditions went back at least to 1369, and its institutions (except during the brief reign of Paolo Guinigi at the beginning of the fifteenth century) had suffered no drastic upheavals, although it had passed gradually from an aristocratic to an oligarchic regime.

Thanks to this continuity in politics and institutions, the small republic had since medieval times acquired and retained a notable reputation in Europe, especially through the activities of its silk merchants and bankers. In the most distant European cities, from Bruges to Paris, from London to Marseilles, from Antwerp to Lyons, from Geneva to Warsaw, as well as in Spain, in Russia and as far afield as Constantinople, there were colonies of Lucchesi. (To mention only two examples, at Avignon there were Lucchesi bankers at the papal court, while at Bruges, Giovanni Arnolfini (known from Jan van Eyck's famous painting in the National Gallery, London) financed the activities of the dukes of Burgundy.) Despite the fact that the political changes taking place in Europe tended towards the formation of nation states, the republic of Lucca succeeded in preserving its independence until 1799. In this it was helped by the ability and determination of its governors, who knew how to ensure peace, order and well-being for the most part at home, and, by their able and discreet diplomacy, to maintain the foreign contacts necessary to protect those Lucchesi active in various European countries.

The ancient republic came to an end on 2 January 1799 with the entry of the French troops:

A dì 2 Gennaio 1799 alle ore 21 circa cominciò ad entrare La Cavalleria in Lucca. Questa era composta di Dragoni, tutta bella gente, e bene vestita. Per rendersi più feroce, e spaventevole al guardo, oltre una longa sciabla fodrata portava un elmo in

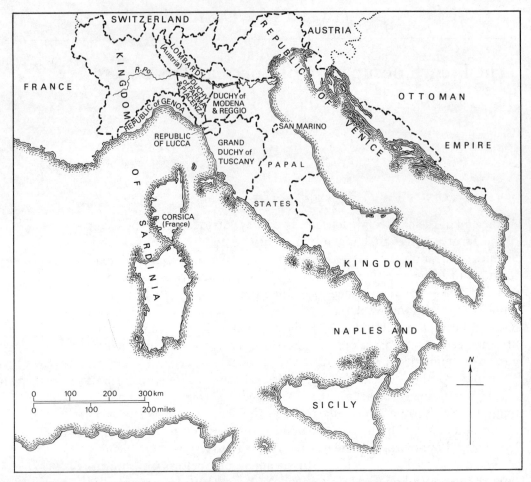

Fig. 1   Italy prior to Napoleon's campaign

testa, dietro al quale vi era una superiormente posta una longa coda di cavallo, che svolazzando per l'aria col correre che faceva questi scarmigliati Dragoni sembravano altrettanti diavoli di Inferno.[1]

On 2 January 1799 at 9.00 pm the cavalry started to enter Lucca. They were composed of dragoons, fine men and well dressed. To make themselves look more ferocious, and fearful to the guard, they carried a long sheathed sabre and wore on

1 J. Chelini, *Zibaldone lucchese*, a manuscript diary in the Archivio di Stato, Lucca (hereafter *I-La*), Archivio Sardini, 165–76: iii, p. 100. Jacopo Chelini (1759–1824) was a viola player in the Cappella Palatina at Lucca from 1781; he was also a cleric, chaplain at the monastery of S. Giustina and family priest to the noble Sardini household. As well as the valuable *Zibaldone*, he has left other diaries and memoirs of fundamental importance to an understanding of, among other things, the crucial period of the fall of the aristocratic republic and the changes in regime that followed. For a general picture of Chelini, see Raffaella Bocconi, 'La società civile lucchese del Settecento veduta da Jacopo Chelini e dai suoi contemporanei', *Bollettino storico lucchese*, xi (1939), pp. 5–35; for references to his musical activities, see L. Nerici, *Storia della musica in Lucca* (Lucca, 1879; reprinted Bologna, 1969), pp. 212, 218 and 247.

their heads a helmet, from the top of which there hung at the back a horsetail which fluttered about in the air as they passed, making these dishevelled dragoons look more like devils from hell.

When, in fact, the troops of General Serurier entered Lucca, most of the population experienced feelings like those expressed in that description of the dragoons – either fear or confusion, but certainly not surprise. In the ten years that had passed since the outbreak of the French Revolution, with all the repercussions it had had in Italy, a French invasion of the country had been thought imminent and inevitable by the inhabitants of Lucca. If one reads the official documents and the chronicles of those years one can see, after the first reports of the Revolution had spread, a growing preoccupation with European events and a growing fear that those events would have consequences at home. Concern increased after the constitution of the Cisalpine Republic on Lucca's borders in 1797, and fear of the French derived also from the imperialistic connotations attached to the old republic of Lucca.[2]

During those ten years the governing class in Lucca had tried desperately, with the means most congenial to them (both diplomacy and the payment of considerable inducements), to save the independence of the aristocratic republic. These desperate efforts were really quite unavailing, since the continuation of Lucca's sovereignty until 1799 was decided by the French for reasons of political expediency and strategy. The government, while treading the paths of diplomacy and payments abroad, sought to minimize feelings of discontent at home by giving more families access to public affairs by means of ennoblement, while adopting a greater paternalism than usual in their dealings with commoners. Repression was nevertheless shown towards some groups of 'Jacobins', or rather 'patriots', who were tried and banished or imprisoned.[3] Among the Jacobins who came from Lucca was a *maestro di cappella*, a certain Giuseppe Rustici,[4] active from 1785 at the

---

2 For a historical account of the period, see P. G. Camaiani, *Un patriziato di fronte alla rivoluzione francese: la repubblica oligarchica di Lucca dal 1789 al 1799* (Florence, 1983). Among earlier writings the following are important: A. Mazzarosa, *Storia di Lucca dalla sua origine fino al 1814* (Lucca, 1833; 3rd edn in *Opere*, v, Lucca, 1866); C. Minutoli, Supplement to G. Tommasi, *Sommario della storia di Lucca* (Florence, 1847; reprinted Bologna, n.d.); C. Massei, *Storia civile di Lucca dall'anno 1796 al 1848* (Lucca, 1878); U. Bernardini, *L'ultimo anno della repubblica aristocratica (1798–1799)* (Perugia, 1928); and A. D'Addario, 'La crisi dell'aristocrazia lucchese alla fine del secolo XVIII, nella storiografia e nelle fonti', *Bollettino storico livornese*, iv (1954), pp. 147–61.
3 On the prosecution of Jacobins in Lucca, see M. D. Orzali, *I processi contro i giacobini lucchesi* (Lucca, 1947); and G. Arrighi, 'Una "trama" contro la repubblica di Lucca organizzata a Livorno nel 1796', *Rivista di Livorno*, v (1956), pp. 1–16. The original proceedings of the trials are in *I-La, Cause delegate*, 101.
4 J. Chelini, *Zibaldone lucchese*, ii, p. 349. Giuseppe Rustici, known as 'il seniore' or 'Rustici di Massa' to distinguish him from another of the same name, was born in Lucca in 1752 and had composed music for the 'Tasche' (see below): in 1783 *Leonida, rè di Sparta* and in 1789 *Bruto*. He met with success in Massa and was made *maestro di cappella* at the cathedral there in 1785, a

primatial church of Massa and therefore possibly influenced by the Cisalpines. Fear of what might come from outside was therefore added to what was hidden inside the country. The entry of the French troops on that day in January 1799 must therefore be considered as an event for which long preparations had been made, and this had an important consequence: that Lucca 'evaded almost completely the most significant experience of Jacobin Italy, that of the period 1796–9' ('si sottrasse quasi completamente all'esperienza più significativa dell'Italia giacobina, quella cioè del triennio 1796–'99').[5]

It may be taken as self-evident that the end of a secular republic governed by statutes and laws almost unchanged for centuries was a disturbing event, and one which had important repercussions on the history of the city. The aim of the present article is to establish whether that historical event was as disturbing to the musical life of Lucca, whether it was anticipated, and whether it affected the subsequent development of music there. The day that signalled, in practical terms, the end of the aristocratic republic also initiated a series of alternations between French and Austrian regimes which resulted from the military events taking place in Italy, and in Europe in general. These may be summarized as follows:

First Democratic Republic	4 February 1799–17 July 1799
First Austrian Regency	18 July 1799–8 July 1800
Second Democratic Republic	9 July 1800–15 September 1800
Second Austrian Regency	15 September 1800–9 October 1800
Third Democratic Republic (or Provisional Government of the Republic)	9 October 1800–31 December 1801
Fourth Democratic Republic	1 January 1802–24 June 1805

On this last date began the rule of Elisa Bonaparte Baciocchi. It need not be stressed what a disturbing effect these frequent changes had on all aspects of life in Lucca. Thousands of soldiers lodged in the convents and churches,[6] the arrival and departure of generals and commanders,

post which he occupied until 1799. He became known in Massa for his open-minded ideas about religion, which incurred the wrath of the Sacred Office, and for his decidedly republican militance, especially at the time when the Cisalpine Republic was formed. See L. Nerici, *Storia della musica in Lucca*, pp. 284 and 386, and S. Giampaoli, *Musica e teatro alla corte di Massa: i Guglielmi* (Massa, 1978), pp. 85 and 87–9.
5 Camaiani, *Un patriziato*, p. 4.
6 Chelini, *Zibaldone lucchese*, iii, pp. 325–6. One reads, for example, in the section 'Danni cagionati dalla Truppa in Lucca': 'In [the church of] S. Francesco ... although the choir stalls were completely closed, some soldiers, by means of portable ladders, climbed over the arches of the facade and down into the choir, where they broke into the stalls where the choirbooks were

endless proclamations and dispatches[7] and conflicting reports coming from the fields of battle – all served to disconcert and disorient the peace-loving inhabitants of Lucca, accustomed to a life of even pace and predictability.

This piling-up of events affected also the musical life of Lucca, which had long followed a regular pattern: liturgical feasts of the Roman Catholic calendar with a tradition of musical involvement; feasts celebrating the saints after whom the city's churches and monasteries were named, again with music performing a traditional role; opera seasons in the Pubblico, Castiglioncelli and Pantera theatres of the city – in autumn (from August to November), during Carnival (from 26 December to the beginning of Lent), in spring (after Easter) and in summer (June and July).[8] Sometimes spoken drama was given during the same season as opera, or substituted for it, especially during the less regular and traditional seasons of spring and summer. To these opportunities for music, which were characteristic of other Italian cities as well, must be added some which were particularly associated with Lucca itself: the feast of S Croce and the celebrations of the *Tasche*, which by the 1790s had centuries of tradition behind them. The feast of S Croce (13–14 September), which was of both civic and religious importance, was observed above all with imposing church music: first and second solemn vespers and a mass for double chorus and orchestra in the cathedral, in which (at least for the whole of the eighteenth century) the most celebrated vocal and instrumental soloists in Italy took part. The *Tasche*, which took place every two or three years, were the most important of all civic occasions: during three consecutive days the chief magistrates of the republic were elected, the voting being preceded by the performance of cantatas or 'political serenatas' which exalted republican values.[9] Obviously the musical life of Lucca included also special occasions which called for celebratory cantatas, vocal and instrumental 'accademie' and so on. As I have shown elsewhere,[10] what distinguished

and took them away. They used the leaves of parchment to repair their drums, which for the most part had broken skins.'

7 For a collection of proclamations, dispatches and *avvisi*, see I-La, Archivio Sardini, 188–91, *Nota de' Proclami, Notificazioni, Leggi etc.* (a collection worked on by Chelini).

8 For a general picture of the history of music in Lucca, see Nerici, *Storia della musica in Lucca*; A. Bonaccorsi, *Giacomo Puccini e i suoi antenati musicali* (Milan, 1950); and G. Biagi Ravenni, 'Lucca', in *Dizionario enciclopedico universale della musica e dei musicisti: il lessico*, iii (Turin, 1984), pp. 13–15. For the history of opera in particular, see A. Pellegrini, *Spettacoli lucchesi nei secoli XVII–XIX* (Lucca, 1941); M. T. Quilici, 'Spettacoli lucchesi nella seconda metà del '700' (diss., University of Pisa, 1986); and G. Biagi Ravenni, 'Lucca', in *The New Grove Dictionary of Opera*, ed. S. Sadie (in course of publication).

9 See G. Biagi Ravenni and C. Gianturco, 'The "Tasche" of Lucca: 150 Years of Political Serenatas', *Proceedings of the Royal Musical Association*, cxi (1984–5), pp. 45–56.

10 G. Biagi Ravenni, 'Musica e potere politico a Lucca tra '700 e '800', a paper read at the inaugural conference for the Ricasoli Collection, *Patrons, Politics, Music and Art in Italy 1738–1859*, Louisville, Kentucky, 14–18 March 1989 (in course of publication).

the situation at Lucca before 1799 was the firm control exercised by the authorities on the most important musical occasions of the city; these had to satisfy standards of decorum and good entertainment, and therefore in effect offer guarantees of quality.

The upset caused by the arrival of the French in 1799 does not seem at first to have affected most of these traditional occasions, except for the *Tasche*, which of course were no longer celebrated; certain minor church feasts observed in street processions were also prohibited, for fear of incidents. A glance at the succession of musical events during the First Democratic Republic shows that new occasions were added to the traditional ones, resulting in an even fuller musical calendar. This combining of the traditional and the novel continued under subsequent regimes, both Austrian and French, although with a gradual diminution in quantity.

The theatre seasons were still the major events for the citizenry and also for French army officers; they continued to furnish abundant material for the chroniclers, even for those primarily interested in the political changes taking place. When the French entered Lucca *I due fratelli Pappamosca*, a *dramma giocoso* by Pietro Guglielmi, had been playing at the Teatro Castiglioncelli since 26 December 1798, and performances continued during the whole of Carnival.[11] Events changed nothing in this case. And yet if one looks for musical precedents, so to speak, for the arrival of the French, the list is a rather short one: a few performances of French pieces and appearances by French artists, but nothing of great significance. Of course, privileged ties existed between Lucca and the Austrian Empire, but important repercussions of French culture were nevertheless felt during the eighteenth century in Lucca: the second edition of the *Encyclopédie* was published there from 1758,[12] as also was the Italian translation of *Le journal encyclopédique* of Liège. But, just as repercussions in the political arena seem not to have strengthened Revolutionary ideology in Lucca, so contacts with French music and culture seem also to have been few and fleeting.

For those contacts that did take place we must again look mainly to the theatre. In spring 1780 *Il Pigmalione azione scenica di Mr. de Rousseau dedicata alle nobilissime ed ornatissime dame di Lucca dal capocomico Pietro Ferrari* was given during a season of spoken drama; the translation was by Ferrari himself. On 21 January 1796 a perform-

---

11 D. Merli, *Diario delle cose riguardanti Lucca dall'anno 1761 al 1836*, MS diary in the Biblioteca Statale, Lucca (hereafter *I-Lg*), MSS 495–9: III, p. 76. A copy of the libretto is in the Biblioteca Marucelliana, Florence.

12 *Encyclopédie ou Dictionnaire raisonné des sciences, des arts et des métiers par une société de gens de lettres, mis en ordre & publié par M. Diderot ... & par M. D'Alembert ... Seconde edition enrichie de notes, & donnée au public par M. Octavien Diodati noble lucquis ... A Lucques Chez Vincent Giuntini Imprimeur, MDCCLVIII.* The same printer issued the *Giornale enciclopedico di Liegi ... tradotto in lingua italiana con nuove aggiunte* (1756–60).

ance of *Pimmalione scena lirica di M. J. J. Rousseau tradotta dal Sig. Sografi e posta in musica dal celebvre Maestro Sig. Cimador, azione drammatica da rappresentarsi nel Teatro alla Pantera* is reported.[13] On 13 and 16 October 1797 concerts were given at the Teatro Pubblico by the violinist Rodolphe Kreutzer. Kreutzer was at this time closely involved in the events of the French Revolution and composed *opéras comiques* based on them, but the diarist to whom we owe these references remarks only on his celebrity, his unique qualities as a violinist and the difficulty of the music he played.[14] In autumn 1798 *L'avviso ai maritati*, with music by Nicolas Isouard, was staged.[15] The composer settled shortly afterwards in Paris, where he collaborated with Kreutzer.

It was precisely in these years, between 1796 and 1798, that the habit of theatre-going changed, as we learn from the *Zibaldone* of Jacopo Chelini:

Il Teatro di Lucca era sempre stato il modello, parlando dell'udienza, del rispetto, della saviezza, e della quiete, né mai si dava il caso che si facesse replicare pezzo alcuno di Musica, o di Ballo, per quanto fosse accetto al pubblico, essendo questo l'uso antico del nostro Teatro. Ora però sono già due anni o tre, che il popolo, animato ancora da qualche persona nobile; è divenuto franco, e sfacciato oltre l'usato, perché in qualcuno vi era entrato le massime correnti di Libertà, ed eguaglianza; Da ciò vi nasce che si faceva lecito, perché già persuaso che non sarebbe stato castigato per quello che hò già detto, non solo di battere smode-ratamente mani, e piedi al Teatro per applaudire, ma di fare degli urli, e voci insoffribili, e fare replicare quelle arie, o Balli, che le piaceva, e di far tornare in scena tutti gli attori, qualora era finita la rappresentanza, al solo oggetto di far nuovi

13 Librettos in, respectively, *I-Lg*, Busta 1140.6 and the Archivio arcivescovile, Lucca, Fondo Martini 113. In the library of the Istituto Musicale 'L. Boccherini', Lucca (hereafter *I-Li*), Fondo Bottini Zbis, there is a score with the title *Pimmalione/Parte Prima/A[n]na T[ere]sa B[otti]ni/1789*, copied by a certain Francesco Ginni, a musician and scribe at Lucca, for Anna Teresa Bottini, a noblewoman and musical amateur, also of Lucca (see below). The music is that by Cimador performed in 1796. It is difficult to account for the date on the title-page, which seems, however, to have been added when the score was bound. On the importance and dissemination of *Pygmalion*, see G. Morelli and E. Surian, 'Pigmalione a Venezia', in *Venezia e il melo-dramma nel settecento*, ed. M. T. Muraro, ii (Florence, 1981), pp. 147–68.
14 Louise Palma Mansi, *Memoires ou notices à l'usage de L. P. M.*, MS diary in *I-La*, Archivio Arnolfini, 191: ii, pp. 7, 9. 'Le jour 13 du même mois d'Octobre, il y aveû au Théâtre un Concert donné par M. Kreutzer célebre Professeur de Violon. Il a été trouvé genéralment unique dans sa profession, sur tout pour executer les choses les plus difficiles.' 'Le jour 16 du même il y aveû un autre Concert du professeur de Violon Kreutzer avec illumination au Théâtre.'
15 Libretto in *I-Lg*, Busta 702–12. It is not known whether the composer was present during the preparation of this opera, which was originally given at Florence in 1794. It is curious to note a connection between the first performance of the Lucca revival, on 18 August, and a plot against the state that was discovered later (see U. Bernardini, *L'ultimo anno della repubblica aristocra-tica...*, p. 38). According to the testimony given by Sebastiano Bossi on 25 August 1798 in the trial of Antonio Biondi and others implicated in the plot, 'conveniva trovare un luogo dove far l'unione dei congiurati per sottoscriversi, la qual unione sarebbe stata meglio, che seguisse nella susseguente sera di sabato [18 agosto], giacché aprendosi in quella sera il Teatro era supponibile che la nostra radunanza non fosse stata da alcuno soggetto scoperta per la distrazione, che richiama la prima volta dell'apertura del Teatro' (*I-La, Cause delegate*, 101, no. 96).

applausi, e ciò con incomodo, e molestia grande della maggior parte dell'udienza, che savia, e morigerata disapprovava la maniera inconveniente con cui pochi discoli turbavano quella bella quiete che per tanti anni si godeva a qualunque spettacolo Teatrale.[16]

The theatre at Lucca, as far as the audience is concerned, has always been a model of respectability, of good behaviour and of quiet attention, and it was never the case that anyone should be made to repeat a piece of music or a dance, no matter how much it pleased the audience, since this was the long-established custom at our theatre. For the last two or three years, though, the public, excited by some member of the nobility, has become outspoken and more than usually bold because someone has taken up the current maxims of Liberty and Equality. As a result it has become permissible (because it is known that it will not be condemned for the reasons I have mentioned) for some members of the audience to applaud not only by clapping their hands and stamping their feet in an immoderate manner, but also by shouting out at the top of their voices, and also for them to have those arias or dances they like repeated, and to have all the cast return to the stage at the end of the performance for the sole purpose of applauding them again. And all this is to the discomfort and great annoyance of most of the audience, who, being well-behaved and orderly, disapprove of the way a few trouble-makers disturb that lovely calm which for so many years one enjoyed at any theatrical performance.

Was it simply a case of applauding 'in an immoderate manner', or had the 'current maxims of Liberty and Equality' had some other effect? Did the change manifest itself in the staging of pieces dealing with the current situation or the new spirit? Perhaps a more detailed examination of the repertories of those companies putting on spoken drama might throw some light on this.[17]

To return to 1799, the presence or absence of Lucchesi at the theatre

---

16 Chelini, *Zibaldone lucchese*, ii, pp. 511–12.
17 Information about drama companies before 1799 is scanty. The presence of the following companies can be gleaned from a reading of Merli, Mansi and Quilici (works cited above):

1789	spring	Luigi Mazzotti
	autumn	Anna Roffi Ferri
1790	spring	Rosa Medembach
1791	autumn	Merli
1792	spring	Pietro Andolfati
	summer	Ferri
1793	spring	a Florentine company
	summer	Pietro Andolfati
	autumn	Giuseppe and Anna Ferri
1794	Carnival	Antonio Goldoni
	spring	Domenico Nerini
1795	spring	Giovanni Battista Mancini
1796	spring	Mataglieni
	summer	Antonio Pelandi
	autumn	Mancini
1797	spring	Luigi del Bono
	summer	Luigi Rossi
1798	Carnival	Salimbeni

To these visiting companies must be added the activities of an amateur group of Lucchesi, the Accademici Impavidi Risvegliati, who each year (except for 1789, 1797 and 1798) presented tragedies, comedies and farces during Carnival.

came to be looked upon as indicating consent or dissent *vis-à-vis* the new course that politics were taking. Chelini in particular was scandalized to learn that Benedetta Mallegni Pozzi, a notorious Jacobin (or 'patriot') put on trial in 1798 and sent to the city lunatic asylum in Lucca, was released by the French on 6 January and dared to show her presence in the theatre on the very same evening.[18] He mentions also that only a small number of Lucchesi frequented the theatre, and that all were people of the lower classes who paraded their Revolutionary views.[19] It was in the theatre that the first official acclamation of the French Republic took place – on that same 6 January, in fact – and this was followed the next day by the singing of *Ça ira*.[20] With a little more time at their disposal, the company of Giovanni Battista Mancini[21] of Florence put on at the Teatro Pubblico a series of prose dramas (in Italian) on decidedly propagandist subjects: *Fénelon* by Marie-Joseph Chénier, *Robert, chef de brigands* by La Martelière, *L'oligarchia di-strutta* and *La presa di Faenza*. Included in the cast was a 'strepitosa', Elisabetta Marchionni, who, according to the critic of *La staffetta del Serchio*, a Jacobin journal managed by the *abbé* Severino Ferloni, 'in *La presa di Faenza* ... instilled strong patriotic feelings for the National

18 The widow Mallegni, *née* Benedetta Toti (sister of Paolo, another Jacobin), had been married a second time to Luigi Pozzi, who shared her revolutionary views. In July 1797 she was arrested, tried and imprisoned together with her husband and a doctor, Domenico Moscheni. Set free at the end of the year, she was arrested, put on trial again and imprisoned, this time with her husband, her brother, Antonio Biondi, Giuseppe Beccari and others. See Orzali, *I processi*, pp. 12–24.

19 'La Mallegni Pozzi, che meritatamente era stata messa fra i pazzi di Fregionaja, è stata liberata questa mattina de' 6 d[ett]o e condotta in Lucca in trionfo ... L'impudenza della Pozzi arrivò tant'oltre, che la stessa prima sera de' 6 si fece vedere al Teatro corteggiata da varj Francesi. Il Teatro oltre i Francesi non vi andavano che de' nostri più sfaccendati Giovinastri. Solo vi andava qualche Dama p[er] la necessità in cui ritrovavasi di compiacere a quegli Offiziali di stato maggiore che alloggiava nella propria casa. Troppo era l'afflizione universale per aver voglia d'andare al Teatro.' (Chelini, *Zibaldone lucchese*, iii, pp. 125–6).

20 See Chelini, *Zibaldone lucchese*, iii, pp. 131 and 133, and Mansi, *Memoires ou notices*, ii, p. 18.

21 'Nota della Compagnia Comica / Elisabetta Marchionni / Teresa Valentini / Pierina Fava / Oliva Bianchi / Giuditta Crespi / Gio. Batt[ist]a Mancini / Fran[ces]co Rinaldi / Agostino Minelli / Vincenzo Broccoletto e Fratello / Vincenzo Valentini / Benedetto Mazzeranghi / Antonio Benichi / Filippo Fava / Angelo Marchionni / Gaetano Brazzini / Luigi Salomoni / Paolo Spada / Gio. Palavicini / Gio. Melani / Teresa Giorgi Agnesa Giorgi cantanti / Io Gio Batt[ist]a Mancini attesto essere le sud[dett]e persone addette alla mia compagnia' (*I-La, Reggenza provvisoria (prima)* 11. *Commissariato di Poliza: lettere e carte diverse*). For earlier appearances of Mancini's company, see note 17, above. It is interesting that this list of the company's members closes with the names of two singers, who were employed to sing the 'patriotic songs' during the intervals. It should not be forgotten also that these years saw the dissemination of the *farsa*, which mixed music and speech. The companies of Luigi Mazzotti (spring 1789), Rosa Medembach (spring 1790) and Giuseppe and Anna Ferri (autumn 1793) also featured performances of music. On this still little-known phenomenon, see *I vicini di Mozart*: i, *Il teatro musicale tra sette e ottocento*, ed. M. T. Muraro, and ii, *La farsa musicale veneziana (1750–1810)*, ed. D. Bryant (Florence, 1989).

Guard'.[22] Chelini's opinion was quite different:

Adesso sì che bisogna confessare essere il Teatro una cosa peccaminosa. ... oggi veramente [scuola] della scostumatezza, della irreligione, e dello scandalo e viemaggiormente adunque risvegliare l'entusiasmo de' Patriotti, da una compagnia di Strioni sono state recitate varie Commedie analoghe alle rivoluzionarie nostre circostanze. ... Una fra queste aveva per titolo *Il Fenellon*. Fra i vari personaggi della medesima vi facevano la prima figura una Monaca incinta, un Vescovo, ed un semplice sacerdote che faceva da Confessore. Un altra per titolo *L'Oligarchia distrutta*: vi erano in questa dentro vari de' nostri ex Senatori, ed una delle nostre ex Dame primarie chiamati col vero nome loro, rivestiti tutti d'un carattere iniquio, ed insultante al maggior segno e renduti oggetto di derisione e d'avvilimento all'esultante uditorio. Con tutte queste, ed altre simili rappresentanze uscite da una penna infernale che si permettono, si ha poi il coraggio di dire, che la Nobiltà, che i Preti, i Frati, e le persone oneste, non vogliono fraternizzare co' Patriotti non lasciandosi più vedere ai Teatri, ai passeggi, luoghi pubblici etc. Ma santo Dio assisteteci![23]

It must be confessed that the theatre is now a sinful place. ... It is today truly [a school] for licentiousness, irreligion and scandal, and a vehicle for arousing enthusiasm in the patriots. A company of actors has put on various plays reflecting our revolutionary times. ... One of these was entitled *Il Fenellon*. Prominent among the cast were a pregnant nun, a bishop and a simple priest who acted as confessor. In another play, *L'oligarchia distrutta*, various former senators and one of our most revered ladies were impersonated. Under their real names they were made objects of derision and scorn for the jeering audience. With all these and other similar spectacles issuing from a cursed pen which is allowed produce them, they then have the face to complain that the nobility, the clerics, the monks and all honest people no longer wish to be friendly with the patriots or to frequent the theatres, the promenades, public places etc. But God help us!

It became the practice to perform 'patriotic' songs during the intervals in place of the usual sinfonias, although this presented some problems for the instrumentalists, who were for the most part members of the old Cappella Palatina, and therefore employees of the oligarchic government. A certain violinist by the name of Giovanni Ubaldo Macarini ended up in jail for having too clearly expressed his displeasure at the imposition of this new repertory.[24] Evidently one's presence in the

22 *La staffetta del Serchio*, no. 9 (1 May 1799). This newspaper, the first to be printed in Lucca, reflected essentially the views of the Jacobin *abbé* Severino Ferloni; it was issued from 6 March to 3 July 1799.
23 Chelini, *Zibaldone lucchese*, iii, pp. 401–2.
24 There are two different reports of the event:

> Se fra i Professori di Musica vi sono delle persone oneste, uno certamente era Gio. Ubaldo Macarini. Le arie Patriottiche adesso sono quelle che si vogliono sentire suonare al Teatro in vece di Sinfonie fra l'uno e l'altro atto della Commedia secondo il gusto e lo stile rivoluzionario. Una sera adunque invece delle arie sud[dett]e ne furono altre sostituite ... le quali però non piacendo all'udienza ed incominciò a gridare il *Sairà*, il *Sairà* ... Il Macarini che di mal'animo erasi indotto a suonare quelle arie nuove, perché supponeva che l'udienza non volesse ascoltarle con qualche atto impaziente si levò davanti quella parte ... chiedendo l'altra del celebre *Sairà*. Osservato da un Patriotta questo atto di disprezzo, e credendo che lo avesse fatto al *Sairà*, diè parte di tale enorme

theatre at performances of this kind could also be understood as showing consent, or at least acceptance, but Chelini must have been right when he reported that few Lucchesi went to the theatre, since the government, responding to pressing requests from the impresario, was forced to issue a proclamation 'inviting' the Lucchesi to frequent the theatre *en masse*.[25]

The theatre was seen, then, as a meeting place and as a testing-ground for the consent obtained by the ruling administration. During the planning stage for the emblematic season of 1799 the new government had decreed that work should be done to adapt the Teatro Pubblico to the new situation (by introducing pictures and by decorating the central box with tricolour cloth) and also to implement new ideas regarding its function, 'to make it more comfortable for the spectators, and adapted to the present system of government, by bringing down the level of the so-called amphitheatre to that of the pit, thus lowering the level of the seating to a proper height' ('per renderlo più commodo per li Spettatori, e adatto all'attual sistema di Governo, consistenti in portare in coerenza dell'Orchestra il così detto Anfiteatro, e indi ridurre le Banche per sedervi ad una proporzionata altezza').[26] A final comment on the significant role the theatre played in the lives of certain Jacobins at Lucca (as it did also in the lives of so many other people in the eighteenth century) is provided by the records of the trial of Benedetta Pozzi in 1797, and in particular by the testimony of Guido Forti. We learn that in the planned uprising against the old aristocratic state it was arranged that the signal for the revolt would be given by her at the theatre. Again, the final meeting to put into effect another conspiracy, that of Biondi in

> delitto al Comandante della piazza Henin, il quale lo condannò a tre giorni di carcere. È da notarsi essere quest'uomo onesto, poco ben veduto dai Patriotti p[er]ché trattava sempre colla ex nobiltà, ed in special modo in casa Ottolini.
>
> (Chelini, *Zibaldone lucchese*, iii, p. 403)

> Il suonatore di violino Macarini ha insultato in Teatro con indecenti parole il Sairà tanto caro ai Patrioti. Il Popolo se n'è sdegnato. Ora da due giorni emenda in carcere il suo Fallo. Si è veduto negli ex-nobili suoi fautori un moto da essi non mai sentito nelle lunghe, e crudeli carcerazioni dei Patriotti. (*La staffetta del Serchio*, no. 6, 10 April 1799)

25 The proclamation by the Ministry of Justice and Police is prefaced by a letter from the commandant of the Piazza di Lucca which refers to the 'complaint' by the theatre director about the poor attendance and recognizes in it the essential features of a genuine crime on the part of the former nobles, that of refusing to fraternize with 'patriots'. The minister expresses astonishment that 'una Classe quasi intera di Cittadini facoltosi, che nei tempi della fastosa Aristocrazia amava più degli altri il Teatro, e che sempre lottava per occupare i primi Palchi, siasene tutt'ad un tratto allontanata per mezzo di una Segreta Coalizione. Si accresce poi lo stupore dal vedere, che ... rifuggono tutti gli spettacoli, e segnatamente i Patriottici.' He exhorts everyone 'a rompere, e dissipare tutte quelle Barriere, che tenevano divisi gli Uomini', and, sure of a prompt and positive response, affirms that 'il numeroso Concorso, e la riunione indistinta di tutti ai pubblici spettacoli, e particolarmente al Teatro, daranno la più luminosa riprova ... di essere eglino in cuore animati da non ostentati, ma da veri e leali principj di sincera Fraternità, e perfetta eguaglianza' (*I-La*, Proclami, i, no. 95).

26 *I-La*, Cura sopra il teatro 1 (1754–1799): deliberazioni, 7 March 1799.

1798, was arranged for the evening of 18 August, the opening night of the autumn season at the Teatro Pubblico, when Isouard's *L'avviso ai maritati* was played.[27]

During the whole of the period preceding the reign of Elisa Bonaparte Baciocchi the theatres continued to animate the life of the city, presenting spoken comedies and plays more than operas, probably because the ample repertory of the drama companies was more easily and quickly adaptable to the changing political situation and to didactic and propagandist requirements.[28] It is no mere chance that on 10 and 11 October 1801 Negrini's company put on *La gran battaglia di Marengo*; the Napoleonic fate of the city seems to have been predictable from the date of that theatrical performance.[29]

From documents and accounts it is clear, in addition, that the seasons of *opera buffa* in autumn 1799, autumn 1800 and Carnival 1801 resulted in serious deficits, and this also could account for the preference for spoken drama.[30] In October 1802 some former members of the ruling class, who in the past had often underwritten opera seasons, and who had frequented not only the theatres in Lucca but also those in

27 See Orzali, *I processi*, p. 13, and Bernardini, *L'ultimo anno della repubblica aristocratica*, p. 38. The exact wording of the testimony given by Guido Forti on 28 August 1797 is as follows:

mi era stato detto dalla S[ignor]a Pozzi, cioè che essendo in Lucca c[om]e essa assicurava, molti li malcontenti del Gov[ern]o e che il partito di q[ue]sti era esteso, e che stavano secreti e molto riguardati, questi alla venuta di d[ett]o G[enera]le [Chabot] al Teatro avrebbero picchiate le mani in segno di acclamaz[ion]e onde con q[ues]to segno si dasse c[om]e essa diceva un principio alla rivoluz[ion]e che si teneva p[er] sicura.

(*I-La, Cause delegate*, 101, no. 92)

For the other episode, see note 15, above.

28 For a provisional chronology of theatrical performances during 1799–1805, see Appendix.

29 The relevant playbill (*I-La, Proclami*, iii, no. 208) places the accent on 'episodi, che si accostino al vero simile. Per renderla poi adorna, e decorata, vi sarà la Banda Militare, Evoluzioni, Combattimenti a fuoco vivo.' It ends with a pressing invitation: 'In questa Sera Tutti devono concorrere al Teatro.'

30 The impresarios who signed a private contract for the season of *opere buffe* with dancing in autumn 1799 were in prison for bankruptcy by the second half of October. Two further administrations had to take over, and it was only through the generosity of the creditors, who forewent part of what was owing to them, that it was possible to complete the season, which lasted from 15 August to 6 November with 44 performances (see the documentation in *I-La, Reggenza provvisoria*, 11).

In autumn 1800 Giacomo Pedrinelli, an impresario engaged in *opera buffa*, having made extensive losses, requested and obtained authorization to introduce the game of tombola in an attempt to recoup them (see Chelini, *Zibaldone lucchese*, v, pp. 119–20, and *I-La, Proclami*, iii, no. 33). But the attempt evidently failed, since on 4 December two singers had recourse to the Deputation of Police to reclaim what was owing to them (*I-La, Reggenza provvisoria (prima)* 10: *atti diversi di polizia*, 179).

Finally, during Carnival 1801 (starting in fact on 30 December 1800) an *opera buffa*, *Le trame deluse*, with comic intermezzi was mounted at the Teatro Castiglioncelli. After only five performances two impresarios fled, leaving the artists themselves to take charge of the management on 10 January for the remaining twenty-five performances. (See Chelini, *Zibaldone lucchese*, v, pp. 414–15, and *I-La, Dono Pellegrini*, 14, *Appunti di spettacoli Lucchesi del sec. XVIII 1751–1804*.)

neighbouring towns when there was an important performance, began to look for a way of remedying the lack of opera, which had not been put on since Carnival 1801. They decided to finance the production of an *opera buffa* in a small theatre erected for the purpose in the Palazzo Cenami, and entrusted the performance to amateur musicians among the erstwhile nobility.[31] The opera met with great success, of course, among the social class that had promoted it, but it provoked not a little displeasure among certain members of the government, who saw in this initiative a strong show of nostalgia for the aristocratic regime. Their displeasure would definitely have led to a ban on the production if it had not been for the ex-nobleman Cosimo Bernardini, who at that moment regained his position as president of the Department of Police, and was one of those aristocrats who had always shown a particular interest in opera. Entry to the small theatre was by invitation only, extended to not more than thirty ladies, either ex-noblewomen or others sympathetic to the nobility, each of whom could be accompanied by two gentlemen. There were thus at the most ninety people in the audience at each of the twelve performances that were given, and the fact that the ladies were all invited more than once suggests that the attendance was even smaller than this. The title of this 'rappresentanza teatrale in musica' was *Il cambio dei due ritratti*.[32]

The enterprise of putting on private operas was repeated in succeeding years, but it must be emphasized that opera seasons of such excellence as that of 1784 were a thing of the past. In that year Cimarosa's *Olimpiade* had been given immediately after its première in Vicenza, with the same star-studded cast.[33]

The city's theatres were used also for the kind of entertainment that was most popular among the Lucchesi, the French, the Austrians and the Poles: the *festa* (or *veglia*) *di ballo*.[34] During the period of the oligarchy such diversions took place only during Carnival, when they constituted

31 The performers were Teresa Bottini, Maria Guinigi, Olimpia Cenami Fatinelli, Giovanni Battista Fatinelli, Bartolomeo Cenami, Costantino Nobili, and a certain Giambastiani (the only commoner); the undertaking was financed by the two Massoni brothers, a certain Caselli and others not named, as well as by members of the cast. (See Chelini, *Zibaldone lucchese*, vi, pp. 341–6; Mansi, *Memoires ou notices*, iii, pp. 83–4; and Merli, *Diario delle cose riguardanti Lucca*, iii, p. 131).
32 See the permission for the production registered in *I-La, Repubblica Lucchese (Quarto Governo Democratico) 68. 1802 Magistrato di Polizia e Forza Armata: deliberazioni*, no. 280 (17 October 1802).
33 The production of *L'Olimpiade* was a notable undertaking and was an outstanding success with the public, as all accounts testify. More than 2200 tickets were sold to visitors for the thirty-nine performances that took place between 21 August and 19 October (the opera had closed in Vicenza on 10 August). The cast included Giuseppe Simoni, Francesca Danzi, Vincenzo Ponticelli, Antonio Balelli and Luigi Marchesi, whose fee was, it seems, the highest ever paid at Lucca to a castrato – 401 *zecchini*, equivalent to about 5875 *lire* in Lucca's currency (see Chelini, *Zibaldone lucchese*, i, pp. 66–7). The libretto is in *I-Lg*, Busta 189.12.
34 See especially Chelini, Mansi and Merli, cited above.

one of the principal attractions. However, after 1799 there were an incredible number of them, in honour of French, Polish or Austrian officialdom, to mark the arrival or departure of a general or to crown some feast day. Various sources transmit amusing comments on the kind of people who went to them, on the quality of the refreshments that were offered and on the appropriateness of the decorations. These lead us to believe that after the breath of democracy that came with the First Republic, during which such occasions served to bring together the different classes of society, there was soon a return to class distinction, with the nobility, or ex-nobility, dancing on the stage and the citizens, or patriots, in the pit, and later with the French teaching the quadrille (not surprisingly the dance most in vogue during the Napoleonic era) to the nobility, or ex-nobility, of Lucca. Social mixing was not favoured by the French generals, who organized exclusive *veglie* in the palaces. It should be noted that *veglie di ballo* were often given free in the theatres, as happened when they were opened for some particular occasion such as the visit to Lucca of Joachim Murat in August 1803.[35] The readiness to extend entry to a new class of people in this way, or rather the wish to gain their support for the regime, is only too clear.

One facet of musical life that underwent an extraordinary increase after the arrival of the French was the ecclesiastical celebration of political events which the authorities deemed worthy of official recognition. Such manifestations of accord between church and state were not wholly new in Lucca, but in the second half of the eighteenth century there were fewer than a dozen celebrations of this kind, almost all of them connected with the death or election of an emperor. In the case of a death, it was a requiem mass that was sung, in the case of an election a high mass, followed by a *Te Deum*.[36] After 2 January 1799 such occasions multiplied. During the First Republic there were six, during the First Regency ten, during the Second Republic one, during the Second Regency two, and during the Third and Fourth Republics fourteen; the practice was continued by the Baciocchi. In all, thirty-three political events were celebrated with special functions in the space of six and a half years. Settings of the *Te Deum* were, of course, sung in profusion all over Italy, but they seem to have been particularly numerous in Lucca, and the reason may be found in the important role

---

35 The government of the Fourth Democratic Republic organized various entertainments for Murat, among them a banquet and a *festa di ballo*, while free entry was allowed to the theatre (*I-La, Offizi sui ricevimenti di principi 6: trattamenti di principi, 1775–1803*, ff. 142v–192).

36 The events celebrated were: the election of Joseph II as King of the Romans (1764); the death of Emperor Francis I (1765); the election of Pope Pius VI (1775); the death of Joseph II (1790); the election of Emperor Leopold II (1790); the death of Leopold II (1792); and the coronation of Francis II (1792). For the death of Leopold II a requiem mass by Antonio Puccini was performed 'd'un gusto patetico e capriccioso', which made 'un ottimo effetto' (Chelini, *Zibaldone lucchese*, i, p. 99).

that religion had always played in the lives of the Lucchesi. Two points will suffice to illustrate this: the motto adopted by the Second and subsequent Republics at Lucca was 'Libertà–Religione–Eguaglianza'; secondly, when Giuseppe Beccari was planning in 1796 to conspire against the aristocratic republic he intended that a *Te Deum* should be sung in the cathedral in gratitude for the liberty obtained.[37] The authorities of the old oligarchy had used religion as a formidable means of control: by respecting the principles and forms of the Catholic faith they could, in exchange, count on the support of the clergy in maintaining their power, and also in avoiding dangerous interference from outside (from the papacy and the Jesuits, for example). This collaboration was most clearly manifested in the feast of S Croce, already mentioned. The new authorities – for the most part new Lucchesi assisted by, or working alongside, the old Lucchesi – sought to continue this 'use' of religion.

The first 'revolutionary' *Te Deum* was sung on 5 February 1799, the day after the installation of a provisional government by the French. It was also the first great festival 'à la française'. A Tree of Liberty was planted in the Piazza S Michele to the accompaniment of a military band; then, after a rousing speech by the *abbé* Ferloni, editor of the Jacobin paper *La staffetta del Serchio*, the *Te Deum* was performed in the cathedral; finally, in the brightly-lit city streets, patriotic songs such as *La Carmagnole* were sung. The text of *La Carmagnole* was adapted to the situation at Lucca by Francesco Bartolucci from Livorno, and consisted in all of twelve four-line strophes in Italian, alternating with a refrain in French. It begins:

Questi Nobili arroganti	Dansons la Carmagnole,
ci vorriano dominar,	vive le son, vive le son,
ma noi altri siamo tanti	dansons la Carmagnole
li possiamo far sospirar.	vive le son du Cannon.

These arrogant noblemen would like to rule us; but we others are many, and we can make them regret it. Let's dance the Carmagnole; long live the sound of the cannon.[38]

One wonders if the Lucchesi were aware that in Paris the singing of *La Carmagnole* had accompanied numerous beheadings during the Terror.

Ten days later, on 15 February, another festival was authorized to give

37 This information derives from the testimony of Benedetto La Borde, an accomplice of Beccari's; see Arrighi, 'Una "trama" contro la repubblica', pp. 15–16. From what he had to say it is clear that for the success of the plot they had to play on the respect that was due to the clergy, as well as on the benefits that could be offered to the common people (see also Camaiani, *Un patriziato*, pp. 11–12): 'Le Mont de Pieté sera ouvert, et les effects engagés rendue gratis aux gens du peuple ... Et les nouvelles Authorités, prècedées du clergé, iront avec pompe à la cathedrale, où l'on chantera le Te Deum en action de grace.'

38 The text of the *Carmagnola lucchese* is given complete in Chelini, *Zibaldone lucchese*, iii, pp. 223–40.

thanks to God for the 'liberation' of Lucca: after the exposition of the Holy Sacrament, the *Te Deum* was again sung in the cathedral by the *cappella* of the former regime.[39] Finally, in June the colours of the newly instituted Civic Guard were blessed (they were of tricolour silk, with the legend, in gold, 'Repubblica Lucchese/Libertà Eguaglianza/Odio all'oligarchia'); on this occasion a solemn mass was sung, followed by the *Te Deum*.[40]

The Austrians, who seized possession of the city on 18 July 1799, were still keener to show their devotion to religion, and politico-liturgical events became even more frequent. On 1 August a solemn *Te Deum* was sung for the taking of Mantua. On 4 August, to give thanks to S Paulinus for liberating Lucca from the French, a 'scelta e copiosa musica a più orchestre' was performed, consisting of music for First and Second Vespers, a mass and a *Te Deum*. On 1 September, as an act of thanksgiving, there took place a procession of the sacred relics of the Precious Blood from the monastery of the Olivetani di S Ponziano to the cathedral and back to the monastery; mass was celebrated 'con scelta e numerosa musica cantata solenne' in S Ponziano; a 'strepitosa' sinfonia was played as the procession entered the cathedral, where a double-chorus setting of the *Vexilla regis* was sung, and there was another 'lunga e strepitosa' sinfonia at S Ponziano, where the *Te Deum* and the *Vexilla regis* were sung by the choir and congregation. Finally, on 12 December a mass and *Te Deum* celebrated the taking of Cuneo.[41]

The taking of Genoa, the last stronghold of the French, at the beginning of June 1800 was celebrated by the Austrians in a way which recalls the practices of the French at their patriotic festivals; a band played 'strepitose sinfonie' in the city streets to announce the important event; a triumphal carriage, or float, moved through the city carrying a military band and singers who performed a 'hymn appropriate to the happy occasion'; in the cathedral a solemn mass 'with copious and choice music for double orchestra' was heard and, after the exposition of the Holy Sacrament, a 'most solemn *Te Deum* with military band composed by Domenico Puccini especially for this long-awaited event, which won universal applause for the mastery with which the military instruments were introduced and for the novel way in which they had been united with the serious and grave expression suited to the church' ('il serio ed il grave adattato alla Chiesa'); there was a *festa di ballo* at the Teatro Pubblico, 'beautifully lit and decorated'; and finally a cantata, *Bella madre degl'inni guerrieri*, with words by Francesco Franceschi and music again by Domenico Puccini, was sung in the open-air.[42]

---

39 Ibid., iii, p. 257.   40 Ibid., iii, pp. 645–6.

41 Ibid., iv, pp. 34, 38, 78–85 and 161–2.

42 Ibid., iv, pp. 403–8. On French patriotic festivals, see B. Brévan, *Les changements de la vie musicale parisienne de 1774 à 1799* (Paris, 1980).

Ex. 1

Ex. 2

Domenico Puccini's *Te Deum* calls for an orchestra (first and second violins, violas, oboes, horns, trumpets, bassoons and bass), a wind band (oboes, clarinets, horns and bass) and two four-part choirs (SATB).[43] The grand solemnity to which Chelini bore witness is confirmed by this unusual and imposing scoring, and by the work's length (a note on the autograph score reads 'dura 43 minuti'), while the novelty mentioned by him is to be found above all in the use of the military band, and consequently in the use also of what might be called 'march and fanfare' rhythms. This is to be observed in the opening Allegro's motif (Ex. 1). The importance of this theme is confirmed by its frequent reappearance in a kind of rondo structure. In the choral sections the text is divided between the two choirs, which contrast or combine with each other in the way one would expect in such a work. The choral texture is predominantly homorhythmic, with the text clearly articulated; in some passages the choir almost recites the words. Regular stresses assist the homorhythm and the correct accentuation of the words. Some passages begin contrapuntally, in fact like double fugues with two themes presented simultaneously, but these are no more than gestures, necessary perhaps to reinforce the element that Chelini described as 'serio e grave adattato alla chiesa'. There are also some solo passages, among them a quite long and highly virtuoso 'Pleni sunt coeli' for tenor, probably sung by Tommaso Santini, a member of the Cappella Palatina. The scoring is nicely calculated, with the kind of variety one would expect in a sectional structure and, in the choral portions, with effective contrasts between voices and instruments and a telling use of rests to lighten the choral textures. The *Te Deum* is, then, an *ad hoc* work, but also one which was carefully composed, given that the occasion for which it was written had been 'long awaited'. This is confirmed by the autograph score, with its frequent and radical corrections; Puccini has often not only cancelled passages but also pasted new paper over them.

43 *Ad M. D. G. / Hymnus / Te Deum / Octo concinnendus vocibus, / ab orchestre Symphonia, / atque Musica Militari / sequtus / cum concertis. / Auctore / Dom[en]ico Puccinio Luc[en]se /*

The hymn *Bella madre degl'inni guerrieri*[44] calls for a wind band (clarinets, oboes, horns and bassoons) suitable for an open-air performance, two soprano soloists and chorus. The fact that it was performed 'in various places in the streets, like a notturno or serenata' is reflected in the music by its march rhythms, its simple, homorhythmic textures, the orchestra's anticipation of the sung melody, a structure which involves exact repetition for every four strophes of the text and the fanfare-like character of the opening motif (Ex. 2).

The idea of the open-air festival, however, was really French, and during the First Republic the Lucchesi had become accustomed to patriotic festivals designed for celebration entirely out of doors. Chelini described how, on the second Sunday in Lent (17 February) 1799, the Festival of the Regeneration was celebrated.[45] It began with a procession through the city streets of two floats symbolizing crafts, arts, sciences and the Graces, with plaster busts of Voltaire and Rousseau and with the accompaniment of a military band. A large construction ('apparato') was erected in the Piazza S Michele by the stage designer Giovanni Antonio de Santi, from Lucca, who, having obtained the government's patent for patriotic spectacles and festivals,[46] recycled parts of 'apparati' designed for earlier special occasions, such as the visit in 1785 of the King and Queen of Naples, the Grand Duke and Grand Duchess of Tuscany and the Archduke of Milan: 'in a large, square enclosure, dressed with laurel and having at each corner an Etruscan vase from which issued the smoke of incense, stood the Tree of Liberty. ... Above was the democratic emblem, a red beret, and lower down the tricolour flags, to the poles of which were attached the Roman consular emblems of fasces and axes. In one corner of the enclosure there was a chair ... Two low columns ... to the right and left of the tree, and at one side of the enclosure a large space which could serve for a big orchestra of musicians'. The busts of Voltaire and Rousseau were placed on these columns, after which a patriotic hymn, *Mentre in riva del Serchio*, composed for the occasion, was performed 'by a large orchestra of

Anno Domini / CI CICC XCIX / immo CI DCCC (Torre del Lago, Museo Puccini, MS 45). The date on the title-page, '1799, or rather 1800', puts back the work's gestation by some months; possibly it was even begun for another occasion. A manuscript score for the second chorus bears the date 7 May 1800: *Te Deum laudamus / Con strumenti obbligati, e Banda militare / Del / Sig[nor]e Domenico Puccini / 1800 / Coro Secondo / 7 Maggio scrip[si]* (I-Li, Fondo Puccini, D. 14).

44 *Inno / Per la resa di Genova / Poesia del Dott[or]e Fran[ces]co Franceschi / musica del Sig[nor]e Dom[eni]co Puccini*, MS score in I-Li, Fondo Puccini, D. 15d. For the text, see I-La, *Proclami*, ii, no. 75.

45 Chelini, *Zibaldone lucchese*, iii, pp. 262–72.

46 I-La, *Cura sopra il teatro*, 1, 4 February 1799: 'avendo il Cittadino Gio. Antonio de Santi fatto istanza al Direttorio per essere incaricato della direzione, e sopraintendenza per tutti quei pubblici Spettacoli Patriottici, e Feste che si dovessero fare in avvenire, e ciò privativam[ent]e ad ogn'altra persona, ha il Direttorio provvisoriam[ent]e eletto e deput[at]o il sudd[etto] Cittadino alla direzione e sopraintendenza come sopra'. Even before 1799 De Santi enjoyed a near-monopoly as theatre designer in Lucca and as a designer of 'apparati' for open-air celebrations.

instruments and voices' both before and after speeches by the *abbé* Ferloni and various representatives of the French and Lucchesi authorities.[47] A meal in the Buonvisi residence, at which the various social classes of the Lucchesi could join together in a new spirit of comradeship, was followed by an *accademia musicale*, rendered patriotic by the singing of the hymn already heard in the Piazza S Michele. Finally, a *festa di ballo* took place at the Teatro Pantera.

Chelini described another celebration, this time a funereal one, on 10 June for the French plenipotentiaries Bonnier and Roberiot, killed (according to the French) by imperial assassins at Ramstadt.[48] In this case the music held a central place in the ceremony. 'In a lovely parterre adorned with cypresses, from which a majestic staircase rose to the tomb of the two ministers placed beside the Tree, with the statue of Liberty above' (another of De Santi's creations), sinfonias and *La Marseillaise* were preceded and followed by a number of speeches condemning imperial violence. Although the occasion was not really a festive one, it did not lack a 'patriotic' meal. The total cost of the ceremony was at least 700 *scudi*, which Chelini considered an enormity, since 'in the three special days which the former government set aside for the *Tasche* only the sum of 100 [later 120] *scudi* per day was spent, and on those occasions, as well as solemn music, there were served in the evening delicious refreshments, and in addition a magnificent dinner was provided for more than 150 people each evening'.

The year 1799, crowded as it was with military and political events, emerges from this picture as a particularly rich and varied one as far as musical occasions are concerned. The new compositions were those that resulted from the increase in number and size of the politico-religious celebrations, with their numerous *Te Deum* settings, and from patriotic festivals; the latter were inevitably occasional pieces. Both sacred and secular compositions used mainly pre-existing music adapted to the occasion (as witness the *Te Deum* with military band, or *La Carmagnole* with a text about Lucca); or, if they were completely new, they were cast in simple strophic forms with a good deal of repetition (for example, the songs with refrain). In either case the attention of the composer, or rather the compiler, is directed primarily towards the text, the bearer of the ideological message and the didactic medium *par excellence*. The proliferation of the occasions for music was thus matched by an increase

47 The text of the hymn, in *I-La, Proclami*, i, no. 48a, consists of four pairs of four-line and eight-line strophes for the chorus, together with a refrain intended for everyone to sing (although Chelini's account does not mention that the public joined in). The words call on the Lucchesi to love their country, now set free, and to inspire themselves with the 'costume severo' of the ancient republics of Rome and Greece. The strophe intended for the 'coro di popolo' is a more energetic and explicit incitement: 'Patriotti s'impugni la spada, / E tremendi si corra, si vada / A discior le catene alle genti / Quai torrenti che il vento gonfiò.' The Serchio is the river that flows past the outskirts of Lucca.
48 Chelini, *Zibaldone lucchese*, iii, pp. 636–40.

in the number, but a decline in the quality, of the musical genres. Patriotic songs, celebratory cantatas and *Te Deum* settings with military band could not, because of their ephemeral nature, deal in profundity, while the speed with which the composition had to be completed encouraged the use of already existing music. In the years leading up to the arrival of the Baciocchi such occasions became less numerous, but the fragmentation seemed somehow to persist, with fewer opera seasons, more performances of spoken drama, public religious functions, musical 'academies' and *veglie di ballo* in the theatres and palaces, celebratory cantatas etc.

After 1799 relations between the musicians and the institutions at Lucca also changed radically. The state was at first the most important patron of musicians, and it was on music as a public function that the number and kind of occasions that called for music depended. Now it was necessary to adapt to ever-changing conditions, to the tastes of the new rulers who came and went, to the ideas of some 'foreign' impresario. Domenico Puccini's career is entirely typical. In 1799 he was at Naples, studying with Paisiello; taken by surprise when the French arrived,[49] he returned to his native city to find the situation there quite different from the one he had left. In 1800 he took on the composition of the *Te Deum* with military band and the cantata on the text by the priest Franceschi, who was later imprisoned by the French for having written it (further proof that it was the words that were considered to be important).[50] By the end of summer 1800 Puccini had prepared another cantata commissioned by the French (it was never performed because of pressing events and the return of the Austrians),[51] so it is not surprising to find that he tried hard to obtain a position under successive Democratic Republics.

To sum up, a firmly established routine which provided incentives to composers and musicians had been swept away by political events and by a proliferation of ephemeral festivals, while on the other hand a succession of Democratic Republics under the French, by reason of their instability and interruptions from Austrian regimes, were unable to establish new customs and to create new relations with musicians. If, as seems to be the case, the year 1799 signals the beginning of a slow but inexorable decline in the quality of musical life in Lucca, this is the result essentially of the difficulty of replacing the old with the new – a situation

---

49 Of particular interest is the letter of 29 January 1799 written by Domenico Puccini from Naples to his father Antonio (*I-La*, Legato Cerù, 94), published in Luigi Volpicella, 'L'anarchia popolare in Napoli nel gennaio 1799 raccontata da Domenico Puccini', *Archivio storico per le province napoletane* (1910), pp. 485–500.

50 See Chelini, *Zibaldone lucchese*, iv, p. 369

51 Ibid., iv, pp. 739–40: '... si pensò a far comporre una Cantata allusiva alla rigenerata Libertà dell'Italia ... Il Sig[nor]e Domenico Puccini ... ne fece la Musica. Fu fatta venire da Firenze una Cantatrice ... e tutto si dispose ... addobbando magnificamente il Pubblico Teatro con Emblemi allusivi ... e se ne incominciarono già a far le prove ...'.

which was to be repeated many times during the half century that
separates these events from the incorporation of the state of Lucca into
the grand-duchy of Tuscany.

Translation by the editor

APPENDIX
Theatrical productions in Lucca, 1799–1805

The following table presents a provisional chronology of theatrical performances in Lucca during the years 1799–1805, that is from the arrival of the French
troops until the reign of the Baciocchi. Titles and names of composers have been
arrived at from a variety of sources. Titles of farces are shown by an asterisk (*),
and where evidence exists for the use of music on the part of companies
producing spoken drama this also is indicated. The chronology is derived
largely from the following sources cited in the notes to the main text: L. Palma
Mansi, ii and iii; D. Merli, iii; M. T. Quilici; *I-La*, Dono Pellegrini, 14 *Appunti
di spettacoli Lucchesi del sec. XVIII 1751–1804*; and from F. Minutoli's MS
diary, *Memorie degli spettacoli teatrali in Lucca*, in *I-La*, Dono Pellegrini, 17.
Titles of farces have been compared with those given in *I vicini di Mozart*, ii (see
note 21) especially pp. 431–55 (D. Bryant), pp. 551–65 (E. Sala) and
pp. 597–624 (R. Verti).

Theatrical performances in Lucca, 1799–1805

Date	Teatro Pubblico	Teatro Castiglioncelli	Teatro Pantera
1799			
Carnival		*I due fratelli Pappamosca* (Guglielmi)	Merli's company
spring	G. B. Mancini's company: *Fenelon*; *Roberto capo dei briganti*; *L'oligarchia di-strutta*; *La presa di Faenza*; patriotic songs during the intervals		
summer	company of low actors		
autumn	*L'astuto in amore* (Paisiello); ballets: *La disfatta di Barbarossa*; *Don Giovanni*		
1800			Teatro Rinaldi
Carnival		*Il matrimonio segreto* (Cimarosa); *La pietra simpatica* (Palma)	Accademici Impavidi Risvegliati: *Verter*; *Diogene*; *Il poeta fanatico*; *La finta ammalata*; *Il calderaio di Vienna*

spring	Pani's company		
autumn	*L'amore platonico (Puccitta); *Le donne cambiate (Portogallo)		

1801

Carnival		Le trame deluse (Cimarosa); comic plays	
spring	Pani's company		
summer	Negrini's company		
autumn	Negrini's company: La battaglia di Marengo		

1802   Palazzo Cenami

_____

Carnival	Negrini's company		
spring	Negrini's company, and/or Luigi del Bono's company		
summer	Morrocchesi's company: 56 tragedies, comedies, farces and ballo buffo		
autumn	Accademici Impavidi Risvegliati		Il cambio dei due ritratti

1803

Carnival		'Comitiva comica Animosi nascenti'	
spring	Luigi del Bono's company: 29 tragedies, comedies and farces; 1 accademia in musica		
summer	Giuseppe Perini's company: 'comiche e musiche rappresentanze', *L'amor soldato, *Lo spazzacamino principe (Portogallo); ballets		
autumn	*La donna di genio volubile (Portogallo); *La donna ve la fa (Gardi); Gli amanti comici; ballets		

1804

Carnival	*La muta, o sia Il medico per forza (Gardi); Il marito geloso (Cimarosa); *Il carretto del venditore di aceto (Mayr); *La donna ve la fa (Gardi); ballets: Cefalo e Procri protetti da Cupido; I pittori olandesi		

spring	Perotti's company	
summer	Gaetano Perotti's company: 45 tragedies, comedies and farces	
autumn	*Ifigenia in Aulide* (G. M. Curcio); ballet: *Fernando e Adelaide*	

1805

Carnival	Accademici Impavidi Risvegliati	**Che originali!* (Mayr)
spring	Francesco Taddei's company: 53 tragedies, comedies and farces; *Cammilla* ('melodramma')	
summer	**La locandiera* (Farinelli); **La Pamela* (Farinelli); ballet: *Amor vince tutto*	

Beethoven and the Revolution: the view of the French musical press

It might seem a commonplace to mention Beethoven and France in the same breath. Indeed, Beethoven has been the subject of musicological research for so long that many scholars have already discussed the question of how far his works were influenced by the period in which he lived – a period which included the dramatic and changing events of the French Revolution and the rise and fall of Napoleon. Two main approaches to this vast subject can be distinguished. Firstly, there exists a wide range of treatises which cover Beethoven's view of the world and his political opinions, and which analyse specific works, such as the opera *Fidelio*, Symphonies nos. 3 and 9 and the 'Battle Symphony' op. 91, that are believed to reflect certain ideas or even actual events. Secondly, there are a few studies, modelled on the approach pioneered by Arnold Schmitz,[1] that concentrate on certain *topoi* (or musical patterns) and themes that are surprisingly analogous to those in other works – on the similarities that exist, for example, between Symphonies nos. 3, 5 and 7 and works in the French repertory by composers such as Gossec, Cherubini, Grétry, Méhul, Le Sueur, Rouget de Lisle and Adrien *l'aîné*.[2] No doubt further research into the influence of French music on Beethoven's own creative work will permit a better understanding of his knowledge of a wide range of music that is little known today.

It is astonishing that the interesting relationship between Beethoven and France used to be regarded by most scholars from only one point of view, that of the influence of French culture and society on Beethoven. For the opposite perspective – the role that Beethoven's music played in France – reference is still made to Leo Schrade's interpretation of the

---

1 A. Schmitz, *Das romantische Beethovenbild: Darstellung und Kritik* (Berlin and Bonn, 1927), pp. 164–73.
2 M. Geck and P. Schleunig, *'Geschrieben auf Bonaparte'. Beethovens 'Eroica': Revolution, Reaktion, Rezeption* (Reinbek, 1989), pp. 138–61; P. Gülke, 'Motive aus französischer Revolutionsmusik in Beethovens fünfter Sinfonie', *Musik und Gesellschaft*, xxi (1971), pp. 636–41, and *Zur Neuausgabe der Sinfonie Nr. 5 von Ludwig van Beethoven: Werk und Edition* (Leipzig, 1978), pp. 49–55; C. V. Palisca, 'French Revolutionary Models in Beethoven's *Eroica* Funeral

reasons underlying the success of Beethoven's symphonies,[3] which is based on his thesis that 'the growth of an idea' was brought to maturity by the French Romanticists, at which point the 'entrance of a genius' became possible.[4] Certainly one should not ignore the importance of François-Antoine Habeneck's performances of Beethoven's works at the Société des Concerts du Conservatoire after 1828 and the importance, too, of the controversies over Victor Hugo's *Hernani* around the same time (1830). Nevertheless, the question remains as to whether Schrade's hypothesis is sufficient to explain why it was especially in France that Beethoven's works dominated the musical scene in such a far-reaching way. In contrast to Schrade's opinion, there are indications that, even before the Romantic period, there existed in France a certain basis of musical composition and appreciation which made French musicians and audiences favourably disposed to accept and integrate Beethoven's music. Carol MacClintock has suggested that for the first Romantics 'the freedom-loving composer and revolutionary musician incarnated their own "liberté, égalité, fraternité" and they heard in the Third and Fifth Symphonies echoes of the idealistic enthusiasm of the great Revolution'.[5] Frédéric Robert recalled that as early as 1809 the funeral march from the Piano Sonata op. 26 was performed in Paris for the first time in an orchestral version, on the occasion of the transferring of Marshal Lannes's ashes to the Panthéon.[6] One might recall, too, the much-quoted anecdote according to which, during a performance of Beethoven's Fifth Symphony, one of Napoleon's veterans jumped to his feet at the beginning of the finale, shouting 'C'est l'empereur! Vive l'empereur!'.[7]

At this point it might be appropriate to examine briefly some articles and comments in the French musical press which show how Beethoven's music was understood by French critics. Sources such as the *Revue musicale*, *Le ménestrel*, the *Revue et gazette musicale de Paris*, *La France musicale* and *Le monde musical* contain an enormous amount of information concerning the reaction to Beethoven's music in France, including some that has never been thoroughly researched. Moreover,

March', in *Music and Context: Essays for John M. Ward*, ed. A. D. Shapiro (Harvard, 1985), pp. 198–209.
3 L. Schrade, *Beethoven and France: the Growth of an Idea* (New Haven, 1942).
4 'The door, then, through which the French admitted the genius of Beethoven into France was opened by the romantics.... Not until romanticism struck the intellectual world like lightning was the way cleared and Beethoven let in. Accompanied by an idea Beethoven enters France, surrounded with ideas he is to remain' (L. Schrade, *Beethoven and France*, p. 36).
5 C. MacClintock, 'Beethoven and France', in *Beethoven Encyclopedia*, ed. P. Nettl (New York, 1956), p. 62.
6 F. Robert, 'Sur l'introduction de Beethoven en France', *Europe*, xlviii (October 1970), p. 119.
7 See K. H. Wörner, *Das Zeitalter der thematischen Prozesse in der Geschichte der Musik* (Regensburg, 1969), pp. 18–19.

these specialized journals are of particular interest, since they were directed at the intended audience of Beethoven's works, and this makes them different from other commentaries, such as those to be found in letters or diaries, or in the daily press.

To illustrate more specifically how Beethoven's music was seen through the eyes of the French musical press, two examples will be taken – those of the Fifth and Seventh Symphonies, since these works seem to have played a particularly important role in French civilization. For example, in 1838 Léon Escudier stated that 'there are two symphonies by Beethoven which already enjoy the accolade of popularity: the Symphony in A [major] and the Symphony in C minor. The *Eroica* Symphony is not yet understood; but it will be.' ('Il est deux symphonies de Beethoven qui jouissent déjà des honneurs de la popularité: la symphonie en la et la symphonie en ut mineur. La symphonie héroïque n'est point encore comprise; mais on y viendra.')[8] In fact, Symphonies nos. 3 and 9, like *Fidelio*, gave rise to involved discussion, whereas the examples chosen here became famous and popular from the time of their first performances in Paris.

The Fifth Symphony can be regarded as the most popular of all Beethoven's works. Constant Pierre showed that it had been performed in April 1808 in Paris during the *Exercices des élèves* at the Conservatoire, even before its first performance in Vienna.[9] During the two decades from the founding of the famous Société des Concerts du Conservatoire to Habeneck's death, this orchestra played the work about forty times, making it the most frequently performed symphony of the time. The earliest commentary on it in the French musical press is by François-Joseph Fétis. Comparing Beethoven to Mozart, Fétis devoted himself exclusively to the last movement and ignored the greater part of the symphony. It seems to have been only this 'march' that aroused his interest:

Mozart n'aurait jamais imaginé cette marche colossale qui ouvre le dernier morceau de la symphonie en ut mineur de Beethoven; et cependant la sublime pensée de cette marche était digne d'un génie si prodigieux. Une semblable création est au-dessus de la musique; ce ne sont plus des flûtes, des cors, des violons et des basses qu'on entend, c'est l'univers qui s'ébranle.[10]

Mozart could never have conceived that colossal march which opens the last movement of Beethoven's Symphony in C minor; and yet the sublime thought behind it was worthy of a genius as prodigious as his. A creation such as this is above music; it is no longer flutes, horns, violins and basses that we hear, but the universe that trembles.

8 *La France musicale*, i/3 (14 January 1838), p. 8.
9 C. Pierre, *Le Conservatoire National de Musique et de Déclamation: documents historiques et administratifs recueillis ou reconstitués* (Paris, 1900), p. 486.
10 *Revue musicale*, iii (February–July 1828), p. 315.

As for the rest of the symphony, we still find the reproach that Beethoven, who made the world tremble with this fanfare at the beginning of the last movement, unfortunately did not have enough taste to make an end at the right moment: 'Malheureusement Beethoven ne sait point finir'.[11] Later, after another performance of the Fifth Symphony, Fétis touched on the other movements as well, but only in a superficial way: 'As for the scherzo, everything about it is perfect, admirable, and the way he ties it to the magnificent march that crowns the work is beyond all praise'. ('Quant au scherzo, tout y est parfait, admirable, et la manière dont il se lie à la marche magnifique qui couronne l'œuvre est au-dessus de tout éloge.')[12] This evaluation can be regarded as the basis for all the critiques of the symphony in the French musical press during the decades that followed: in France it was the beginning of the finale that was considered the essence of the entire work. Among all the reviews and commentaries, those of E. T. A. Hoffmann, published in French in the *Revue musicale*,[13] and the famous detailed analysis of all four movements by Hector Berlioz[14] are notable exceptions. When, in an article entitled 'Correspondance particulière', Henri Panofka recalled an anecdote about Beethoven which he had heard from Schindler, he quoted Beethoven's remark that the four notes at the beginning of the Fifth Symphony are symbolic of Fate knocking at Beethoven's door, but he put it in such a way that it was completely hidden in an eclectic juxtaposition of various facts and anecdotes.[15] Thus in France, at least during the first half of the nineteenth century, Beethoven's Fifth Symphony was not commonly known as the 'Fate' Symphony. Critics described the first, second and third movements in favourable but unenthusiastic terms; often they ventured no opinion of the composition as a whole, but considered only the effect the finale had on the audience. Only occasionally did they admit that the meaning of the work as a whole escaped them. Their positive comments can therefore be interpreted as a means of hiding the fact that they simply did not know what to say about the work. On the other hand, certain skilful critics pretended that everything there was to say about the Fifth Symphony had already been said, and that there was no need to repeat comments already made[16] – an elegant evasion of the critic's proper role.

As it was the finale that made the Fifth Symphony the most popular of Beethoven's works in France, reviews of this piece are representative of

11 Ibid., p. 316.   12 Ibid., p. 343.

13 'Opuscules de E.-T.-A. Hoffmann. Kreisleriana. Sur la musique instrumentale de Beethoven', *Revue musicale*, x (4 December 1830), pp. 97–104.

14 *Revue et gazette musicale de Paris*, v/4 (28 January 1838), pp. 35–7.

15 Ibid., iv/35 (27 August 1837), pp. 390–91.

16 See, for example, *Le ménestrel*, v/32 (8 July 1838), p. [1]; *Revue musicale*, xv/14 (5 April 1835), p. 109; *Revue et gazette musicale de Paris*, x/12 (19 March 1843), p. 102, and xv/15 (9 April 1848), p. 112; *Le monde musical*, iv/11 (15 March 1843), p. 37.

the public's entire evaluation of Beethoven. The last movement, which bears no designation such as 'alla marcia', was christened 'marche gigantesque',[17] 'grande marche',[18] 'marche colossale',[19] 'chant de victoire',[20] 'marche triomphale',[21] or even 'marche militaire'[22] by French critics at the time. Orchestras formed after the foundation of the Société des Concerts du Conservatoire (whose conductor, Habeneck, set an excellent example of how to interpret and perform Beethoven) tried to make their name by performing this famous work. Thus, for example, the Concerts Saint-Honoré, founded by Henri-Justin-Joseph Valentino in 1837, played the Fifth Symphony at one of their first performances. Sometimes only the finale was played,[23] as it was when Berlioz conducted an enormous orchestra during the Grand Festival de l'Industrie in 1844.[24] And when François Stoepel, in 1845, organized a concert to demonstrate his arrangements of symphonic music for pianos, the first piece performed by the twenty pianists on ten pianos was again Beethoven's Fifth Symphony. This curious event, executed by an 'armée de pianistes', was considered by *La France musicale* to be among the most interesting concerts of the season.[25]

Whenever in France a concert was intended to arouse interest in a particular event, or to lend importance to it, the Fifth Symphony was played; it regularly appeared in the programme of the second of the Concerts Spirituels de la Société des Concerts. A review of one of these occasions by Maurice Bourges draws comparisons of a military nature:

On peut vraiment douter que l'armée du grand Frédéric fût plus scrupuleusement disciplinée et manœvrât avec une harmonie aussi complète. Le moyen de résister à celle de M. Habeneck, lorsqu'elle attaque avec une foudroyante énergie le finale de la symphonie en ut mineur? C'est beau comme tout ce qu'il y a de beau dans le monde. C'est étourdissant de pompe et de majesté. Il eût fallu cette musique et cet orchestre pour régler le pas du cortège triomphal d'Alexandre à Babylone.[26]

One must really doubt whether the army of Frederick the Great was more meticulously disciplined, and whether it manœuvred in such complete harmony. How can one resist M. Habeneck's when it attacks with enormous energy the finale of the Symphony in C minor? There is nothing finer in the whole world. It has

---

17 *Revue musicale* v (February–July 1829), p. 348.
18 Ibid., vii (February–May 1830), p. 345.
19 Ibid., xi/5 (5 March 1831), p. 37.
20 *Revue et gazette musicale de Paris*, v/4 (28 January 1838), p. 37.
21 Ibid., v/4 (28 January 1838), p. 37; ibid., xiv/19 (9 May 1847), p. 156; *Le monde musical*, ii/16 (2 April 1841), p. [2]; ibid., iv/11 (15 March 1843), p. 37; *La France musicale*, v/14 (3 April 1842), p. 129.
22 *Revue et gazette musicale de Paris*, v/12 (25 March 1838), p. 131.
23 Ibid., viii/27 (4 April 1841), p. 215.
24 *Le ménestrel*, xi/35 (28 July 1844), p. [1], and xi/36 (4 August 1844), p. [1].
25 See *La France musicale*, viii/9 (2 March 1845), p. 70, and *Le monde musical*, vi/11 (13 March 1845), p. [4].
26 *Revue et gazette musicale de Paris*, x/17 (23 April 1843), p. 143.

astounding pomp and majesty. This music and this orchestra ought to have been there to set the pace for the triumphal cortège of Alexander at Babylon.

Finally, on the subject of Beethoven's most popular work in France, the importance of a 'concert extraordinaire' at the Conservatoire on 5 March 1848, a benefit performance for those wounded during the February Revolution, should not be ignored. The programme opened with the *Marseillaise* in Gossec's arrangement, and this was followed by Beethoven's Fifth Symphony. Its inclusion exemplifies the eminence that Beethoven's music had attained, and a commentary on the performance by Auguste Morel points out precisely the status of the work:

Presque tous les morceaux composant le programme avaient été choisis en vue d'une allusion ou d'un rapport quelconque au but patriotique du concert. La symphonie en ut mineur de Beethoven n'exprime sans doute aucune idée déterminée, mais elle offre un caractère éminemment martial, et il est certain que toutes les fois qu'il s'agira de célébrer un triomphe on saura rien trouver de mieux que son sublime finale.[27]

Nearly all the pieces on the programme had been chosen because they had some connection with the patriotic aim of the concert. Beethoven's Symphony in C minor does not, of course, express any specific idea, but it conveys an eminently martial tone, and when it comes to celebrating a triumph one could not find anything better than its sublime finale.

To turn now to the critical reaction to the Seventh Symphony, we find that it was again only one movement that enjoyed conspicuous success and caused the work to assume a position of particular importance in France; this was the second movement, Allegretto, which can be regarded as the second most famous of Beethoven's works. In contemporary French music criticism it was called the 'Andante' or 'Adagio' (in the same way that the terms 'Scherzo' and 'Menuet' were often used as synonyms), ignoring the composer's indication.

Edouard Fétis was among the first to express the opinion that 'this movement alone is worth a whole symphony' ('ce morceau à lui seul vaut une symphonie').[28] It seems that when the Seventh Symphony was performed, this movement was frequently played as an encore because of the tremendous impression it made on the public compared with the rest of the work, which did not arouse as much interest. It could therefore be used in an attempt to secure a good reception for pieces that an audience might otherwise not have taken to. It did not always succeed in

27 *Le monde musical*, ix/9 (9 March 1848), p. [2]. The other works performed on this occasion were Weber's 'Affranchissons notre patrie' (a chorus from *Euryanthe*) and Handel's 'Chantons victoire' (from *Judas Maccabaeus*). Except for the *Marseillaise*, no French music appeared on the programme.
28 *Revue musicale*, v (February–July 1829), p. 347.

this, however. According to several critical reports, in the 1820s Beethoven's First Symphony was performed in Paris with the famous 'Andante' of the Seventh replacing its own Andante,[29] but even this could not save the First Symphony from neglect; it became one of Beethoven's least played works, and Habeneck gave only five performances of it in approximately twenty years.

It became customary to include the Fifth Symphony in the programme of the Concert Spirituel de Conservatoire on Easter Sunday, and the Seventh was often played on Good Friday. The Allegretto was frequently performed on other occasions, for example as funeral music during the commemoration of Antoine Reicha in 1836:

Musique Religieuse. On sait que les élèves et amis du feu Reicha se sont réunis et contisés pour subvenir au frais d'une messe funèbre en l'honneur de leur savant professeur.... Puis, l'orchestre a exécuté le magnifique andante en la de la symphonie de Beethoven.[30]

Sacred Music. It is well known that the students and friends of the late Reicha joined in contributing to the expenses of a requiem mass in honour of their learned professor.... Then the orchestra performed the magnificent Andante in A [minor] from the symphony by Beethoven.

Again, most critics described the effect on the public of this movement only. Their comments are quite vague, but they are sufficient to give some idea of why the Allegretto became such an important piece of music. As Edouard Fétis put it, 'how could anyone resist the deep hue of sadness that pervades this piece?...The same idea is restated in a thousand different ways; and when it seems to have been lost it returns richer and more shining than ever.' ('Comment résister à la profonde teinte de tristesse répandue sur ce morceau?...La même idée s'y représente sous mille formes différentes; et lorsqu'on croit l'avoir perdue, elle revient plus riche et brillante que jamais'.)[31] Hector Berlioz confirmed this interpretation in a review of 1834: 'the sublime lament rises up with the accents of a vast, limitless suffering, like that of the prophet of the Lamentations' ('la sublime plainte s'élève en accens d'une souffrance immense sans bornes, comme celle du prophète des Lamentations').[32] Indeed, when Berlioz published his detailed analysis of the Seventh Symphony a few years later, he started his article with the following statement:

La septième symphonie (en la) est célèbre par son andante.... Le rhythme, un rhythme simple ... est encore la cause principale de l'incroyable effet produit par l'andante. Il consiste uniquement dans un dactyle suivi d'un spondée, frappés sans

29 See, for example, Joseph d'Ortigue in *La France musicale*, vii/14 (7 April 1844), p. 106.
30 *Le ménestrel*, iii/33 (17 July 1836), p. [4].
31 *Revue musicale*, v (February–July 1829), p. 347.
32 *Gazette musicale de Paris*, i/17 (27 April 1834), p. 134.

relâche ... Là-dessus la mélodieuse plainte, émise avec plus d'énergie, prend le
caractère d'un gémissement convulsif ... Mais une lueur d'espoir vient de naître: à
ces accents déchirants succède une vaporeuse mélodie, pure, simple, douce,... Les
basses seules continuent leur inexorable rhythme sous cet arc-en-ciel mélodieux...[33]

The seventh symphony (in A major) is celebrated for its Andante.... The rhythm, a
simple one, is again the principal source of the incredible effect produced by the
Andante. It consists only of a dactyl followed by a spondee, repeated continuously
... Above, the melodious lament, sounded with more strength, takes on the
character of a convulsive wailing ... But a ray of hope is born: these harrowing
accents are succeeded by a delicate melody, pure, simple and gentle.... Only the
basses continue with their inexorable rhythm beneath this melodious rainbow.

It was thus precisely the combination of the simple, constantly repeated
rhythm, like that of a funeral march, and the impressive melody restated
with varying timbre and instrumentation that made the slow movement
such a popular piece. The Allegretto was admired not only for its
plangent character but also for its splendour, its 'pompe orientale', as
Maurice Bourges put it.[34] Consequently, as part of the celebrations to
mark the state visit of the Queen of England to France in 1843, the
Allegretto was performed by 'La Musique de Roi' as the second piece,
after the overture to *La gazza ladra*.[35]

The enormous success of the Allegretto nevertheless generated hys-
teria, as Maurice Bourges emphasized in his review: 'Rapture develops
into a state of ecstasy, enthusiasm becomes fanaticism and continues
even beyond this exemplary performance...' ('Le transport passe à l'état
d'extase, l'enthousiasme devient fanatisme et se prolonge au-delà même
de cette éxécution modèle ...').[36]

The question arises as to whether these reviews of two of Beethoven's
symphonies convey a true idea of the relationship between Beethoven's
music and French civilization. We have to admit that during the first half
of the nineteenth century reviews were relatively imprecise, and consequently we must draw our conclusions about the significance of
Beethoven's music in France from the context in which it was performed
and from the preferences shown by the French public. It is surprising
that in each of the works considered here the movement that led to
acceptance of the whole symphony can be regarded as a continuation of
French musical history: in the case of the Fifth Symphony it was the
'military march' with its fanfares that aroused interest, while the famous
'Andante' of the Seventh Symphony recalls those funeral marches

33 *Revue et gazette musicale de Paris*, v/6 (11 February 1838), pp. 64–5.
34 Ibid., x/6 (5 February 1843), p. 47.
35 Ibid., x/37 (10 September 1843), p. 318.   36 Ibid., x/6 (5 February 1843), p. 47.

performed in France on many public occasions during the decades immediately after the Revolution.

When we say that the impact of the Revolution on Beethoven's works was not really discussed by the critics, we should remember that these French music periodicals were published during a period of monarchy. Critics seem to have been clearly aware that the Conservatoire, which played an enormous role in making Beethoven's music popular, owed its foundation to the Revolution. Thus, in 1847 it was stated that 'Beethoven's first two symphonies had been performed at the former Paris Conservatoire before that celebrated school was destroyed in 1815, in hatred of the revolution that had given birth to it'. ('Les deux premières symphonies de Beethoven avaient été exécutées aux anciens Conservatoires de Paris, avant que cette école célèbre fût détruite en 1815, en haine de la révolution qui lui avait donné naissance.')[37] Revolutionary interpretations of Beethoven's works were therefore not possible until after the overthrow of the monarchy, which is why this aspect could not appear in the reviews. It nevertheless surfaced, remarkably enough, during the short period of the February Revolution. Maurice Bourges concluded a review of a performance of the 'ouverture de Léonore' at the Conservatoire in March 1848 with these words:

C'est le flambeau de la vie, c'est l'air vif de la liberté. Cette ouverture serait bien vite comprise des condamnés politiques, dont notre République a rouvert les cachots. Eux seuls pourraient dire tout ce qu'il y a dans cette vaste inspiration de poésie vraie et sublime. C'est tout un plaidoyer de sentiment contre l'ancien régime pénitentiaire.[38]

It is the torch of life, it is the crisp air of liberty. This overture would be easily understood by the political prisoners whose dungeons the Republic has opened. They alone could say how much true and sublime poetry there is in this great inspiration. It is nothing other than a deeply felt defence plea against the shackles of the *ancien régime*.

Nothing like this would have been published during the years of monarchy, but, reading between the lines of the reviews, it seems that some of Beethoven's works owed their success to their revolutionary spirit. And it should be remembered that the musicians who introduced Beethoven to the French public would have known the music performed in France during the preceding period: Habeneck, for example, was born in 1781 the son of a regimental musician, and we can therefore be sure that he was familiar with the military music of that period. The biographies of other musicians involved in the introduction of Beethoven's works in France show that, despite the numerous changes in political life, there was some continuity in the musical life of the French capital.

37 Ibid., xiv/19 (9 May 1847), p. 156.   38 Ibid., xv/12 (19 March 1848), p. 89.

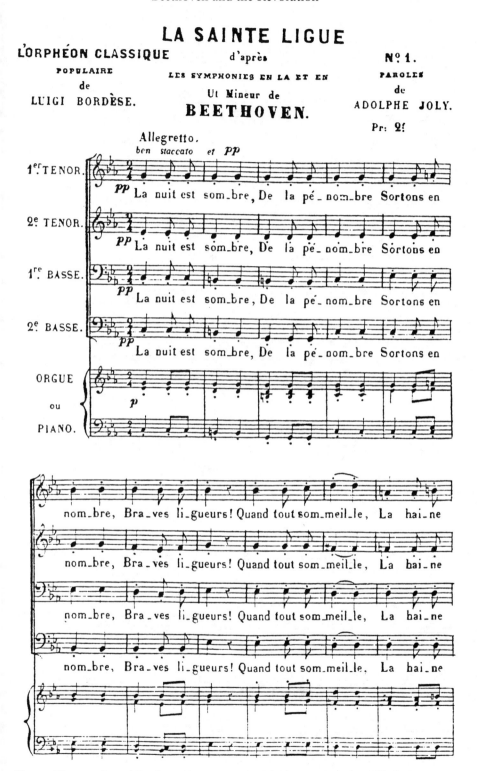

Fig. 1 The opening of *La Sainte Ligue*, arranged by Luigi Bordèse from Beethoven's Fifth and Seventh Symphonies

Fig. 2   *La Sainte Ligue*: transition to the second part, and final bars

-tyr, ven - geons le mar-tyr le mar-tyr de
-tyr, ven - geons le mar-tyr le mar-tyr de
-tyr, ven - geons le mar-tyr le mar-tyr de
-tyr, Vengeons la grande om-bre de Guise, Vengeons le saint mar-tyr de

(...)

de Va - lois, frap - pons frap - pons Hen - ry de Va - lois!
de Va - lois, frap - pons frap - pons Hen - ry de Va - lois!
de Va - lois, frap - pons frap - pons Hen - ry de Va - lois!
de Va - lois, frap - pous frap - pons Hen - ry de Va - lois!
ucelot, 27 r. C. des P. Champs.

Some of the points made above are illustrated in a piece for four-part male choir and organ (or piano) published by *Le ménestrel* in 1863.[39] This is an arrangement by Luigi Bordèse (1815–86), a composer of Italian origin, in which words by Adolphe Joly are put to the Allegretto of Beethoven's Seventh Symphony and the finale of his Fifth. It is given a historical setting (as was also Beethoven's *Fidelio* when it was performed in 1860 at the Théâtre-Lyrique with a text by Jules Barbier and Michel Carré set in the late fifteenth century during the reign of Charles VIII of France). The 'action' of *La Sainte Ligue* takes place during the last of the religious wars, when Henry III was king of France. The members of the Holy League meet at night to avenge the death of the Duc de Guise, who, together with his brother, was murdered in the château at Blois in 1588 by order of the king. The slow movement of the Seventh Symphony comes at the beginning of the chorus; the members of the League are urged to oppose oppression and to declare war on the impious king and his favourites. The music serves also as a funeral march for the Duc de Guise, a hero who died for his faith and his country (see Fig. 1). At the precise moment when the decision to advance to the attack is made, the finale of Beethoven's Fifth Symphony bursts forth (see Fig. 2). This is the 'chant de victoire' sung to the words 'Vengeons la grande ombre de Guise, frappons au cœur Henry de Valois' ('Let us avenge the great shade of De Guise, and strike Henry de Valois to the heart').

This curious arrangement can be regarded as highly illustrative, since it consists of two marches. The Allegretto in this case not only recalls the past and serves to commemorate a 'reign of terror'; it also functions as a stimulus to action. When it is combined with the finale of the Fifth Symphony, used here as a direct call to tyrannicide, the result is like the proclamation of a revolution.

One might argue that this survey has overemphasized the revolutionary aspects of the works and critiques discussed, while neglecting the Romantic aspects of the repertory. However, the works were chosen precisely to counterbalance a bias which has been predominant in recent studies of the period. A study of, for example, the piano works as assessed in the French musical press would have produced different results. But the examples presented here have shown that the French public responded spontaneously and directly to Beethoven's music, and especially to those movements that were closest to their own musical traditions and experiences. Certainly, with respect to an important part of Beethoven's works one may conclude that he was integrated into French culture as the successor to Gossec.

39 Advertised for the first time in *Le ménestrel*, xxx/10 (8 February 1863), p. 80.

Index

Abel, Carl Friedrich, 76
Abraham, Gerald, 2n
Abréviateur universel, 126n, 137n
Académie de Musique (Paris), 195,
    196–7, 198; *see also* Conservatoire
    (Paris)
Académie Française, 172
Académie Royale de Musique (Paris), 16,
    37, 39, 41–3, 44, 52n, 54ff, 107,
    224; *see also* Opéra (Paris)
Accademici Impavidi Risvegliati, 284n,
    299
Accorimboni, Agostino, 61
Adam, Jean-Louis, 64f, 67
Adam, Maître
    Meunier de Nevers, Le, 271
Adrien, Martin Joseph, 26, 302
Affiches, annonces et avis divers, 108n,
    125n, 126n, 127n, 136n, 137n,
    226n
Agus, Henri-Joseph, 206n
Ah! ça ira; *see* Ça ira
Aix-la-Chapelle, Treaty of, 279
Albanese, Egide-Joseph-Ignace-Antoine,
    273
Algarotti, Francesco, 22
Amar, André, 115n
Amboise, 165
American War of Independence, 95
Amsterdam, 74
Anderson, Emily, 50n
Andolfati, Pietro, 286n
André, Johann, 5, 66
Andreozzi, Gaetano, 61
Andriès, L., 236n, 237n
Anfossi, Pasquale, 43, 44
    Avaro, L', 48, 55
    Curioso indiscreto, Il, 56
    Finta giardiniera, La, 55
    Geloso in cimento, Il, 55
    Incognita perseguitata, L', 42, 54f

Angermüller, Rudolph, 24n
Anglesey, 174n
'Anti-Marchant', 237–75
Antwerp, 279
Aristotle, 233n
Arles, 77, 261
Arnault, Antoine Vincent, 156, 185, 188
Arnolfini, Giovanni, 279
Arnould, Jean François [pseud.]; *see*
    Musset, Jean François
Arnould, Sophie, 26, 188
Arrighi, Gino, 281n, 293n
Artois, Countess d', 97, 100
assignats, 115, 248, 257
Auber, Daniel-François-Esprit, 10
    Muette de Portici, La, 186
Auch, Martin, d', 121
Aucoc, Léon, 203n
Audinot, Nicolas Medard, 188
Augustine, St, 226
Aulard, François Victor Alphonse, 110n
Avignon, 261, 279
Azaïs, Pierre-Hyacinthe, 195n

Baccelli, Domenico, 54
Bach, Johann Christian, 222n
Baciocchi, Elisa Bonaparte, 282, 290
Baciocchi family, 292, 298f
Bagge, Charles Ernest, Baron de, 74
Bailleux, publisher, 59, 74n
Baillon, publisher, 62
Baillot, Pierre, 87, 92, 207n
Bailly, Jean-Sylvain, 111, 121, 224
Balelli, Antonio, 291n
Ballard, publishers, 26, 57
Balle, 55
ballet, 16, 27–31, 41, 43f, 109f, 297ff
Ballière de Laisement,
    Charles-Louis-Denis, 193n
Bambini, Felice, 58
Barber, William Henry 95n

Barbier, Jules, 312
Barère, Bertrand, 128n
Barfoot, Terry, 187–8
Barnave, Antoine-Pierre, 158
Barouillet, Marie-Joseph Désiré Martin,
    126, 138n, 139, 155
Barra, Joseph, 114
Barré, Pierre-Yon, 188
Barthes, Roland, 17n, 18n
Bartlet, M. Elizabeth C., 2n, 5n, 6n, 7,
    54, 108n, 139n, 149n, 157n, 175n,
    178n, 179n
Bartolucci, Francesco, 293
Baudron, Antoine Laurent, 75–6, 92
Beaumarchais, Pierre Augustin Caron de,
    1, 46–7, 110, 156, 224
Beaumont d'Avantois, Marie-François,
    93n
Beaurepaire, 113, 127
Beauvarlet-Charpentier, Jean-Jacques,
    58, 61
Beccari, Giuseppe, 287n, 293
Beethoven, Ludwig van, 1–2, 5, 10, 93,
    302–314
    An die ferne Geliebte, 236
    'Battle Symphony', op.91, 300
    Fidelio, 2, 157, 168, 173, 181, 187,
        302, 304, 314
    Piano sonata in Ab, op. 26, 303
    Symphony no. 1, op. 21, 308
    Symphony no. 3, op. 55, 302ff
    Symphony no. 5, op. 67, 303, 304–7,
        311, 314
    Symphony no. 7, op. 92, 302, 304,
        307–9, 311, 314
    Symphony no. 9, op. 125, 302, 304
Beffroy de Rigny, Louis Abel, 136, 155
    Nicomède dans la lune, 260, 262, 271
Bemetzrieder, Anton, 194–8, 201,
    202–3, 205, 208
Benaut, publisher, 58n
Benichi, Antonio, 285n
Benoît, Bruno, 132n
Berlin, 78, 80n
Berlioz, Hector, 10, 209n, 305f, 308–9
Bernardini, Cosimo, 291
Bernardini, Ugo, 281n, 285n, 290n
Bernier, Nicolas, 94
Bertaud, J.-P., 114n
Berthault, Pierre, 113n
Berton, Henri-Montan, 7n, 207n
    Nouveau d'Assas, Le, 175
    Oriflamme, L', 154
    Rigueurs du cloître, Les, 179, 183,
        187f
Bertoni, Ferdinando, 16n
Betzwieser, Thomas, 250n

Béziers, 2
Biagi Ravenni, Gabriella, 283n
Bianchi, Francesco, 61
Bianchi, Oliva, 287n
Bindman, D., 123n
Biondi, Antonio, 285n, 287n, 289–90
Blanchard, abbé, 94
Bloch-Michel, A., 4n
Blume, Friedrich, 211n
Bobillier, Marie, 74n
Boccherini, Luigi, 58, 74, 76
Bocconi, Rafaella, 280n
Boieldieu, Adrien, 10
Bonaccorsi, Alfredo, 283n
Bonaparte, Napoléon, see Napoleon I
Bonnet, Jean Claude, 41n
Bonnier d'Alco, Ange-Louis-Antoine, 297
Bordeaux, 25n
Bordes, Philippe, 120n, 121n
Bordèse, Luigi, 311–14
Bossi, Sebastiano, 285n
Bottarelli, Giovanni Gualberto, 16n
Bottini, Anna Teresa, 285n, 291n
Bouilly, Jean-Nicolas, 2, 3, 157–68,
    173–4, 180f, 182n, 184, 188
Bouquet, Marie-Thérèse, 201n
Bouquier, Gabriel, 137, 155
Bourbons, 1
Bourdon de la Crosnière, Léonard, 111ff,
    115ff, 123–4
Bourges, Maurice, 306, 309f
Boyer, publisher, 59, 62–5
Brazzini, Gaetano, 287n
Brécy, Robert, 239
Brenet, Michel [pseud.]; see Bobillier,
    Marie
Brenet, Nicolas Guy. 116
Brenner, Clarence D., 6n, 38n, 41n, 171n
Brett, Raymond Laurence, 186n
Brévan, Bruno, 203n, 294n
Broccoletto, Vincenzo, 287n
Brook, Barry S., 211n
Browne, Richmond, 192n
Bruges, 279
Bruni, Antonio Bartolomeo, 56
Brussels, 55, 66
Bryant, David, 285n, 299
Bürckhoffer, J. G., 58
Burney, Charles, 20n
Busserole, Jacques-Xavier Carré de; see
    Carré de Busserole, Jacques-Xavier

Ça ira, 5, 132, 137, 240n, 287, 288n,
    289n
Caldara, Antonio, 16n
calendar, Revolutionary, ix–x, 3, 101f
Calzabigi, Raniero, 15, 24

Camaiani, Pier Giorgio, 281n, 282n, 293n
Cambini, Giuseppe Maria, 48, 55, 86
Cambrai, 238
Cambridge
  King's College, 74n, 80
Campra, André, 272
Candeille, Pierre Joseph
  Patrie reconnaissante, La, 126f, 129f, 133, 137–8, 147n, 154
Capece, Carlo Sigismondo, 16n
Carlez, Jules A., 207n
Carmagnole, La, 5, 293, 297
Carra, Jean Louis, 262
Carré, Michel, 314
Carré de Busserole, Jacques-Xavier, 159n, 162n, 165n, 166n
Caselli, impresario, 291n
Castel, L., 170n, 175n
Castil-Blaze, 15n
Castinel, Nathalie, 86n
Catel, Charles-Simon, 154, 191, 206–10
  Bataille de Fleurus, La, 5
Celoniati, Ignazio, 58n
Cenami, Bartolomeo, 291n
Cerati, M., 114n, 115n
César, Pierre Antoine, 61f
Český Krumlov, 86n
Chabanon, Michel-Paul-Guy de, 211–20
Chabot, General, 290n
Chabran, Gaetano; *see* Chiabrano, Gaetano
Chabroud, Jean-Baptiste-Charles, 245n
Challamel, Jean Baptiste Marie Augustin, 211, 230, 235
Champein, Stanislas, 273
Chardiny, Louis Armand, 55
Charles VIII, King, 314
Charles X, King, 15, 97
Charlton, David, 5n, 6n, 27n, 42n, 171n, 174n, 180n, 181n, 185n
Chassaing, Jean-François, 206n
Chastellux, François Jean de, 22, 231
Chelini, Jacopo, 280n, 282n, 283n, 285, 286n, 287ff, 290n, 292n, 293n, 295ff
Chénier, Marie-Joseph, 154, 199, 201n, 221, 223–35, 287
Chéron, 26
Chéron, Mme, 26
Cherubini, Luigi, 2, 8, 10, 154, 206n, 208, 227, 230, 302
  Deux journées, Les, 170, 178f, 183n, 188
  Eliza, 175, 178, 185f, 188
  Lodoïska, 176f, 179, 182, 188
  Médée, 178

Chiabrano, Carlo, 77
Chiabrano, Gaetano, 58n
Chinon, 165
Choron, Alexandre, 209–10
Chrétien, Gilles-Louis, 95–7
Christina, Queen of Sweden, 99
Chronique de Paris, 226
Chronique du manège, 238
Church, 3, 4, 10, 17, 111, 122, 202, 223, 225, 227, 246, 283, 292–3
Cigna-Santi, Vittorio Amedeo, 16n
Cimador, Giambattista
  Pimmalione, 285
Cimarosa, Domenico, 43, 44
  Gianniana e Bernardone, 44
  Impresario in angustie, L', 56
  Italiana in Londra, L', 44, 56
  Marito geloso, Il, 300
  Matrimonio segreto, Il, 299
  Olimpiade, 291
Cisalpine Republic, 281f
Civil Constitution of the Clergy, 227
Clarke, Martyn, 27n
Clément, Charles-François, 58, 61
Clementi, Muzio, 64f, 67, 70
Clerval, J.-Alexandre, 201n
Cobban, Alfred, 180n
Coleridge, Samuel Taylor, 186
Collette, Armand Romain, 201n
Collot d'Herbois, Jean-Marie, 236, 239
Comédie-Française, 41, 76n, 172, 223
Comédie-Italienne, 6, 37ff, 40ff, 54ff, 171f, 174, 175n, 197n
comédie mêlée d'ariettes, 37–8, 40f
comédie-vaudeville, 37
Committee of Public Instruction, 102, 111, 167f, 199, 201, 205n, 218, 231
Committee of Public Safety, 109f, 162
Committee for General Security, 115n
Compiègne, 99
Comte d'Artois; *see* Charles X
Concert de la Loge Olympique, 1, 76
Concert des Amateurs, 211f
Concerts Saint-Honoré, 306
Concert Spirituel, 4, 64, 70, 76f, 94, 217, 222, 224
Concerts de la rue de Cléry, 5
Concerts Spirituels de la Société des Concerts, 306
Condorcet, Marie Jean Antoine Nicolas Caritat, Marquis de, 262
Conservatoire (Paris), 5, 8, 86, 92f, 98, 100f, 103f, 191–210, 218, 225n, 304, 307, 310; *see also* Académie de Musique (Paris)
Constantinople, 279
constitution, 120ff, 236–75

of 1791, 236–75 *passim*
of 24 June 1793, 114
of An III/1795, 205n
of An VIII/1799, 205n
Conti, Louis François de Bourbon, Prince de, 74, 77
Convention, 111, 114n, 117n, 124, 137, 154f, 191, 199, 201, 205n, 230
Coquéau, Claude-Philibert, 195, 196n
Corday, Charlotte, 101
Cordeliers, 224
Corelli, Arcangelo, 193
Corneille, Pierre, 139
Correspondance littéraire (Grimm, Diderot *et al*), 23, 28n, 38f, 50n, 197–8
Corsica, 49n
Cosson, M.-D., publisher, 103
Cotte, Roger, 1n, 93n, 100n, 211n, 213–14
Courier français, 116n
Courrier des spectacles, 86n, 167f
Coupigny, 229
Cousineau, publishers, 42, 50n, 59
Coy, Adelheid, 2n
Crajenschot, J. T., publisher, 77n
Crespi, Giuditta, 287n
Croll, Gerhard, 16n
Crow, Thomas, 118n
Cucuel, Georges, 177n
Cuneo, 294
Curcio, Giuseppe Maria
    Ifigenia in Aulide, 301

D., M., 121n
D'Addario, Arnaldo, 281n
Daguerre, Louis Jacques Mandé, 95
Dalayrac, Nicolas-Marie
    Azémia, 271
    Camille, 175f, 182, 187f
    Léhéman, 180, 185, 188
    Léon, 175f, 186, 188
    Raoul, Sire de Créqui, 178, 183f, 188
    Renaud d'Ast, 274
    Sargines, 273
D'Alembert, Jean le Rond, 94, 192n, 193n
Damcke, B., 17n
Dannery, *maître de chapelle*, 102
Danou, Claude-François, 201n, 203n
Danton, Georges Jacques, 111, 224, 262
Danzi, Francesca, 291n
Da Ponte, Lorenzo, 1
Dashwood, Sir Francis, 80n
Dashwood, Henry, 80
Dauvergne, Antoine, 37, 94
Davaux, Jean-Baptiste, 74n, 77–8, 80

David, François, 122n
David, Jacques Louis, 1, 114n, 118–21, 139
Dean, Winton, 2n, 7n, 34n, 169, 175, 187
Decadist cults, 231
Declaration of the Rights of Man and Citizen, 121, 132
Dejaure, Jean-Elie-Bédénd, 175n, 188
De La Haye, Mme, 47
De la Marelle, Louis Basset, 95
Delaunay d'Angers, Joseph, 113, 127
Del Bono, Luigi, 286n, 300
Delcroix, Maurice, 17n
Delormel, publisher, 26
Delrieu, Etienne Joseph Bernard, 101
Dent, Edward J., 7, 169, 178, 186
De Piis, Pierre-Antoine Augustin, 188
    Amours d'été, Les, 258, 271ff
Depping, Georges-Bernard, 167n
De Santi, Giovanni Antonio, 296f
Désaugiers, Marc-Antoine
    Albanèse, 271
    Florine, 271
    Prise de la Bastille, La, 5
Descartes, René, 99
Desfontaines [pseud.]; *see* Fouques, François-Georges
Desmoulins, Camille, 224
Desrosier, 238n
Devienne, François, 64f, 67, 69
Devries, Anik, 58n
Dezède, Nicolas
    Barbier de Séville, Le, 274
    Péronne sauvée, 110, 174
    Trois fermiers, Les, 272
Dibdin, Charles, 80n
Diderot, Denis, 183n; *see also* *Correspondance littéraire*, *Encyclopédie*
Dietz, Max, 7n, 170n
Directory, 3, 5, 90, 149, 210n, 203
Dittersdorf, Carl Ditters von, 58
Dowd, David L., 8n, 118n, 120n
Dubech, Lucien, 17n
Dubreuil, Alphonse Ducongé, 185, 188
Dubuisson, Paul Ulric, 44f, 49–50, 55f
Duchemin, 112–13
Duchez, Marie-Elisabeth, 192n
Duchow, Marvin, 53n
Dudley, Walter Sherwood, 8n, 110n
Duhet, P. M., 114n, 115n
Dumouriez, Charles, 111
Duni, Egidio, 37, 39
Durante, Francesco, 38, 39
Durey, Albert, 205n
Dussek, Jan Ladislav, 64f, 69f
Dutilh, 154, 175

Index

Ecole Royale de Chant et de Déclamation (Paris), 197ff, 207, 222, 225; *see also* Conservatoire (Paris)
Ehrard, Jean, 93n, 208n
Eidous, Marc-Antoine, 176n
Einstein, Alfred, 20, 32
émigrés, 4, 239, 248–9, 267f
Encyclopédie, 38f, 282
Enlightenment, 31, 34, 35–6, 95, 99, 234
Epidor, Mathieu de l', 98
Epinay, Louise Florence Pétronille Tardieu d'Esclavelles, Dame de La Live d', 53n
Erskine, Thomas Alexander; *see* Kelly, Thomas Alexander Erskine, 6th Earl of
Escudier, Léon, 302
Estandoux, Cailhava d', 54
Euripides, 18, 22

Fainstein, Norman, 220
Fairclough, Peter, 176n
Farinelli, Giuseppe
  Locandiera, La, 301
  Pamela, La, 301
Fatinelli, Giovanni Battista, 291n
Fatinelli, Olimpia Cenami, 291n
Fava, Filippo, 287n
Fava, Pierina, 287n
Favier, Jean, 7n
Favières, Etienne Guillaume François de, 185, 188
Favre, Georges, 5
Fayolle, François, 209–10
Fellinger, Imogen, 57
Ferloni, Severino, 287f, 297
Ferrari, Pietro, 284
Ferri, Anna Roffi, 286n, 287n
Ferri, Giuseppe, 286n, 287n
festa di ballo; *see veglia di ballo*
festa teatrale, 21
festival, patriotic, 8–9, 101, 107n, 114n, 118, 120, 128, 139, 145, 191, 199ff, 204–5, 209, 219, 221f, 226, 228f, 231, 235, 293–7
  of Agriculture, 90
  of the Federation, 9, 121, 205n, 224–7
  of Industry (1844), 306
  of the Regeneration, 296–7
  of the Supreme Being, 9
  of the Unity and Indivisibility of the Republic, 159
Fétis, Edouard, 307f
Fétis, François-Joseph, 77n, 86n, 93, 95, 104, 207n, 304–5
Feuille de salut public, 115n

Fiévée, Joseph, 179n, 188
Fillette-Loraux, Claude-François, 188
Fink, Gottfried Wilhelm, 170n
First Republic, 2
Florence, 284n, 287
Floros, C., 32n
Flothuis, Marius, 17n, 36
Focillon, Henri, 10
Fodor, Carolus [Charles] Emanuel, 61, 64f, 67
Fontainebleau, 42f, 54
Fontanier, Pierre, 232
Fontenelle, Bernard le Bovier de, 222
Forgeot, Nicolas-Julien, 188
Forti, Guido, 289, 290n
Fouché, Joseph, 98
Fouques, François-Georges ('Desfontaines'), 172, 174, 188
Framery, Nicolas Etienne, 40, 41n, 45ff, 52n, 53, 54f, 177, 211, 212n, 217–18, 231, 235n
France musicale, La, 303, 304n, 306
Franceschi, Francesco, 294, 296n, 298
Franchi, Carlo, 16n
Francis I, Emperor, 292n
Francis, II, Emperor, 292n
Francisconi, Giovanni, 58n
Franklin, Benjamin, 234
Frederick the Great, King of Prussia, 36, 306
freemasonry, 1, 94–5, 97f; *see also* masonic lodges
Fridzeri, Alessandro Mario Antonio, 58n
Fried, Michael, 120n
Friedrich II, King; *see* Frederick the Great
Frishberg Saloman, Ora, 1n, 215n, 220n

Galliver, David, 2n, 157n, 166n, 174
Gardel, Pierre Gabriel, 110, 156
Gardi, Francesco
  Donna ve la fa, 300
  Muta, La, 300
Garnier, Michèle, 6
Gauffier, Louis, 116
Gauzarges, Charles, 94
Gaveaux, Pierre, 7n, 167
  Amour filial, L', 167
  Léonore, ou L'amour conjugal, 2, 3, 167–8, 188
  Réveil du peuple contre les terroristes, Le, 2–3
Gaviniès, Pierre, 222
Gazette nationale; see Moniteur universel, Le
Gazzaniga, Giuseppe, 44, 61
Geck, Martin, 302n
Geneva, 279

Genoa, 294
Gerle, Dom, 121
Gérold, Théodore, 177n
Gessele, Cynthia M., 1n
Giambastiani, 291n
Giampaoli, Stefano, 282n
Gianturco, Carolyn, 283n
Giardini, Felice, 58, 80n
Ginni, Francesco, 285n
Giorgi, Agnese, 287n
Giorgi, Teresa, 287n
Girey-Dupré, Joseph Marie, 238
Girondins, 101, 115
Giroust, François, 1n, 93–104, 225n
   Apothéose de Marat et Le Peletier, 101
   Appel à la bien faisance, 103
   Cantate à l'Eternel, 102
   Concert des octogénaires, 102–3
   Gédéon, 98–9
   Hymne à l'Eternel, 102
   Hymne au Grand Architecte, 102
   Hymne des versaillais, 101
   Inquiétudes et les charmes de l'amitié, Les, 99
   Irruption de l'océan, 99
   Ombre de Samuel, L', 99
   Scène dityrambique, 101
   Thélèphe, 100
Gluck, Christoph Willibald, 16, 28, 107, 110, 132f, 137ff, 145, 197, 213, 223
   Alceste, 19, 21, 32, 35, 133, 145, 178
   Armide, 5, 17, 31, 142–4
   Don Juan, 21
   Iphigénie en Aulide, 6, 15–36, 138, 197, 222
   Iphigénie en Tauride, 16n, 17, 27, 31, 138, 222
   Orfeo ed Euridice, 19, 21, 35, 178
   Paride ed Elena, 21
   Semiramis, 16n
Godecharle, Eugène, 58n
Godechot, Jacques, 201n, 204n, 205n, 239n
Goldoni, Antonio, 284n
Goldoni, Carlo, 49, 56
Gorsas, Antoine Joseph, 245, 261ff
Gossec, François-Joseph, 8–9, 31, 58, 74, 76–7, 198f, 201, 206n, 208, 211, 221–35, 302, 307, 314
   Athalie, 139, 140, 142, 230
   Chant de Châteauvieux, Le, 5
   Chant du 14 juillet, 226n
   Choeur à la liberté, 228n
   Double déguisement, Le, 222
   Grande messe des morts, 224f
   Hymne à Jean-Jacques Rousseau, 229

   Hymne à la liberté, 228n, 230
   Hymne à l'Etre Suprème, 5, 228
   Hymne du IX Thermidor, 231
   Marche lugubre, 8, 9, 133, 230
   Nativité, La, 224f
   O salutaris hostia, 223, 225, 230
   Prise de Toulon, La, 229
   Sabinus, 15–16, 222f
   Serment républicain, 228n, 230
   Symphonies, op. 3, 222
   Symphony in 17 parts, 222
   Te Deum, 225–6
   Thésée, 223
   Triomphe de la République, La, 126, 128, 154
Gouffé, A., 274
Gouges, Olympe de, 115
Goulet, Antoine, 94
Gourbillon, Joseph Antoine de, 55f
Gray, A., 24n
Grégoire, abbé Henri, 121
Grenier, Gabriel, 61
Grétry, André-Ernest-Modeste, 7, 37, 39n, 107, 110, 168, 222, 230, 251, 302
   Amant jaloux, L', 1n
   Amitié à l'épreuve, L', 273
   Andromaque, 31
   Aucassin et Nicolette, 188
   Caravane du Caire, 43
   Cécile et Ermancé, 155
   Céphale et Procris, 16
   Colinette à la cour, 43
   Comte d'Albert, Le, 183–4
   Denys le tyran, 156
   Huron, Le, 222
   Mariages samnites, Les, 174
   Panurge dans l'isle, 43
   Pierre le grand, 157
   Prisonnier anglais, Le, 172, 183n
   Richard Coeur-de-lion, 174, 178, 183n, 187
   Rosière de Salancy, La, 271
   Rosière républicaine, ou La fête de la vertu, La, 155
Grétry, Antoinette, 158, 161, 165
Gribenski, Jean, 5
Grimaud, Louis, 205n
Grimm, F. W. von, 23n, 24n, 53n; see also Correspondance littéraire
Grout, Donald Jay, 169, 178, 187
Guettard, Jean Etienne, 177n
Guglielmi, Pietro Alessandro, 16n, 44
   Due fratelli Pappamosca, I, 284, 299
Guichard, François
   La fête des bons gens, 272
Guillard, Nicolas François, 139, 155, 174

Index

Guillaume, James, 200n
Guillot, Georges, 226n
Guines, Adrien-Louis Bonnières de Sodastre, Comte de, 78n
Guinguené, Pierre Louis, 54, 212n
Guinigi, Maria, 291n
Guinigi, Paolo, 279
Guise, Duc de, 314
Gülke, Peter, 302n
Gustav III, King of Sweden, 36

Habeneck, François-Antoine, 303f, 306, 308, 310
Haberkamp, Gertraud, 78n
Hague, The, 66, 74
Halévy, Fromental, 10
Hamburg, 66
Handel, George Frideric
    Alcina, 178
    Judas Maccabaeus, 305n
Harden, Jean, 77n
Haspot, Erick, 211n
Hasquin, Hervé, 10n
Hasse, Johann Adolf, 39
Haydn, Joseph, 1, 64f, 67f, 70, 72, 74, 80, 86f, 90, 92, 100, 218, 222
    Symphony in C, 5
Haye, de la, fermier-général, 74
Hayez, F., publisher, 50n
Headington, Christopher, 169, 175, 178n, 187–8
Heartz, Daniel, 22n
Hellouin, Frédéric, 207n
Hemmerlein, Joseph, 64f, 70
Hennequin, Réné, 95n
Henry III, King, 314
Herding, K., 236n, 237n
Herman, Martin, 214n
Hérold, Ferdinand, 10
Héron, Louis-Julien-Simon, 160, 162, 165
Heurtault-Lamerville, Jean-Marie, 203
Hippolyte; see Leroux, Hippolyte
Hoffman, E. T. A., 27n, 305
Hoffman, François-Benoît, 170–72, 175f, 178, 180, 186, 188
Holmes, Eleanor, 210n
Holmes, Rachel, 210n
Homet, Louis, 93–4
Horace [Quintus Horatius Flaccus], 113, 164, 226, 233n
Hugo, Victor, 234–5, 303
Hüllmandel, Nicolas-Joseph, 64f, 68
Hummel, publishers, 74n, 77n
Hunt, Lynn, 110n
Hus, August, 156
Hussey, Dyneley, 170

Imbault, Jean-Jérôme, 5
Institut National de Musique, 4, 8, 199, 201, 205, 206n, 207; see also Conservatoire (Paris)
Isouard, Nicolas
    Avviso ai maritati, L', 285, 290

Jacobins, 2, 115n, 118, 123, 126, 237f, 242n, 245, 247, 249n, 257ff, 261ff, 269f, 281–82, 287, 288n, 289, 293
Jadin, Hyacinthe, 86–92
Jadin, Louis-Emmanuel, 64f, 70, 90
    Siège de Thionville, Le, 126, 128, 130–31, 134, 136, 137n, 138, 145–6, 147n, 154, 175
Jam, Jean-Louis, 2n, 10, 208n, 225n, 226n, 227n, 231n
Jamard, T., theorist, 193–4, 205
Jansenism, 23
Joan of Arc, 178n
Johansson, Carl, 74n
Joigny, 7n
Joly, Adolphe, 311–14
Jommelli, Nicolò, 16n, 38
Jones, A. R., 186n
Joseph II, Emperor of Austria, 36, 290n
Journal de musique, 194
Journal de Paris national, 125, 128–9, 137n, 138n, 146n, 147n, 152n, 168, 208
Journal des spectacles, 136n, 146n, 152n, 207n
Journal des théâtres et des fêtes nationales, 129n, 137n
Journal encyclopédique, 24, 27n, 193, 194n, 284
Journal général de France; see Affiches, annonces et avis divers
Julien, Jean-Rémy, 2n, 6n, 10, 238n, 254n
Jullien, Adolphe, 107n

Kammel, Antonín, 76
Karro, Françoise, 10n
Keiler, Allan R., 192n
Kelly, Thomas Alexander Erskine, 6th Earl of, 78
Killen, Alice M., 177, 185n
King's Theatre (London), 44, 177n
Kirtlington, 80
Klein, Jean-Claude, 6n, 10, 254n
Klob, Karl M., 170
Kosellech, Reinhard, 236n
Kozeluch, Leopold, 64f, 67f, 70
Krauss, Werner, 95n
Kreutzer, Rodolphe, 285
    Brigand, Le, 175, 188

Lodoiska, 182, 188
Paul et Virginie, 175, 185, 188
Kruthoffer, Franz, 26n, 31n
Küffner, Johan Jakob Paul, 64f, 68
Kuhn, Anton Leoni, 64f, 69

La Borde, Benedetto, 291n
La Borde, Jean Benjamin de, 177n, 198n
Labrousse, engraver, 113n
Lacépède, Bernard Germain Etienne Médard de la Ville-sur-Illon, Comte de, 173, 214f
La Chevardière, publisher, 58
Lacombe, Claire, 115
La Fayette, Marie Joseph Yves Gilbert du Motier, Marquis de, 111, 121, 131, 262
La Fontaine, 183
La Harpe, Jean François de, 122–3, 273
Lainez, Etienne, 6–7, 26, 139
Lajarte, Théodore de, 42n
La Martelière, Jean Henri Ferdinand, 287
Lamartine, Alphonse de, 232
La May, T., 15n
Lambesc, Charles Eugène, Prince de, 270
Lameth, Charles de, 245n, 261
Lancaster, Henry Carrington, 127n
Langlé, Honoré-François-Marie, 206n
Langlois, Marie Louise, 161
Lannes, Jean, 303
La Révelliere-Lépeaux, Louis-Marie de, 201n
Larousse, Pierre, 217n
Larrivé, Henri, 35
Lasceux, Guillaume, 58, 61
Laujon, P., 271
Launay, Denise, 107n, 193n, 201n
Lauvernier, Dominique, 10n
Lavillat, Bernard, 201n
Leblond, Gaspard Michel, *dit*, 15n, 107n, 197n
Leboeuf, Jean-Joseph, 127, 154
Le Breton, Joachim, 9n
Lebrun, Jean-Baptiste-Pierre, 5
Le Cerf de la Viéville, Jean Laurent, 193
Leclair, Jean-Marie, *l'aîné*, 217
Leclerc, Jean-Baptiste, 191, 201–4, 208, 211, 218–19, 222n, 228
Leclerc, publisher, 58n
Leduc, publishers, 50n, 59, 61
Leduc, Simon, 222
Lefébure, Louis-François Henri, 211, 216
Legislative Assembly, 230
Legouvé, Ernest, 163
Legrand, Raphaëlle, 10n
Legros, Joseph, 27, 139
Leith, James Andress, 179n, 203n, 206n

Le Jeune, Nicolas, 122n
Le Moigne-Mussat, Marie-Claire, 10n
Lemoyne, Jean-Baptiste
Electre, 31–2
Louis IX en Egypte, 108, 110
Miltiade à Marathon, 125ff, 135, 145, 146n, 148–50, 151, 155
Toute la Grèce, 108n, 125f, 129, 133, 136, 145, 146n, 148, 151, 155
Leopold I, Emperor, 180
Leopold II, Emperor, 292n
Lepeletier de Saint-Fargeau, Louis Michel, Marquis de, 101
Lépidor, M. J. Mattieu de, 54
Le Pin, Henry-Noël, 64f, 70
Leroux, Hippolyte, 56
Lesage, Alain-René, 175
Le Sueur, Jean-François, 8, 10, 154, 206n, 208, 209, 211, 214–16, 225n, 230, 302
Caverne, La, 175, 182, 184, 188
Paul et Virginie, 175
Lesueur, 117n
Lesure, François, 15n, 57n, 58n, 67n, 196n
Levasseur, Rosalie, 26
Lévêque, Jean-Jacques, 117n, 118n, 120n, 122n
Lewis, Anthony, 9
Lille, 7, 203n
Lippman, Edward A., 212n
Livigni, Filippo, 188
Livorno, 293
Lobel, Mary D., 80n
Loches, 165
Loeschmann, Horst B., 24n
Loewenberg, Alfred, 54
Loge Olympique; *see* Concert de la Loge Olympique
Loire, 113
London, 74, 77, 78n, 279
    Hellfire Club, 80n
    National Gallery, 279
    see also King's Theatre
London und Paris, 238
Longyear, Rey Morgan, 170, 173, 175f
Louis XIV, 58, 108, 121
Louis XV, 16, 34, 162
Louis XVI, 1, 28, 94, 97, 107, 108n, 110, 118, 121ff, 131f, 225n, 251, 257
Louis XVIII, 163–4
Lucca, 279–301
Lully, Jean-Baptiste, 125, 192–3
Isis, 272
Roland, 27n, 177n
Lyons, 86n, 279

Macarini, Giovanni Ubaldo, 288–9
MacClintock, Carol, 303
Magasin de Musique (Paris), 199, 205
Maillard, singer, 26
Mamczarz, Irene, 38n
Mancini, Giovanni Battista, 286n, 287, 299
Maniates, Maria Rika, 214
Mansi, Louise Palma, 285n, 286n, 287n, 291n, 299
Mantua, 294
Marand-Fouquet, C., 114n
Marat, Jean-Paul, 101, 261
Marchant, François, 237–75
Marchesi, Luigi, 291n
Marchionni, Angelo, 287n
Marchionni, Elisabetta, 287
Maréchal, Pierre Sylvain, 155, 156
Marie Antoinette, 16, 40, 107, 115n, 157, 241, 267
Marivaux, Pierre Carlet de Chamblain de, 171
Marmontel, Jean François, 15n, 170n, 174, 197, 273
Marseillaise, La; see Rouget de Lisle, Claude-Joseph
Marseilles, 279
Marsollier, Benoît-Joseph, 180, 188
Martin, George, 187
Martín y Soler, Vicente, 44
    Abore di Diana, L', 56
Martini, Johann Paul Ægidius, 8, 58, 100, 272
    Complainte de Marie Stuart, 267, 271
    Droit de seigneur, Le, 174
    Henri IV, 174
    Rosière de Salency, La, 271
    Sapho, 7n
Mason, William, 174n
masonic lodges
    Olympique de la Parfaite Estime, 95
    Orient de la Cour, de l', 94–5, 99
    Patriotisme, Le, 95, 98, 102
    Saint-Louis de la Martinique, 95
Massa, 279n, 282
Massai, Carlo, 281n
Massip, Catherine, 5
Massoni brothers, impresarios, 291n
Mataglieni, impresario, 286n
Mayenne, 113
Mayr, Simon
    Carretto del venditore de aceto, Il, 300
    Che originali!, 301
Mazzarosa, Antonio, 281n
Mazzeranghi, Benedetto, 287n
Mazzotti, Luigi, 286n, 287n
Medembach, Rosa, 286n, 287n

Méhul, Etienne-Nicolas, 5, 8, 10, 154, 157, 206n, 208, 227f, 230, 302
    Camille, 182n, 188
    Caverne, La, 175, 178, 188
    Chant du départ, Le, 5, 9, 228
    Chant du retour, Le, 3
    Cora, 108
    Doria, 179n
    Euphrosine, 182, 188
    Horatius Coclès, 126, 132, 133–4, 137, 145, 149, 151, 153, 156
    Jeune Henri, Le, 157, 167
    Jugement de Pâris, Le, 151, 156
    Mélidore et Phrosine, 185f, 188
    Symphony 'no. 0' in C, 5
Melani, Giovanni, 287n
Ménestrel, Le, 303, 305n, 306n, 308n, 312
Mengozzi, Bernardo, 44
Menou, Jacques François de Boussay, Baron de, 245n, 261
Mercier, Elisabeth, 161ff, 165
Mercier, Louis-Sébastien, 10, 179
Mercier, Nicolas-Jean, 162
Mercier family, 160–61, 162f
Mercure de France, 16n, 21, 23, 28n, 42ff, 47, 50n, 55f, 172n, 174n, 194, 195n, 197
Méreaux, Nicolas-Jean Le Froid de, 54
    Fabius, 125f, 129, 131, 135, 137, 145, 146n, 147–9, 152n, 155
Merli, D., 284n, 286n, 291n, 299
Meude-Monpas, writer, 237n
Meyer, Philippe-Jacques, 58n
Mezger, Franz, 61, 64f, 68ff, 72
Miller, Ernest Louis, 110
Minelli, Agostino, 285n
Minutoli, Carlo, 281n
Minutoli, Francesco, 299
Mirabeau, Honoré-Gabriel Riqueti, Comte de, 111, 158, 224
Miroglio, Jean-Baptiste, 58
modinha, 66
Moitte, Adelaïde, Marie Anne Castellas, 116, 117
Moitte, Jean Guillaume, 116
Moline, Pierre-Louis, 42f, 49–50, 52n, 54f, 137, 155
Monde musical, Le, 303, 305n, 306n, 307n
Mongrédien, Jean, 2n, 5, 10, 74n, 203n, 208n, 209n, 214n, 238n
Moniteur universel, Le, 113n, 114n, 115n, 116n, 122n, 125n, 128n, 163n, 180n
Monsigny, Pierre-Alexandre, 37, 230, 244

Déserteur, Le, 80n, 178, 183n, 184, 188, 251, 256, 273f
Roy et le fermier, Le, 251, 257, 265, 272
Montenoy, Charles Palissot de, 223
Montesquieu, Charles Louis de Secondat, Baron de la Brède et de, 158
Monvel, Jacques-Marie Boutet de, 174–5, 184n, 188
Morange, Jean, 206n
Moreau, Jean Michel, 118n
Morel, Auguste, 307
Morelli, Giovanni, 285n
Morrochesi, impresario, 300
Mortier, Roland, 10n
Moscheni, Domenico, 287n
Mozart, Wolfgang Amadeus, 1, 5, 50n, 64f, 68f, 78n, 87, 93, 304
  Così fan tutte, 5
  Don Giovanni, 181
  Idomeneo, 32, 34ff
  Nozze di Figaro, Le, 110, 156
  String Quartet in C, K465, 88
  Symphony in G minor, K550, 5
  Zauberflöte, Die, 36, 98
Mozin, Benoit, 64f, 72
Mueller von Asow, Erich H., 25n, 26n, 31n
Mueller von Asow, Hedwig, 25n, 26n, 31n
Muraro, Maria Teresa, 285n, 287n
Murat, Joachim, 292
Musée de Paris, 102
Mussot, Jean François ('Arnould'), 188

Napier, publisher, 78f
Napoleon I, 1, 3, 90, 97, 301
National Assembly, 111, 113, 116, 120, 122, 158, 224, 234, 239, 240, 242, 247–8, 257ff, 265ff, 269
National Convention; *see* Convention
National Guard, 4, 8, 104, 111, 121f, 179, 199, 207, 219, 224, 228
Negrini, impresario, 290, 300
Nerici, Luigi, 280n, 282n, 283n
Nerini, Domenico, 286n
Nettl, Paul, 303n
Newman, Ernest, 210n
Niepce, Joseph, 95
Nobili, Constantino, 291n
Nogaret, Félix, 97–104
Noiray, Michel, 41n, 45n, 54
Notaris, François, 156

Oboussier, Philippe, 6, 80n, 86n
Och, Andreas, 58n

Ogny, Baron d'; *see* Rigoley d'Ogny, Baron
Olivet, Antoine Fabre d', 155
Olivier, Gabriel-Raimond-Jean de Dieu-François d', 211, 219
opera buffa, 37–56, 290–1
opéra comique, 6, 10, 15, 37–56, 61, 174, 180, 186, 222, 250, 285
Opéra (Paris), 6, 7, 15–16, 25, 27f, 107–56, 174, 175n, 177, 197, 209, 229
Opéra-Comique (Paris), 6f, 37f, 136, 167, 170
opera seria, 15f, 49, 182
Orlandini, Giuseppe Maria, 16n
Orleans, 94, 178n, 260, 262
Orléans, Louis-Philippe-Joseph, Duc d' (Philippe-Egalité), 223–4
Ortigue, Joseph d', 308n
Orzali, Maria Domitilla, 281n, 287n, 290n
Oxford, 80
Ozi, publisher, 62
Ozouf, Mona, 8n, 179n, 201n, 205n

Paisiello, Giovanni, 40, 43, 44, 56, 298
  Astuto in amore, L', 299
  Barbiere di Siviglia, Il, 42, 46, 52n, 53, 55
  Credulo deluso, Il, 53n, 54
  Due contesse, Le, 55
  Duello, Il, 54
  Filosofi immaginari, I, 55
  Frascatana, La, 47–8, 54, 177, 188
  Gare generose, Le, 44, 55f
  Gran Cid, Il, 48
  Grotta di Trofonio, La, 55
  Matrimonio inaspettato, Il, 55
  Re Teodoro in Venezia, Il, 42ff, 46, 49, 55
  Schiavi per amore, Gli, 55f
  Tamburo, Il, 48, 54
Palat-Dercy, 188
Palavicini, Giovanni, 287n
Palisca, Claude V., 302n
Palma, Silvestro
  Pietra simpatica, La, 299
Pani, impresario, 300
Panofka, Henri, 305
Paris, 2, 34, 35, 54, 74, 77, 93, 102, 158f, 191, 238, 262, 267, 279
  Bastille, 114, 179–80, 224, 262
  Café de Chartres, 3
  Champs-de-Mars, 122
  Cirque, 4
  Hôtel du Musée, 4
  Les Halles, 129

Index

Notre Dame, 93, 225n
Palais Royal, 41, 45, 55, 159
Panthéon, 9, 101, 113, 229, 234, 303
Salle Favart, 6
St-Germain l'Auxerrois, 94
Sts-Innocents, 94
Tuileries, 4, 55, 100, 229, 230, 262
see also Académie Royale de Musique,
    Comédie-Française,
    Comédie-Italienne, Conservatoire,
    Ecole Royale de Chant, Opéra,
    Opéra-Comique, Théâtre Beaujolais,
    Théâtre de la République, Théâtre
    de Monsieur, Théâtre Feydeau,
    Théâtre Français, Théâtre-Italien,
    Théâtre Montansier
Pariseau, Pierre Germain, 56
Parker, Harold Talbot, 125n
Peake, Luise Eitel, 236n
Pedrinelli, Giacomo, 290n
Pelandi, Antonio, 286n
Pellegrini, Almachilde, 283n
Pelletan, F., 17n
Pendle, Karin, 179n, 183n
Pergolesi, Giovanni Battista, 38f
    La serva padrona, 38
Perini, Giuseppe, 300
Péronne, 174n
Perotti, Gaetano, 301
Perrière, 128n, 149n
Peters, Antoine de, 58
Pétion, Jérôme, 245n, 257
Philidor, François-André Danican, 37,
    94, 273
    Ernelinde, 5, 15–16, 23, 139–40, 174
    Thémistocle, 140n
    Tom Jones, 208n
Philippe-Egalité; *see* Orléans,
    Louis-Philippe-Joseph, Duc d'
Philippon, A., 158, 159n, 166n
physionotrace, 95–7
Picard, Joseph, 207n
Piccinni, Niccolò, 41n, 44, 56, 107, 132,
    137, 140, 222f, 230
    Buona figliuola, La, 40, 48, 54
    Didon, 127, 139ff
    Stravaganti, Gli, 50, 54
Pichon, Thomas Jean, 118n
Pierre, Constant, 2n, 3n, 4n, 8n, 9n, 93n,
    101n, 102n, 139n, 198n, 199n,
    200n, 201n, 203n, 204n, 205n,
    207n, 221n, 226n, 230n, 238f,
    249–50, 255, 304
Piis, Pierre-Antoine Augustin; *see* De Piis,
    Pierre-Antoine Augustin
Pillnitz Declaration, 234
Pius VI, Pope, 292n

Pixérécourt, René-Charles Guilbert de,
    172n
Place, Adélaïde de, 4n, 5
Plasson, Michel, 9n
Pleyel, Ignace Joseph, 8, 64f, 69, 86n
Poinsinet, Antoine Alexandre Henri, 174
Ponteil, Felix, 203n
Ponticelli, Vincenzo, 291n
Porpora, Nicola, 16n
Porro, publisher, 61
Porta, Bernardo,
    Réunion du dix août, La, 110, 126,
        128f, 137, 145, 152, 155
Porta, Giovanni, 16n
Portogallo, Marcus Antônio
    Donna de genio volubile, La, 300
    Donne cambiate, Le, 300
    Spazzacamino principe, Lo, 300
Pougin, Arthur, 86n
Pozzi, Benedetta Mallegni, 287, 289,
    290n
Pozzi, Luigi, 287n
Prieur, Jean-Louis, 117n
Prim, *abbé* Jean, 93, 100
Prod'homme, Jacques Gabriel, 23n, 108n
Provence, Comte, de, 6, 41
Puccini, Antonio, 292n, 298n
Puccini, Domenico, 294–6, 298
    Bella madre degli'inni guerrieri, 294,
        296, 298
    Te Deum, 294–5, 298
Puccitta, Vincenzo,
    Amore platonico, L', 300

Querelle des Bouffons, 37f, 107
Quilici, Maria Teresa, 283n, 286n, 299
Quinault, Philippe, 125

Rabaut Saint-Etienne, Jean Paul, 121
Racine, Jean, 16ff, 21ff, 31, 34, 139, 230
Radcliffe, Anne, 177, 185
Ragué, Louis-Charles, 64f, 68
    Muses, Les, 156
Raguenet, François, 193
Rákóczi, Prince Francis II, 180
Rameau, Jean-Philippe, 107, 191–3,
    194–5, 203, 206f, 208n, 213
    Hippolyte et Aricie, 27n
Ramstadt, 297
Rasetti, Amadeo, 64f, 69
Reason, cult of, 103
Reicha, Antoine, 308
Reichardt, Johann Friedrich, 238
Reichardt, Rolf, 107m, 236n, 237n,
    242n, 250n
Reichenburg, Louisette, 107n
'rescue' opera, 169–88

325

Rétat, Pierre, 57
Rével, Eugénie, 161, 165, 166–7
Révellier-Lépeaux, Louis-Marie de la; see
    La Révelliere-Lépeaux, Louis-Marie
    de
Revue et gazette musicale de Paris, 303,
    305n, 306n, 308n, 309n, 310n
Revue musicale, 303, 305, 306n, 307n,
    308n
Rey, Alain, 218n
Rheims, 118
Rieger, D., 250n
Riemann, Hugo, 169
Rigel, organist, 61
Rigel, publisher, 51n
Rigel, Henri-Jean, 64, 206n
Rigel, Henri-Joseph, 64f, 67, 69, 72
Rigoley d'Ogny, Baron, 74
Rinaldi, Francesco, 287n
Riom, 226n
Roberiot, plenipotentiary, 297
Robert, Frédéric, 303
Robespierre, Maximilien de, 2, 103,
    114n, 166, 205n, 245n, 246, 257,
    261f, 269
Robinson, Michael F., 6, 39n, 48n
Rochefort, Jean-Baptiste, 55
    Toulon soumis, 126, 128f, 134, 136,
    155
Rodolphe, Jean-Joseph, 195n
    Aveugle de Palmyre, L', 208n, 272
Roland, Eudora, 115n
Rolli, Paolo, 16n
Rosenthal, Harold, 169, 178n, 187
Rösing, Helmut, 78n
Rossi, Luigi, 286n
Rossini, Gioachino
    Gazza ladra, La, 309
    Guillaume Tell, 154, 178
Rouget de Lisle, Claude-Joseph, 301
    Marseillaise, La, 3, 5, 9, 132, 297, 307
Roullet, Marie François Louis Gand
    Lebland, 16ff, 22ff, 28–9
Rousseau, Jean-Jacques, 38–9, 158, 193,
    212, 227, 229, 253–4, 272, 296
    Pygmalion, 284–5
Rousseau, Thomas, 120, 238
Roussier, Pierre-Joseph, 194n
Rozoy, Barnabé Farmian de, 42, 54ff,
    174n
Rudé, George, 172n
Rushton, Julian, 6, 139n, 143
Rustici, Giuseppe, 281–82

Sacchini, Antonio, 40, 107, 110, 132
    Arvire et Evélina, 174
    Dardanus, 31

Isola d'amore, L', 40, 53f
Sade, Alphonse François, Marquis de,
    183n
Sadie, Stanley, 16n, 77n, 187, 211n,
    236n, 283n
Saint-Ange, Ange-François Fariau de,
    211, 217
Saint-Cyr, Jacques-Antoine de Révéroni,
    185, 188
Saint-Foix, G. F. P. de, 22n
St Petersburg, 40, 66
Saint-Pierre, Bernadin de, 185–6
Saisselin, Rémy, 213
Sala, Emilio, 299
Salieri, Antonio, 44, 107, 132
    Horaces, Les, 139
    Tarare, 250n, 272
Salimbeni, impresario, 286n
Salins, Gabiot de, 48, 55
Salle Favart; see Paris
Salomoni, Luigi, 287n
San Rafaele, Benevento di, 58n
sans-culottes, 114
Santi Giovanni Antonio de; see De Santi
    Giovanni Antonio
Sarcey, Sedaine de, 56
Sarrette, Bernard, 8, 191, 199ff, 203–4,
    206, 209
Sarti, Giuseppe, 43f, 61
    Fra i due litiganti, 55
    Nozze di Dorina, Le, 55
Saulnier, N. F. Guillaume, 154, 175n
Sauvigny, Edmé-Louis Billardon de, 174n
Scarlatti, Domenico, 16n
Schama, Simon, 9
Schelling, Friedrich von, 188
Schindler, Anton Felix, 305
Schizzi, Folchino, 40n
Schleunig, Peter, 299n
Schmale, Wolfgang, 242n
Schmidt, Adolph, 128n
Schmitz, Arnold, 301
Schneider, Herbert, 10, 107n, 238n,
    250n
Scholes, Percy, 20n
Schrade, Leo, 302–304
Schröter, Johann Samuel, 64f, 70
Schubert, Franz, 90
Schwarz, Boris, 4n
Schwarzendorf, Johann Paul Aegidius;
    see Martini, Johann Paul Aegidius
Scribe, Eugène, 186
Sedain, Michael-Jean, 171–2, 174n,
    176–7, 180–81, 182–3, 188, 243,
    251, 252
Séjan, Nicolas, 61
Sénar, Gabriel-Jérome, 165

Index

September Massacres, 4
Serurier, Jean-Mathieu-Philibert, 281
Shakespeare, William, 176
Shapiro, Anne Dhu, 301n
Sheridan, Alan, 8n, 179n, 201n
Sheridan, Richard Brinsley, 172
Sicard, *abbé* Roch Ambroise Cucurron, 164n
Sieber, publisher, 80
Sillery, Madame de, 174n
Simoni, Giuseppe, 291n
Simrock, publisher, 5
Slonimsky, Nicolas, 216n
Smith, Patrick. J., 22n
Smith, Theodore, 58n
Snyders, Georges, 211n
Société Apolonienne, 102
Société des Amis de la Constitution, 158
Société des Concerts du Conservatoire, 303, 304, 306
Société Philotechnique, 167
Sografi, Antonio Simone, 285
Soissons, 102
Sonnleithner, Joseph, 2
Sorel-Nitzberg, Alice, 211n
Souriguère, Jean Marcel, 2
Spada, Paolo, 287n
Spectacles de Paris, Les, 4
Spontini, Gaspare
    Fernand Cortez, 154
Staël Germaine de, 157
Staffetta del Serchio, La, 287f, 293
Stamitz, Carl, 76
Starbinski, Jean, 117f, 120–21
Steibelt, Daniel, 8, 64f, 70ff
Sterkel, Johann Franz Xaver, 64f, 67ff
Sternfeld, F. W., 19n
Stockholm, 25n
Stoepel François, 306
Storace, Stephen, 44
    Sposi malcontenti, Gli, 56
Strasbourg, 9, 54f, 177
Suard, Jean-Baptiste-Antoine, 197
Sucy-sur-Marne, 225n
Supičič, Ivo, 214
Supreme Being, cult of, 103; *see also* festivals, patriotic
Surian, Elvidio, 285n
Swanzy, David P., 8n
Swebach-Desfontaines, Jacques François, 113n

Tackett, Timothy, 122n
Taddei, Francesco, 301
Talma, François Joseph, 224
Tapray, Jean-François, 64f, 67
Tarchi, Angelo, 44

Tasche, 279n, 281–2, 297
Tatin, J.-J., 236n
Terror, the, 3, 109f, 114, 123n, 154, 161, 166, 175, 180, 188, 235, 293
Théâtre Beaujolais (Paris), 41, 45n, 48, 55
Théâtre de la République (Paris), 164n, 167
Théâtre de Monsieur (Paris), 6, 40f, 44, 50n, 54ff
Théâtre Feydeau (Paris), 2ff, 45, 167f
Théâtre Français (Paris), 224
Théâtre-Italien (Paris), 157
Théâtre Montansier (Paris), 40, 45, 54ff, 102
Théâtre Montansier (Versailles), 98
Theodor von Neuhof, Baron, 49n
Theophilanthropists, 103, 201
Third Estate, 120
Thoinant, E., 93n
Tiedge, F. A., 236n
Tiersot, Julien, 100n, 205n, 223n
timbres, 249–68, 271–4
Tommasi, Girolamo, 281n
Toti, Benedetta; *see* Pozzi, Benedetta Mallegni
Toti, Paolo, 287n
Toulouse, 203n
Tourneux, Maurice, 39n, 198n
Tours, 158, 160, 165
Tovey, Donald, 18n
Traetta, Tommaso, 61
tragédie lyrique, 15f, 21, 37, 177n, 222
Trial, Antoine, 7n
Trial, Armand-Emmanuel
    Cécile et Julien, 7
Trimpert, D. L., 74n
Tritto, Giacomo, 44
Tuileries Gardens; *see* Paris

Vachon, Pierre, 74, 77–86, 90
Valentini, Teresa, 287n
Valentini, Vincenzo, 287n
Valentino, Henri-Justin-Joseph, 306
Valmy, 111
Valois d'Orville
    Revenants, Les, 271
Van Eyck, Jan, 279
Vanhal, Johann Baptist, 64f, 67
Varennes, 234
veglia di ballo, 291–92, 293, 297, 298
Venier, publisher, 80n
Verazi, Mattia, 16n
Verdi, Giuseppe
    Don Carlos, 17
Verdun, 113

Versailles, 15, 43ff, 54, 86n, 97, 100ff, 267
  Hôtel des Chevau-légers, 98
  Notre Dame, 102
  see also Théâtre Montansier
Verti, Roberto, 299
Viala, Agricole, 114n
Viallaneix, Paul, 93n, 208n
Vicenza, 291
Victoria, Queen, 309
Vidal, publisher, 61
Vienna, 46
Vigué, writer, 211, 214
Villers, Clemence de, 195n
Villiers, Pierre-Antoine-Jean-Baptiste de, 238
Vincennes, 262
Vinci, Leonardo, 39
Viotti, Giovanni, Battista, 4, 64f, 71, 86f
Virgil, 140
Vogel, Johann Christoph
  Démophon, 5
Vogler, Georg Joseph, 64f, 68
Voidel, a Jacobin, 245n, 262
Volpicella, Luigi, 298n

Voltaire, 9, 49, 176, 223, 234, 296
Vovelle, Michel, 113n, 116n, 117n, 120n, 121n, 122n, 123n

Wagner, Richard, 24, 32n
Wallon, S., 254n
Walpole, Horace, 176, 182
Warrack, John, 169, 178n, 180n, 187
Warsaw, 279
Weber, Carl Maria von, 180
  Euryanthe, 307n
Weber, William, 211n
Weismann, Wilhelm, 17n, 18–19, 24, 35
Wenck, August Heinrich, 55, 62
Westbrook, Roy, 187–8
Westrup, Jack, 19n
West Wycombe, 80n
Whittall, Mary, 24n
Wild, Nicole, 6n
Wordsworth, William, 186n
  Prelude, The, 7–8
Wörner, Karl H., 301n

Zeno, Apostolo, 16n
Zingarelli, Niccolò Antonio, 61